UNHOLY ALLIANCE

A Tigress Publishing Book

ISBN: 978-0-980-1510-9-1
Library of Congress Control Number: 2011934566
Printed in the United States of America

Book Design: Steve Montiglio
Editor: Peter Atkins

10 9 8 7 6 5 4 3 2 1

Requests for such permission should be submitted to:
Tigress Publishing
1301 First Ave. #1807
Seattle, Washington 98101

In memory of my father, Donald Addison Low, who exemplified personal strength, courage and moral integrity.

Patrolman Ben Kearney stood patiently in the late night's misty rain at Twelfth Avenue and South Jackson Street, quietly listening to jazz music escaping from the neighborhood's nearby clubs. As Sergeant McMurphy parked his prowl car under a street light in front of him, Kearney snuck a peek at the watch on his thick wrist. It had been twenty minutes since he'd summoned his supervisor with a request to meet him.

The sergeant set the parking brake, threw open the car door, and caught his balance after staggering into the street. Leaving the door opened wide into the traffic lane, he climbed the curb and approached the oversized beat cop standing in front of a police callbox, kitty corner from the Black and Tan Club, the major draw in the area known as Jazz Alley.

"What's this about?" asked Sergeant McMurphy, before quickly scanning the darkness that threatened to suck them into its void, a range of muted shades, from dull gray to inky black, the ethereal shroud that continually hung over the men who worked graveyard shift. "And where's Hack Sawyer?"

Kearney shrugged and slowly shook his large head, well situated on an immense frame that packed too much weight for common bathroom scales to withstand. Despite his size,

1

there wasn't a lot of fat on Big Ben's thick bones.

"Haven't seen him since a half hour into the shift, around 11:30," Kearney said. "That's why I had Radio call you."

McMurphy glanced at his watch and then up to Kearney. "I took an early lunch in Chinatown, and then I shook a couple of whores right after that, which put me out of earshot of the radio."

Kearney nodded impassively.

McMurphy glanced at the open call box, checked his watch, and then shot a look back toward his patrol car, as if to blame the police radio mounted under his dash for not getting hold of him sooner. "Right," he said, as if needing more time to think. Then he shrugged nonchalantly. "When I got back to the car, I heard dispatch squawking about something, but I didn't want to ask him to repeat himself. It must have taken him a little time to catch up with me. So Hacksaw didn't ring in at 2:00 o'clock—that's what this is about?"

"Actually, he didn't ring the 1:00 o'clock bell either," said Kearney flatly. "I did that for him. I figured that since the two of you just got off suspension, I'd help out a little, keep him out of trouble."

"You're new up here, Kearney," said McMurphy, "but you've been warned that doing that could cost you two days off?"

It was Kearney's turn to shrug. He shook his head, resigned to accept his fate. "Sometimes you got to hurt a little to help your friends."

"I didn't know Hacksaw had any friends," said McMurphy.

"You're still sore at him, Sarge?"

"I just had fifteen days off without pay because he wasn't taking care of the whores in *his* beat, which happens to be in *my* sector," said McMurphy. "I have a right to be sore, but I think the problem looks worse to the brass because you've chased all of the hookers from your beat to his."

"Supply and demand economics is all it is," said Kearney. "Hack's got Thirteenth and Yesler. There've always been whores there, which is the supply part of the equation. Every cabbie downtown knows that, and they bring eager customers here, which creates the demand. It also racks up a few extra miles for them and gets them a nice tip. This has been going on since they first put a horse in front of a buggy, and it won't ever change, at least not in our lifetimes. Maybe someday they'll knock down all these bars, jazz clubs, and flop houses and put up a convent or a school, but until then, it'll be filled with pimps, whores, drug dealers, and winos."

"The class of Seattle."

"Hack's probably okay," said Big Ben, "but it's half past another check-in, and I was getting just a little worried. I expected he'd show by now."

"You hear anything that sounded suspicious?" asked McMurphy.

"Just the usual shouts and laughter from the clubs, about the time they push their drunks outside. Seems like they've all got an early start on St. Patty's Day."

"No harm in that," said McMurphy, "but you didn't hear Hack's whistle, screams for help, 'bombs bursting in air,' that kind of thing?"

"None of that. Just the usual St. Patty's Day thing about Erin going around in her bra."

McMurphy scrunched his brow into a frown as he thought. "It's *Erin go bragh*," he said. "Ireland Forever!"

Big Ben rolled his eyes. "Kearneys are Scotsmen, not Irish."

"I'm Ulster-Irish myself, an Orangeman by birth. But amazingly they let us both on the department," said McMurphy. "Thank God for the Masons. But that's not why we're here, is it?" He pushed his police hat back on his head so that more of his forehead showed under the short brim. "Alright then, let's take a look around his beat. If we don't find him by 3:00 A.M., we better have Radio raise the alarm and notify the Watch Captain."

"Should we split up?"

"No!" McMurphy said sharply. "If Hack stepped into something deep, it might take both of us to pull him out. Besides, I've got a radio in my car. If we find trouble, it's a lot faster getting help with the two-way than you running back to a callbox."

McMurphy slid behind the steering wheel of his cruiser, and Big Ben eased his large frame into the passenger seat, causing the car to settle a couple inches lower, so that the door nearly scraped against the high sidewalk as he pulled it closed. He adjusted himself in the seat and reached down to the floorboard to pick up a wet pair of black gloves he'd just stepped on.

McMurphy stared at the gloves in Kearney's hands. "Those fell out of my back pocket smack dab into a crater sized mud puddle. They're almost brand new, so wouldn't you know it? I'm lucky I didn't drown pulling them out."

Kearney sniffed and scrunched his nose. "They smell of lavender," he said, while also thinking that McMurphy's breath stank of booze. Curiously, though, his speech wasn't as slurred as Kearney would have expected with that strong of an alcohol smell oozing from his body.

"You never know what ends up in these puddles around here," said McMurphy. "Could be anything from horse piss to sewer waste. So I washed them in a sink in Chinatown, hoping to get the germs out and kill any stink." McMurphy canted his head toward the rear. "Just toss them in the back on the floor. Give them some time to dry out. In a day or two, they'll be good as…used."

For the next twenty-five minutes, the sergeant drove slowly up and down every street and alley in Sawyer's beat, which ranged over to Fourteenth and Yesler. In places where there were taverns or clubs, Kearney got out of the car and knocked on doors and peeked into windows, but Hack Sawyer was nowhere to be found.

At 2:55 A.M., Sergeant McMurphy called Captain Hodges at headquarters to make a report. The captain told him to keep on looking, and if he didn't find Sawyer by 3:15, he would send more officers to help with the search.

At 3:05 A.M., McMurphy stopped the police car in front of the Main Street Garage at 1242 South Main Street. He climbed out and again left his car door open. Kearney closed the passenger door before joining McMurphy in front of the two large wooden doors to the garage, which were padlocked shut. Adjoining the bay doors was a regular shop door with glass panes over a wooden panel. McMurphy shook the doorknob. "While we're here, we might as well check where he parks his car," he said.

"He wouldn't be napping, if that's what you're thinking," said Kearney. "It's too early in the shift for that. Things don't slow down enough for anyone to draw a yawn until about 4:30. He wouldn't want to miss out on any of the action before that."

"I still say we check," said the sergeant. "He might have found a jug and a young lady, and they could've wanted a little privacy."

"He's married, isn't he?" asked Kearney.

"Yeah, he is. And for that matter, if he found a jug of liquor that would be illegal too, but we're not in the business of hearing confessions or enforcing religious morality—at least not so far as I see it."

"He was stone sober when I last saw him," said Kearney. "I can't see him getting liquored up that fast to a state where

5

he'd forget to check in…"

McMurphy shook his head and banged on the garage's door several times with his nightstick. "Me neither, and that has me worried that the worst may have happened."

"Why's that?" asked Kearney.

McMurphy groaned with a grimace. "It's just a feeling I've got. There's a history of bad blood here in this building. The garage's former owner is a guy named Steve Savage. He's holding a grudge against us, more so for Hack than me. We busted him and his brother Scott for liquor possession a year back, and he got six months in the county jail for it. Since Scott had a prior offense, he got felony time—a year in Monroe. Should be out any time now. The brothers claim Hack and I planted the booze in question, set them up so to speak. So Steve ended up selling the garage to a guy named Rinaldi, before doing his time in the county pokey. After he got out of jail, he came back, and now he works for Rinaldi. He's not happy about that."

Kearney chewed on that a moment. "Why didn't Hack just find another place to park?" he asked. "Why pick at old scabs?"

"I don't know. Rinaldi could be letting him park here for free, since Hacksaw would be keeping an eye on the place while checking on his car, or Maybe Hack's just a creature of habit. He's thickheaded that way."

Kearney shook his head thoughtfully. "So did you two plant the booze?"

McMurphy bent over and picked up a stray brick near the corner of the garage and stepped up to the door. He glanced at Kearney as he sized up the window glass. "You don't expect me to answer that, do you?"

Kearney creased a wry smile. "I suppose not."

McMurphy held the chunk in front of him as if he were an instructor making a point in a classroom. "No sense

6

chewing up a perfectly good nightstick breaking glass," he said, hefting the brick up and down in his hand. Cocking his arm, he slammed the brick into the glass pane closest to the door knob. The glass shattered, shards falling inside the garage onto the wooden plank floor, and McMurphy tossed the brick aside on the sidewalk. He plucked at the few remaining pieces of glass, which stuck out menacingly like shark's teeth, pulling them out carefully, one at a time, with his left hand.

"Who pays for the window?" asked Kearney.

"If Rinaldi gets his knickers in a twist, he can bill the city," McMurphy said, gently setting the broken glass down on the sidewalk. He stood up and reached through the empty window pane and twisted the knob, unlocking the door. As he pulled his hand back through the opening, he raked a knuckle across a tiny shard that still clung to the frame. "Damn!" he said, and shook his head. "After all the noggins I've busted with these dukes, you'd think my skin would be so scarred it wouldn't bleed anymore."

"Is that why they call you Knuckles?" Kearney asked. "For breaking heads?"

McMurphy nodded as he dug in his pocket for a handkerchief to press against the cut. "Yeah, that and the bounty hunting work I did as a bail bondsman. That was just after I got into police work, but the bosses made me give it up. They called it a conflict of interest and said they didn't want us boys collecting debts either. But while I was doing it, I found that a sharp blast or two with these to the ribs to be very effective. I had less problems if I introduced myself to my captures with a knuckle sandwich—just to get their attention. Once my point was made, I almost never had a problem after that. Then the word got around, and guys knew not to mess with me."

McMurphy wrapped the hanky tight around his hand,

7

pressed the flashlight against the makeshift bandage, and pushed open the side door with his shoulder. Kearney slid a flashlight into his left hand, unholstered his revolver, and held it low against his leg, before following the sergeant inside the garage. Immediately inside and to the left of the door was a bank of light switches. McMurphy passed a light beam over them quickly and then reached with his cut hand to turn on the switches one by one. As he did, the hanging light fixtures sprang to life in sets of three, working their way from the back of the garage to the front.

"Let there be light," McMurphy quipped, but the barroom humor was wasted on Kearney.

As the lights came on, illuminating the garage floor, Kearney doused his flashlight and glanced back toward McMurphy. "Is that your blood on the light switches, or was it already there?" he asked.

McMurphy gazed back at the switch plate and then down at his blood-soaked handkerchief. "I can't be sure," he said as he shook his head, acknowledging his carelessness.

Kearney frowned at the sergeant like he would a rookie cop, but quickly caught himself and forced an indulgent grin. Then he turned away and headed into the center aisle of the garage. "Remind me...which car's Sawyer's?" he asked.

"He's got a 1930 Buick, four door—black of course," the sergeant said. "He usually parks about half way down on the left."

Kearney nodded and continued on ahead. "I see it now," he said. And then he abruptly stopped next to a LaSalle Fleetwood, the first car in line, which he had nearly passed. Kearney back pedaled away from the car, like it was a coiled rattlesnake waiting in the bushes for a passing pair of legs. He brought his revolver up to eye level and pointed it toward the rear car door, which was gaping open, exposing what was inside the backseat. Dangling across the car's running board was a pair of legs, their bare skin exposed above black socks and below navy blue pants. The skin was pasty white, lacking any color. On the garage's wooden floor, next to the parked LaSalle, were several droplets of blood.

Kearney shook his head and closed his eyes. Then he opened them quickly and instinctively glanced around the entirety of the shop, glaring over the top of his revolver for any signs someone else might still be inside. Seeing no indications of the presence of others, he returned his gaze to the rear of the LaSalle and focused on a bullet hole near the lower edge of the rear window's glass, which he initially had missed while walking past the car. "I've got something here, Sarge, and it ain't going to be pretty."

Kearney cautiously approached the protruding legs, with McMurphy now close at his side. He exhaled contemptuously, holstered his revolver, and flicked on his flashlight. The body was on the floorboards of the car, wedged between the seats. The bloodied head was canted forward against the officer's chest at an unnatural angle. After confirming the dead man was Officer Hack Sawyer, and that he had obviously suffered gunshot trauma to the head, Kearney began a more careful search of the car's interior, slowly running his flashlight beam up the dead man's legs, across a dark reddish stain on Sawyer's left leg, and over the gloved hands that protruded from the sleeves of the beatman's blouse. The arms were extended straight out and crossed, as if pinched together by the small space where the body was wedged. On top of the officer's waist, next to his hands, was a police revolver covered in blood and pointing toward the officer's face. In the middle of the rear seat was a congealed mass of blood, so thick that Kearney first thought it might have been a human organ, possibly a man's liver.

"Is it Hacksaw?" McMurphy asked, standing slightly behind Kearney, his gun hand resting on top of his coat, where his revolver would be holstered.

Kearney nodded quietly, almost reverently. Then he glanced back and lowered his eyes to McMurphy's bloodied left hand. "You're still leaking, Sarge. We can't do anything for him now. So don't get any closer to the car with that mitt of yours. It'll just confuse the detectives if you drip blood in the mess that's already here."

Kearney resumed inspecting the interior of the car, starting this time with the front, where he found Officer Sawyer's hat flipped upside down on the front seat. Kearney brought his flashlight beam back to Officer Sawyer's body and continued working up his chest to the bloodied face. Sawyer had a bullet hole in his left cheek and a ragged tear near the back of his jaw where it joined the neck. It appeared that gaping injury was the exit wound from which a lot of blood had pumped out. Farther up in the middle of Sawyer's forehead was another hole, positioned almost exactly between the middle of his eyes. There was very little blood around the entry wound. At the top of Sawyer's head was yet another small wound, a gash of some kind, possibly a blunt object strike from the butt of a gun.

Kearney flashed his light beam up on the ceiling of the car and didn't find any blood spatter patterns there. He leaned in closer to the body and shined his light inside Sawyer's hat. There was a folded over packet of paper with a spray of red. Kearney presumed the paper to be a police bulletin, which was accompanied by two fresh cigars wedged into the crown of the hat.

"What do you see?" asked McMurphy, from ten feet back.

"He's been shot twice in the face and maybe once again in the leg," said Kearney. "I can't be sure about that without checking closer, but since he's one of ours, I don't want to

10

risk screwing it up. I'll let Homicide take it from here."

"Good idea," said McMurphy.

"On top of his head there's another wound. Just a rough guess, but he might've been clocked with something hard— like a gun or ballpeen hammer, maybe."

"Not suicide?" asked McMurphy, as he ran his tongue across his upper lip thoughtfully.

"Not with that many wounds," said Kearney. "Unless he's the world's worst shot—in all of recorded history. I mean…who misses at that range? Or shoots himself in the face, anyway? Twice, no less."

"Sounds like you've given the concept some thought."

Kearney shook his large head. "No, not me personally, but I've seen where it's happened. Times are tough. Who would've guessed the Depression would run this long? There've been a lot of people who've taken the shortcut out of here. It's raised my curiosity, and I've checked out so many books on death and dying that the librarian thinks I'm incurably morbid. But I read them because someday I want to work Homicide."

"You put your time in on the street, stay out of trouble— which is something I've never been able to do—and you might get your shot at it," said McMurphy. Then he looked behind him to the garage's entrance. "I've got to call this in."

As soon as Vera Deward and Alan Stewart arrived at

the union building off Denny Way, Alice advised them that George Brinkman had important company in his office, and that Alice was to send them in. Alan held Brinkman's door open for Vera, and when she entered, Mike Ketchum stood tall, smiled broadly, and shook their hands, which was a more formal greeting than Alan was used to receiving from the police department's Chief of Detectives.

After all were seated around Mr. Brinkman's desk, the boss opened his cigar case and indicated with a nod that others could join him with a smoke, as if it were a peace pipe ceremony, an integral part of conducting important business. Vera and Alan politely declined. So did Ketchum, which again was out of the ordinary. Alan figured the Chief had something weighing heavy on his mind.

Brinkman lit his cigar, nodded at Ketchum, and waved his hand, indicating that the floor was open for him to speak.

"Because of the fine work you've done for us both, I'm coming to you again," Ketchum said in his heavy Irish brogue. "George has given me permission to discuss with you a police case that I'd like your help with, if you don't mind?"

13

Alan glanced at Vera, and she at him. Then she nodded for Ketchum to continue.

"It involves the suspicious death of one of our boys several years back. At the time it was ruled a suicide by the Homicide captain, despite the outcry from reformers and the press that there had been a cover up. Personally, I believe the good captain at the time made an honest mistake, but he was a friend of mine and mentor, so I might be a little too forgiving of his faults. He meant well, but I've always felt strongly that he was wrong. I believe the officer was killed in the line of duty."

Vera reached over and squeezed Alan's hand. Alan knew what the signal meant. She was excited to be working on another case with teeth in it, instead of trying to catch the cheats and frauds, the fairly routine pension cases that filled their days when they weren't providing personal security for their boss.

Ketchum continued, "Of course you're under no obligation to take this case to help the police department if you don't want to, for whatever reason that inclines you one way or the other. It's outside the realm of what you do here for George, and the cold reality is that it could be dangerous for the both of you. If you agree to take it, however, George will let you work it on the union's clock. You won't be out any money, and in fact you might stand to make a little extra cash."

Mr. Brinkman stirred in his chair. "That's just my way of saying thanks to the police department for their extraordinary help with the McNeary matter," he said with a quiet nod, before closing his eyes.

"How would it be dangerous for us?" asked Vera, gazing intently at Ketchum.

Ketchum nodded several times and sucked in his hollow cheeks before answering. "The killer or killers have never

14

been identified, not even tentatively," he said. "Since they've never been caught, they'll obviously want to make sure it stays that way, and then there's always the problem with outsiders nosing around in the department's dirty laundry. Policemen don't like it when that happens. They circle the wagons and load the carbines. They won't stand for outside intervention—especially if the shooter—or shooters—turns out to be one of our own."

Alan glanced again at Mr. Brinkman, seeking additional clarity or verification that the boss was fine with where Chief Ketchum was heading with his request, but Mr. B sat quietly and blew cigar smoke across his thick mustache and closed his eyes again.

"Nine years ago this month, the department lost an officer in a garage at 1242 Main Street," said Chief Ketchum. "Name was Charles Sawyer. We called him Hacksaw because of his time in the Dry Squad working for me. Right after he started chasing moonshine, *Life* magazine published a picture of him chopping up a still with a double-bladed axe, out in the Woodinville-Duvall area, hence the nickname Hack. During his time with me he must have chopped up a junkyard full of stills and dumped out a cargo ship full of hooch. He was always my biggest producer, month after month, up till the early part of 1931. But it turns out his focus wasn't really to rid the city of the scourge of 'demon rum,' as the preachers liked to call it, but instead to eliminate the competition for his friends. So of course he made a lot of bitter enemies during his time, while making a lot of extra money on the side—or so we suspect but were never able to prove. Lord only knows what he did with all his money. His widow claims he left her penniless when he died. His great success, if that's what you want to call it, was because his tips came from his buddies who ratted each other out. The rats were the ones protected, and they paid Hacksaw

15

well. But he wasn't the only copper with a hand in other people's wallets. Of that we're damn sure."

Since Vera would have known Brinkman and Alan's father's involvement in the liquor wars, Alan glanced at her to see if Ketchum might be treading on sacred ground that they might want to avoid, but she nodded for Ketchum to continue.

"Hack took two bullets to the face in '32," said Ketchum.

Alan nodded thoughtfully. "I remember that," he said.

"Really?" asked Ketchum. "You must have been only twelve or thirteen at the time."

"That's right," said Alan. I delivered the *Post Intelligencer* in the mornings back then. After my route I read the story to Dad at breakfast. The *P.I.* said the Homicide captain wrote his report to the Mayor officially declaring the case a suicide, which meant the police officer's wife wouldn't get her husband's pension."

"That's correct," said Ketchum, "which is just one of the reasons we want to take another look at this. If he was really killed in the line of duty, even if it was one crooked cop killing another, then she's entitled to a survivor's pension."

"Dad wondered how somebody could beat himself on the head with the butt of his own gun and then shoot himself three times with just two bullets, once in the leg and twice in the face."

"Actually it was just the two bullets to the face," said Ketchum. "The bullet to his forehead split upon entry, the main part of the slug went through his brain pan, but a fragment went out the top of his head. It knocked his cap off, and the chip and hat both landed in the front seat. There was a heavy saturation of blood on Sawyer's left leg, like what was also found in the back seat, but there was no bullet hole to go with it, according to the autopsy reports, which we can be sure were reliable. It was probably blood that drained from one of his facial wounds, when he came to rest with his head pitched forward. The early story about the leg wound was pure conjecture on the part of the press. One of the patrol boys or the sergeant yakked to a reporter when he should've been standing his post and keeping those vultures at bay, not acting as a cub reporter for them."

"But still," said Alan, "how would the officer have shot himself in the face? Dad used my brother's cap gun to show me how impossible that would be. The officer, Hack Sawyer, would have had to bend his hand completely around and then pull the trigger away from himself, which I can't do."

Chief Ketchum raised his brow thoughtfully and gazed at Alan evenly. "Officer Sawyer might have used his thumb," he said. "Slid it inside the trigger and pressed down and away from himself."

Alan shook his head as he tried to imagine how that would work. "Do you train your officers to shoot with their thumbs?" he asked.

"NO!" Ketchum said emphatically, "and that's why I came here to talk with you. I agree with your analysis…so far, that is. Anybody who knows anything about shooting a gun, like policemen necessarily do, knows how killing works. With suicide, the idea is to end the pain quickly, not see how much you can inflict on yourself before you die, dragging it out needlessly. So guys intent on shooting themselves either stick their smoke poles under their chins, into their mouths, or they press them flat against their temples, say a prayer, and squeeze the trigger, hoping for instant oblivion. And cops also know they're supposed to squeeze, not jerk the trigger. You jerk the trigger and the barrel moves off target. Either way, it should be a one-shot proposition that doesn't involve the face, a lot of pain, or a lingering death."

"Mackie and I also talked about this case," Vera said, lightly squeezing Alan's hand as if to apologize for her disclosing a point of intimacy with his late father. She was the kind of person who needed to touch others, and having grown up in a house where that kind of touching wasn't done, Alan relished that part of her. It was their way of connecting, even though there was a lingering issue between them that had not yet been resolved.

"And wasn't Sawyer's sergeant arrested for smuggling liquor a little while after Sawyer's death?" she asked.

Alan nodded as Vera spoke, recalling more of the details of the newspaper accounts of the minor scandal.

"That's right," said Ketchum. "Knuckles McMurphy was caught at the Canadian Border by US Customs with a trunk load of Canadian Whiskey. Both the booze and the car were confiscated. I was asked to consult with the Police Chief on the discipline for that case, and I concurred with his recommendation to fire Knuckles for *Conduct Unbecoming a Police Officer*, as well as leaving the State and City Limits without written or oral permission. And I can guess you're probably asking yourself the same questions we did at the time: why would Knuckles assume he could drive a carload of liquor through the border and not get caught? Was he flat out stupid or brazen as hell?"

Vera and Alan both nodded in agreement.

"We think he'd paid off a Customs agent to look the other way while he made a regular run, but something went wrong at the border that morning. We're not sure what, but it could have been as simple as the guy who was supposed to wave him through choosing the wrong time to take a potty break, or a new supervisor just happened to wander out of his office and conducted a spot inspection on Knuckle's car, or the opponents on the other team made a better offer to the Custom's agent—eliminating their competition."

Alan grinned.

"There's an axiom in police work," said Ketchum. "Most of the best work gets done by accident, more so than by design, which means we catch crooks because there are hundreds of ways for them to get caught. All they have to do is screw up one time and we've got them—that is if we happen to be paying attention at the moment. On the other hand, police can screw up hundreds of times during their investigations and life goes on. We only have to get it right once to catch a crook, but sooner or later, we will get them all, because even the best ones eventually make mistakes. That might have been all that happened here—a simple screw up."

"So does the fact he got caught smuggling booze make him the suspect in Officer Sawyer's death?" asked Vera. "If that's all it takes—"

"George and I have come to an understanding on all of our pasts," said Ketchum. "Nobody in this room is without sin, and as far as the Police Department is concerned, St. James Cathedral could build a bank of confessionals and staff it late into the wee hours every Saturday night just so our Catholic officers could take Holy Communion on Sunday." He shook his head wearily. "But I'm absolutely confident that neither George Brinkman nor Mackie Stewart had anything to do with Hack Sawyer's death—nor with his circle of friends, nor with his partners in crime, nor with his other enemies for that matter. Otherwise, I wouldn't be here."

Vera nodded for Ketchum to continue.

"Knuckles stands by his story that he had nothing to do with Hack's death," said Ketchum. "It might just be that Knuckles is a skunk with an overactive stink gland, not a murderer who leaves a foul odor on everybody and everything he comes into contact with. As a matter of fact, we had him in for routine questioning last year, following the death of another one of our beatmen. This one was gunned down at Seventh and Union while checking out three suspicious characters at a low rent hotel. Another police officer heard the gunshots and gave chase, hot on their heels, but the trio jumped into a car and fled town before our man could squeeze off a shot at them. The trio was caught later, down in Kent. The car they 'stole' belonged to none other than our former sergeant, Knuckles McMurphy."

Alan's eyebrows creased low into a scowl. "I'd say that's too unlikely to be a coincidence."

"That's my take on it too, but Knuckles held tight to his story," said Ketchum.

"Were your detectives persuasive in their techniques?" asked Vera, raising her brow knowingly.

Ketchum nodded, indicating he understood her meaning. "With Knuckles being a former bull—albeit a bad one at that—the boys were loath to lay the leather to him," he said. "You might call it professional courtesy or a fraternal honor system, because just like them, he once wore a blue uniform, but I see that kind of thing as misplaced allegiance to the old blue code: protect your brother officer, no matter what he did. In this kind of case the blue code makes for an unholy alliance with the criminal sector. My position is that I'm against that courtesy when it applies to those who've taken a walk on the dark side, committed a crime, whether they were a copper or not, but not everyone sees it my way."

Vera pushed out her lips into a thinking frown and shook her head. "Who were Sawyer's other enemies?" she asked.

Ketchum shook his head as he thought for a moment. "Let's start with the two brothers named Savage, one of whom used to own the garage where the shooting occurred. Then there's a Chinatown mobster named Goon Dip Wong, who runs opium, whores, booze, gambling, numbers, and smuggles illegal immigrants. Or it could be any of a score of bootleggers Hacksaw put out of business. Or it could be any of forty policemen who hold grudges and carry firearms."

"Is that all?" asked Alan sarcastically, shaking his head.

"There's another thing you'll learn soon enough when you read the file," Ketchum said, clearing his throat and glancing nervously at Vera. "Hacksaw's overcoat and shirt were pulled open at the top, and it seems his fly was pulled all the way down."

Alan's eyebrows knitted low as he tried to figure where Ketchum was going with that and why he had paused.

"Do you think he was having sex?" Vera asked, cutting to the point and easing the tension in the air.

"It might have been that," said Ketchum, "or it could have been that he had relieved himself in the alley and was surprised before he got himself zipped up again. He might have been shot outside and then dragged into the garage— that theory has been advanced."

Alan shook his head, more for himself than the others.

"Why'd you come to us?" asked Vera. "Why not have Sergeant Watkins or Detective Ballard work this case?"

"It hits too close to home for us, darling. I trust Spud and Sean well enough, but the Chief has told us to stand down on this. He doesn't want us spending anymore of the taxpayers' dollars trying to make this suicide into a homicide just so the widow can secure a pension from the City. And with him taking a strong position on this, it would be very difficult to get the boys to put their heart into the case."

"Is that all it is for the Chief, saving the City some money?" asked Vera.

21

Ketchum shook his head again. "I don't buy that for a minute," he said. "Hack's death tore apart the Department in '32. Those who favored the old ways lined up on one side, the honest cops on the other. Chief Galloway, an attorney with no police or management experience, was brought in to clean up the department and improve morale, which often are mutually exclusive terms. You can't do both at the same time, at least not quickly. To make drastic changes with an institution this large and so set in its ways, you have to make haste slowly. Within four years, we had a palace revolt and Galloway was forced out. We now have Clement, who's a consummate politician. He knows there are two secrets to keeping his job. The first is to start each year off with a vigorous vice sweep, affirming that he will not tolerate licentious behavior. The second secret is to pretend to everyone that there are no bones, whether handcuffed, bound in sisal coils, or wrapped in chains, hidden away in our closets, despite our checkered past. That way he keeps the department's tenured carnivores happy, and it also keeps the public from looking too closely at the shady dealings that are still going on. This way the Chief also avoids the sticky business of having to deal with Sawyer's murderer being a fellow copper, should that turn out to be the case. He's content crossing his heart and hoping that whoever did it doesn't strike again."

"So you've come to us to do more digging," said Vera. "Won't Clement eventually hear about it and tell us to stay out of the department's business?"

"Very likely," said Ketchum.

"And won't he figure we're actually working for you, his Chief of Detectives?" asked Alan.

"Not unless you tell him, and that's a risk I'm prepared to take, given my tenure and the circumstances here. As private detectives, you're obliged to your client *not* to reveal who he or she is to anyone who asks. If pressed, you might imply that it's the Mayor's office, but no one can make you say who it really is."

"Tell me more about the missing money," said Vera. "You said he was heavily involved in graft and yet his widow was left with nothing. How could that be? Has that been verified?"

"This information isn't to leave this room," Ketchum said, glancing back and forth between Vera and Alan, "because I don't want to read it in the newspaper some day. Talking against the department that's fed and clothed me all these years would make me appear ungrateful, which is absolutely not the case. I love the department but think it can do a lot better than it has. The old ways are dying and should already have been buried."

Vera and Alan nodded their agreement.

"First of all, seventy percent of our officers are reasonably honest, church going men," said Ketchum. "They're true blue loyal to the Department and their fellow officers— right or wrong—which means they won't rat out the corrupt ones. As for the remaining thirty percent, you have the grass eaters and the meat eaters. For grass eaters, the normal perks and kickbacks from ignoring code violations or making referrals to attorneys, bail bond companies, tow trucks, ambulances, and the money that exchanges hands giving traffic warnings can more than double their income. The carnivores who tip off their close buddies to vice raids or liquor busts, along with pay offs from the whore houses, gambling dens, bingo halls, narcotics peddlers and everyone else they can bully into tithing, can *easily* triple their salary, leaving a trail that snakes all the way up to the Chief's office and across the street to the Mayor. The City Attorney and the County Prosecutor's Offices have their own problems as well. Unfortunately, the carnivores have ruled the roost here for too long. When police are tasked with enforcing the city's morals, it begs for judgment on ourselves, and we can't yet meet that scrutiny with a straight face and unblinking eye."

Ketchum inhaled deeply and sucked in his cheeks, as if he were chewing on something tart. "I blame the Volstead Act," he said. "Outlawing the sale of liquor caused us more grief than all of the other laws combined. Police officers who were known to vigorously enforce every other ordinance and criminal statute deliberately turned a blind eye to liquor laws, because they saw no harm in booze. Others, who had been morally honest and law abiding, found a profit in it, like Lieutenant Roy Olmstead, who spent six years in prison during the '20's. During the height of Prohibition our motorcycle officers followed and arrested three federal agents selling a car load of confiscated liquor to the bars on First Avenue, and then the feds promptly retaliated by arresting all but two of my Dry Squad detectives—on solid cases. They also had their sights set on me, but they didn't have what they needed. So Chief Severyns told them to leave me alone or the war would continue, and he would make it more embarrassing for them than they could possibly do for us. When Severyns took over the department in '22, right off the bat a detective sent an emissary to him, offering $60,000 in cash if he would place the detective in charge of the Morals Unit, which oversaw the Dry Squad. Severyns refused the bribe, transferred the detective to the sticks, and put me in charge of the squad. He said that if the feds didn't leave me alone, he was prepared to advise the Seattle P.I. about that former detective, who after leaving the department, coincidentally found a job working for the feds. How would they like to explain that?"

Alan closed his eyes, forcing out a memory of Harry Frantz, the corrupt lieutenant who had wreaked havoc on Alan's life and that of his family. Hungry Harry was a carnivore Alan had given a comeuppance, but the danger lingered that he'd recover from his wounds soon enough and come after Alan.

"We never saw the likes of Elliot Ness out here," said Ketchum, "either as a Fed or as one of us. I have no doubt that Hack Sawyer was a carnivore of the highest order. I would guess conservatively that he quadrupled his income with his greed and sticky fingers, just during the time he worked for me. But I've been to see his widow on Beacon Hill, and her home and way of living is more in keeping with an honest copper's salary: it's neither poor nor shabby, but it's not middle class either. I'd say Sawyer's squirreled away a small fortune in a box somewhere, and given how long he was at it, we're talking several thousands of dollars. I'd guess somewhere between one-hundred-fifty to two-hundred thousand dollars, easily. It very well could be double that. If you happen to find that for the widow, the standard finder's fee of ten percent should apply."

Alan quickly tallied the figures. Splitting fifteen to twenty thousand with Vera was a very attractive proposition.

"Why wouldn't his wife know where the money is?" Alan asked, even though he was already beginning to form his own idea as to why.

Alan spotted Chief Ketchum's unmarked police car in the parking lot for the Ballard Locks. Rather than sliding the Union's Buick into a spot next to the empty car, Alan parked several stalls away, in case anyone was watching the lot and might connect them together. "Why'd he want to meet us here?" Alan asked Vera. "The gardens won't be in full bloom for another month yet."

"Mike's not here for the flowers," Vera said. "He likes to watch the boats come and go, and it's just far enough away from downtown that we won't have to worry about prying eyes."

Alan and Vera passed the visitor's center, the gardens, and found Ketchum leaning over the large lock, doing just what Vera said he'd be doing: staring at the boats as they queued up in the locks for the raising and lowering of the canal's water, which allowed ships and boats to travel up the canal or down, depending on whether their destination was the freshwater of the inland lakes or the saltwater of Puget Sound.

"Which ones are your favorites, Mike?" Vera asked.

"I've got my eye on that *Sparkman and Stephens M42*," said Ketchum. "That'd be a nice way to spend my retirement, don't you think?"

"I know just the houseboat you could tie it up to," said Vera. "Professor McCoy's got a vacancy down on Portage Bay. It's near a boat works where Alan's got an eye on a *Chris Craft* runabout."

"Oh, very good," said Ketchum with a grin towards Alan. "Are you interested in boats, lad?"

Alan sucked in his cheeks, knowing where Vera was headed with this, preparing to take his licks.

"He's more interested in Robbie, who's rebuilding the little honey," Vera said.

Ketchum's eyebrows drooped into a puzzled scowl.

"She's the daughter of the owner down at Baumgartner's," said Alan. "She salvaged a 19-foot Capri this winter and has done all the restoration work herself."

Ketchum nodded knowingly, the grin returning to his face. "A girl who's handy like that, you wouldn't want to let her get away, lad," he said. "Throw all the others back. That one would be the keeper."

Vera reached out and touched the large brown accordion file wrapped with an elastic band that Ketchum was holding. "Is that for us?" she asked.

"It is, darling," said Ketchum. "It's the entirety of the case. It's signed out to me, so keep it locked up and don't lose it, because it's now considered an open investigation. I'm responsible, if there's ever an audit."

"Everything's in here?" asked Vera.

"Everything that's left," said Ketchum. "Because the case was first ruled a suicide, it was scheduled for destruction, but I put a stop to that."

"Why destroy it?" asked Alan.

"The Department does that on a regular business, every five years or thereabouts, so we don't get buried in paperwork—literally. Except for open Homicides, we purge cases with no leads or where the Statute of Limitations has run out, leaving no chance of prosecution. In a suicide case, there should be no suspects and no one to prosecute, so we dump them. The problem comes when you've got a case like this where some people want it saved and others want it tossed. That's when crime scene photos start disappearing."

"Why's that?" asked Vera.

"Some of the lads filch pictures and sell them to magazines or the tabloids, or they give them to girlfriends or people they're trying to impress with their stories of derring-do."

"People want pictures of dead bodies?" Vera asked.

"It would appear so," said Ketchum. "Society has always had a fascination with death and insanity. All you have to do is take a look at the great operas, like Lucia di Lammermoor. A mad woman singing an aria with blood dripping down her wedding gown captivates an audience like nothing else. People are fascinated by what others might be capable of doing, because it means they might be, too. They secretly wonder if they would kill because of passion, answering a primitive murder lust deep inside them."

Alan nodded slowly, taking in what the chief had said. "Do you think anything's missing here?" he asked.

"I'd expected to find more pictures of the theater of the crime," said Ketchum. "There should also have been more photos of the car, the corpse, the wounds, and all the extra bullet holes in the garage."

"I thought that there had only been two shots fired," said Alan.

"Two holes in Officer Sawyer," said Ketchum. "We can account for those, and according to Captain Merit's report, Sawyer's gun had been fired twice. As I said before, the majority of one slug was recovered inside Sawyer's head during the autopsy, and the wedge that fragmented and went out the top of his skull was found in the front seat. We didn't have much of a Crime Lab then, so the lads took the two pieces to a pharmacist and compared them to another bullet removed from department issued ammo, which would be a .38. Together the pieces weighed the same."

"But wouldn't that also match with a lot of other .38 caliber ammunition, like what I could walk in and buy at Warshall's?" asked Alan.

"That would be about right," said Ketchum. "And then there's the bullet that went through Sawyer's jaw and passed out his neck, which is believed to be the same one that went through the rear window of the car, but was never recovered."

"Is that unusual?" asked Vera. "Don't you normally recover all the spent bullets?"

"Not really," said Ketchum. "There's a hole in the wall, which has a busy street behind it. The round could have tumbled out there and been picked up by a car tire or knocked into a drain. That happens."

"But you said 'extra bullet holes,' as in plural," said Alan.

Ketchum nodded. "Directly in front of where the LaSalle was parked, where they overhaul engines, there were five holes in the wooden floor in a group, all fired from a .38, which of course is the same caliber as Sawyer's gun. So the detectives grilled the Savage brothers about the holes, and one or the other said they'd fired a pistol into the floor—their floor—testing a gun several months before Sawyer's shooting. The detectives recovered the spent rounds from the soil underneath the garage and had them all tested, by the lab, which had little more than a magnifying glass back then. None of those slugs looked enough like the piece found inside Sawyer's head."

"What was Captain Merit's theory on this?" asked Vera.

"What made him think it was a suicide?"

"A copy of his letter to the Mayor is inside the folder," said Ketchum, who turned to take another look at the M42 as the gates to the locks opened and it cast off its lines and started into the freshwater canal, heading up stream to Lake Union and likely to Lake Washington.

"That's a thing of beauty, isn't it?" he asked rhetorically.

Alan and Vera both smiled.

"In his review of the facts," Ketchum continued. "Merit said that Sawyer had been complaining about severe headaches for a couple of days, which the captain took to mean depression, even though there's no other indication Hack had been diagnosed with that condition or sounded depressed to the neighboring beat officer. Hell, he had two new cigars tucked away in his hat. Why would he buy them if he'd planned to shoot himself? What would be the point?"

Ketchum shook his head angrily as he thought. "No one at all thought he seemed despondent," said Ketchum. "Merit bases his theory primarily on one of the neighbors in an apartment nearby the garage. A colored man reported he'd heard two shots. The man was lying in bed awake, between midnight and one o'clock. He said he heard the second shot about two minutes after the first one, which would generally not be the case if it was a heated gun battle."

"He's the only witness?" asked Alan.

"The only one who spoke up," said Ketchum.

"So Merit said it appears Hack shot himself in the face," Ketchum said, "and that bullet passed through his jaw, out his neck, and out the rear window, causing significant but not fatal blood loss. A lot of blood was found on the backseat of the LaSalle, such a quantity that it congealed into a lumpy mass. The first officer thought he'd found a human organ. That first shot must have stunned Sawyer, enough so that he passed out for two minutes, if you believe this version. When he came around and discovered he was still alive, he stood up into a crouch, which would have been the best he could do inside the LaSalle. He stumbled forward and pitched his head out through the open window on the right side of the car, for some unknown reason, where some of his blood dripped on the far running board and the garage floor. Then he pushed himself backward, and pointed his gun again at his head and fired one more time, with the bullet fragment knocking his cap off. The fragment and the cap were found in the front seat. The detectives found blood spatter under the bill of the hat, which might indicate he was shot at fairly close range."

Alan glanced at Vera to see if she was also picturing how this might have happened.

"After the second shot, he fell backwards," said Ketchum, "into the area between the seats, and his body slumped to the floor. Merit figures this wedging between the seats pushed his shirt and overcoat up his torso, causing the fabric to bunch towards his shoulders, pulling out the tail of his shirt. Sawyer's legs flopped spasmodically, while he was in his death throes, and extended partially out the rear door, from the mid-calf down. His head wedged against the far door and ended up pressed against his chest."

Vera scrunched her eyes close together and shook her head. "I'm not getting why he would stand up inside the car and make himself a moving target," she said. "If his first shot didn't do the trick, why wouldn't he make absolutely sure the second one would, by sitting still on the car seat or propping his arm against something solid?"

"Exactly my point," said Ketchum. "I have the utmost respect for Charles Merit, but I think he's wrong on this case."

"Was there any blood around the bullet hole in the rear

window?" asked Alan.

"You'll have to check the file, but I don't recall reading that."

"What about the other windows in the LaSalle?" asked Alan. "Were they open or shut?"

"I believe they were all down," said Ketchum.

"Any powder burns around the wound?" asked Alan.

Chief Ketchum nodded his head and smiled. "You do catch on fast, son," he said, "which makes me feel better about asking you two to take this case. To answer your question; yes, there was a heavy concentration of gunpowder around the hole to the right side of his face, indicating the weapon was discharged very close to his skin, but that's not the case with the wound to the forehead, which did not have a very heavy powder concentration or tattooing, as we call it. Merit believes that somehow the bill of Sawyer's hat deflected the majority of gunpowder from this shot, but that would only account for some of it not being there—and it also would mean for Sawyer to shoot himself in the face, his hand would have held the gun further away from his face than would be humanly possible. If Sawyer had been the one squeezing the trigger, he would have had to have six-foot arms and been double-jointed."

"Did the police lab do an analysis?" asked Alan.

"Remember, there was only the one bullet recovered," said Ketchum, "and it had fragmented. In 1932, our Crime Lab wasn't much at all. We didn't have a comparison microscope or even a scale to weigh the pieces. With the case being ruled a suicide, the lab saw no sense in holding onto what was left of the bullet. I'm afraid it's no longer there."

"Does its disappearance look deliberate?" asked Vera.

Ketchum shook his head. "I'd lay the blame on the department's growing pains, not malfeasance."

"So what is it you'd like us to do, Mike?" asked Vera.

"Where do we start?"

"I'd say start with this file," said Ketchum, handing it to Vera. "Review it carefully. See if Merit or his crew missed anything. Then ask around the garage and Sawyer's old beat. Talk to the people the detectives interviewed years ago. Often times after a little time has passed, loyalties change. You might find someone now who's no longer afraid to say what they wouldn't nine years ago."

"You mentioned Goon Dip Wong, yesterday," said Alan. "Was there anything in particular that points to him?"

"There's a note in the file from Officer Ben Kearney," said Ketchum. "He sent the detectives a tip a couple of days after the shooting that Merit thought was sketchy. An informant on Kearney's beat told him Hack had been talking to a man and a woman dressed in sporting attire. This was around midnight in front of the garage. Sawyer let them into the garage to talk private business."

"Was that followed-up on?" asked Vera. "That doesn't sound sketchy to me at all."

"Check for yourself, but I didn't read anything that said it was, which was not all that unusual back them."

"Why's that?" asked Vera.

"There are a couple of fragmented camps in the police department," said Ketchum. "In one camp you have the Masons and the other the Catholics. They both work against each other, trying to secure the 'softest' beats for those who view life and religion the way they do. 'Soft' beats are a euphemism for where the most payoffs can be found, like on First Avenue, Chinatown, and the Negro area. The other division is between the detectives and the beat cops, whom the detectives refer to as 'flatfoots.' Sad to say but there have been many cases where the detectives let a perfectly good arrest go free, putting the public at unnecessary risk, just so they can come back later and arrest the guy on their own, allowing them to take all the credit, leaving none for the beat cop. During my years I've experienced the religious conflict, and now I'm trying to abolish the elitism system."

"What kind of description did this informant give?" asked Alan.

"The woman was young," said Ketchum, "and dressed for the evening—'sporting' it said. There's nothing on the man with her."

"Would she have been a prostitute?" asked Vera.

"And the man her pimp?" asked Ketchum in reply. "I believe that's what 'sporting' means, but that's probably a question best put to Officer Kearney. Only remember to keep my name out of the conversation, for now anyway."

"And where's he working?" asked Alan.

Alan stood six-feet-two inches tall in his stocking feet, but when he introduced himself to Officer Kearney, he felt like David meeting Goliath. Only this time the meeting was friendly and the giant was wearing a beat cop's uniform, not animal skins and a helmet. Alan flashed his private detective's badge and stuck out his hand, which was quickly swallowed by a paw the size of a fielder's mitt. The grip was surprisingly gentle, and after letting go of Alan's hand, Kearney touched the bill of his cap, acknowledging Vera with a warm smile. He didn't stare at her the way the majority of men always did, hungry with unapologetic lust. Instead, Kearney's focus was the badge in her hand.

"A lady detective?" Kearney asked in a soft husky voice. "You're the first I've met."

"The first lady?" quipped Vera.

Kearney grinned broadly, his eyes sparkled, and this time he chuckled. "First lady shamus—with a real brass badge, no less."

"We're making an inquiry into Officer Hack Sawyer's death," said Alan. "We understand you were the one who found his body."

"That's right," said Kearney. "Sergeant McMurphy and I

found the body."

"We'd like to talk to you about that night, if you don't mind?" asked Alan.

Officer Kearney nodded and then paused a moment under the street light to gaze around Chinatown, staring with penetrating eyes down King Street and then across Maynard Avenue, like a shepherd keeping track of his flock, protecting them from the creatures of the night. "I'm due to ring in soon, and then we can chat over dinner. You like Chinese food?"

"We love Chinese," said Vera, "and we'll even buy. You just pick the restaurant."

"Since you two are in the business—cousins to police work, so to speak—you can call me Ben."

Vera and Alan followed a short distance behind Kearney to the call box at the corner. "Are you sure about picking up the tab for Ben?" Alan asked discreetly. "I bet he could tip down a fully loaded dim sum cart, wheels and all."

Vera smiled the way Alan liked to see her, full of confidence and a touch of humor. "You know that saying about the Army travelling on its stomach? Well, that applies to everyone else that you want to keep happy. We take care of Big Ben's appetite, and it's money well spent."

Officer Kearney inserted an oversized brass key and unlocked the blue call box door. As it opened wide, he adjusted the inside pointer to an embossed number under a label that said reports, and then he spun the crank around, generating an electric signal, before he shut the door and removed the key. "That will let them know that I'm okay… for an hour or so," he said.

"I always wondered what was inside those boxes," said Alan. "I thought they were just storage lockers where you kept your lunches."

"Or our liquor bottles?" asked Kearney non-threateningly.

Alan nodded. "I'd heard tell of that."

"There's really not enough room in there for anything more than a hip flask," said Kearney, "which hardly seems worth the bother, especially after the Repeal. There're plenty of bartenders willing to pour any of the boys in blue a free glass, and those so inclined to want more carry pints in their topcoats. It's been said to keep the chill away."

"Where to, now?" asked Vera.

"The King Café is up at the top of the block," he said while pointing. "It's a little short on ambience, but the food more than makes up for that."

"Do they serve dim sum this late in the day?" asked Alan.

"That's pretty well over with by two or three in the afternoon," said Kearney. "I heard it's bad form to serve it after that, but I never heard why. It must have something to do with tradition and staying true to the old Chinese ways."

As soon as the three were seated, the waiter brought a plate of barbecue pork, with teacups and a pot of tea. "Is there anything special you'd like, or do you trust me to pick out a few items?" asked Kearney.

Vera and Alan shared a look and then nodded for Kearney to go ahead, which he did without the need to consult a menu. Alan took a scoop of the hot mustard and began mixing it with the hot sauce, before cutting it again with soy sauce. Kearney looked down at the mixture with approval. "The beat man's brew," he said. "Where'd you learn that? Most people assume it's too hot mixed that way."

Alan smiled. "An old friend of ours, name of Vic Morrison, showed me this before he retired."

"Well good for Vic, on both accounts," said Kearney, "but I'd guess you're more interested in hearing what happened to Hacksaw than swapping recipes with me."

"If you don't mind," said Vera.

"Not at all. Where do you want me to start?"

"How about when you found the body?" asked Vera.

"That's a good a place as any," said Kearney. "So I'll start with what's been bugging me all these years." He glanced at Alan, as if he were checking with him also to see if it was okay for him to steer the conversation on his own.

Alan nodded for Kearney to continue, thinking there was something about this guy he liked.

"First off, I have to say I was a little surprised that Knuckles—that's what we called Sergeant McMurphy back then—was so quick to break the window to get inside the garage. Normally, we only do that kind of thing after we've established that we have exigent circumstances," Kearney said, glancing up to see if he needed to explain the terminology. "But I didn't think we had what the courts would call an urgent need, not at that point. I thought we were still at the 'concerned' threshold, which is a much lower standard for the courts. We weren't in the frantic mode yet. I was still assuming Hack was merely missing, not dead or injured. After I turned it over in my brain several times I began to wonder why Knuckles was so quick to break in. So eventually, like everyone else, I began to suspect that he probably knew all along that Hacksaw was inside there dead—so why wait?"

"Do you still think that way?" asked Vera.

"I'm not so sure at the moment," said Kearney. "Knuckles was pretty casual with me up to that point, not tense like I'd expect of someone who'd just shot a man twice in the face. Of course Knuckles was stinking of alcohol, which might have loosened him up, but if he did that—shot Hacksaw that way and then acted as if nothing had ever happened—he's either a damn fine actor or a cold-blooded psychopath."

"What about the car Hacksaw's body was found inside?" asked Alan. "We saw the pictures, but between the black and white and shades of gray it's hard to tell what's blood and what's something else. We thought you could fill in the details for us."

"You don't mind talking about this over dinner?" Kearney asked, glancing cautiously towards Vera.

"Thank you for asking," Vera said, "but we've both seen death and dying before, which is never pretty."

With chopsticks held like an old pro, Officer Kearney dipped a piece of barbecued pork into Alan's sauce mixture and then slid it into his mouth. After chewing delicately, swallowing, and sipping from his cup of tea, he nodded for Alan to continue with his questions.

"The pictures show Sawyer's gun resting above his lap, up around his chest," Alan said. "It was covered in blood, and I'm wondering why that would be?"

"I heard the suicide theory," said Kearney, "and if what Captain Merit thinks is true, it would mean that Sawyer shot himself in the face, in the middle of his left cheek with the first bullet. That shot wouldn't have been fatal, but it would have been bloody and terribly painful. It would be like having the worst visit to a dentist you could possibly imagine, and take away the Novocain. It must have been excruciatingly awful. I think that shot might have happened while he was sitting down in the back seat—or just before that, which would explain the pool of blood in the back. If Hack recovered from that wound a couple minutes later, like they think he did, he might have brought his left hand up to his jaw to check the wound, but that would be almost pointless."

"Maybe he tried to stop the blood loss," suggested Alan.

"Yeah," said Kearney. "He might have tried to put pressure on it to stop the bleeding. All cops have seen enough bleeding to know that's the first thing you do, but if you're trying to kill yourself, you don't want to stop the bleeding. What's the point of that?"

Alan nodded and picked up a piece of pork with his chopsticks and dipped it in the mustard brew. "You're right. That wouldn't make sense, and then would that mean that Sawyer would've grabbed onto the gun with his left hand to do what? Steady it for the next shot?"

"Possibly. He might've used the weak hand to make sure the gun was pointed at his forehead for the second shot."

"Were there any fingerprints on the gun?" asked Alan.

"Not that I've heard, and from what I saw that night, it's more like the revolver might have been wiped in blood."

"What do you mean 'wiped'?" asked Vera.

"You know how it is when you get wet paint on your hand and then touch something smooth?" asked Kearney. "You leave an impression of your fingerprints. Blood smears do the same thing, generally speaking, but this wasn't like that. It was smooth looking and heavily coated, not like it had been simply gripped by a hand that had blood on it— but soaked in it—maybe to cover what was underneath it."

"Wouldn't Sawyer's hands have been so bloody that they smoothed out the blood?" Vera asked.

"From the pictures it's hard to tell, but I don't recall them being bloody at all," said Kearney. "And remember the gun wasn't in his hands when I saw it. It was on top of his chest, like he'd dropped it—or someone dropped it—and it landed up there, or had been tossed up there."

Alan nodded, picturing what Kearney had said.

"That reminds me of something else I never told Merit's men," said Kearney. "McMurphy had washed his gloves before he met me that night. They were sopping wet on the floor of his car when he picked me up, smelling of soap. He said they fell into something rank earlier in the evening, so he rinsed them out while he was down here in Chinatown eating."

"Really?" asked Vera. "That's convenient."

Alan thought for a moment. "What about the rest of Officer Sawyer's clothing?" he asked. "Merit's report said his collar was open, his shirt tail pulled out, and his fly pulled down. Merit says most of that happened when he fell backwards between the seats."

"I saw the overcoat and shirt collar open," said Kearney, "but I didn't check the shirt tail or his fly. I can understand that the shirt tail got pulled up some, but Hacksaw wasn't so big that his shirt would've pulled out easily. But I'm not positive of that. As far as his fly being pulled down, I supposed he could've forgotten to zip it up after he relieved himself, but…"

Alan inhaled deeply as he considered the likelihood of that.

"Was there a note in the file about the cut on Knuckle's hand?" asked Kearney.

Alan shrugged and glanced at Vera. She shook her head, confirming what Alan remembered from the file. "Not that we saw," he said.

"There's another possibility," said Kearney. "Knuckles cut himself while breaking the shop window, and then he was the one who turned on the lights to the garage with his cut hand. When I looked over at the light switches, I saw blood on them, which might have come from Knuckles—or it could have been there already."

"More blood than would have come from the cut on his hand?" asked Vera.

"He wrapped his hand after he cut it, and that caught most of the blood. But some leaked through the bandage. Now thinking back on it, I don't remember there being enough to mark up the switch-plates like they were. Later, I just assumed that whoever murdered Hacksaw left a trail of blood going out of the shop."

"So, even that night, you thought he was murdered?" asked Vera.

"I'm still thinking that way," said Kearney, "but I don't have any evidence to prove it."

"We understand that you sent in a report to the detectives," said Vera, "that mentioned Officer Sawyer having company in the garage that night—possibly a young woman."

Kearney scooped a large serving of chow mein onto his plate next to the fried rice and egg foo young. He set the platter down and glanced back and forth between Alan and Vera, while thoughtfully nodding. "You two don't miss anything, do you? And you're the first to ask me about that. The detectives didn't seem to care. I got the feeling that if the case was going to be cracked, they wanted to do it without the help of a lowly beat officer."

Alan smiled. "I believe you reported she was 'dressed sportingly.' What exactly does that mean?"

"That information comes from an informant who wanted to keep their name out of it," said Officer Kearney.

"'Their' as in more than one person?" asked Vera, "or 'their' as in you don't want to tell us if it was a man or woman?"

"The latter," said Kearney. "But enough time's passed now, and I haven't seen her in years. She used to work the area up there, but she kept her nose fairly clean and maintained a low profile, so I didn't ride her as hard as I did the hookers who were cheats and thieves. She never dressed sportingly; that wasn't her style, or maybe she spent her money on other expenses. Sporting attire would have been worn at the upscale whore houses, like the one Lou Graham ran at Second and Washington or Madam Damndable's at First and King. Ones like those advertised that they were sporting houses. It's a euphemism—a rose by any other name—"

"Would smell as sweet," said Vera. "You read Shakespeare,

Ben?"

"From time to time," said Kearney. "When I get a night off work I like to attend the University's drama productions. But if you have any concerns that I was extra friendly with the rosebush we're talking about here, she was a bit on the thorny side and too short on blooms for my taste."

"Did your rosebush say what the woman looked like? Age? Race?" asked Alan.

"'Rosebush' is a great nom de plume," said Kearney. "We'll just call her that for now. She was holding something back. Maybe hoping to sell what she had, if the detectives came a-calling, peddling one piece at a time to them, increasing its worth—or on the other hand, she might have been afraid those involved in the shooting would come after her."

"Do you think that happened?" asked Alan. "Did someone go after her?"

"I haven't seen her in years, but girls in that line of work come and go all the time, never sticking around long," said Kearney. "She was a little older than the other working girls, maybe close to thirty. That's long-in-the-tooth for a prostitute. Thinking back, I had a feeling she might have a family in town that she was taking care of—so she might be a local who just left the business."

"Did Rosebush say if the lady was from up here?" asked Vera

"No she didn't, but if the young lady she'd seen was wearing sporting attire, she likely was from a downtown cathouse. We didn't have anything that fancy near Twelfth and Jackson or Thirteenth and Yesler. But of course there's always Goon Dip Wong's place over on Seventh Avenue, which takes up all the floors of a building that's just west of here. They have Chinese gambling in the basement, which they call the first floor; a western style casino on the main floor, which they call the second floor; run of the mill working girls on the third floor, which you get the picture... And cream of the crop working girls work the next floor up. There's one more floor on top of the building, but I don't know what's up there. As far as I know it's the main residence for the Wong family."

"Yes," said Alan nodding. "The floor numbers are off because the streets were raised."

"That's right," said Kearney. "Now the people here call that area the down-unders, and there's always something going on underneath the streets at night. I've nosed around there once or twice, but the sergeant told me to stay the hell out of there. He said what goes on down there is none of our concern, and if I went down there and got lost, they'd never find me, because he wouldn't come looking."

Alan knew about the catacombs. He nodded for Kearney to continue.

"So some of those ladies from the top floor make outcalls," said Kearney, "and it would have only been a five block walk from Seventh up to the garage on Twelfth. Goon Dip dresses the girls well—in everything from sporting attire, to lingerie, to top of the line leather and riding crops."

"Is there any indication that Officer Sawyer had adventurous tastes like that?" asked Vera.

"That's a nice way to put it," Kearney said with a smile toward Vera, "but I don't know. He may have developed a taste for *adventure* while working Vice and the Dry Squad, but if he did want that kind of thing, it seems it'd be a waste to indulge his high-end appetite up here in a garage—on duty, no less. Why not wait till after work to fully enjoy it and get what you're paying for? Why do it up there?"

"Would Goon Dip's girls all be Chinese?" asked Alan.

"Mostly, but not all," said Kearney. "I can't be certain because the Vice detectives won't let the beat cops go inside Goon Dip's."

"Why not?" asked Vera. "Can they do that?"

"Yes they can," said Kearney, "because my bosses in Patrol say they can." Kearney looked around at the other tables and then glanced outside while he thought a moment. "I'll have to ask you not to repeat this, but the brass finds that I'm a problem, when it comes to the system they have."

"Go on," encouraged Vera.

"I work nights. Not by choice, but because I won't be a good *sport*—which in my line of work is a gentlemanly reference to cops on the take. And in this case it means I won't be a bag man, pick up the payoffs the day crew is expected to collect, and pass them up the line. If I don't collect the graft, the bosses don't get their cut, which they look at as ripe fruit left to rot on the tree. They see my approach as a waste of a golden opportunity that life is presenting them. If it's out there, and people are willing to pay, why not pick the fruit? I told the lieutenant I'd seen enough chicanery while I was a wrestler, and I didn't want to be part of it anymore. I just wanted to do my job and collect a pension some day. So this is my punishment."

"You wrestled professionally?" asked Alan.

"Yeah, under the name Hurricane Alley. I scholarshiped through school playing football and was asked to play pro when I graduated, but there was more money in wrestling— and a lot less chance of ending up a cripple. Wrestling involves tumbling and pratfalls, so no one ever gets hurt. But after a couple years of butting heads with the promoter about who was supposed to win and who wasn't, I came back to Seattle. That was in '28."

"You were about to say something about Goon Dip Wong," Vera reminded him.

"Just that whoever's in charge of Vice doesn't want any beat cops interfering with Goon Dip or his operation. Officially, they tell us that if we follow-up on a lead that

47

takes us inside there on our own, we might throw off their plans for a raid they might have scheduled, maybe even for that very day."

"Is that a possibility?" asked Vera.

"I've been in Chinatown seven years," said Kearney. "There's never been a raid. Even if Vice finally gets the probable cause they need for a warrant, everybody and everything would be cleaned out before the detectives reached the second floor. Also, the detectives need to have an Asian informant willing to risk his life as a turncoat to show them around, or they could end up getting lost in the maze the locals call the smuggler's passage. Without a compass, they'd start out here but end up inside a building down on the waterfront—inside one they didn't have a warrant for."

"Are there smugglers' passages inside all these buildings?" asked Alan.

"The large ones, yes," said Kearney. "But I'm not so sure they're all for smuggling as much as they're designed to befuddle their rivals—" Kearney stopped mid-sentence. "I'm sorry for the big words, it's just that I live alone and like to read a lot."

Vera grinned and nodded at Alan, who was thinking the same thing. "You remind us of the old friend we mentioned earlier," said Alan. "When Vic used big words, something was troubling him—or someone was about to feel his wrath."

"It's a good memory for us," said Vera, "but you were saying?"

"The mazes I've been inside look like they were designed to confuse would-be robbers from rival tongs, the Immigration Service, or our vice cops, should they actually remember they work for the taxpayers and not the highest bidder. In one hotel room I saw a potbellied stove mounted on castors. There were people playing house in the room, with their children and all, but then they rolled the stove aside, including the flue and chimney stack, to access the passageway. As I see it, the Chinese wouldn't need that much protection to stall for time from the Vice Squad. It only takes a ten-second delay for them to make a high stakes game look legit, but if they were worried about a take-over robbery from rivals, they'd want the kind of time a ruse like that would buy them, so they could move their money to safety and shield their wealthy patrons."

"Amazing," said Vera, "but was there anymore of a description on the girl or the man who was with her?"

"Since we've covered this much, telling you a little more isn't going to hurt her reputation anymore," Kearney said. "Rosebush was in the alley next to the garage, rearranging her wardrobe after turning a trick with a customer. As she was about to leave, Hacksaw walked by, heading to the garage, accompanied by a young woman and her business manager, or least that's what Rose figured."

"How young?" asked Vera.

Kearney sat back and sighed. "Jail bait young, or close to it," he said. "An Asian-Caucasian mix, she thought. Very pretty."

"A mixed race girl?" asked Vera. "Would that be rare in Chinatown?"

"Yes and no," said Kearney. "You don't see many of them out during the day, working in the restaurants, garment shops, or selling produce on the street corners, but as I make my rounds at night and handle complaints, my work takes me inside some of the sporting houses that make up Chinatown. That's where you see them. It seems like every large house has one or two girls fitting that description, some have more. No one's confirmed it, but I have the feeling their contracts are purchased and they get moved

49

around between houses."

"Like slavery?" asked Vera.

"They'd never call it that," said Kearney. "Some of the girls who're brought in from China have financial arrangements with their sponsors. So they're working off a loan or debt their family incurred back home. As soon as their family's debt is paid, which typically runs until the girl's looks are gone, then she works on commission, up until she has enough to bring over the rest of their family members. What you find with a lot of the mixed-race babies, is that they were born into the business, born in brothels—they're the ones called 'trick babies.' They usually end up working inside the nicer houses—and they go for top dollar, if that's any consolation."

"Why the nicer houses?" asked Alan.

"A lot of their customers are well-to-do whites," said Kearney. "They're mostly men—but sometimes women—looking for a taste of the exotic, while finding comfort in the familiar."

Alan thought for a moment, processing what he'd just heard. "What about the man with her?" he asked.

Officer Kearney set down his chopsticks and topped off each of their tea cups. "She didn't get that good a look, but he was older than the girl and on the tall side. My guess would be that he was likely White or mixed race, because of the height, but that's not for sure. Rose described him as a little over six feet—about your height," Kearney said, inclining his head toward Alan. "Clean shaven and well tailored."

"Wouldn't he stand out in a crowd down here?" Alan asked. "No pun intended."

"Actually, I know a young man who fits that description, except for the age," said Kearney. "The one I'm thinking of works inside Goon Dip's now, but he would still have been dealing with puberty when Sawyer was killed."

"If we were to wander next door and hang around awhile, wouldn't we eventually see a likely candidate or two?"

"Well, that would be supposing he was from Goon Dip's, and then you would be assuming that he still works there," said Kearney, shaking his head. "So, maybe you'd find him there, but you wouldn't be able to get inside tonight. Too many eyes have seen you talking to me."

"Let me explain," Kearney went on. "You've probably noticed those balconies on the upper floors of all the buildings in Chinatown. There's a reason for them. That's where the tongs are located. They say they're the benevolent associations for the large families who share the same name, but these have spotters who watch the streets below. They look out for their own. They pass the word along building to building, street to street, making sure there are no surprises—no raids by rival gangs, no Immigration visits—no vice cops for that matter. When you leave here, they'll watch you until you're gone. You're better off coming back during the late morning or early afternoon, when dim sum is served. That's your best chance of catching him— when he's out and about. But I doubt you'll see her outside without an escort."

"Why's that?" asked Vera.

"Too much of a chance she might wander off and not come back. She's too valuable to Goon Dip for him to let her run off with a rich patron."

"What about my going inside as a customer?" asked Alan. "Would I have any problems fitting in?"

"Since you're young and Caucasian, they might worry that you were a rogue deputy sheriff or state trooper out to shake them down, so they might not let you gamble in a high stakes game until they got to know you. That could take several visits. They'd be less worried about you if you went in looking for a girl, but whoever snuggles up to you will find a way during the flirting and caressing to check you for a gun or badge, anything that'd indicate you might be a threat to them."

Alan scowled as he thought. There would be no way the direct approach would work inside a brothel. If he pulled out his detective badge and announced what he was after, they'd toss him out the back door into the alley, and he'd be lucky to escape with a few broken bones. His experience had also taught him that the Asians liked to fight with their feet. He'd taken a heavy kick to the face before, while his hands were tied behind his back, but he eventually delivered his own kicks to the coward, repaying the favor. Even though his assailant eventually paid with his life, Alan didn't look forward to another donnybrook, either here or in Japan Town, where the numbers would be stacked against him. They could come at him in waves, using their numbers to wear him down.

"Did you get any names at all?" asked Vera.

"Hua," said Kearney. "Or something with Hua in it."

"That sounds very Asian," said Alan. "Not a working girl's nickname."

"That's right," said Kearney. "Rosebush thought she'd heard the man call her that, but she's not positive."

"Is there any chance we might be able to find your Rosebush?" asked Vera. "I'd like to start with her, if you don't mind?"

Kearney slowly shook his head. "It's not that I mind, I just haven't seen her in years. I'm not sure she's still around—or still alive for that matter—but there's a slim chance I might be able to find her picture in our mug shot files. The problem is that I don't know her real name. Not too many people living on the edge of the law like to introduce themselves formally to us, so I'll have to search through every picture in the department's files. The next time I go to court, I'll wander up to the I.D. Bureau and take a look."

Vera took Alan's arm and tucked it in close to her as they walked west on King Street, back toward where Alan had parked the Buick. He normally loved the familiarity they shared, but this time his senses were tuned to the dangers that Officer Kearney had alerted them to a half hour before. He had seen the balconies in Chinatown on his other visits and had heard the chattering above the street in their strange dialect, but he'd assumed it was neighbors visiting, talking about their kids or the weather, speaking in a language that was most comfortable to them. He hadn't thought that what he had seen and heard might involve lookouts watching the streets below, keeping track of who came and went.

Alan and Vera passed underneath a balcony built out over the street. They continued on down the sidewalk to the corner. Alan waited until they were most of the way across Seventh Avenue before he glanced over his shoulder at the large brick building they had just passed. A third of the way down on the left was a nondescript entrance with double glass doors. There was no signage to indicate what was inside and up the stairs behind the door. Two sturdy Asian men, Chinese he guessed, stood near the door, each looking over the other's shoulders, like beat cops watching their partner's backs. They were the gate keepers he would have to get past.

Alan held the car door for Vera, before climbing in the driver's seat. He let the engine idle for a moment as he thought. "You know I'm going to have to go inside there, don't you?" he asked.

"I gather it's not where you and Vic hid out a few months ago." said Vera.

Alan shook his head and stared west on King Street toward the railroad stations a few blocks away.

"But with your taste for Asian women, that shouldn't pose any problem for you," Vera said.

Alan smiled wryly, knowing his blushing was obvious, which was the exact response Vera wanted from him.

"And I don't imagine you'd have a problem pretending you're a horny young man with a bulge in your pants, pockets full of cash, and looking for an exotic beauty—or two," said Vera with a wicked grin.

Alan stared at her a moment, wondering how much she knew about there having been two his first time. He couldn't imagine that his friend Vic had disclosed his coming of age experience, while they were on the run together, hiding out in a Chinese brothel. Alan had learned that Vera was crafty enough to pretend she knew more than she actually did, a ploy she'd used to manipulate Alan into disclosing more than he otherwise would have. He wasn't going to let her have the upper hand this time and confirm what she might only be guessing at. But there had been two women—she was right about that—both named after flowers, which was common in Vic's lair. But Vera didn't need to know the details, information she would be sure to taunt him with at her pleasure.

"I think I could manage to look eager," he said. "I could

pull that off."

Vera twisted slightly in her seat and reached over and squeezed Alan's thigh. "I know you'll have a good time without the need to pretend," she said. "And I think you're getting excited just thinking about it," she said as she brushed her hand up his leg towards his waist. "I know I am, but how will your sweet Alice feel about it?"

Alan spun sideways in his seat, drawing his leg up part way, ensuring there was a barrier between them. Over the past few months, he'd continued to enjoy her teasing and touching, but his deep ardor for her had cooled, starting the night he learned she was taking care of a problem for Mr. Brinkman which involved the murder of a woman who was about to escape the clutches of justice, at least according to Mr. B's interpretation of how the laws and vengeance applied to his needs. In Alan's mind, murder in self-defense or defense of somebody else was understandable; on the other hand, plotting a murder for the sake of revenge was another thing altogether. It required cold calculation and a lack of conscience, the very thing that separated humans from beasts. For a person to do what she had done for Brinkman, he figured she had to be flawed, maybe unrepairable, and to make it worse, she refused to talk to him about it. She said she had sworn to keep the details a secret, a condition Mr. B had insisted on. But despite her secrets and the murder, Vera still had a magnetism Alan could neither walk away from nor deny. He was drawn to her red hot flame, helplessly hypnotized, blinded to the fear he knew he should feel.

"You're getting excited about my going inside there?" Alan asked, not sure if he should let the conversation head off in the direction she had steered it. "Is that what you said?"

Vera rested her arm on Alan's knee. "Sure," she said. "Imagine what you could learn about yourself in there: what you'll want to see more of, what you'll want to see less of, what kind of things scratch your itches, and what chafes up a rash when you think too long about it. Just remember to wear a condom during all that play time. You might even want to take several of them along with you, because you wouldn't want to bring something dangerous back and pass it along to the woman you love."

Alan glanced down at Vera's arm, comfortably positioned above his knee, as if his thigh provided a convenient arm rest for her. He leaned back and draped his arm across the back of the seat and pushed the fedora back on his head. "Okay Vera, your mouth is saying one thing, but I'm sensing you're thinking—"

"You'll need to be safe," Vera said sharply. Then she pushed her lips into a hard pout, turned forward in her seat, and stared straight ahead.

In the several months he'd known her, Vera was seemingly always under control, or so he thought. This was one of the rare moments she was off her game. He wondered how far he should push to see what was bothering her.

"Of course I'll be safe," he said. Then he knitted his brows into a frown. "Are we talking about safe—snooping around for clues—or safe as in sex?"

Vera withdrew her arm and crossed her legs in front of her. Then she pressed the hem of her skirt down with the palms of her hand, a mannerism of modesty that continued to amaze him, given her past as a burlesque performer.

"They both can be fatal if you're not careful," Vera said. "And you heard Officer Kearney describing the inside of that place. It's a fortress with secret passages, hidden portals, and guards at every door. If they dismembered your body and threw you out with the trash, how would I know? How would I know when to come for you?"

Alan stared at her, forgetting his concerns about the

depth of her soul and now remembering how her passions for the people she loved ran to uncharted depths, like when they were aboard the Japanese merchant ship, the Hiye Maru, rescuing her daughter Jennifer. Throughout that whole ordeal, Vera battled her own mother bear instincts, supplanting them with well-reasoned calculation, emotional control, and focused lethalness, protecting the daughter she loved. Now, here she was again, a case of extreme contradictions that defied explanation: she was capable of murder on the one hand—he was certain of that—but she was also able to care deeply on the other, and right now he was pretty sure the deep love which was unsettling her was directed at him. That was it, wasn't it? Love?

Alan reached out and squeezed her hand. "I'll be careful. Trust me."

"If anything happens to you while you're inside there, darling, I'll leave that building a burnt out mausoleum full of lost souls."

Alan leaned close to her and with the back of his hand lightly brushed the side of her cheek and ran his fingers across her jaw line, where it met her graceful neck. Vera closed her eyes to the caress but then inclined her head toward the passenger door, away from him, which exposed more of her tantalizing neck. He reached behind her head, cupped it in his hand, and gently pulled her to him. He slid further across the bench seat and met her face as she turned back to face him. His nose slid past hers as he searched for her open lips with his and found them. He brushed his gently against hers and then forced her lips wider as he opened her mouth with his. After a brief hesitation her lips parted and accepted his tongue as he pushed it into her mouth, exploring.

Her chest arched with pleasure toward him, and on its rise one of her mounds met Alan's left hand, which he let drop gently across her, before squeezing the softness. He delicately slid his fingers inside her unbuttoned coat and over the top of her blouse, kneading and probing, wishing the blouse would pop open and reveal the splendor he knew it protected.

Vera moaned and whispered his name softly, and then she suddenly grabbed his hand and made him stop. "Alan, not here. Not now!"

"Why?" he asked. "You want it too."

"Look around you. Did you forget where we're at or why we're here?"

Alan withdrew his hand and leaned back to better see her. Outside on the sidewalk, beside the car, were two pairs of legs standing close by. He decided to ignore them, bent forward, and again kissed her full lips gently. "The hell with them," he said.

Vera grabbed Alan's tie, half way up his chest, first tugging on it one moment, pulling him tighter toward her, and then pushing it against him the next moment, breaking the connection between their lips. "Where'd that come from?" she asked. "You've been so distant lately, I thought you didn't care anymore."

"I've been working on a problem," he said. "Mulling it over."

"'Mulling?'" she asked. "No one talks that way anymore."

"When my mind goes blank, like it does when I'm with you, that's what comes out. That's the best I can do. You drive me nuts, and I've been mulling that over."

"I've been pawed, mauled, and muzzled, but this is my first for mulling," said Vera.

"Did you charge extra for the muzzling?" Alan asked as he leaned his body into her hand, stretched his neck, and kissed her lightly, as close friends do before parting.

"Of course," she said with a grin. "Same as the bad girls uptown."

Alan sat up and glanced out the window at the elderly Chinese men unabashedly staring through the car window at them as if they were actors on the silver screen. "You're right," Alan said. "I better let you go before the neighbors fetch Officer Kearney and report a rape."

"If this is a rape, I better wipe the smile off my face."

"Each time I kiss you, Vera, I've felt the need to apologize. But this time I'm not going to, because you had it coming, and I think you know it. I don't understand how you do it, but you bring out the lust in me."

"I'm not about to apologize for that, but I should apologize to your friend Alice for—"

"That's probably not a good idea," said Alan. "I'll take care of that—if it ever becomes necessary, which is just one of the things I'm mulling over. In the meantime, I need to remind myself to behave better. Keep my mitts—and lips—off you."

The following evening Alan parked the Buick in the 800 block of Main Street in the middle of Nihonmachi, otherwise known to Whites as Japan Town. Alan was dressed casually, compared to what he usually wore to work, with a leather jacket and wool slacks. And compared to how well she normally dressed, Vera's attire was also very casual. She wore a black sweater underneath her coat, over dark wools slacks, designed more for function than form. Although her curves were somewhat muted in this outfit, there was no camouflaging her womanliness.

Alan took her arm as they strolled down the sidewalk to the theater on the corner. As they rounded it, there was a small queue of people gathered at the ticket booth, finishing their purchases with the cashier. Alan glanced at a poster in an enclosed glass display, proclaiming the praises of "Nishizumi senshacho-den" the film currently running. "It's a war movie," said Alan. "Helmets, tanks, horses, and heroes. I can handle that."

"I've heard about this movie," said Vera. "It's got something to do with Japan's march on Nanking."

"Oh," Alan said dryly, a hint of a scowl on his face. "Nippon's glorious victory. I'd forgotten that. Will it show the rape and murder of the innocent women and children?"

"To see that version we'd have to find a theater in Chinatown. Up here we'll see only what Japan wants the world to see, the sanitized version."

Vera stood off to the side as Alan paid for their tickets. The young Japanese woman waiting on them didn't act surprised that two White people would be attending the showing. In the little conversation she and Alan had, her English was flawless. He figured she was second, if not third generation American. After entering the theater, Alan asked Vera if she wanted popcorn. Vera scowled playfully at him, apparently waiting to see if he was serious or not. "Hopefully we won't be here that long," she said.

While most of the movie patrons sat in a bunch towards the middle of the theater, Alan and Vera moved down close towards the screen, which hung down in front of the burgundy stage curtains. They took seats close to the aisle, away from the others.

"Follow my lead," whispered Vera. "This is where my skills are strongest. We'll move when the bombs are bursting in air and there's a lot of chaos on the screen. Tuck behind the curtain's edge and slide backstage as quickly as you can. Try not to ruffle the screen."

"Yes, ma—"

"Don't you dare call me that, you rascal!" Vera said as she smacked the side of Alan's leg playfully. "You absolutely hate it when I give you orders."

"Not really," Alan said with a smirk, "but I have to tease you when I can, pay you back for all the times you taunt me."

"So, it's revenge you want?" she asked. "Is that it?"

"It's your reaction I want. That's what I like to see."

"You're incurable. We'll stay long enough to let our eyes adapt to the dark, no more than that."

64

Ten minutes into the movie, Vera wound her hair into a ponytail, took a wool beret from her coat pocket, and pulled it down, tucking much of her hair up into it. She prodded Alan's leg with hers, and he climbed from his seat to the aisle, stepping out of her way. She quickly passed in front of him, and he followed her to the outer reaches of the raised stage, ten feet from the movie screen, where she sat back against the ledge, pushed herself up, spun around, and stood up. She braced her back against the theater's wall, as deep into the darkness as she could get. Alan followed her motions exactly, finally standing next to her, his feet near the edge of the stage. After a brief glance toward the audience, Vera slid her hand behind the curtain and pulled the heavy fabric out just far enough for her to pass behind, economizing her motion. Alan did his best to imitate her movements and was fast on her heels.

There was very little light that found its way to the back of the stage from behind the closed curtain, but that didn't pose a problem, since Vera and Alan knew their way around, having used this portal to the catacombs on other occasions. They quietly crossed the main stage, heading directly for the door that led to the stairwell. Vera reached it first, pushed down on the lever, and opened the door to total darkness.

"Wait till it's completely closed before you strike a match," Vera whispered. "We don't want to alert anyone we're here."

"Pistols out?" asked Alan as he stepped inside the stairwell and closed the door quietly, shutting out all the light, while manipulating the lever so that it wouldn't make a noise while clicking shut.

"Not yet," Vera whispered, her voice helping to guide Alan's way through the darkness. "I prefer to save the firepower for the back-up plan, when my feet or fists are overmatched, not lead with it."

Alan stepped down to the stair Vera was on, and in the crowded confines he listened quietly and felt her soft breaths on his shoulder, and then without explanation her breath moved several inches over and now landed on his neck. She was behind and close to him. He savored it, wanted it to last. She was leaning in closer than she needed, he sensed that she must be enjoying their closeness as much as he delighted in it. He wanted to spin around, clutch her tightly, run his hands up and down her body, and kiss her again, but knew he shouldn't. They had a job to do. Her breath was warm and inviting, but he wasn't exactly sure where she was at. He dipped his hand into his pocket to pull out a box of matches. In doing so, his elbow banged heavily into one of her breasts. "Oops, sorry," he whispered, as he instinctively drew his hand back and almost patted her mounds, reassuring them that he didn't mean to bruise them, but then he caught himself, realizing that would only compound his error. He was relieved she couldn't see his clumsiness in the dark.

"That's alright, darling" Vera whispered from close by. "They've had worse abuse."

Alan wanted to ask her to explain what she meant by that, but instead he forced his mind to focus, get off Vera's physicality. He slid the match box part way open and shook it gently, until one match jumped up above the rest where he could pinch hold of it, and pull it free.

Vera's bosoms pressed against his left arm, but she didn't pull them back—and he didn't want her to. Okay, he thought, this time the contact was all her doing and had to be deliberate. She had to know what she was doing and wanted the contact. He wasn't about to give ground to her and step away until the match was lit. Alan closed the small box and struck the match, bringing it to life on the second strike.

66

"Cup it with your hands," Vera said. "So it doesn't blind us to the darkness beyond."

Alan squeezed the match box closed and held it with the last two fingers of one hand, while forming his remaining fingers into a shield of sorts, reflecting the light down the steps that would take them to the sub-stage and then continue down to another level, located below the theater, the one that was the portal to the brick-lined chambers beneath the streets of Japan Town, Chinatown, and much more, traveling westward all the way to Pioneer Square and the waterfront.

Vera lightly laced her arm through Alan's as they tiptoed down to the bottom. Alan figured this gesture was one of reassurance from her, not dependence or fear. "Remind me," said Alan. "Why didn't we bring a flashlight?"

Alan lit another match, and while doing so he had to admit that he loved this contact with her. He'd heard of chakras and auras but hadn't given them or the Eastern concept of mystic thought much credence. If such things really existed, inside and around a person, and flawed ones could be made whole in some mysterious way, then Vera was exactly the person who could perform such magic. On the occasions she rubbed up against him, radiating her feminine mystique, she left him energized for weeks afterward.

"We could have brought a flashlight," said Vera, "but then it'd be that much more gear I'd have to carry and be sure not to lose. My flashlights are government issued, remember? If I left one down here for someone to find, it'd cause wide-spread panic."

Alan managed a chuckle before he and Vera stepped down from the wooden stairs to the brick pavers that lined the catacombs, to where it formed a three-way junction of tunnels outside the entrance to the theater. They had been down the tunnel that was straight in front of them before, following it for a couple of blocks, knowing that it ran to the west past a Buddhist temple and past the Panama Hotel, which had its own secret portal. The farther west they had traveled in the tunnel, the stronger the saltwater smell had become. They had reason to believe the brick-lined passage ran all the way to the waterfront, providing the perfect route for smuggling everything that wouldn't make it through Customs, or more importantly for the Asians, bypassing Immigration and the Chinese Exclusion Act.

The tunnel to the right wasn't a concern for them at this time, because it continued up the hill eastward, presumably heading into the higher reaches of Japan Town, up toward Harborview Hospital. It was the tunnel to the left they were going to take. An associate of theirs, Gunny Manheim, had taken that course a few months back and reported that it led down the grade to the south, underneath Jackson Street, into the heart of Chinatown. Gunny had used this southern tunnel to deliver a wounded enemy, a Japanese agent they shot during a skirmish with the White Dragon. Gunny overpaid an opium den's Chinese operators, enough so they kept their common foe "medicated" and out of everyone's way for a week. The den had been easy to find, according to Gunny, because there were boxes and a number of broken opium pipes left near the entrance.

Vera took down a lantern hanging from a peg on a post and shook it near her ear. "This one has plenty of kerosene," she said, passing the lantern to Alan.

Alan twisted the knob, increasing the amount of wick that was exposed, pulled up the glass, and lit the flame. The lantern flickered to life, casting a warm glow that surrounded them like a gigantic aura, a golden glow that was in sharp contrast to the inky darkness they had been climbing through. Alan slid the glass back into place,

68

protecting the flame from sudden movements and gusts of air. Vera took another lantern down from a peg and shook it also, as she had with the first. "This one has enough juice for a back up. We won't light it, unless we need it."

Alan carried the lantern he'd lit with his hand extended out and away from his body, while keeping his gun hand free. He was aware from other forays through the catacombs that the lantern was the proverbial two-edged sword. It provided them with the ability to see where they were going, but it also alerted others to Alan and Vera's approach, making them perfect targets. The danger was increased down here because the tunnels restricted their ability to zigzag or dive out of the way to safety. There was no safe place to dive when inside a tight tunnel. After traveling a dozen yards, Alan pulled the lantern closer to him, reduced the wick, diming its flame, and then he held it out away from him again. Vera clasped her hand lightly around Alan's arm, offering reassurance.

They cautiously passed two side spur tunnels, one on each side of the main tunnel, while traveling down the hill. When they reached the bottom of the grade, they came to a crossroads. Alan leaned close to Vera and pressed his lips close to her ear. "This crossing tunnel has to be Jackson Street," he said.

"Of course," said Vera, as she glanced east and then west. "The tunnel has a sharper pitched arch above us, which would sustain the greater weight of a busy street and the streetcars that pass above. Jackson's the main arterial, but we want to continue south, get as close to Goon Dip's place and King Street as we can."

Alan lowered the lantern close to the floor pavers and swept the light back and forth, examining the moistened grit on the worn pavers. "Lots of foot traffic through here," he said. "All directions."

Vera squeezed Alan's arm gently, and he again led them forward. Almost immediately on the other side of the Jackson Street crossing were more side spurs, entrances to the buildings that rose above ground level. Alan swung the lantern cautiously in front of him, glancing up each portal, looking for people lurking about, as well as the broken opium pipes and shipping boxes Gunny had described. Not seeing either, they continued to the next spur, which wasn't more than thirty feet past the last one. "You get the feeling we're getting close to the center of the beehive?" Alan asked.

Vera pressed against him. "Expect to see some bees before we get there, and if we do, act like we belong in the hive."

"And how do we do that?" Alan asked. "Act like we're hop heads looking for a bowl to smoke?"

Vera nudged Alan with her shoulder, "No, silly. Don't make eye contact with anyone. Act like we're minding our own business."

Not too far ahead was the end of this segment of the tunnel. It finished with a portal on either side. The one on the right was closer to them, and the one on the left was another thirty feet past that one. They slowed and cautiously peeked around the corner of the one to their right, where a wheelbarrow was tipped on its side. "This is it," said Alan. "Gunny's wheelbarrow. I bet this is the one he used to roll Riki down the hill…"

"Of course," said Vera. "Riki was in such a state…he couldn't walk."

Alan nodded sheepishly. "We only did what we had to. I hope sparing his life won't come back to haunt us some day. By the way," he added, "I stopped to visit Gunny the other night, and he's on the mend. He's using a cane, but otherwise he's moving around very well."

"That was nice, Champ. He told me how much he

appreciated your visit."

"So you've seen him too?"

"Of course I have. He and I go back a ways. We did a few black bag jobs together, but that's about as much as I can say, for now that is."

Beyond the overturned wheelbarrow at the mouth of the side spur was a raised curb and underground sidewalk, partially illuminated by the purplish light from above. Past what Alan could see of the sidewalk was the entrance to a building, which had a dust coated brick and terra cotta foundation, along with storefront windows that included painted signage in Chinese characters and English writing: "Deng's Herbal Remedies and Acupuncture." Scattered on the sidewalk in front of it were broken shipping boxes, along with shards from opium pipes, porcelain bowls, and dark green wine bottles. In the middle of the disarray was a pair of black silk slippers—with pasty colored feet sticking out of them, but no socks. Alan stopped to stare at the darkly clad, stupefied figure sprawled on the pavers outside the entrance to the shop. "What do you make of that?" he asked, with a nod toward the building in the background.

"I'd heard stories that the streets used to be lower," said Vera, "but I thought that was only in the old part of Seattle, down by Pioneer Square and Occidental Avenue. But it would make sense that when they graded off Beacon Hill and made the cut for Jackson Street that they'd also leveled out the low spots down here at the same time. This must have been one of the low spots, because this is the original entrance to the building."

"Sure," said Alan, "There's a curb and sidewalk. We're standing on what was probably the original street. So the catacombs actually merge with the old sidewalks down here. I wasn't sure how that would work. I wonder how much of it there is? And I hadn't thought about it, but the streets above us have a steady slope that leads toward the water, all the way from Twelfth Avenue down to Fourth, which isn't a natural occurrence. You don't find that kind of evenness in nature. She's never that forgiving. All the knolls, gulches, bumps and ant hills are gone, and then there's the light we're seeing from the purple glass, embedded in the sidewalks."

Alan dimmed the lantern's glow as far as he could, without losing the wick. He led Vera past the unconscious man on the ground, slouched against a thick wooden post at the opening to the tunnel. Alan took a protective position between Vera and the man, keeping himself between the two, even though he knew that if the inebriate was playing possum and suddenly lunged at them, Vera would handle that type of threat better than he could.

Vera's fighting skills were unparalleled—but she was still a lady in Alan's eyes. His upbringing had taught him to treat her as a gentleman would, and she seemed to savor that kind of attention from him. But she was more than capable of playing rough with the boys when she needed. In fact, the best move he could make to protect them both would be to get out of her way and give her room to work.

Alan glanced briefly at the man's Asian features, his wispy beard, mustache, and small flat nose. Then he paused to stare at his abdomen, searching for signs of life. The man's diaphragm finally pushed outward as he inhaled, and then it slowly dropped to let out air. Alan finally inhaled, himself, and stepped over the man onto the sidewalk.

Extending out from the terra cotta of the old building was an old gas lamp that appeared intact and functional, but it was unlit. Below the herbal medicine and acupuncture sign, painted in gold leaf, were the remnants of another word that had been scraped off the window: *Opium*. Alan reached out and touched the glass, drawing Vera's attention to the details as he traced the word with his finger.

Vera nodded. "Chinatown used to be wide-open here," she said. "This building's old enough that it pre-dates the laws against smoking opium. Those in charge probably figured opium was a scourge that only affected the Chinese, keeping their voices silent and docile. Because of that, the politicians didn't see the need to ban it."

A shadow crossed over them from the sidewalk above. Alan glanced up and stared at the thick purple glass, inlaid in the sidewalk above, supported from below by arched metal beams every few feet. The walls closest to the street were crudely constructed with an emphasis on sturdiness and holding back the fill dirt from the re-grade that raised the streets to their new level, no concern for esthetics, while the walls of the adjacent building still maintained most of their original grace and style. The thick post the man was lying against was part of the frame that created the portal to the catacombs. It had wooden dowels bored into it high up, and there were four lanterns on the various pegs. At the foot of the post, near the lying man was a five gallon can of kerosene. Alan inclined his head towards the direction they were heading. "I think I can guess where we're at," he said. "There's a large hotel above us that takes up most of this block. It used to have a Chinese name, but I think it's called the Milwaukie or something close to that. Its entrance is around the corner on King Street, which is about fifty feet south of us to your left. Goon Dip Wong's place would be on the other side of King and back across Seventh Avenue. The street level entrance we saw last night was about a hundred feet past the southeast corner of the intersection that's coming up. Do we want to see how close we can get?"

"If you mean Goon Dip Wong's," Vera said, "sure we do. It's totally *amazing* down here."

Alan paused and scrunched his eyes, taking a moment to

get the play on words. "Yes, *amazing*," he said. "The problem is we can't get very far in a straight line."

Alan held out the lantern to arms length, indicating the path they should take. "I'm going to hold onto this, even though we can see where we're going." He reached back and lightly clasped Vera's elbow. "Just in case."

"You're a regular Boy Scout," Vera said teasingly. "But I agree. We don't want to get into a scrape and then wished we'd had it when we didn't."

They reached the corner, and the door to the herb shop behind them opened. The voices that emanated from it were in an Asian dialect. Alan leaned close to Vera. "Remind me again: what's our story, should anyone want to know?"

"We're just minding our own business," said Vera. "If you're worried that we're the only white people who've ever come down here, I doubt that's true. After Gunny dropped Riki off, he didn't make a big deal about their response to seeing him here. We don't owe anybody an explanation."

Around the corner and ten feet down was another timber-braced tunnel with an unrecognizable Asian word painted above the entrance. It was directly across the sidewalk from a wood and glass front door to a darkened business with Asian characters painted on the window in red, black, and gold. In front of the door were discarded scraps of papers, printed with Asian characters. "Chinese Lottery tickets," said Vera.

Alan paused a moment to stare at the trash and then glanced over his shoulder. "This is where we cross under King Street."

"You can read Chinese?" Vera said with a smirk.

Alan grinned and shook his head, still enjoying her humor. "It's just my guess. Old fashioned dead reckoning."

Alan let out more wick to the lantern, increasing its glow and tugged lightly on Vera's arm, hoping to put some distance between them and whoever had just come out of the opium den. He was having second thoughts about their plan, not the part about going into the brothel alone, but the part that included Vera staying behind, hanging back to protect him. Who protects her while I'm gone? he wondered. Thinking about her fighting skills with her feet and la canne, he knew she didn't need his protecting, but his inner voice was telling him it was something he was born to do. He couldn't let her get hurt. Although their relationship wasn't at the point it had been two months before, it was almost back on track and improving. He knew he would be completely devastated if something happened to her, so much so that he wouldn't be able to hide his grief from Alice, his siblings, or his mother. He switched the lantern back to his left hand, freeing up his right, in case he needed to pull his large pistol.

Vera clasped his arm reassuringly to her side as they stepped into the narrow tunnel. Before they reached the halfway point under King Street, two silhouettes appeared on the other side and started to enter, but stopped to allow them to pass. Vera tugged Alan close to whisper like lovers would do. "Keep your hand away from your gun. If there's trouble, swing the lantern at their faces, keep them distracted and give me room to work."

Taking advantage of their closeness, Alan pressed his lips against her cheek for a quick kiss, like he was a school boy at recess. "Yes, ma'am," he whispered.

Vera threw her hip into Alan's, bumping him sideways and making him miss a step. "Rascal!" she said, in faux rage.

Nearing the exit to the tunnel, Alan heard laughter and voices speaking in conversational tones, which meant other people couldn't be too far away. He extended the lantern, pushing it straight out ahead of them. He quickly scanned the path and found the two dark silhouettes waiting just to the left. They weren't the source of the voices he had heard. They bowed their heads in his direction, a polite greeting. The men were Chinese, as expected, and dressed in the ubiquitous workers' garb of dark, drab coats buttoned to the neck, nondescript hats that showed ample signs of wear, and thick brogans on their feet. Alan returned their demure greeting instinctively, although his bow wasn't as deep, was more of a nod than theirs had been. He wanted to convey mutual respect, while not showing fear or giving the appearance that he and Vera were a threat to whatever was going on under the streets. Alan's mind flashed to a Gary Cooper western, where the hero met with distrustful Indians to arrange safe passage for a wagon train. That's what they wanted here, safe passage through new territory.

As Vera followed Alan out of the tunnel, the men raised their gazes to her, but then they bowed quickly again. Alan half-bowed, caught himself, and rolled his eyes while keeping himself between the men and Vera. He couldn't help but want to be her protector.

Alan and Vera passed more men and paused underneath another set of glass skylights to gather their bearings. The men glanced up at Vera, said something to each other in their dialect, and then ducked into the tunnel they had been waiting to use.

While listening to other voices, which must have been nearby, Alan sniffed in the air. "I smell food," he said.

Vera nodded in agreement. "Noodles," she said. "Like from won ton soup."

"I bet that's what it is," said Alan.

"And cigarette smoke," said Vera, wrinkling her nose.

"That's right," Alan said. "You don't smoke."

Vera shook her head. "I know it's all of a sudden a glamorous thing, but I think there are risks. I've never thought the smoker's cough was very becoming to anyone."

They followed their noses less than a dozen feet to the corner and then continued around it. Ten to twelve feet down Seventh was another tunnel to the left, which would cross under the street and take them closer to Goon Dip's. Less than ten feet past the tunnel, on the right, was a shop door propped open, which belonged to a restaurant, the source of the voices and the aromas. The steamy storefront window had a depiction of a large bowl with chopsticks hovering above it, accompanied by Chinese characters.

Alan glanced sideways at Vera, "You want to take a look inside?"

"Of course, darling. It always pays to know your environment—know what you might be up against or where you might find a safe haven when the storm strikes."

Alan twisted the knob on the lantern, reducing the wick all the way. He raised the glass and blew out what remained of the flame. He set the lantern down on the ancient sidewalk next to where a footing for the building jutted out. "I think this might look out of place in there."

Vera nodded. "Leaving it here will free up your hands, in case you need them."

Alan offered his elbow to Vera. She reached through the crook he made and took his arm. He boldly led her through the open door into the open noodle shop, exuding more confidence than he felt. There were fifteen to twenty men sitting around large round tables, communal style, like they were familiar with each other. They all momentarily paused to check out the new visitors, as did the hired help. Most of the men were attired in similar clothing as the two Vera and Alan had just passed at the tunnel entrance, while others in the café had finer quality Asian attire. Their buttoned up coats were made of silk, their hats newer and better kept, and their shoes were much lighter in construction than the brogans, more of a slipper than a shoe, indicating the owners didn't spend much time out of doors or up on the street level during the winter. Sitting at the counter, back near the kitchen, were three men in high end western attire: wool suits, shirts, and bright silk ties. Similar in age and size, their fedoras closely matched the color of their suits, and their shoes were highly polished, making them stand out in this small crowd. The common denominator for all of the patrons was their penchant for cigarette smoking, which contributed to the haze that hung in the air.

A small, graying man in a long, bright, red silk coat approached Alan and Vera with a smile. He gestured for them to enter the shop. "You take seat, please," he said, indicating an open table over by the wall.

Vera smiled broadly but shook her head no. "Perhaps later," she said. "We just wanted to see what you serve."

While Vera spoke with the manager, Alan glanced about. Many of the men had returned their attention to their bowls of soup, except a few who continued to stare at Vera, already forgetting that Alan was there. Two waitresses working the front were soon joined by a third. All three of them were young, pretty, and seemingly out of place in the otherwise male environment. They reminded Alan of the young women he had seen working inside the brothel where he and Vic hid out after the shootout they'd been involved in at the Kasbah a few months back. Alan suspected the young women had also been "sold" by their families as indentured servants, then smuggled into this country, and were now having to work off their debt to win their freedom. Vic had tried to explain how the system worked, rescuing the girls' families from abject poverty. He said that it wasn't as cruel as whites thought it to be, because everyone involved in the agreements seemed to benefit, particularly those who held the girls' contracts.

The last part to the puzzle, the piece Alan still didn't understand, was what the girls got out of the arrangement. They were cast out like anchors from boats adrift, with their families' hopes that when they had paid their debt to the men who'd bought them, they would then dutifully continue working in order to bring the rest of their families over to this country where the anchor caught fast—the land of the free, which was full of bountiful opportunity. Given that there was little in it for the girls, Alan wondered why they would cooperate with it? Why not just walk away and fade into the American mainstream someplace? In the brothel business, Vic had told him that the girls worked on settling their debt "until the bloom fell off the rose." With the bloom gone, how would they then find husbands that would still want them and start families of their own? Would that opportunity ever be there for them?

Alan wondered if his patronage was good for the girls or not. Poppy, the young woman he'd spent most of his time with certainly seemed to enjoy his company while he was there, particularly their love making sessions. She jealously kept him for herself as much as she could, and it was she who snuggled up to him at night, often initiating another round of sexual passion, waking him for what she hungered for in the middle of the night, grabbing him by his penis, craving the largeness of his erection.

Vic's advice for Alan was encouragement that he treat the girls nicely, leaving a large tip under their pillow, giving them something extra that Mama San couldn't touch, for their families.

Without glancing up at Alan, the girl who had come from the kitchen stopped at a table nearby to clear the bowls into a tub. She was beautiful like Poppy, with similarly fine features. Her hair was pulled back into a bun, held in place by a hairnet, but he could imagine how it would drape softly when she let it down. He wondered if she also took the name of a flower, like the girls at the brothel. He stared at her porcelain like hands as she efficiently swept the bowls into the tub. His nostrils flared and his eyebrows arched.

Vera reached out and clasped Alan's arm, disturbing his reverie. "Down, Rover," she said, pushing her lips out into a thoughtful pout. Then she smiled knowingly. "You do have an eye for the Asian beauties."

Alan blinked apologetically.

"Does she remind you of someone you knew recently?" Vera asked.

Alan dropped his gaze to the tiled floor, but realized instantly that his silence had already told her too much. He nodded, but didn't answer.

"Some time you'll have to tell me all about her, Champ."

"You don't really want to know the details, do you?"

"Why not, Champ? Maybe that kind of thing excites me, and it would probably excite you to tell me. That's not such a bad thing. Look, you're twenty-one and free. I don't think that even your precious Alice hopes you saved yourself for her. And since you're not wearing a wedding ring, I'd say you're entitled to explore whatever's out there and willing to be explored."

Alan sucked his tongue back as far as it would go and then pushed out his cheek as he thought. Was Vera encouraging him to play around on Alice? Did she hope he'd get in trouble doing so, and did she hope that would send him wandering back in the direction of Vera's camp? Was that her way of subtly driving a wedge between Alice, him, and what they had?

The manager was still chatting in a heavy accent, focusing his attention on Vera, trying to hustle her and Alan to a table. Vera raised her hand elegantly, indicating they needed a moment to discuss something. "I'll be back in a minute," she told the waiter, and then she turned away from him and leaned close to Alan. "I'll walk you through the tunnel, and if it's clear on the other side, leave me your gun, and I'll wait here for you."

Alan brushed close to Vera's cheek. "This reminds me of my mother walking me to school on my first day. Are you going to give me a kiss on the forehead too?"

Vera leaned back sharply and shot Alan a hard glare, an expression he wasn't used to seeing from her, especially directed at him.

"I'm just kidding," he said apologetically. "I don't think of you as older…I mean…like my mother, who isn't that old…"

Vera licked her lips and then her frown began to soften. "Please don't compare me to Mary."

"I didn't mean for it to come out that way."

Vera shook her head and forced a smile that was weak around the edges. "It's not the age," she said. "But for the record, I'm two years younger than her."

"So, it's something else between you two?" Alan asked.

"Yes, something that will have to wait for later, if ever."

"It's dad, of course."

Vera lightly clasped Alan's elbow and ever so slightly guided him toward the door. "Mary and I have some unresolved conflicts," she said. "Let's just leave it at that."

Alan led them to the cross-street tunnel entrance. He glanced down at the lantern on the old sidewalk and then peered through the tunnel, sizing it up. "I can see well enough now that I vote we skip the lantern."

Vera paused for a moment. "Don't light it, but hand it to me. That way I'll have it, if I need to bash a noggin or set someone on fire."

Vera laced her arm into Alan's and pulled it tight to her body. "Let's continue to act like a couple," she said, as Alan

81

stepped into the tunnel.

They walked side by side under the street. This tunnel was lower and narrower than the others they had walked through. Vera's hips brushed against Alan's, and he wondered if that was deliberate, her way of telling him to have a good time while in the brothel—but not too good a time, and of course making sure he would think about her.

When they reached the far side, Alan slowed to glance around the corner to their right, with Vera right behind him. They stopped quietly and slipped back into the tunnel and peeked out again. Thirty feet from the porthole were two gas lamps mounted on either side of an entrance, at the top of a small stack of cut granite steps. They illuminated a Chinese man sitting on the lowest step with his legs drawn up close, more like he was squatting. He was dressed in black silk, with a pillbox hat that covered gray hair pulled into a long queue in the back. He was smoking a pipe with an overly long stem, quietly contemplating the brick wall in front of him.

"I didn't know any of the Chinese still wore their hair like that," Alan said.

"Me neither. He's definitely old school."

Alan turned to face Vera, putting his back toward the watchman and the building's entrance. He withdrew his pistol from his jacket pocket, along with his detective badge and passed them to her, the gun butt first. She slipped the items inside her coat and pulled the lapels shut.

Alan reached out and lightly clasped her arm, tugging her close to him. "So up above us they have two bruisers watching the door," he said. "It must be the main entrance, and down here they have a guy whose best years were in the last century."

Vera stood on her toes and peeked over Alan's shoulder, brushing his cheek with hers and licking her lips as she thought. "I'm going to guess this is the employees' entrance…and maybe it also serves close friends. They just need a warm body to monitor the traffic down here and sound an alarm in case there's a surprise attack."

"Police?"

"From our chat with Kearney, I don't think that's what they're afraid of, because in reality they'd have plenty of time to tidy things up before the police could make it to the upper floors, which would give them time to make it look like a social club instead of a gambling den. I'd say it's more likely a rival gang they're worried about, not the police—or possibly somebody angry about losing a large poker stake and wanting to bring a few friends with him to settle a score."

Alan put both hands on Vera's sides and gazed deep into her eyes. "A kiss for luck?" he asked.

Vera smiled warmly, the dimples flashing under her amazing cheekbones, the confident way he liked to see her. "Why sure," she said. "A short one here, and a longer one when you return."

Alan leaned forward, and Vera met her mouth with his. She kissed softly, but when he began to pull away, she chased after his lips with her teeth, catching the lower lip playfully. The not quite painful gesture caught him by surprise, sending a jolt from the back of his neck down through his loins, like a lightning strike, causing him to shiver like he had a nervous tic. He wanted to grab Vera tightly, squeeze her breasts, and kiss her long and hard, but he knew that this wasn't the time or place. Obviously she was aware of that too, or so he thought, but she was willing to take risks, test her luck when she shouldn't. Maybe she got off on adrenalin thrills like he did, he wondered.

Alan pushed himself away from Vera and headed down the underground sidewalk into the light.

Alan dug his hands deep into his pockets, trying to appear casual and nonthreatening. The old Chinese man withdrew the pipe from his mouth and exhaled smoke that had a pleasant tobacco aroma. It reminded Alan of the one his dad favored while he read the evening paper in the living room after dinner. It was a good memory for Alan. He hated to let it go.

He slowed to a stop, his feet scraping on damp brick grit that covered the sidewalk, while his eyes followed the water flow across the walkway, along the side of the building, to where a steady flow ran down the bricks through a dense patch of dark green moss. On the step the Chinese man put out his palm, face up. "Two dollars," he said flatly.

The price of admission, Alan thought. He dug out his wallet and peeled out two singles, without complaint, and began to hand the cash to the man.

The man's hand struck Alan's like a snake bite, snatching the money before clasping Alan's fingertips in a vice grip hold that could loosen rusty lugs on an old tractor. "What kind of work you do?" demanded the man as he examined Alan's palm intently.

"I'm a chauffeur," said Alan. "I drive a car for my boss."

Alan instinctively tried to tug his hand away, but the more he struggled the tighter the grip became, and the man began bending Alan's fingers back, forcing him up onto his toes.

"You policeman?" the man asked, while continuing to puff casually on his pipe.

"No," Alan said, shaking his head for emphasis, while considering punching the man to make him release his grip, which he knew somehow would be a grave mistake.

"You have strong hands but skin is soft from easy work," said the man. "You not have policeman's hands or eyes, but you too young to be a chauffeur. A man should work hard before becoming a driver. What do you want here?"

"I heard it was a good place for a single man to party… with girls…and play cards."

"You have face for play with girls, but not a poker face. Who did you hear about this place from?" asked the man as he relaxed his leverage on Alan's hand, allowing him to stand flat-footed again.

"Vic Morrison told me about this place."

The Chinese man took the pipe out of his mouth and stared up at Alan without saying a word.

"Vic used to spend a lot of time at Mama San's place," said Alan, "about a block east of here. He told me about this place."

"Vic is welcome here, but you're not. Where is Vic now?" asked the man.

"He bought out his girl's contract and took her home to China."

"Girl's name?" asked the man.

"Iris," said Alan.

The man nodded thoughtfully. "Iris is gone now, along with others."

"Vic took her to China," said Alan. "Poppy was one of the others…and Rose." Both women held a special spot in

Alan's life. They had shared a hot bath with him after the gun battle at the Kasbah, and they had guided him through his first sexual experience, a surprise present from Vic, grateful that Alan saved his life.

The man let go of Alan's hand. "When you come here, bring money, not your wallet. Wallets have a way of getting lost, they disappear. Makes you look like cherry boy, not a friend of Vic."

There was that term again. Vic had teased him about being a cherry boy, as had Poppy and Rose during the loss of his virginity. Alan smiled sheepishly and nodded politely.

The man put the pipe in his mouth, took another puff, and resumed staring at the wall. He slid the two dollars in his pocket. "Pai Gow on bottom floor is mostly for Chinese people; Casino and restaurant are on two, everybody plays; girls you want on three; girls too much for young man who carries wallet, on four; booze on every floor."

Alan climbed the steps, paused for a moment. "What's on five?"

"Big trouble," said the man. "Nobody is up there but family and old servants who never go out."

Alan paused for a moment, waiting to see if more instructions were to follow from the sole sentry. While staring at the man's long queue, Alan couldn't help but compare and contrast his attitude to those of the maître d' hotels he had done business with since becoming Mr. Brinkman's driver. They served a similar purpose as gatekeepers, but they did it with grace, garnering large tips in the process. Maybe this man had little interest in the money, and instead he saw pleasantries and courtesy as meaningless frivolity. Oddly though, that gave him his own endearing charm.

Alan opened the door, which had Chinese characters in gold leafing on the glass, along with the numbers from

87

a street address, another reminder that this once had been the original street level.

Vera watched after Alan for a moment as he walked away from her, before retracing her path through the tunnel, back to the noodle shop. She fought the urge to protect him from what might lie ahead. He would have to learn his own lessons in life, fight his own skirmishes, and come back to her with his stories of derring-do. As she exited the tunnel, the three men who had been at the counter at the noodle shop were leaving. The first one, a little on the heavy side, waited at the door for the two behind him, who followed at their own pace. The third one, who was taller than Alan, slowed to a stop in the doorway as if he owned all the space around him, enough so that Vera had to pause a moment and wait for him to step aside. His dark eyes stared as if he was studying her the way an artist might a model he was about to sketch. Finally he touched the brim of his hat, a courtesy gesture.

Vera met his unsettling gaze, which she thought might be what he'd wanted. He was in his mid-twenties, handsome, and sure of himself. His eyes were almond shaped and exotic, not as slanted as she had expected. She excused herself as she stepped past him, heading for the table the manager had pointed out to her earlier. She didn't hear footsteps walking away, so she guessed the man was continuing to stare after her, checking her posterior and her walk, attention she was used to receiving from men. The manager met her at the table and pulled the chair out for her. When she glanced up again the man was walking away, joining the other young men headed into the tunnel.

The manager stood eagerly. "Would you like a pot of tea to start with?" he asked.

Vera reached up and lightly touched his hand. "Yes, please, and do you mind telling me who the nice young man was who just left?"

The manager took a half step backward and winced. He knitted his brow and frowned. He leaned down close so that only Vera could hear. "He not so nice a young man. He Nelson Wong."

"Nelson?" Vera asked, wanting to be sure.

The manager smiled doubtfully. "That may just be his American name, but it's what he's known by."

"I see," said Vera, deciding that she had done enough prying for the evening, not wanting to draw undue attention to herself.

Alan was met with a gush of cigarette smoke as he entered the hall foyer on the first level, which had dark wainscoting that climbed six feet up the walls, above the ubiquitous small white octagonal tiles so common to buildings of the turn of the century era. Alan heard the hum of male voices, speaking in one or more dialects which he assumed were Chinese, though he couldn't be sure. The occasional shout, laugh, and teasing taunt punctuated the noisy drone of excited chatter. Alan stepped forward and glanced into the room to his right, which had four or more large round tables covered in green felt, surrounded by Asian men sitting shoulder to shoulder, their attention focused on the action on the tables in front of them that included black tiles and stacks of poker chips. The room was full of men in common working attire, similar to what Vera and Alan had seen in the noodle shop. A few young Asian women in black kimonos with gold trim and slits up the side that exposed ample portions of their upper legs carried trays with drinks to the tables.

Just inside the room was an ornate teller's cage, which Alan guessed to be 75 to 100 years old. A middle-aged Chinese woman in a golden kimono with a high collar

91

worked the booth. A few feet behind her stood a young Chinese man in a gray business suit. He sized Alan up, giving him the once over as he entered the room. He must be the muscle, Alan thought. Probably good with his fists and feet and packing heat under his coat.

As Alan wandered toward the booth, he heard the happy squeal of a woman's voice from the back of the room. He scanned for the source of the excitement and saw a number of women's heads gathered around a table that was apparently reserved just for them.

"Are you interested in Pai Gow?" asked the woman in the teller's booth.

Alan smiled at her and shrugged his shoulders. "Never played it before," he said.

"You can have a drink and watch awhile," she said. "When you think you're ready to join the play, come back for chips. But you might be more comfortable trying the roulette or Black Jack tables on the next floor up."

Alan smiled, appreciating her concern. Behind her, the bouncer winced as he stared past Alan.

Alan resisted the impulse to quickly turn and see what made the hired muscle jerk nervously. He waited a five count and then casually rotated his head toward the doorway. Filling the opening and scanning the crowded room were the same three Chinese men Alan had seen moments before in the noodle shop. The tallest of the men stood slightly ahead of the other two, surveying the room like he was the prince and all present were his subjects. He was broader shouldered than Alan remembered, but of course in the noodle shop he had been sitting on a stool at the counter. The man's eyes worked their way around the room and landed on Alan, staring unabashedly, giving him the same head to toe chilling appraisal that the muscle behind the cage had given him moments before.

"Your lady friend would be welcome here with you, but you came alone," he said to Alan.

"She has an aversion to gaming," said Alan, meeting the man's gaze.

"But she doesn't mind you going it alone? Here? Where there might be other temptations for a man?"

"In those respects, she can be very tolerant," said Alan, not sure what part of his brain the banter was coming from. Given his strict religious upbringing, he always felt he was artless, with not a single skill in verbal deception, but then here he was playing the role of an urbane sophisticate, in deep, way over his head. "She lets me off the leash if I don't stray too far, spend too much money."

The taller man smiled knowingly, more so in judgment of Alan than in a shared camaraderie. He stuck out his hand. "I'm Nelson Wong, this is my place."

Alan met Nelson's hand with his, knowing full well the offered grip would be firm and assertive, which it was. "Alan Stewart," he countered with a slight nod, and then his brow knitted thoughtfully. "But I thought this was Goon Dip's place?"

"That is correct. My father is much older now and lets me run the business for him. I am his son and the manager— your host, is what I should have said. Is there something in particular you are looking for? A game, a drink, an herb, a potion, or perhaps a woman with special skills?"

Alan's eyebrow arched at the last request, and he knew they did as soon as it happened. *The old doorman was right,* Alan thought—he didn't have a poker face, but he could use this to his advantage. Lowering his eyes and his voice, playing the part of a proper gentleman who would only discuss this kind of subject in whispers, he quickly glanced at his pocket watch as if he were on a schedule. "What kind of skills would this woman have?"

Nelson Wong's not quite almond shaped eyes brightened. "It depends on your interests and what your pocket book can afford. We have girls who specialize in fellatio and enjoy both cunnilingus and anal. And of course there is masturbation, bondage, domination, spankings, flogging, voyeurism, and multiple partners—if that's what you wish and your purse can afford. The only things we don't offer are boys, physical abuse, or mutilation...of course. If you want those, you need to go further east, out of Chinatown. I've heard there is such a place on the edge of Japan Town, but I wouldn't know for sure."

"Of course," said Alan, trying to pretend he was at least familiar with all of the terms and their meanings.

"Let me show you upstairs," said the host, as he made a grand gesture and slid his arm over Alan's shoulder and around his back, as if he was leading a dance partner in a tango across the floor.

Nelson's hand deftly worked its way down Alan's back, and during their short walk to the hallway, the host had managed to lightly touch each of Alan's sides, but not thoroughly. *He's checking to see if I'm armed*, Alan thought.

In the hallway Nelson shook off the other two men, who turned back, returning to the gaming room. Alan and Nelson Wong stopped at the foot of an open stairway with a padded red carpet, tucked in place by brass rods. "Are all of your girls Chinese?" asked Alan.

Nelson shook his head. "Most of our girls are Chinese, but we have all kinds here, ones that appeal to every taste: Blacks, Whites, Indians, and some who are in-between."

"In-between?" Alan asked, even though he was sure what Wong meant.

"Yes. You know, those of mixed breeds. Half Black-half Chinese, half White-half Chinese."

Just like Nelson, Alan thought.

"If that's what you prefer," said Nelson. "Those girls can be more expensive, depending on their beauty and skills. They usually have a regular clientele and would of course be on the fourth floor."

Alan and Nelson took the stairs up to the second floor, where a young man in a page's uniform waited, standing by a red velvet rope with a brass hook. Nelson nodded at the youth, who pulled the rope back to let them through. They stepped into a larger room, more open than the one they had been in on the first floor. It wasn't as noisy on this floor. Off to the left was a Chinese restaurant, more upscale than Alan was used to seeing. It was full of patrons. To his right was the gaming room, where the clicking of the roulette ball could be heard over the occasional celebratory shriek, as the steel ball tap-danced around the spinning wheel before settling into a numbered slot. Cigarette and blue-grey cigar smoke clung heavily in the air, but not nearly to the extent that it had on the more crowded floor below. Nelson said something in Chinese to the youth, who suddenly glanced toward Alan and nodded as if understanding an instruction.

Nelson smiled perfunctorily. "I told him that should you choose to leave through the down-unders, he was to allow you to do so."

"Did I come in through the wrong door?"

"I'm afraid so."

"But I paid the guard outside an admission fee," said Alan.

"We have no guard at the down-under entrance," said Nelson, "and there is no entry fee."

Alan's brow knitted low over his eyes as he stared at Nelson to see if he was teasing him. "An older Chinese man with a long queue in the back," Alan said, using his hands to indicate what the hair looked like. "I paid him two dollars."

"A queue?" asked Nelson, a puzzled expression on his face. "No one wears their hair in a queue anymore. For most men, it's been that way since the 1910s. The last Emperor of China cut his in '22. After that, no one has worn it that way."

Alan decided not to pursue the subject further. Apparently the old Chinese man had run a dodge on him, taking him for two bucks, and Alan had fallen for it. Lesson learned. The man must have taken the money and disappeared down the sidewalk before Nelson and his friends arrived, but given the phantom's knowledge of the workings of the place, surely Nelson must have seen him around. No matter, Alan thought.

Alan surveyed the room in front of him, which was exactly as the man he had paid had described it. It was very much like a casino, with card tables, craps, and Black Jack stations with small clutches of people huddled around, almost all of them sipping drinks. Many of these customers were White, a lot more than Alan had expected to see in Chinatown, and some of them were policemen who wore the same type of blue tunic that Officer Ben Kearney wore, except theirs had more brass and bars on their collars. There must have been five or six of them gathered near a banquet room next to the restaurant, holding drinks, and watching the front entrance.

So it was just like Kearney described, Alan thought. Members of the police department were in bed, probably literally, with those who ran this place. Curious to whether he'd recognize any of the police, Alan tried to catch a glimpse of their faces, while at the same time hoping to not get caught doing so. He didn't want to raise the concern of Nelson Wong.

Alan wandered off to the right into the casino area, continuing to check out the rest of the floor. Unlike what he'd found downstairs, the women on this floor were dressed more provocatively and stood next to their men, many playing alongside them, a mix of hired escorts and well-dressed women out on the town. It suddenly occurred to Alan that this would have been the kind of place Vera might have frequented with his father. He wondered how long ago that might have been. Perhaps that's why Vera was on edge; she knew what went on inside this establishment.

"Do any of these games appeal to you?" asked Nelson.

Alan's eyes hooded thoughtfully as he pushed out his lower lip.

"Not so much, I suppose," said Nelson. "Perhaps then it is the young women you are here for."

Alan's brow flicked and a grin worked its way across his face.

Nelson Wong gracefully gestured with one hand toward the stairway that continued upstairs, while lightly clasping Alan's elbow with his other hand familiarly. "This way—"

A roaring cheer burst out of the banquet room where the policemen had been gathering and covered every other sound in the casino. Alan stopped on the stairs and glanced at the back of a man in a beige overcoat with a bright, silk scarf wrapped around his neck standing in the middle of policemen in their dress uniforms. Wearing a light-colored Homburg tilted rakishly to the side of his head, the man paused for a moment before stepping into the room. As soon as he took a step inside, the many gathered greeted him again: "WELCOME BACK, HARRY!" The heroic tribute was followed quickly by a spontaneous salute, lead by a piano played loudly inside the room. "FOR HE'S A JOLLY GOOD FELLOW, FOR..."

Alan stared open mouthed, and muttered an oath under his breath. "Hungry Harry," he sighed.

"You know Lieutenant Frantz?" asked Nelson Wong.

Alan stared for a moment at the back of Frantz's head

as the lieutenant took off his hat and waved to his well-wishers. Alan had shot Frantz twice, in the months before, once with the lieutenant's dropped pistol, and the other time with an M-1 Garand—both wounds to the head, while trying to avenge his father's murder. But Frantz had survived somehow, even though the last bullet had torn through his mouth, gouged a divot through his tongue, and knocked out two of his teeth. So…the bad lieutenant was finally out of the hospital, Alan thought, and that meant Harry was capable of coming after him now, if he chose to do so.

Mr. Brinkman had told Alan that Frantz officially reported his shooter as being either Benny Hile or Vic Morrison, both of whom were believed to have escaped to Vancouver, Canada, but Alan suspected that Harry really knew who his shooter was. Alan just didn't know why Harry had held that information back when filing his report. Perhaps he would have had to tell Chief Ketchum that Alan was actually holding him and the police department accountable for the killing of his father, Mackie Stewart.

"Do you know Lieutenant Frantz, Mr. Stewart? Would you like to wish him well?"

"No," said Alan, sharply, and then he shook his head slowly, realizing he had conveyed too much information with his abrupt reply. "We've had some encounters in the past, when I was younger. I doubt he'd welcome my interruption. I guess you could say he's not a fan of mine."

"Nor you of him, Mr. Stewart?"

"No, not exactly," Alan said, hoping to change the direction of the conversation. "Let's just leave it at that."

The sound of laughter from the party below grew weaker as they walked up the flight of stairs to the third floor, supplanted by the music on the next floor, which grew louder. The stairwell opened into a large foyer with large rooms on both sides. Even though he anticipated that it was coming, Alan was surprised by the enormity of it, finding the open area packed with women in bedroom attire. What the women wore was nothing like what his sister owned, at least as far as he knew. It was more like what he thought Vera would have on hand for entertaining company, or might have once used in her burlesque act, or what she possibly kept for her own enjoyment. Alan's eyes flashed wide, trying to take it all in, there would be no hiding that from Nelson. The clothing the twenty or so women wore was more exotic and upscale than Alan had seen during his extended stay at Mama San's brothel, which Vic, his mentor, affectionately referred to as his Ritz. At Vic's Ritz the women generally wore silk kimonos or more modest night gowns, designed for sleeping, not play.

During his upbringing, Alan had seen bras, panties, and garters in his mother's laundry basket, but he'd only heard of corsets, camisoles, merry widows, and silk teddies. Their lore was supplanted in his memory by drawings sprinkled throughout his father's detective magazines of vulnerable women dressed provocatively, always in distress, waiting to be rescued by tough-as-nails detectives, but this was his first experience at seeing such apparel on real live, breathing, women of unquestioned beauty, who knew what they had and were happy to show it.

Alan stared at a brunette woman who sat close to where he stood. She wore too much lipstick for his taste, but she suddenly came to life as if he'd pushed her "on" button, causing her to writhe about on her lounge seat, turning her shoulders square to him, and arching her back, making a spectacular presentation of cleavage. He didn't care for that much war paint, but he sure liked the way she filled out her merry widow, which was pulled together tightly in the front, causing her bosoms to spill out over the top. Attached to the garment's bottom were garter straps that tugged lazily at the dark silk hose that rose above her knees, covering her crossed legs.

Next to her was another brunette, not as busty as the first or as heavily made-up, but her smaller bosoms were nicely proportioned, set off well by her cinched-tight corset, which also made her hips look fuller, shapelier, something for a man to grab onto. Her legs were drawn up tight on the sofa exposing the side of her thigh and the curve of her buttocks. She had to wait a moment to catch one of Alan's eyes with hers, but as soon as she did she lowered one of her legs to the Persian carpet, which exposed her smooth inner thighs all the way up to her pink, silk panties.

Alan's eyebrow arched high as he inhaled deeply, slowly, through flared nostrils, as if he were trying to smell the scent of these women from ten feet away. He did so unconsciously, but while doing so, he realized on another level that Nelson Wong was paying close attention to his physical reactions, continuing to evaluate Alan and his purpose for being there. *This part is easy*, Alan thought. He didn't have to put on an act to pretend these women aroused him.

Two young women—Chinese, Alan thought—dressed similarly in pastel teddies with bare legs, slid off the sofa they shared together and approached Alan directly. One of them glanced quickly toward Nelson, as a child might when seeking approval from a parent. Each of the young ladies took one of Alan's arms, tugging him lightly, pulling him away from Nelson toward the inner circle of lounging women who were available and eager. "You like two girls?" one of them asked demurely.

Alan smiled wolfishly, and shrugged slightly, again inhaling deeply as he had before. Although he tried to take in all the beauty in front of him, he was still aware of the women's hands caressing his back and working their way around his sides. The same beauty who had glanced toward Nelson a moment earlier turned slightly again in his direction and shook her head. *No, I'm not armed*, Alan thought, or carrying a badge either. *If that's their concern.*

The partner to the young woman sending signals slid her hand around to Alan's front, across his belt and up his chest. "You have strong muscles," she purred.

Despite knowing what the women were up to, Alan couldn't help but enjoy the touching, the gentle caresses. He flashed back again to his first adventure at Vic's hideaway, which wasn't that long ago. He remembered fondly what Rose and Poppy had done for him, and how well they worked together to satisfy him, despite each of them wanting him as their own steady customer.

The woman doing the signals slid her hand up Alan's chest, massaging his pectoral muscles. She, too, cooed and arched her brows and flared her nostrils. *She's playing her role*, Alan thought, *but she likes what she sees*. He tried reminding himself of what Vera had taught him when she had recruited him to moonlight working a more dangerous job for Naval Intelligence: "Losing your focus could cost you your life!" she had said. "Keep your mind on business and the final goal!"

As he thought about that night with Vera, she had grabbed him by his crotch and offered to do a routine from her burlesque days for him, a thought that was arousing all by itself, even without the pleasurable groping. *Keep your mind on business!* He reminded himself. The only acting he would have to do was to pretend he wasn't interested in any of the girls on this floor, but instead he was looking for a particular girl who might be with a customer somewhere else in the building.

The second Chinese woman suddenly raked her hand across Alan's chest, skipping lightly across his belt, and then slowing as she firmly pressed her hand against his genitals. She let out a loud squeal, announcing she was pleased with her discovery. "You so big!" she said.

Alan felt the blood rush to his face, which competed with all that was flowing to his scrotum. Before he could say anything in protest, the lookout dropped her hand to Alan's fly, joining her partner in the prodding exploration of what was inside his pants. Alan turned his head to glance back at Nelson Wong, who shrugged in mild bemusement. Whatever happened next was Alan's call. Nelson didn't appear to care what the women might do to him in this open area of the floor.

Both of the young women continued their exploration of Alan's body, with one of them feeling for the fly, catching the zipper tab and quickly tugging it down. The other women, who had been sitting nearby, slid off their perches and started to gather around in a huddle, all staring at

Alan's crotch. "Pull it out!" one of them said from off to his side, encouraging the two who were working on him. "I want to see it!" said another.

The second Chinese woman slid her fingers inside Alan's open fly and hooked it around the shaft of his penis, ready to tug it sideways through the opening, outside his pants. Alan dropped his hands quickly, caught her hand, and pulled her fingers out of his pants, while making sure his penis stayed exactly where he wanted it, which wasn't difficult, because it had grown in size, while stiffening with enjoyment. Pulling it out now would be like walking a plank sideways through a door. His penis knew what it liked, despite Alan's conscious mind trying to rule the libido.

"Not yet!" Alan said, firmly but kindly, as he stepped back and struggled to zip his fly over the growing bulge.

Nelson Wong stepped forward a pace, a look of concern on his face. "Is something wrong?" he asked.

Alan shook his head and forced a smile, willing his face to take on the façade of nonchalance, hoping he appeared more experienced than he actually was in the ways of the world. "Everything's fine," he said. "These women are very beautiful. Very appealing. I'd like to have them all someday, one at a time, but my fantasy tonight was for a woman of mixed race—one of the in-betweens. Possibly one who has both Chinese and White parents."

Nelson leaned back, arching away from him, as Alan had seen the beat cops do when they were sizing up a tough customer, trying to intimidate the person into bending to their will, which always seemed to work for the police, at least the times Alan had been with them when they used that approach.

"Is there someone in particular you're looking for?" Nelson asked.

"No," Alan said, shaking his head. "When you described

an in-between downstairs, I just thought that sounded very appealing—something more exotic than I've had before."

"You've had all of these before?" Nelson asked. "A blonde, a brunette, and two Chinese girls at the same time?"

Alan nodded, confident that two out of three questions was close enough, while fully aware that there was no way Nelson could verify the accuracy of what he claimed.

Nelson stepped closer, a wry smile crossing his face. "And these experiences you've always paid for?"

"Not always," said Alan.

Nelson leaned closer still, keeping the conversation just between them. "You could have any girl here for five dollars, but you would like to go up a floor, where services run thirty to forty dollars. Pardon me for saying, but unless you're going up there for the opium, the fourth floor is a little rich for a young man's purse…and it's more tailored for experienced tastes."

Alan was somewhat relieved that the forty-dollar figure had been brought up, although the numbers were very high. Before he entered the establishment he had absolutely no idea what to expect in the way of pricing. "I feel like treating myself to something special tonight," he said.

"What? Is it your Birthday?" Nelson asked.

"No, that's not for a few months yet. I just have an itch I wanted scratched."

"The woman friend you were with earlier in the noodle shop, she doesn't scratch that itch for you?" Nelson asked.

He remembers everything, Alan thought. He's right on top of his game.

"No," Alan said, not denying the obvious. "She's very good at raising a rash on me, but I can't ask her to scratch every itch for me. She might not understand."

Nelson stared at Alan evenly, evaluating, but he didn't respond.

"There are certain cravings I would just as soon not discuss with her," Alan said.

"But won't she ask what you were doing inside The House of Wong? After all, what we do here is known to all. For gambling our customers can be assured that even if they have an unfortunate run of luck, losing everything they brought with them, we will see to it that they have enough of a purse to catch a cab ride home. And as for our other services, we have a nasty—but honest—reputation for what we provide. It is well known that we dabble in the exotic, and perhaps you will leave with passion scratches—or marks from lashings—that will take days to heal? Wouldn't that be hard to explain? Your woman might be concerned."

Just what is it they do upstairs? Alan wondered, and then he forced a smile. "She's actually very tolerant and doesn't expect to satisfy all my needs, and there are those I'd just as soon she didn't know about."

"Then you're a lucky man to have such a woman, especially in this country," said Nelson. "Although half the blood that runs through my veins is like yours, I've been raised Chinese, and speaking for the rest of the world, American society perplexes us. It has laws governing much of what you can do in your personal life: what is permissible in your bedroom, with whom you might sleep, how old that person must be and that they must be of the opposite sex, but then you have voted to give women the right to vote alongside you, treating them as equals. And most amazing of all, America denied both sexes access to alcohol, even though it was obvious that so many people wanted and needed it. Yours is a culture of mixed messages, but then those same prohibitions are what drive the free-spirited here to our House. You have created a demand for this establishment and what we provide, and I should be grateful."

"But you're not grateful?"

Nelson shrugged indifferently. "The woman who is waiting for you in the down-unders, perhaps with her you've found your equal, and it is me who must learn something new."

Alan smiled evenly, careful how that gesture might be interpreted, not wanting to provoke an argument or further a discussion that might keep him from his goal: finding the mixed-race woman who might have been with Hacksaw Sawyer the night he was killed.

"I'd never thought about our friendship in those terms before," Alan said, "but that's very accurate. It's often me who learns from her, which makes her my friend."

Nelson Wong stared at Alan a moment, appraisingly, and then he reached lightly for his elbow while grandly gesturing toward the carpeted steps with his other hand. "This way to the fourth floor, Mr. Stewart, where you will find whips, riding crops, bondage, domination, fetishes, exotic massages, and opium for the discerning customer."

What am I getting myself into? Alan wondered, as he forced a smile that he hoped made him appear both hungry and urbane at the same time.

10

As Nelson Wong and Alan crested the top step, Alan realized that the higher they had climbed the less the wool carpet showed wear and tear, and at the top of the steps, the red themed colors seemed brighter, fresher. There were far fewer women here on this floor than on the floor below, but what they lacked in numbers they made up for in beauty.

A buxom blonde with a Veronica Lake peek-a-boo hairstyle sat by herself on a divan in a reclining position, wearing a white bodice with pink satin trim, while four other women stood a few feet away in a group, chatting amicably among themselves. The blonde had sad blue eyes and a disinterested countenance, lost in her own thoughts. She stared at the male intruders as if they disturbed her reverie, first at Nelson Wong and then Alan, as if she were studying actors entering a stage. Then she shifted her weight forward, as if suddenly remembering a role she was supposed to act out in this play, and she gracefully stood up, facing Alan squarely, pulling her shoulders back, assuming her part. When she gazed again at him, her eyes showed a spark of interest, like a lantern coming to life, drawing oxygen from the room into its flickering flame.

Her beauty was compelling, and Alan had trouble

taking his eyes away from hers to check on the other ladies nearby, who were belatedly turning around to see their new customer. Alan glanced back at the blonde as her bodice scooped open when she leaned forward, generously exposing cleavage, more of which spilled out over the top. Her porcelain colored bosoms disturbingly bore traces of pink and red welts that hadn't completely faded. Alan stared at the marks, forgetting the soft mounds they disgraced, puzzling over how incongruous the wounds appeared on something so exquisite. Having been strapped a time or two on the backside while growing up, he could guess what caused the marks. His tanning had been delivered with a willow switch to his behind, which had always been covered in public, so he couldn't imagine why this woman's welts would be on a part of her body that was so beautiful and likely to be exposed, especially given her profession, and which should have been a source of pride and pleasure for both her and her partner. As the woman drew a pink silk wrap around herself, Alan saw similar markings on her upper arms. Did she want to be whipped, or had she been punished? Did she have a choice in this matter? Was it something she wanted done? After all, Alan had read tales in *Black Mask* magazine that some women liked that sort of thing. Were the girls up here allowed to say 'No' if they didn't want to play rough with the customers? And if he engaged one of them for an hour at these high prices, would flogging her with a cat-o-nine tails or a crop be what she expected of him while he tried to ask questions? How would his mentor Vic Morrison have handled this? Would Vic have played along to get the information he wanted? Could Vic have hurt a woman, even one who pretended she liked that kind of thing?

The other four women opened their tiny circle and faced Alan directly but remained standing together, as if they were sisters and shared a common bond. The brunette on the left had amazing cheekbones and hazel eyes with penciled-in brows arching high, giving her a fresh Loretta Young look. Under her open red silk robe she wore a red merry widow with black satin trim, garter straps, and black hose that fell short of her red panties. She pulled back the robe with her right hand, arched her back slightly, and shifted her weight onto a long, shapely leg, while pushing her fist defiantly down on the hip, as if she were about to thrust the other side directly into Alan's path, should he try to move around her. She stared at him, sizing him up approvingly, daring him to choose anybody but her.

On her immediate left was a woman of mixed heritage, White and Chinese, Alan guessed. Could this be the mysterious Hua, he wondered; but of course that all depended on whether Kearney's informant, Rosebush, had gotten the woman's name right in the first place.

The Asian woman's black hair was parted on the side and pulled back into a bun behind her head. Long fancy chopsticks stuck through the bun like crossed swords. Her eyes were dark and almond shape with a slight upward cast, which along with her erect posture bespoke confidence and mild curiosity in the man in front of her. She wore a dark blue silk kimono with a bold design. Alan thought he remembered seeing a Bengal tiger, while her back was turned to him, but he wasn't sure. Her robe was loosely tied together around her waist, but it was pulled open enough to show that she was bare in front, down through her cleavage. She made no effort to cinch the robe and cover her delights.

Next to her was a darker brunette with luscious curls and dark, striking eyes. She also was of mixed blood, but Alan couldn't be sure which gene pools had donated their best to create her. She was at least half White, if not more, with light African coloring and something else. Her hair's curl was natural and soft, not a perm or process which would make it stiff and coarse. Alan guessed she had Cherokee or Seminole in her family tree. He remembered a college professor at the U.W. telling him about the mixing of slaves and Indians in the Deep South, before the Trail of Tears displaced them. Whatever the admixture, she was stunning, and her full lips hinted that she would have a large capacity for passion. She wore a black silk wrap over a short nightgown in matching colors. Her long legs were lean and bare, and she set her weight over them evenly.

The last in the standing group was another of White and Chinese mix. She was close enough in height, weight, and stature to be a sister to the other Asian woman. She also had perfect posture, her head held erect and proud, as if she were of noble birth. Her hair was parted on the opposite side than the first woman's, and it was also pulled back into a bun—only without the hair sticks—giving her more of a stern look which went well with the rest of her leather outfit. She wore a black bustier, cinched so tight that it didn't require shoulder straps. Beneath that she sported black leather shorts that must have been a size too small, which barely covered her bottom and hinted at her body's crevices. Her thighs were naked to just above her knees, where they slid into very tall black boots, which were folded over at the top like a pirate's. Hanging loosely from her right hand was a short whip with far more straps than a cat-o-nine tails. It was the kind of whip that could have left the welts Alan had seen on the blonde.

Alan figured that with his luck this would be Hua, and if he were to take her into a private room for an hour, he would have to play along and submit to some kind of torture that involved binding his wrists and ankles, while she applied vigorous lashings to him, while he lay helpless and naked. Given his memories of lashings as a kid, this wasn't exactly his idea of fun.

Alan chewed on the inside of his lip, trying to decide how he would handle this. He turned square to the blonde, who was closest to him, and extended his hand. "I'm Alan. Alan Stewart," he said.

The woman stared down at his hand for a moment and then reached for it, taking it softly into hers. She pulled it close to her like Vera would do. "I'm Ruth," she said.

"Pleased to meet you, Ruth."

Alan smiled broadly, feigning confidence he didn't really feel, and canted his head sideways to glance at the other women. The four stood silently, their carriage relaxing some, as if they had assumed Alan had made his choice, which didn't include any of them.

Alan pulled his hand away from Ruth and stepped toward the other women, who quickly renewed their enthusiasm. The darker one with the striking eyes reached for Alan's hand and clasped it gently.

"I'm Lena," she said.

Alan smiled broadly and nodded. He couldn't help it. He liked the touching. The women closed in around him, petting and stroking his back and upper arms. Here and there a soft breast bumped against his triceps and forearms. "I'm Alan Stewart," he repeated.

"You're such a gentleman," said the brunette on his left. "I'm Laurie." She reached for his hand and tugged it gently toward her.

Alan sensed he was onto something with the handshaking. The young women seemed to like it too, but it also appeared they weren't used to having it done up here. He wondered why that would be. Wouldn't their normal cast of clients shake hands with the women they were about to have sex with? He'd have to ask Vera about that to see if she could explain what was going on.

"I'm Mei," said the woman in black leather. She also grabbed Alan's hand, but unlike the others she made a point to squeeze it firmly. She's staying in character, he guessed, where the others had lowered their guard and communicated like they would with a friend. *Mei*, Alan repeated in his mind, wondering how that might pass for Hua.

"Is that what your clients call you?" he asked, being careful with his choice of words.

Mei's brow dipped low, matching Alan's. "Not usually," she said sternly. "They call me Mistress Mei—when I give them permission to speak."

Alan's mouth involuntarily formed a small circle as he slowly processed her response, still holding and shaking her hand. He tried to imagine how an encounter with Mistress Mei behind locked doors might play out, wondering why anyone would want to put up with a stern, unloving bitch who'd flog them painfully. He'd heard about domination and submission but couldn't grasp it. His understanding was that men in powerful positions had the need to surrender complete control to a dominatrix, which was completely the opposite reality of the rest of their lives, where they called in past due notes and ordered foreclosures, grinding other men's hopes and fortunes into dust, along with their bones. He couldn't conceive how the role reversal would work. It would only work for him if at some point the dynamics of the dominatrix session changed. For him to play the weak submissive worm licking Mei's spiked heels and tasting her whip, there would have to be a furious, heated, passionate battle for control in the end. He could imagine at the climactic point he would tear off Mei's leather and hungrily ravage her body with his hands, smothering her screams with his mouth covering her open lips, his legs intertwined with hers, forcing them apart, showing her who was boss.

Suddenly, a session with Mistress Mei sounded strangely appealing to him, something he'd never thought of before but might want to try—if not this night, perhaps another. Maybe he would end up giving her a few lashings with that whip of hers—if that's what she wanted—or he wanted.

"I'm Lynn," interrupted the young Asian woman in the silk robe.

Alan paused for a moment, processing what he had just heard. *Stay in the moment*, he urged himself. *Your life might depend on it*. Then he repeated the name in his head. *Lynn*, he thought. That still didn't sound at all like Hua, which is what Rosebush thought she'd heard.

Alan canted his head sideways and carefully appraised her. She stuck her hand out to meet his. Alan withdrew his from Mistress Mei's, licked his lips unconsciously, and turned to face Lynn, who stood erect with her shoulders back and her chest out slightly. He glanced down to make sure his hand met hers squarely and saw that her robe was still draped open to the waist, exposing the smooth furrow between her breasts. He forced his eyes up to meet hers, noting again the resemblance between her and Mei.

Alan winked and smiled. "Are you two related?" Alan asked, his eyes dancing back and forth between the two women."

"We are sisters," they both said at the same time.

Alan tried to guess at their ages, but couldn't be sure. The dominatrix outfit made Mei appear more mature, authoritative, and adult like. From what he and Vera had learned from Officer Kearney, the mystery woman could be anywhere in age from twenty-three to twenty-eight years old now, depending on how young she was when she'd started in the business, and both of these young women appeared to fit in at the low end of the age spectrum.

"I'm nearly two years older," said Mei, "if that's what

you're wondering, but we're not about to tell you exactly what that would be."

Alan's brow flashed high, and then he turned his gaze back to Lynn. "What do I call you?" he asked.

"I prefer Lynn."

"Of course," Alan said, and then he leaned back to glance at all of the young women, one by one, admiring their unique beauty. "And what is it that each of you do?" he asked.

Nelson Wong moved up close behind Alan. "Anything that would please you, Mr. Stewart."

Alan swung his head slightly so that he could see Nelson better.

"But I should caution you," said Nelson, "that the girls on this floor prefer customers who are loyal to them, not one who is likely to be a butterfly and would sample the nectar from every flower in sight. Of course this house favors the customer's preference, but I must say that harmony in the bedroom—even when you're paying for it—can bring priceless joy. The girls have a way of expressing their gratitude, and I like to minimize bickering, which is only human and understandable. Do you understand what I'm saying?"

"I believe you're saying: Choose wisely."

"If you don't mind," Nelson said. "Now would you like some time to make your decision?"

Alan raised an eyebrow and smiled wolfishly.

"I'll get you a drink," said Nelson. "There's no hurry, unless your waiting friend will grow impatient. What would you like?"

"How about a scotch on the rocks?" Alan asked.

"Any preference?"

"Something smooth—that won't bite my head off."

"If you don't want biting, then perhaps you should stay

114

away from Lena," Nelson said, a hint of a smile on his face.

Alan glanced quickly at the dark beauty, who made a face at Nelson, while he stepped behind an open fully stocked bar. Is there something going on between those two? Alan wondered. Lena seems comfortable challenging his authority and not worried about his retaliating against her. But then Nelson would likely have his pick of any of the women in here anytime he wanted, unless the butterfly issue also applied to him.

Not realizing he was still holding Lynn's hand—and she holding his, rubbing it gently, Alan glanced at the rooms on the far side of the bar, where a small mix of male customers lingered about, representing White and Asian cultures. "What's over there?" he asked.

"Those are the premium opium rooms," Lynn said. "They're for discerning customers who prefer privacy and a personal attendant. They're smaller than the ones on the first floor and really just compartments for individuals to seek pleasure, or sometimes add a friend or two."

"A lot of times that company goes by the name of Lynn," said Ruth.

Lynn snarled impishly at Ruth, and then she resumed a more amicable smile, which she flashed at Alan. "That's not true," she said. "I'm not allowed in there."

They're posturing, Alan thought, wanting my approval, and hoping I'll select one of them over the others. The stakes must be pretty high up here.

"So, which one of us do you want?" purred Laurie. "I know I could satisfy all your needs, from fellatio to anal, if that's what you'd like?"

Alan's eyebrow flicked high quickly. *I'd like each and every one of you*, he thought impulsively—but kept to himself— one right after the other, two or three times a night, every night. I'd be a sultan and a stallion with the world's most impressive harem, but...I need to stay focused on getting the information from one of these girls, most likely Lynn.

Alan grinned sheepishly at Lynn. "And what's your specialty?" he asked, glancing down at his hand, which she was kneading the knots out of.

"I do massages, of course."

"Massages!" said Alan, repeating what he heard, making sure it wasn't just wishful thinking on his part. Getting a massage would be a perfect way for him to ask questions. It would also be relaxing, and there wouldn't be any sex involved. So that way he could maintain his faithfulness to Alice—and Vera, for that matter. His love life was complicated enough as it was without dragging in another woman, especially one highly skilled in pleasuring a man.

Nelson Wong returned, holding a large tumbler full of ice surrounded by a golden liquid. He extended his arm and the glass to Alan. "Will Glenfiddich do?" Nelson asked. "I believe this one is twenty-years old. We also have Chivas Regal, if you'd prefer that."

"Glennfiddich is perfect," said Alan, accepting the glass, which he figured must have four or five healthy shots of Scotland's finest in it.

"While you were away, I made my choice," Alan said, and as soon as he did the other women started peeling away from the clutch, leaving him alone with Lynn.

"Lynn specializes in exotic massages," said Nelson. "Excellent choice, Mr. Stewart."

Pleased with his decision, Alan took a sip from his drink, being careful not to take in too much, which would make him gag and look like a cherry boy, as Vic would say. Alan glanced back to Lynn, and she eagerly returned his smile, withdrew her hand and adjusted her robe, tugging at the sections between her breasts, which only caused the robe's silk material to fluff forward, exposing the inner circles of her soft, round mounds. With her other hand, she tugged Alan's hand, pulling him away from the gathering, past a darkened set of steps that disappeared into the darkness above them.

Two hours later, Alan plopped silently in a chair across from Vera, still sitting in the down-under noodle shop. Her arms were folded in front of her and her legs were crossed. After a moment Alan exhaled and glanced up shyly.

Vera sucked in her cheeks and closed her eyes for a moment. "You've been drinking," she said. "I can smell it from here."

Alan nodded, suddenly tired and fighting to stay awake.

"Are you drunk?"

"Uhmm…not so much," Alan said with a slight slur.

"What does that mean?"

"That I should probably have a few cups of coffee and something to eat."

"Well, you're not going to be driving like that. That's for sure."

Vera caught the manager's eye and indicated with a tilt of her head for him to come over. "Do you have strong coffee?" she asked.

"No coffee, Lady, just tea."

Vera rolled her eyes. "Bring a hot pot of tea then, and a bowl of your beef noodles, like the one I had—two hours ago!" She glared at Alan, indicating the last part of the message was directed at him.

"I didn't realize it would take that long," Alan said sheepishly.

"That what would take that long, Champ? Boozing, gambling, or fucking all the girls in Chinatown?"

"Vera!" Alan said surprised. He couldn't recall her using strong language like that ever—not that he was a prude or offended by it, but it just wasn't like her. She always seemed to be under control. "I didn't fu...no that's not right...I had a...massage. At least—"

"At least it started out as a massage..." Vera said.

"Yeah," Alan said, apologetically. "That's what it was supposed to be. That's all I wanted, but..."

"But it was an exotic massage," interrupted Vera.

"Yeah," said Alan. "You're finishing my thoughts, but how would you know about their massages?"

"You're not the only one who reads books, Champ, and it appears you need to broaden your reading material. Personally, I have my own collection of under-the-counter books. Most of mine are in French. Someday I might interpret a story for you—that is if you're a bad boy and misbehave enough."

Alan's brow knitted low over his watery, bloodshot eyes. "What?"

Vera shook her head, leaned forward, and reached across the table for his hand. "I'm teasing you, and you're having trouble staying up with it."

So, was she mad at him or not? Alan wondered. He clasped her hand tightly, affirming their friendship, and she immediately began stroking and massaging the top of his knuckles, like Lynn had done upstairs in Goon Dip's, before she dragged him off into a private room to have her way with him. Alan sighed lazily, recalling the session of

120

bliss with Lynn. That was an experience that would rival anything he had with the girls inside Vic's hideout.

"So, are you going to tell me about it, or are you just going to roll on your side and want your belly scratched, like a dog that's had a big meal?" asked Vera.

Alan glanced around nervously, but the shop was mostly empty, and he and Vera had the corner to themselves. "What parts do you want to know about?" he asked cautiously.

Vera pulled on Alan's arm, tugging him closer to the table, while she also leaned across it. "I want to know all of it. Every detail."

Alan gazed at the table surface and then off towards the kitchen in the back while he thought. "Including the massage?"

"Yes, that too," Vera said, while rubbing his hand like it was a magic lantern.

"You don't mind the lurid details?" Alan asked, even though he was now sure that Vera seemed somehow excited about what he had been through. He still had reservations about telling her everything. He was still trying to understand how it had all happened himself. He'd thought he was just going to get a rub down, and he figured that exotic meant he would strip to his undies, nothing more than that. He didn't know that he'd be able to explain his innocence in a way that would portray him as anything other than a horny twenty-one year old with twice as much libido as brains. His head hurt just thinking about the complexities of it all, and with the second tumbler of scotch that magically appeared during his massage, he had enough liquor in him now that what happened in Goon Dip's somehow sounded right and proper.

"Tell me the lurid details. I'm fine with them. I'm just glad you're safe."

"Thank you..." Alan was tempted to call her ma'am,

again, which he normally did just to rile her, but he decided this would not be the appropriate time.

"I think I found our girl," he said. "Her name's Lien, but she goes by Lynn. She's the masseuse."

"She's the one who laid you?"

Alan raised his head and his hand to object, but then he lowered both. "That would be correct, but it didn't start out that way."

"How did it start, Champ?"

Alan described his guided tour through each level of the building—and the services available on each floor—including the "welcome back" party for Hungry Harry. He described the young women on level three, the pat down they gave him while fondling him, and then the five women he found on four.

Alan stopped his narrative as the Asian waitress he had admired earlier in the evening delivered his noodles and tea. Without thinking about it, Alan watched her as she walked back to the kitchen.

Vera playfully backhanded Alan's upper arm. "You just got laid and you're already looking for your next conquest?" Vera teased.

Alan rolled his eyes and half smiled. "I wasn't thinking that at all. I was just waiting until she got out of earshot."

"Trust me," said Vera. "She hasn't been here long enough to speak the language. But as I was saying, apparently you and Lynn hit it off."

"Once we got inside the room, she asked me to take my clothes off and climb up on a narrow massage table. So I stripped down to my underwear and was just standing there for a moment."

"Why was that?"

"I was giving my erection time to settle down."

"You had an erection already?"

"Well, yeah. She was naked under the robe, and as she was spreading the linen out on the table, her robe draped open, showing me everything. Of course she knew I was watching, but she didn't say anything. So there I was looking at all she had, and she didn't—"

"So she was nice to look at?" Vera asked, now pulling on Alan's fingers.

"Very nice," he said dreamily. "And then she looked at me standing there in my underwear, reached out with both her hands, and yanked them down, before I could say anything. When she passed by my penis, it almost poked her in the eye."

Vera snickered, glanced away, and then smiled at Alan. "I'm sorry," she said. "I just had an image of how that would happen. So that's when she jumped on top of you?"

"No, that didn't come till much later. First, she had me lie on my stomach and tuck my equipment out of the way. Then she gave me a full back massage, and we talked."

"About what?"

"How long she'd been working there, but she wasn't sure. She thought she started before Roosevelt was elected President, because she remembers a customer complaining, worrying about the country and all the giveaway programs."

Vera suddenly stopped massaging Alan's hand. "Now that's just plain sick!" she said. "There's no way that girls that age should even know about what goes on inside a place like Goon Dip's."

"That's what I was thinking," said Alan. "Which took a lot away from the moment, until I finally worked it out in my head that she's really twenty-four now, which makes her three years older than me and okay to be with, because she's old enough to make decisions for herself."

"I wonder though if she really has any say, even now,"

Alan continued. "I think if you're born into it, there's no getting out until you've got nothing left that's bankable for the house. They'll use the girls and then put them out to pasture, which could include working in the kitchens or tailor shops as seamstresses."

Alan leaned back in his chair and sighed. After a moment he wiped his face with his dry hands and shook his head dejectedly and took a sip of tea.

"So I asked her how she felt about that," Alan said, "and she told me there was a high demand for younger girls, particularly those of mixed origins. Older men pay big money to be with them. So I asked if she had a fortune stashed away, but she said, 'Not so much.' Most of it has gone to a worthy cause."

"'Worthy cause' likely means the house pimp's bank account."

"She seems smart enough to have figured that out," said Alan, "so I think it's a lot more complicated than that. There's another floor to the building, which isn't part of the business. Lynn didn't want to tell me where she came from or how she ended up in Goon Dip's, but I've got a feeling she's got a connection to the top floor."

"Really? But wouldn't that be where the house girls live?"

"I think they live in rooms in the back corners on each of the floors—three and four for sure. The girls on the upper floor might have a little more room, because they treat them special."

"They must be thrilled about that," said Vera.

"And you know what else is weird? Remember the old guy with the queue sitting on the front step when we peeked around the corner?"

"Sure I do."

"He charged me two dollars to go inside. Later, one of the

124

men we'd seen here ended up being my escort throughout the building. His name is—"

"Nelson Wong," interrupted Vera.

Alan knitted his brow and sat up in his chair. "How would you know that?"

"Because he made a point to stare at me, like a man who has never had a woman say 'No' to him before. He left moments after I said goodbye to you. The manager here told me his name and said he wasn't a very nice fellow."

"Nelson noticed you alright," said Alan. "But when I told him about the old man with the queue who took my money, he said they didn't have anyone working the door—and no one wears their hair that way anymore!"

"Really?" asked Vera. "How odd. I wonder where he could have gone so fast?"

"When I left Goon Dip's, I glanced around on the sidewalk, but the rest of the block on that side was sealed off with bricks and mortar. There were a couple of green side doors, the nondescript kind you see in Chinatown, which lead to small walk-up apartments, bachelor flats, that kind of thing."

"That's something to think about," Vera said, "but what else did your masseuse tell you before she humped you and turned your brains to mush?"

Alan snickered. "After I realized the massage was going in a different direction than I had figured, I asked her about the party downstairs for Hungry Harry."

"So he was actually across the street?"

"In the flesh," Alan said, "with a whole host of police brass who filled a banquet room, cheering his return."

Vera rolled her eyes. "Tell me please that Mike Ketchum wasn't in their group!"

Alan shook his head. "He wasn't, as far as I could see, but I got the feeling Lynn recognized Harry's name, even though she didn't say anything. So, I asked her if she was worried about the cops from the party coming upstairs and busting them—with me in her room—and she said of course not. The house paid handsomely to be left alone. She said that whenever the police stopped by on business, Nelson would give them a silver token that they could use for any of the girls on the third floor."

"Really?"

"So I asked if any police officers ever came up to the fourth floor as customers. She stopped the massage at that point, which made me think I'd gone too far. But then a moment later she rolled me over onto my back. And there she was, standing there naked. She climbs up on the table and sits down on top of my chest. That's when I found out that exotic meant a lot more than I thought."

"Come on, Champ. What'd you think it meant?"

"There were candles and a very fancy sculpture of a dragon mounted on the wall. Other than that I didn't have much time to think about it. I assumed there might be a nude dance or a show of some kind, but I had no idea she could use her body to do what she did."

"A dragon sculpture?"

"Yeah," Alan said. "So of course I thought of your old friend, the White Dragon, and hesitated a moment, but I could see into the next room down, and it had a Tiger on the wall. They both might have been done by the same artist."

"You should have taken the room with the Tiger."

"Lynn was plenty enough tiger all by herself."

Vera leaned back in her chair, crossed her arms, shook her head, and pushed her lips out, like she'd swallowed too much ice cream.

Alan leaned forward and kept his voice low. "A few minutes into it she said something like: 'I don't take police customers anymore, but I still get politicians and judges.'"

Vera nodded thoughtfully. "Her saying 'anymore' would imply she used to do them, so that's interesting. She told you this in the middle of sex?"

"Not then," Alan said. "This was way before that, when she was using her body to rub oil over me."

"I see," said Vera. "Like a human paint brush with boobs."

"Yes, that's exactly what it was."

"Well I hoped she made you use a condom!"

"She did, when it got to the point that I couldn't take anymore of the massage. Condoms are one of the House rules."

"Well Champ, you got a surprising amount of information, despite what was going on in your sexual *Playland*. But I'm wondering if she stopped turning tricks with policemen after Sawyer met his demise. If she did, maybe there's a connection."

"I thought that too, but I couldn't think of how to bring up the subject."

"If my knowledge of the law is accurate," said Vera, "an adult who had sex with your little masseuse before she turned fifteen could be charged with Carnal Knowledge, as well they should be, whether she was willing and able, paid or not. This is a case where 'fourteen gets you twenty,' as in twenty years in prison. Even if she was fifteen or older, that could still get him fifteen years in the joint, which is likely a death sentence for a cop. So if the dearly departed Hacksaw was one of her customers, he gave the House a lot of leverage to hold over him and drop anytime they wanted."

"Sure," said Alan, "but what would they've done with that kind of hammer? Skip their payoffs? Get the police department to back off? That might work on Hacksaw, but I doubt that the rest of the department would feel obliged to honor his debts."

"I don't know, but since he once had been part of the Dry Squad, he'd have known the best liquor suppliers, and Goon Dip could have forced him to grease the way for him and his house—keep the Canadian liquor coming at a more competitive rate."

Alan sighed heavily and then smiled dreamily. "I'll need to go up there again for more information."

Vera smirked, shook her head, and kicked him playfully with the side of her foot. "Eat your noodles, Champ."

"Sure, and then I want to talk with Officer Kearney," Alan said. "I'm curious about Goon Dip's Phantom of the Opera. I wonder if Kearney's ever seen him before."

"We can't meet Big Ben anywhere near Chinatown tonight, or you'll risk being able to get back inside to visit your new friend."

Alan grinned. "You know her older sister also works up there with her. Did I mention that? They're both mixed race: half White, half Chinese. Her name's Mei. She dresses in black leather and carries a whip."

"Hmm," said Vera. "The whip would be for bad boys like you who need a spanking."

"But why would guys pay for that?" asked Alan. "Wouldn't that hurt? I don't see the pleasure in that at all."

"If we ever went that far, I'd be sure to make you feel better afterwards."

Alan opened his mouth to say something snappy, witty, but then he thought about what she'd just said, changed his mind, and began to wonder.

Noodles Smith, the owner of the Black and Tan at Twelfth and Jackson, wore a nasty scowl on his dark brown face. He shook his head, marched away from the bouncers monitoring the arrival of guests, and stopped sharply midway down the eclectic mix of customers waiting patiently outside his jazz club for a chance to hear Lena Horne. His dark eyes widened. He took the cigar out of his mouth with one hand, while cocking his other hand back behind his body. Then he let it loose, sending it flying solidly toward Big Ben Kearney's outstretched mitt. The two hands clashed like mountain goats fighting over a jagged mountain arête, before they finally meshed into a friendly grip, back slapping, and ending in a brotherly hug.

"How ya doing, old soul!" said Smith.

"Just fine, Noodles. I thought my friends and I would have a little conversation and catch a late show here tonight," Kearney said, indicating Vera and Alan with a tilt of his large head.

"Late shows are always the best," said Smith. "That's why I'm so busy, and it's been that way all around jazz alley the past couple of weeks. Been a lot of headliners in town. They all come up here after playing the White clubs downtown.

Nothing worth doing starts up in the Jazz Alley until late."

Smith stood tall, leaned back for a better view, almost stepping into the street, and he quickly focused on Vera, then Alan, flashing them each a grin which revealed a shiny gold tooth where an upper incisor should have been.

Kearney made the introductions for everybody, sticking to names, not occupations. This was the only area of the city where the races mixed in relative harmony. Adding that you were a detective, even a private detective, would unsettle the balance of nature at the water hole.

Smith put the cigar back in his mouth, clamped down on it with his teeth, and waved a bouncer over from the entrance door that led to the downstairs. Smith peeled a twenty dollar bill from a roll and folded it into the young man's hand. "These are my personal guests tonight, Miles. I want you to take them inside and give them my table. Whatever they want to eat or drink is on me, understood?"

"Yes, sir."

The coal black bouncer led the threesome down the steps into a dimly lit room, through the tightly packed audience of White, Black, and Asian customers, up to where there was a table with four chairs set in a semi-circle facing the stage. On top of the tablecloth was a *Reserved* placard, a candle, and a heavy glass ashtray. The bouncer held a chair for Vera, while Alan and Big Ben took seats on either side of her. Alan glanced around the packed club at people staring jealously at them and whispering to each other. The bouncer picked up the owner's placard and tucked it under his arm. "I'll send a waitress right over," he said. "You are Mr. Smith's guests tonight. Please do not insult him by tipping his staff. He's given me enough to provide for them later."

Alan grinned and glanced to Vera and then Kearney. She nodded assuredly, as if she had received the high roller treatment on many occasions. No doubt that would have been during her headliner days, Alan thought.

Vera leaned close and patted Kearney's thick shoulder. "It would appear you're in tight with Noodles," she whispered.

Kearney shrugged, almost apologetically. "More so than I'd imagined. Noodles has always had trouble with the law—not Seattle Police but the King County Sheriff—and the State. It seems that those who live above the Yesler line are upset that a Black man could do so well during the Depression, when they couldn't. Noodles pays his tributes to the department, sure enough, but he runs a clean house, at least as far as taxes and health codes go. So we leave him alone, but every now and then the outsiders come in and demand a piece of the action. Sometimes they make trouble."

"They can do that?" Vera asked.

"Other coppers look at it as fishing in a fella's private pond, but it can be done—and they do it. The Police and the Sheriff are always having turf wars: who can arrest whom, who should be warned ahead of time before a raid is made, that kind of thing."

Kearney leaned in close over the table, so he could be heard over the noise in the crowded room. Alan and Vera followed suit. "Remember, I told you that back before the Repeal I had the beat up here?" Kearney asked. "Well, one night a couple of drunken deputies made a ruckus in here, all because Noodles ignored their attempt to shake him down. He's paying enough to the police department, why pay more? The deputies raised their voices, interrupted the musicians, stopped the performance, and then all of a sudden, someone turned the lights out. The two deputies took a pretty good beating. I got word of it on the street and got here just as the lights came back on. I helped the deputies to their feet and dusted them off. They couldn't— or wouldn't—say who did what to them and why, so I sent them on their way. Figured they'd learned their lesson, justice had been served, and that's the last we'd see of them.

"But no good deed goes unpunished. Those two came back the next day and punched one of the bouncers in the nose. I got word of it right away, showed up, and I took the boys around back for a private discussion, just between me and them. They called me a 'nigger lover' and in general showed they'd had a very poor upbringing, when it comes to manners and the niceties of life. So I grabbed each one by an ear and asked if they wanted to hear what coconuts sounded like when they're slammed together real hard. Of course they didn't want to hear that, but I thought a modest demonstration was appropriate. It was a teachable moment. After a couple of knocks together, a little bongo music to go with the jazz inside the club, I instructed them not to come back into my beat or I'd arrest them for attempting to solicit prostitution—with teenage boys."

Vera stifled a laugh and gave Kearney that confident grin that Alan loved to see. "Very nice," she said.

"They didn't come back," said Kearney.

"I don't imagine they would," said Alan with a chuckle. The more he was around Kearney, the more he was reminded of his mentor, Vic Morrison, who was reportedly living out his retirement somewhere off the coast of China, in the middle of a war zone.

"So, are you a big fan of jazz, Ben?" asked Vera.

"That I am, and even more so I'm a big fan of Lena Horne." Kearney's smile fractured as he spoke, bemused.

"I said something funny?" asked Vera.

"Because of my size, whatever I do or like is punctuated with the adjective 'big,' whether it's baseball, stage plays, or opera, 'big' is always part of it."

"I'm sorry," said Vera. "I'll try not to make any references to your size."

"I'm teasing," said Kearney. "I really don't mind at all."

The already dim house lights darkened further so that only the candles were casting light on the tables, and up on stage the musicians were taking seats on bent cane chairs, while picking up their instruments. The energy in the room changed, like a radio seeking a new channel, from loud and electric to one of eager anticipation. Voices changed from conversational tones to urgent whispers.

"I heard Walter Winchell gave Miss Horne a plug on the radio," said Alan. "Is that why there's such a crowd?"

"A plug from Winchell or Damon Runyon's always a good thing," whispered Kearney, "but if she didn't have great pipes, great looks, great legs, or high class, these people wouldn't be here. So how about you, Alan, do you like jazz?"

"I like music best when there's a singer with the group, especially a trio. If it's just the music, not so much."

In the darkness Alan felt a presence behind him, and then a slender hand lightly clasped his shoulder and gave it a gentle squeeze. He glanced around cautiously as a beautiful young face leaned down close, in between his and Vera's. "I'm Lena Horne," she said. "Noodles said you were some of my biggest fans."

Alan's mouth sagged open speechless as he gaped wide-eyed at the sparkling beauty so intimately close.

"Thank you for coming to my show," Miss Horne said. "I'm very flattered. I've asked the club to deliver champagne to your table. There will be a fourth glass, which will be for me."

"Thank you," said Vera graciously, a sentiment that was quickly echoed by Alan and Ben.

"I hope you enjoy the show," said Miss Horne as she stood tall and stepped into the spotlight that was directed at the stage. Applause broke out throughout the room, which

Miss Horne met with a warm smile. She scooted sideways past Big Ben, playfully leaned over him, reached around his girth, and squeezed his thickly muscled shoulders, before turning to the crowd with exaggerated pleasure at her discovery. The crowd laughed on cue, indicating she already had them locked under her spell. She took off her mink wrap to reveal a shimmering blue floor-length sarong with high side vents. The gown had a single shoulder sash that delicately crossed over her left side, adding a sense of playfulness.

Miss Horne casually let the fur slide off her arms into Ben's lap. "Watch this for me, will you, handsome?"

Vera leaned close to Alan, her breath soft on his ear. "I see you checking out her legs, but just so you know, she was a fan dancer when she started out at the Cotton Club in Harlem."

Alan grabbed Vera before she could get away and whispered in her ear, his lips touching her lobe. "Sure, I can imagine that."

Vera sat back in her chair, nodded, and frowned impishly as the music started. "Rascal!" she said, exaggerating the enunciation so Alan could easily read her lips.

After the applause from the first set subsided, Miss Horne stopped by the table, picked up her champagne glass, and took a sip while resting a hand on Ben's shoulder. "If you don't mind, I'd like to say hello to some friends in the crowd. I'll be back before you know it."

Big Ben toasted Miss Horne with his glass and took a sip. "Isn't she something?" he asked.

Vera nodded approvingly, while Alan tried to assume an air of casualness.

"This place is totally amazing, Ben," said Vera. "As much

as I like jazz, I don't know why I've never come up here before."

Ben inclined his head over the table and shrugged. "Maybe it's because no one's ever asked you," he said.

Not wanting to be left out, Alan leaned in closer looking for an opportunity to contribute.

"You don't need an invitation to come up here," said Ben, "It's very safe, but if you'd like an escort some night after my shift, I'd be happy to show you around. There's maybe two dozen jazz clubs in the area, some trying to catch on in the business and some going out of business. Noodles also owns the *Ubangi* and the *New Harlem*, but this is where the big names come."

"While we've got a minute, Ben," Alan interrupted, "I was wondering if we could talk about Goon Dip's place. Do you mind?"

"Not at all."

Vera shot Alan a sideways look, and he guessed that he might have jumped into too soon with talk of work. Maybe she felt he was too focused on the case and not enjoying the moment. Doubtless, she would tell him later.

"Have you ever been in the down-unders?" Alan asked.

Ben creased a smile and nodded. "As a matter of fact I have. Another beat cop and I were meeting at our call box, the same one I met you at that first night. And while talking, we saw something that caught our eye. It resulted in our finding a portal underneath the Milwaukie Hotel."

"Really?" said Vera. "Tell us about it."

"We'd seen a known gambler," Kearney said. "A Chinese guy who goes by the name of Sonny Jim. We watched him slide into a garment shop, but he was wearing a shirt and slacks that were way too thin for the weather. While staring through the shop windows, I caught a glimpse of a door closing, off to the side in the back of the shop. After a good

135

ten minutes he never came back out. So Sully and I—"

"Would the Sully you're referring to be John L. Sullivan?" asked Vera.

"Yes, indeed. You know him?"

"Yes, we do," both Vera and Alan said together. Alan playfully nudged Vera with his arm, but she ignored him.

"So Sully and I went inside the shop, like we were paying the store a courtesy visit, looking over their wares, and just being neighborly. While I'm talking with the shop owner and his wife, Sully wanders over to the door I mentioned. As soon as he grabs the handle, the merchant yells at Sully in Chinese, probably something along the lines of 'you can't go down there.' And as I'm glancing over my shoulder to watch Sully, the guy's wife flips up the lid on a brass tube and drops something ceramic looking into it, before letting the lid drop quickly so I wouldn't see what she'd done.

"Sully hears it too and knows something's up, so he jerks open the door, and I'm right behind him as he stomps down the steps. We're banging our billy clubs on the handrails, making as much racket as we can, like angry bulls that have been nicked with swords by those sissies in the bull ring with the tight pants. When we get to the bottom step, there are three tables full of Chinese men playing cards with various sized stacks of chips in front of them. Sully says to them, 'Gentlemen, it would appear you're gambling here, in flagrant violation of Seattle City codes.' And one of the men speaks up for the others, 'This is just a friendly card game. There's no money involved.'"

Alan nodded thoughtfully, following the logic.

"So, I'm busy scouring the room for our friend Sonny," said Kearney, "but I don't see him anywhere, so I point this out to Sully. He nods thoughtfully and scowls at the gamblers, and he raises his billy club for emphasis, like a band conductor about to launch the brass section into something zesty. He says, 'So, if money's not involved, what are the chips for?'"

"The same guy answers, 'Nothing. Chips don't mean anything, except that's how we keep track of who's the better player. That's all.' So Sully smacks his club down on the green felt between two of the players, and then quick as you sneeze he knocks all the stacks of chips into the center of the table with the tip of his club. He pounces from one table to the next, and the gamblers are too stunned to react before Sully's wreaked total chaos on their holdings. And Sully growls at them, 'If the chips don't mean nothin', then you fellas won't mind starting over.'"

"Oh, my word!" said Vera. "If I know Chinese gamblers, there could have been thousands of dollars on the table. How would they ever sort that out?"

"They were angry as hell, but they knew better than to take on Sully when he had that fire in his eyes, and they were much more worried about their neighbors picking up and running off with chips that weren't theirs to start with. And it's not like we really cared about their gambling; after all, this is Chinatown. It's their way of life down here. Nothing we say or do is going to ever change that. And furthermore, neither of us cared a whit that they hadn't paid off the Vice Squad. I think what happened was a reaction to how they handled our visit. They'd lied to us, and that made us angry. Treated us like we were thick-headed Irishmen—and by the way Kearney's are Scots."

Alan nodded thoughtfully. "Duly noted."

"But it doesn't end there," said Kearney. "Because I looked up at the ceiling where I can see the bottom of the brass tube, coming right out of the floorboards above me, down from where the merchant's wife would have been standing. Directly below it, I see white porcelain shards smashed on the floor. It's the remnants from the pot that the missus dropped from above. It had been full of ashes of some kind, and there's a foot print in the middle of the shards and ashes that leads directly toward a back wall with very nice wainscoting, below the wood paneling. I walk over to the footprint, take a gander, and a few feet further on I see part of another print, but the rest of it is somehow swallowed up into the wall.

"So I ask myself how that could happen. Are some of the Chinese spiritual apparitions who spend half their time in the physical world and the other half in the paranormal?" Kearney asked rhetorically.

"Meanwhile, the Chinese men are all out of their seats bouncing up and down on their toes excitedly," said Kearney, "grappling over the mess Sully made on their tables, grabbing fistfuls of chips, jabbing fingers in each other's faces, yakking in high pitched tones, and not paying any attention to me. It was like a three ring circus, with a different show at each table. So I press my hands against the wall that had only half a footprint at its base. About four feet up the wall is a varnished trim board that runs across the wainscoting, and I see that it has a fingernail nicks just above the rail board on the paneling, with an arching pattern of scratch marks below the board, scraping across the wainscoting. So I reach up and tug down gently on the board, and it moves like a lever. That releases a catch and the door suddenly pops open and swings toward me. So I'm standing there right inside the gambling parlor, and I'm feeling a gush of sea breeze. And down on the hidden floor, just before it runs out onto brick pavers, is the rest of the footprint."

Vera sucked in her cheeks and shared a glance with Alan, who nodded knowingly.

"I stared through the gaping hole in the wall into the passageway," said Kearney, "and I see Sonny's shadow, backlit by a lantern, along with another shape, staring at me, and then both men suddenly take off running towards the west. I call to Sully, indicate the hidden passageway to him, and he runs over and follows me through the door and into the catacombs.

"Now, we carry flashlights as part of our gear," Kearney continued, "but I'm not wanting to run smack dab into the darkest depths of hell, unless I know I've got enough battery power to get me all the way back to the sunshine again. But worry not, because hanging on a post where this spur meets the main tunnel were five or six more lanterns. I grabbed one of them that was still warm, full of kerosene, and lit it. We start after Sonny and his friend, and we can see down ahead of us the glow of their lantern reflecting off the top of the tunnel as it flows down hill to the west."

Vera nodded for Kearney to continue.

"Figuring that if I can see their lantern, they'd be able to look back and do the same, I reduced the flame just enough to keep it lit. After about a hundred yards, the tunnel veered north and met up with another one heading due west, toward the water. We followed their glow past a few dozen portals getting closer to the salt water smell, which got stronger, and then we went under the railroad tracks—"

"How did you know when you were going under the tracks?" asked Alan.

Big Ben's brow furrowed as he thought a moment. "I'm not absolutely positive that's where we were, because I had no way of checking, but I'm guessing that was it because of how straight and professionally crafted that stretch of tunnel was. At that point, it narrowed enough that Sully and I had to walk in single file, and it had a serious arch to it, which would support a lot of weight, like those Gothic Cathedrals you see in France with the buttresses. The rest of the tunnel we'd been in could have been put together by an everyday work crew, but that particular stretch of tunnel was well made—union craftsmanship. I'm surprised there weren't handrails and overhead lights, along with a comfort station with an attendant at either end."

"You've been to France, Ben?"

Kearney nodded. "Back during my wrestling days, the promoters took the show on the road. We were like Buffalo Bill Cody's Wild West show, only the French saw us more as a freak show than American culture. I didn't enjoy that part of the travel, but I did like how the rest of days and nights went while I was over there. But as I was saying, we continued underneath the tracks, and I thought we were just going to end up connecting to the old underground in Pioneer Square, but instead the tunnel branched again, with a main shaft heading due north to Lord knows where, probably under the middle of First Avenue, up past Madison Street, I would guess. We didn't follow it, so we didn't find out; instead, we stayed on our westerly course and eventually came out through the seawall, underneath a pier near Washington Street. A catwalk of some kind wound its way under the pier, but we didn't follow it out over the water. We stopped next to pilings encrusted in barnacles, and there must have been fifteen or twenty lanterns on a post, along with a five gallon can of kerosene."

"Any sign of Sonny?" asked Alan.

Kearney shook his head. "We lost sight of the lantern's glow when we went under the railroad and never picked it up again. I'm guessing they went north or ducked out through another portal near Pioneer Square. Chinatown originally started near First Avenue, and I'm sure they knew their way around better than we did. But by then, the curiosity of what we were in got the better of us, and we wanted to see where it ended. And sure enough, we found that. They have a very sophisticated smuggler's passage in place down there, and I'm not sure who all knows or cares."

"You didn't report what you found?" asked Vera.

Kearney winced and shook his head. "Given the way the laws are written now and how the politicos and brass decide which ones they want us to enforce and which to tolerate, neither of us felt like weighing into the battle. Neither Sully nor I have much use for those who want to keep the country safe for only the descendants of the Europeans. There's enough room for all of us. Those leaders are the same ones who want to send those stolen from Africa back to their homelands. It's funny that after all their years of servitude the leaders have had a change of heart about human larceny, and now they want to make amends. And then there're the Chinese Exclusion Acts, barring Asian immigration. Prohibition and the Exclusion Acts have been a financial windfall to those running the show because of what people are forced to pay to get around them. So I don't see any harm in letting the needy escape the greedy's clutches."

Alan nodded thoughtfully.

"You asked me about the down-unders for a reason, Champ?" Ben asked. "You've been in them yourself, I take it."

Alan nodded. "That's how I got inside Goon Dip's the other night."

"Very clever," said Kearney, tilting his head back and smiling approvingly. "And what'd you find?"

"Right off I ran into an old Chinese man, dressed in silks with a small box hat and a long queue in the back. He acted like he was the bouncer for the House," said Alan. "He charged me two bucks to get in, but later when I met Nelson Wong, he told me they didn't have a doorman on that level—and no one wore their hair like that anymore."

Kearney shook his head and smiled. "The shaved head with the long pony tail? I haven't seen that before, other than in paintings and old books."

"So part of me is thinking he's a phantom," said Alan, "but then what use would money be to a phantom? What would he need to buy? Cigarettes? Opium? And this phantom had a strong grip and told me what I would find on each of the floors."

Kearney's brow knitted low and he shook his head. "Can't say that I've ever seen him, but then as I've just told you, my time in the down-unders has been very short and was for a single purpose. So, that doesn't mean he doesn't exist."

"What can you tell me about Nelson Wong?" asked Alan.

"I think I mentioned him before," said Kearney, "but I think he would be too young to be our man. He's mixed ancestry. Rumor has it that he's one of Goon Dip's children, product of a liaison with one of the working girls in years past, but because Goon is married to a Chinese woman, that technically makes Nelson his bastard child, who's not eligible for property inheritance. At any rate, he has no arrests, no criminal record, and I hear that he's college educated, degree in business. It appears that he's Goon Dip's designated successor for running the operation—but not for owning it. The legitimate children would be the ones in-line for ownership of his holdings."

"Looks like Nelson runs the show to me," said Alan. "Everyone was on their toes when he walked around, very deferential if not outright afraid."

"Yes," said Kearney, brow furrowed low in thought. "But that might be just because he's a tyrannical ass. But I've heard there's trouble afoot in Goon Dip's pleasure emporium. Either Nelson's planning a palace coup, or he might be getting ready to branch off on his own, start up

142

his own place. But if he does either of those, he better have everything in place, several contingency plans, and a moat dug around his new castle, because Goon Dip will see his leaving as treason and either he or his minions will come raging after Nelson. Heads will roll."

Alan pushed out his lips into a thoughtful frown. "I'll file that away for future use. But for now, after our meeting on the first floor, Nelson became my tour guide and led me through the upper floors. When we reached the second floor, I found that almost the entirety of the Seattle Police Department brass was throwing Hungry Harry a rousing welcome back party. Nelson even asked me if I wanted to pay my respects to Harry, but I declined."

"So, Harry's back…" said Kearney, letting the thought trail away.

"A little worse for the wear, but he was up and about, partying with the brass. So Nelson took me up to the third floor, where there was an assortment of girls, any of whom I could have had for five dollars. Nelson was surprised that I wanted to pass them up to see what was on the fourth floor, but he took me up there anyway."

"Why was he surprised?" asked Kearney.

"He said the upper floor was for those with more adventurous tastes," said Alan, "which I took to mean: more expensive, but that's where I met Lien and her sister Mei, who are both half Chinese and half white. Lien of course goes by Lynn."

Kearney smiled. "Neither of those sounds close to Hua," he said. "But my source wasn't that clear…which I should probably explain a little more. Rosebush also used to work for Goon Dip, probably on the third floor. Girls who work inside places like Goon Dip's are treated fairly well, from what I understand, and they make a lot more money there than they can turning tricks on street corners. But Rose spent too much of the company's time in the opium rooms, and not enough time on her back, so Goon Dip kicked her out. Once she was out on the street, she made the transition from opium to spiking heroin in her skinny arms. When I last spoke with her, she was crashing after a drugged high. She said that when Hacksaw was shot she had been with a customer, but I'm thinking she was probably cooking up a spoonful in the alley behind the garage. So what I'm saying is that her information's very sketchy, and it's never going to get any better than what we've got now."

"So that would explain how Rosebush knew who Hacksaw had been seeing before he was shot, wouldn't it?" asked Vera. "Could Rosebush have known or remembered her from her days—and nights—working at Goon Dip's? Maybe she just didn't overhear a name mentioned in the darkness, she very well could have known Miss Hua."

Kearney nodded, following Vera's train of thought.

"Back to Nelson Wong," said Vera. "You don't think he could be our man, Ben? After all, think how old Billy the Kid was when he started shooting people? Wasn't he in his teens?"

"And what about Lynn?" asked Alan. "Wouldn't she have been too young? If she was really the mystery woman, she would have been thirteen and change at the time, but Mei, on the other hand, would have been around sixteen. So, if it was one of them, wouldn't it make more sense that it was Mei? Wouldn't Rosebush have noticed that the girl was fresh into her teens, if it had been Lynn?"

"Gosh! That's so young!" said Vera.

"You're thinking the way churchgoers with morals do," said Kearney, "and that could be a mistake in this case. You can't assume that the people involved here—and their customers for that matter—think exactly the way you and I do. What makes us sick to our stomachs might actually be a turn-on for them. And if money can be made selling young women for sex, then it would be a turn-on for Goon Dip and his operation."

Alan nodded and ran his hand through his hair, as if his fingers were chasing after an old memory that had snuck out. "You're absolutely right on that," he said. "In fact, the way you said it reminded me again of my old friend Vic. He had a way of digging past the caramel pop corn and getting to the prize at the bottom of the box."

"Well...I'll take that as a good thing then," said Kearney, "because you seem to regard his friendship so highly, and by the way, I love *Cracker Jacks*."

"What about Rosebush?" asked Vera. "Do you think there's any possibility that she's alive and well somewhere in Seattle?"

"I never did find out if the name I knew her by was real or not," said Kearney. "I checked through all the arrest records and mug shots we have on file, and I never found a thing on her, which means she most likely has a clean record, never arrested."

"Is that possible?" asked Alan, "given her drug use and prostitution?"

"She spent years inside a protected establishment, and I never arrested her," said Kearney. "I think I told you before that she never gave me any problems, moved along when I asked her to, and I never saw her with a pimp."

"But you're being careful not to tell us her real name," said Vera.

"Agatha Perkins," said Kearney begrudgingly. "Normally I wouldn't give that up, because I told her I would keep her name out of it, but I got the feeling she's long gone—as in not alive anymore. From what I know of heroin, it's a slippery slope to self-destruction. I've never seen anyone come back from the depths it takes them."

The musicians had taken the stage again and were

finishing their cigarettes as they waited patiently for Miss Horne. Alan craned his neck to scan over the audience behind them, to where Miss Horne was engaged in an animated but friendly conversation with a striking brunette wearing theatrical makeup and wrapped in a feather boa. Alan leaned close to Vera and whispered, "Who's that she's talking to?"

Vera paused a moment before glancing casually behind her. Then she quickly turned around and smiled confidently. "That would be Gypsy Rose Lee," she whispered.

"The one and only Gypsy Rose?" Alan asked, keeping his voice low.

"The very same. I had already retired by the time she started in the business."

"So, will you introduce me?" Alan asked, his voice returning to a normal level.

Vera backhanded Alan playfully across his upper arm. "Honestly, Champ. You really know how to sweet talk a lady, don't you?"

Alan stopped close to Vera in front of the noodle shop where she'd waited for him the last time. "Why don't you come in with me this time?" he asked.

"Because at some point you would have to leave me alone on the gambling floor, while you went up to see Lynn," said Vera, "and I don't think Nelson Wong would approve of an unescorted lady roaming about his establishment, gambling or not. He might end up saying something inappropriate to me, and then I might get mad and hurt him. And then there's the possibility of running into Hungry Harry while I'm waiting. What would I say to him? 'Gee, Harry, haven't seen you in years, since you used to hang out and catch my show. Are you still leaking cranial fluid where Alan shot you?'"

Alan grinned knowingly. "Alright, I forgot you'd know him," he said, "I just don't like the idea of leaving you here while I'm—"

"Banging Lynn?"

Alan pushed his fedora back and scratched his head. "I'm going to pay her the standard fee and ask if we can just have a private conversation, and see how that goes. I'm sure she'll be surprised at that. It'll probably be a first for any of the girls on the fourth floor, but how else will we find

147

out if she knew Hacksaw or Knuckles, write her a letter?"

"But the direct approach could be dangerous!" protested Vera.

"Why? If she doesn't like the questions, she doesn't have to answer them."

"But, Champ, she may have been involved in Hacksaw's death, and you're on her home turf, which operates entirely outside of the law. It's like its own tiny little island country with its very own set of rules and diplomatic immunity. If she doesn't like your questions, all she has to do is scream for Nelson Wong to haul you out of there, chop you up into fish bait in the kitchen, and feed you to the chum salmon in the harbor."

"Why don't you escort me to the entrance, just in case our phantom is sitting on the stoop waiting for another pigeon?"

Vera reached behind Alan's head and flipped his hat forward, down over his nose. "A pigeon like you? Do you want me to hold your hand, too?" she said as she took his arm in his and tugged it close to her side.

"Yes, ma'am, I would."

Vera stopped abruptly, shot him a scowl, and shook her head. "You incurable rascal. You know how I hate that word!"

Alan did know that, but he could also see Vera was fighting to hold back a smile that was busting to get loose and race across her face, betraying her playfulness. He fought an almost overwhelming desire to grab her at that point, push her up against a brick wall, and kiss her passionately, while pawing at her bosoms, but instead she forced him to hurry along so he could stay up with her as she led him through the tunnel to the other side of the street. When they reached the end, she peeked out as they had done on their first visit. Alan pressed his hand on her back and leaned out alongside her. "He's not there," they both said in unison.

Alan gently squeezed Vera's arm, behind the elbow. "Alright then, I go it alone from here."

Alan leaned over to kiss her on the lips, but Vera brushed past his lips and kissed him on the cheek, before sliding her arm around his back and giving him a gentle push towards the steps. "You'll get your kiss when you come back safely— that is if you behave yourself while you're gone, Mister."

Vera ducked back into the tunnel, and Alan headed directly to the steps. As he reached the top, he sensed motion to his right. He stopped just past the terra cotta brick trim to see what had moved. He leaned back for a better view, and emerging from the green door at the far end of the building was the elderly gatekeeper who had taken his two dollars the week before.

Alan waited quietly in the shadows for the phantom to work his way towards where he was standing. As far as specters went, he was the oddest looking one Alan could imagine. Under his black box like hat, his head was shaved on the front to the ears, leaving the long, gray queue in back to dance across his back as he walked. Adding to the picture, the man held a long-stemmed pipe in one hand and pressed it to his mouth.

The phantom paused under a section of skylights in the sidewalk above him. He pulled a pouch from his quilted silk coat, took a pinch of tobacco, and tamped it down inside the bowl. With his attention focused exclusively on the pipe and not his walking, he struck a match and proceeded to light up.

"I was beginning to think you weren't real," said Alan, startling the man, sending him into a coughing jag.

"Well, if it isn't the young chauffeur!" said the phantom as he hacked out a trail of smoke that he had swallowed. "You're back so soon. You must have found something here you liked."

"Yes, indeed," said Alan.

"And you were waiting here for me so you could pay your entry fee tonight?"

Alan's brows flicked high as he grinned in amusement. "Nelson Wong says you don't exist."

"Nelson Wong wishes I didn't exist."

"Why's that?"

"I come from the old country and prefer the old ways, like things were before the last emperor. Nelson prefers the new ways...his own ways. You Americans have an expression that fits: He crawls under my skin, so I crawl under his."

Alan nodded. "That's not exactly how it goes, but I get what you're saying. No matter how hard you try, there're people in life you'll just never get along with."

"The trick is in how you handle those people," said the phantom. "As in Kung Fu, you have to learn to deflect your opponent's blow, roll with it, and use his energy against him."

"Do you teach Kung Fu?" asked Alan.

"I am Shifu, a teacher of many things. I teach what is necessary, when it is necessary, and to whom it is necessary."

"Like when to pay two dollars and when not to?" he asked.

Shifu grinned. "Precisely. With the two dollars you spent, you are already becoming wise to the ways of the world. For another two dollars, I will teach you more."

Alan stared at Shifu a long moment, appraisingly. Then he pulled out a small roll of cash and peeled off two dollars, handing it to the phantom, while staying casually vigilant, guarding against another wrist grab. Shifu took the crisp two dollars and slid it into his silk robe.

"What'd you do with the two bucks?" asked Alan.

"I buy tobacco," said Shifu. "It's a nasty indulgence I've

had since my youth."

Alan shook his head sympathetically. "My dad was a smoker."

"What, he smokes no more?"

Alan grimaced. "He was killed two years ago."

"I'm sorry to hear that. I see bitterness in your eyes," said Shifu. "The matter hasn't been satisfied to your liking."

Alan forced a smile. "There's been a reckoning of sorts."

"I understand," said Shifu, "but when one loses a family member, no amount of blood letting ever seems to make it right."

Alan nodded quietly.

"I see that you no longer carry your wallet," said Shifu, "which means you've learned another lesson from your last visit."

A grin creased Alan's lips. He would enjoy having this man as a teacher, a boxing coach, or old friend.

"Here's your next lesson," said Shifu. "I teach Kung Fu no more."

"Why's that?" asked Alan, his brow pinched into a thoughtful frown.

"Kung Fu is a martial art that is for self defense, not for making a man into a bully. It is also a way of life intended to benefit a man or woman on a physical, mental, and spiritual level. One of my last pupils could never seem to grasp the philosophy that is at the core of Kung Fu."

Alan waited a long moment for Shifu to continue, but he didn't. Alan shifted his weight and chewed at his lip. "Would that person be Nelson Wong?"

"Yes," said Shifu with a trace of bitterness in his voice. "He is physically gifted and very athletic, but he can be very mean. He doesn't understand the words stop or enough—in any language. Be careful around him. That is my advice for you today."

"Duly noted," said Alan with a nod of respect. He reached behind, opened the door, and went inside to Goon Dip's lower lobby. As he passed the gaming room on his way to the stairs he glanced to his left at the hallway he hadn't explored before. There were six to eight Chinese men sitting on padded benches, each one lost in thought. Unlike the young women upstairs, none of these men shared a conversation with the others, and there were no ladies of pleasure hanging about the men, trying to entice them into a bedroom romp on a mattress. Alan figured that this was where the main opium den was, and these men were waiting for a spot and someone to bring them a pipe.

Alan continued up the stairs to the second level, thinking about Nelson Wong and the two bouncers he had seen with him on his first visit there. Doubtless they also knew Kung Fu, the fighting which involved hard kicks with the feet. Alan remembered taking a couple of kicks a few months back during an encounter in Japan Town. The trick he learned was to watch his opponent's eyes and remember the strike could come from hand or foot. If he ended up in a row with Nelson or the bouncers, it would be as dangerous as a boxing match in front of a blindfolded referee, and from what Shifu had said, Alan should never expect mercy from Nelson Wong.

The man tending the velvet rope on the second level recognized Alan from his previous visit and let him pass. Alan slowed his pace as he took the steps to the third level, spending more time observing his surroundings, like a tourist might do at a museum. He sensed that Nelson Wong was about the premises somewhere, and Alan wanted to make a point to pay his respects, stay on Nelson's good side as long as he could. While taking the stairs, Alan tried to absorb as many details as his mind could handle, memorizing and filing away what was around him, just in case he would need to recall it again.

When Alan reached the third floor landing, one of the young women he had met before recognized him and quickly alerted the others around her. Alan smiled broadly at those who turned his way, acknowledging them with a half-wave that resembled a modified salute. Three of the girls waved back at him, like he was a friend they recognized across a school playground. Somehow this simple act made them seem different to him, in a more human way he had trouble defining. He thought about this as he climbed the steps to the fourth floor.

Alan slowed as he reached the top, again glancing around to absorb as many details as he could. He quickly located the darkened stairs that led to the fifth floor, but there wasn't enough light in the stairwell for him to discern any secrets the building might be harboring. He guessed that there must be a door at the top of the steps that blocked out light that normally would fill the well and show off its architectural details.

Gathered around one of the two divans were three of the young women from last week. Alan forced his memory to give back the names he had heard during introductions. Lena was the dark beauty with Indian and Black genes, and Laurie was the Loretta Young brunette with the amazing cheekbones and long legs. Lynn was again wearing the silk robe that she was careless about tying tightly. Missing were Mistress Mei and Ruth, the blonde. They must be out with customers, Alan presumed—at least that's the way he understood how it worked, based on time he spent in Vic Morrison's brothel.

Laurie was the first to see Alan coming upstairs. She stepped around the divan, set her feet shoulder width apart, and pushed her hip to the side. Alan recalled that she had done something similar on their first meeting, and whatever she was doing to draw all the attention in the room to her was working. His eyes locked on hers and he walked towards her trance like, before he finally broke away to exchange greetings with Lena and Lynn.

The young women were all in an exaggerated flirt mode, apparently testing Alan to see if he was committed to spending another evening with Lynn or was going to sample another selection. Then it occurred to him that perhaps Lynn had returned to the group after their liaison and spun a tale of his virility—or so he hoped. Alan chuckled as the thought occurred to him, sure that if Lynn had spun a tale it had more to do with the generous tip he'd left than anything else.

Alan reached out and grabbed Lynn by her wrists, which she had folded across in front of her lower abdomen, almost coyishly. He tugged her away from the edges of the circle toward him, letting them all know that she was his choice again. As she stepped forward awkwardly, her bosoms shook inside her open silk robe. Alan realized that his plan of just talking—without sex—was going to be more difficult than he'd thought.

Lynn warmed to Alan's selection and eagerly led him off towards the rooms. As they passed an open door, Alan saw the tiger artwork on the wall and pulled Lynn to a stop. "How about this one?" he asked.

"I usually take the Dragon room if it's open," said Lynn, "but here's fine if you'd like."

"Sure, I'd like this one," Alan said, inclining his head towards the room. "Tigers bring me luck."

"Really?" asked Lynn. "I thought luck was just something that only we made a big deal of here in Chinatown, only I just don't seem to catch my share of it."

"I believe in luck," said Alan, "but I believe in the kind you make for yourself; you know what I mean? Like when you work hard at something, learn new skills, figure out a new way of looking at old problems. That's when your luck changes."

"I think I know what you're saying," said Lynn, as she directed Alan to the small bed by the wall. "Help me pull it into the middle of the room where it will work better for the massage."

Lynn bent over and took hold of the bed frame, with Alan doing the same. After dragging the bed a few feet from the wall, she tugged her sash loose and let her robe drape open. Alan grabbed her lightly by the wrist and pulled her close. Her dark eyes flashed wide, as if she liked the direction this session was heading. With their bodies pressed tightly together, Alan put his lips near her ear to whisper.

"This could be your lucky night," said Alan, "in that you won't have to do anything but talk."

"I don't understand," whispered Lynn. "Sometimes men who want that will visit the girls on the third floor, but that kind of thing never happens up here. This floor is too expensive."

"I'll pay your rate," said Alan, "and if you can answer what I need to know, I'll pay more. We don't have to have sex tonight."

Lynn reached down for Alan's hands and clasped each one in hers. She drew them up, slid them inside her robe, and pressed them against her breasts. "So…you want information, is that it?"

"Yes," said Alan, his eyes darting down to where he felt the smooth skin and the eager softness of her bosom.

"Information can be dangerous, because the walls have eyes and ears," Lynn said, as she shook out of the robe and let it fall to the floor. She left Alan's hands to continue their exploration around to her back and down to her butt cheeks. She leaned forward and brushed her lips against his ear. "Do you understand what I'm saying?"

"I think so," said Alan. "Somebody's watching us?"

Lynn pulled off Alan's coat, forcing it down his back and over his arms. "Maybe not now, maybe not tonight, but probably. You have to count on it."

Alan pulled Lynn close to him again and kissed her on her neck near her ear, the place he enjoyed most on women. "Where?" he whispered.

Lynn returned the kiss, brushing his cheek gently, before nibbling on the lobe of his ear. "The tiger's eyes, but please don't stare or echo back what I tell you. Can you do that?"

"Yes."

"This will only work if you take your clothes off and I give you the massage as before. When we get to the end, you don't have to ejaculate inside me, if you don't like me."

"That's not it," said Alan. "That's not it at all. The problem is I like what I see and what you're doing too much, but there are complications."

Lynn unbuckled Alan's belt and unhooked his pants, pulling them down quickly past his knees. "Complications— like you're married or have a woman?"

Alan sat back on the bed that was little more than a fancy cot. "Close enough," said Alan. He let Lynn take off his shoes, socks, and pants, and fold them into a neat pile before setting them to the side.

Lynn undid her hair, letting it fall around her shoulders, and knelt down in front of Alan. He gazed dreamily at the entirety of her body before seeing an expectant look on her face. "What?" he whispered.

"Your skivvies, sailor," she whispered. "Play along, unless you want me to get mineral oil all over them."

Alan stood in front of the cot but hesitated a moment, his crotch several inches from Lynn's face.

Lynn gazed into his eyes, apparently perplexed as to

why he was stalling. "It's not like I haven't seen it before," she said.

Alan bent low, brushed her hair back on the side of her cheek, and whispered. "But what about the others?"

She nodded her understanding and dropped her gaze to his undershorts where she stared at the erection pushing the plaid fabric out toward her face. "Oh my!" she whispered. "I didn't realize you were already ready for me."

As Alan rolled his eyes in embarrassment, Lynn tugged at the shorts, pulling them down roughly over his hardened penis, all the way to the floor. "Now tuck that up and lie on your stomach," she said matter-of-factly, not bothering to whisper.

Alan did as he was told, and Lynn climbed up on his back and straddled his hips, before leaning forward and letting her hair dance across his broad shoulders. "What is it that's so important to you?" she whispered.

"First of all, who's watching us?"

"I'm not sure," she said, while rubbing his shoulders with the palms of her hands, occasionally kneading them with an elbow. "It depends. Sometimes, I'm sure it's Nelson. Other times it's the men who work for him, and there may be others, like people who pay to watch."

"How about other girls from the floor?" asked Alan.

"Not that I've ever heard. We're not allowed to go back there."

"Why do they watch?" Alan asked.

Lynn took her time thinking before leaning forward again. "To see what the customer likes; to make sure he doesn't get seconds without paying the house their cut of the action; to make sure we don't get hurt or marked up—which is only because they're more concerned about damage that would diminish our beauty and lower our value, rather than in the pain it causes; and sometimes for the viewer's enjoyment, whoever that might be."

"Do all the rooms on this floor have eyes?" asked Alan, thinking of the secret passages he had been through in Mama San's brothel with Vic.

"All the rooms in this building have eyes," said Lynn, pulling on one of Alan's arms, stretching it back and out to the side.

"How do you get inside the passages?"

"Why? Do you want to watch *me* or the other girls?"

"I'd love to watch *you* in action," Alan said, letting what he really wanted slip out before he thought it through, "but that's not why I'm asking."

"Why are you asking?"

"I'm just curious what I'm up against," Alan said.

"So this must be important, this thing you want to talk to me about?"

"Yes," said Alan, "but before I go there, can you tell me if you're ever allowed to leave here?"

"You mean outcalls?"

"Yes, exactly," said Alan. "Outcalls or go shopping downtown, that kind of thing."

"Both," said Lynn, "but only if I have a chaperone to go along with me."

"They're worried about you wandering off then?"

"That's a big reason why they watch us. They're worried a regular customer might grow attached and want to steal us away from the House without buying out the contracts first."

"I'd assumed you were born here in the states," said Alan, "but you're indentured?"

"I was born in Seattle, but yes, it's a lot like that."

"But you have a price for your freedom?"

"I have a very high price."

"How high?

"Why are you asking? Are you going to buy my way out

of here?"

"You never know… Actually, I'm curious about an old friend who might have been a customer of yours, guy by the name of Charles Sawyer. His police friends called him Hacksaw."

Lynn paused for a moment to think. "I used to see him around here and I heard his name a lot, not in a good way, but he wasn't one of my customers."

"You sure?"

Lynn leaned close to Alan's ear again. "Yes, I'm sure, and please don't repeat questions. That's our deal."

"How about if the question is about your *going* price?"

"You can ask that one again, but only if you're serious about it. Then we'll talk, but I don't want you to tease and get my hopes up. There's no discounts for leading me on."

"Since you were born in the states, this is slavery isn't it?"

"Alan… May I call you Alan?"

"Certainly."

"The first night you were here, wasn't there a party going on downstairs for a policeman, and a lot of government officials were there?" Lynn asked.

"Yes, a welcome back party for the one and only Lieutenant Harry Frantz," Alan said.

Lynn stopped her massage and grabbed Alan's trapezius muscle, near his neck. "Now how would you remember his name? Do you work for him? Is he one of your friends?"

"No, not in any way. He and I have never been properly introduced, although we each know who the other is," Alan's voice lowered to a growl as his jaw clinched tightly.

"You don't like him then?"

"I probably shouldn't be telling you this, but no, not in the least."

"Well, that's actually good to know," said Lynn, as she leaned low over Alan's back, dragging her breasts across his shoulder blades and planting her lips next to his ear. "I've got bad memories of him that I'm never supposed to mention."

"Really? What about?"

Lynn slid off Alan's well oiled back and moved around to the front of the bed, to where she leaned over the top of him and pushed her hands rhythmically down his sides, while her upper thighs and pubic region touched at the top and side of his head. "You're tense," she said. "I can feel it. Let go of whatever's bothering you and enjoy the moment; otherwise, this is a waste of your time and money."

"This is definitely not a waste, but the point is I came here to talk to you. So if I let go and enjoy myself, I'll never… never mind."

"Harry took me when I was very young," said Lynn with a forced flatness to her tone.

"You say that like he was your first sexual experience," said Alan.

"Yes, because he was," Lynn said, before pausing a moment, and moving around to Alan's side, where she continued pushing down on his muscles, running her hands over his buttocks. "I was born in this House—literally. The world outside here doesn't even know I exist. There's no record of me anywhere. No birth certificate, no nothing. Inside here, everyone works at something, contributing what they can to the House. I worked in the kitchen as part of the wait staff."

"How old were you?"

"Thirteen," Lynn said with a guttural sigh. "The life I lead now wasn't to be for me. My mother was promised something better for her children, but first one and then another were pressed into the business. My day came when Harry saw me working in the kitchen. He would settle for nothing else but me. The House made him pay dearly, and they decided I offered more value to them than a vague unwritten promise to an old whore already in her grave. I went from simple waitress to a dolled up hooker in less than thirty minutes. The loss of my virginity was painful. The loss of my dignity can never be repaired."

"I'm sorry that happened to you," said Alan, not feeling the least bit amorous any longer. "I guess I just saw the glamour and glitz and assumed everyone was having a great time."

"There are moments I enjoy," said Lynn. "I like the camaraderie I have with the other girls. We look after each other, and there's enough business to go around so that we don't have to compete for customers."

"But given the circumstances, I suppose you've seen too much and don't enjoy the sex at all."

"Then you supposed wrong, because there are times when I do enjoy what I do," said Lynn.

"Like when?"

"Like when a man tastes me with his tongue or takes the time to satisfy me."

"Does that happen often?"

"Maybe not every night, maybe not every week, but enough for me to enjoy it."

Alan glanced sideways at Lynn as she lifted a glass cruet to pour more oil on his backside. "Like right now," she said. She smiled and pushed his head back down toward the table. "I'm enjoying looking at you right now as you are me," she said, "even these scars near your neck. What are they from?"

"Those are bullet holes," said Alan. "I was lucky on those, but I don't want to talk about them right now, if that's okay?"

"You're the customer," Lynn said.

"Are they ugly?"

"The bullet holes?" she asked. "By themselves they are, but you have plenty else to make up for it. So I'm thinking now they add character to you, like lines will to your face one day."

Alan exhaled noisily as he contemplated what Lynn had said.

She raked her nails lightly down his spine, all the way to his tailbone, sending an electric tingle along the way. "And I like touching your body," she said. "You have nice muscles and no handles. Yours is much nicer than what I normally get to see."

"Really?" asked Alan.

"Yes really," said Lynn, "and your body responds very well to my caresses, like what I'm doing here, when I run my hand down your bottom and slide it through your legs. I can see that you like that, you bad boy."

Alan stepped out on the landing underneath the twin gas lamps, and glanced down the steps and up the old underground sidewalk to where Shifu had come out of the door at the far end of Goon Dip Wong's building an hour-and-a-half earlier. He stared at the green door a moment, before wandering over for a closer inspection, glancing ahead and then quickly behind him into the darkness, making sure no one would surprise him—or he them.

There was nothing fancy to the aged brass doorknob, not even a slot for a key. Alan clasped hold of the knob, turned it, and pushed the door open into a darkened hallway, one that reminded him of a side entrance to a low rent tenement. The only light inside was from a bare bulb that dangled low from the ceiling, hanging just a few feet over Alan's head like a dwarf piñata begging for a beating. The light's meager output couldn't have totaled more than twenty-five watts. Plain wooden steps with a handyman's railing butted up against the brick wall at the far end of the building on the right. To Alan's left was a chalky plaster wall that formed a narrow passage just wide enough to allow access to a door at the back of the short hallway. Alan calculated that the plaster wall was most likely the exterior wall of the lower level gambling parlor. He sensed that the floors above him would be similar in construction, and the doors at the rear of the hallways would provide access to the viewing rooms and other secret passages.

Alan slid past the steps and stopped short of the varnished door and examined its doorknob, checking it for a locking mechanism. There was a slot for a skeleton key underneath the knob. He pressed his ear against the door and listened carefully for a long moment. Then he clasped the knob gently and gave it a light tug. The knob flexed sideways in his hand as if it wanted to turn, but the door wouldn't open.

Alan backpedaled and turned to leave, but he stopped when he heard the soft padding of shoes approaching from a floor or more above his. If he dashed for the door, then whoever was coming down the steps would see him scurrying away, and the battle would be on. Instead, Alan reached inside his coat pocket, withdrew the sap Chief Ketchum had given him, and slid sideways under the steps, pressing his lean shape deep into the dark shadows, up against the rough brick wall, where the mortar had been allowed to slop over the seams before drying into a constant nuisance. He held his breath as the noise of the feet coming down the steps grew louder. Multiple pairs of shoes pounded above his head, kicking loose a light shower of dust onto the top of his fedora, which he'd pulled low over his face.

From Alan's vantage point, there was a thin gap between the boards that he could peek through, where the riser had shrunken away from the tread. Alan cautiously peered through the slit at the two silhouettes stopped near the foot of the stairs, leaving the third man a couple of steps up from the floor. The faces were obscured by the man's legs standing on the steps, but it didn't matter because the shape nearest the door spoke to the others in English, and

Alan recognized it as Nelson Wong. The man on the steps shifted his weight, allowing Alan a glimpse of Nelson, as he reached into his suit coat's pocket and pulled out a Leica 35mm Rangefinder, opened the back, pulled out a roll of film, and handed it to the man on the steps.

"On second thought, Louie, let's not wait until the roll is full," said Nelson. "I want you to go back upstairs, put this in a container, and take it to Donnie's. I want it developed tonight. He is not to sell any of these pictures until I say so—even the one's where you can't recognize the clients' faces. I have this feeling that one of our American associates just might recognize our Mr. Stewart. Have Donnie file these in my sister's drawer, and remind him that I don't want extra copies floating around—which also applies to you two clowns."

"Which sister?" the man on the steps asked cautiously.

"That was Lynn," said Nelson, his impatience showing.

"Sorry, boss," said Louie. "I thought it might've been her, but she was in Mei's room, and I didn't get enough of a peek to be sure. Charlie was hogging the glass."

"You spend half your life in the closets watching the girls screw," said Nelson. "How could you not tell them apart?"

The third man, who was apparently Charlie, laughed heartily, reveling in Louie's discomfort, apparently glad the focus wasn't on him.

This is like *The Three Stooges*, Alan thought, with Nelson Wong playing the part of the mean one.

"What're you laughing at?" asked Nelson of Charlie. "You're up there almost as much as he is."

Nelson slid the camera back in his coat pocket. "I'm going inside to check the Pai Gow tables, and then I want to meet over at the noodle shop in twenty minutes."

As soon as Nelson and Charlie left through the side door, Louie spun around and marched back up the stairs.

165

Alan desperately wanted the roll of film Louie had in his possession, not wanting to become a black market porn star, either in Hong Kong or Seattle. He considered for a moment pouncing on Louie when he returned down the stairs, laying his head open with the sap, and stealing the film, like a bandit would do. But then Alan had to question the usefulness of that approach, especially since there was probably a developed roll of film out there from his first encounter with Lynn a week ago. Alan figured his best bet was to follow Louie to Donnie's photography business, find out where the film was developed, and hopefully where it was stored. Once he had that information he could develop a plan for stealing it back, thereby protecting his privacy.

Alan passed through the open door to the noodle shop and hurried over to where Vera was sitting in a corner with her back to the wall. She suddenly sat up, alert to Alan's sense of urgency. Alan leaned across the table toward her, like he was going to kiss her on the cheek.

"There's someone we need to follow," he said. "He'll either be passing the tunnel on the other side or coming through this one any minute."

Vera dropped enough cash on the table to pay for two meals and indicated to the manager he could keep the change. She quickly slid into her coat and followed Alan out the door to the entrance to the tunnel.

"What's going on?" she asked, her voice just above a whisper, as she handed Alan the pistol she had been holding for him.

"Nelson Wong is running some kind of porno and blackmail scheme on the side," said Alan. "One of his goons is going to deliver a roll of film to a shop where they'll develop and store it."

"How do you know that?" she asked.

"I did a little snooping, overheard them talking."

"And you're on that roll of film, aren't you? Is that why you want to follow him?"

Alan closed his eyes and lowered his head. "There's a lot more to it than that. It looks like they've been taking pictures of everyone, maybe doing it for years. I'd like to find out how far back their records go."

"Behind you," said Vera. "Someone's coming our way."

Alan heard the scraping of footsteps and tucked the .45 in his belt. Without turning around, he grabbed Vera by the arm and reached out to kiss her, hoping that Louie would ignore an amorous couple who couldn't contain themselves. Vera met Alan's kiss, as he'd hoped, but something was missing from her half of the equation. Alan sensed that she wasn't putting anything into it, that she was only playing her part, adding nothing of her usual playfulness. As soon as Louie passed them, she put her hand on Alan's chest and pushed him away.

"What were you thinking, Champ?" she asked. "Getting caught on film? You need to be more careful."

Alan's brow drooped at the sides, puppy dog like, as he gazed at Vera. She slid out of his grasp with her eyes locked on their prey, who now was almost to the corner.

Alan worried that he'd let his partner down, disappointed her because of his passion for women.

Reaching where the sidewalk branched with a tunnel under King Street, Louie turned to his left, continuing down the grade of the sidewalk to the west. Along with the occasional gas lamp in front of a business there was enough ambient light that shone through the embedded glass blocks above them that they didn't need a lantern to follow their quarry.

"I went in there absolutely convinced I wouldn't let it go

that far," Alan said in a voice just above a whisper.

Vera rocked her head back and forth like a *Jack-In-The-Box* toy, weighing what he was saying. "We'll talk about it later," she whispered.

"It was stupid of me to kiss you, after doing what I did."

"No worries, Champ. I just wonder if she gave you a fortune cookie after you were done."

"Why would she give me a fortune cookie?" Alan asked. "I didn't eat… Alright…I see. You're being really funny tonight."

"I'm not jealous, Champ—well, maybe a little—but the kiss was fine. I've used that trick before on black ops jobs. I learned it from the best. It works every time."

Alan wasn't so sure he wanted to hear that, thinking how it was Vera's opinion above all others that he valued most. He didn't want her thinking he was a slave to his libido, incapable of being loyal to a friend. Damn, how she could drive him nuts.

"From the best?" he asked.

"Did I say best? That must have slipped out, but don't worry about. And for right now, don't say or do anything that will draw attention to us. We'll move from doorway to doorway, ducking out of view when we can. Unless he's completely clueless, he should turn around before he gets to his destination. And if he sees us, we act like we're on our way to an herb store or tea shop, like we have a purpose or errand. Now step up, put your arm in mine, and point to something in the window."

Although this would be the time Alan would typically sass Vera and call her ma'am, he decided against it. "Understood," he grumbled.

Vera slid her hand down to grab his. "Let's catch up a little on him when he's not looking, like we're playing

Kick the Can.

When Louie reached the far corner of the building that stretched all the way to where the alley used to be, he turned into an alcove.

"He didn't look around once," said Alan.

"No he didn't. He acts like a great white shark that has no known enemies,"

"—Except for man," said Alan.

Vera reached back and flipped Alan's hat forward, sliding it down his nose. "And the humpback whale," she said, "if you want to get technical."

Alan pushed his hat back in place, somehow relieved that she wasn't holding a grudge, or so he hoped. "What? Like Moby Dick?" he asked, enjoying the banter.

"Moby Dick was a sperm whale, silly."

Alan chuckled quietly.

Vera clasped Alan's hand and pulled down on his arm, like it was a brake. "Be careful," she said. "He could be lying in wait."

Alan matched his pace to Vera's, acknowledging that her Naval Intelligence background gave her the edge in tailing and shadowing people. Unlike the street level above, where shop entrances fronted on the sidewalk with no set-backs, those below street level were once the primary entrances before the Regrade, and they had proper glass alcoves with street numbers embedded in the small white tiles that marked their entrances.

Vera stopped a few feet shy of the shop's windows. "We can't just wander out in front of the window and stare inside at whoever's there," said Vera. "You wait here while I take a peek."

Vera shimmied along the side of the building, slid a compact from her coat pocket, held it up to eye level, and angled the mirror to reflect around the edge of the glass. As

169

she tilted and adjusted the mirror for a better view inside, Alan slid in close to her.

"Your guy is talking to a man behind the counter," said Vera.

Alan leaned away from the building and studied the shop's name on the large window. "*Donnie Chang's Herbs, Potions, and Acupuncture Shop*," Alan said." That matches with where Nelson told him to go."

"So," said Vera, letting the word hang in the air for a long moment, "do you want to go in there guns blazing and get your sex film back right now? We could always kill them both, teach them a lesson. Or we could wait for the proprietor to develop the film, so you can hang the pictures on your wall at home. But knowing your mother's church going ways, I don't think she would appreciate that."

Alan leaned back against the glass and ran his tongue around his mouth, sucking on a sour note. "Alright, I deserved that. So what do you recommend?"

"It sounds like the film will be safe inside here for awhile, so let's come back tomorrow night at O-dark-thirty, when everyone's in bed, and see what this quack has in his store."

"If we're going to do night operations, how about we stop by Goon Dip's too. I'd like to see what's going on behind those walls on the upper floors."

"And why's that?" asked Vera. "See if they've pinned a poster of their new matinee idol on the wall: 'Super stud bangs Lynn from behind?'"

Alan reached up and grabbed Vera playfully by the nape of the neck, like he was going to wring her head from its shoulders. "There's a lot more to tell you," he said. "First of all, Lynn is Nelson's younger sister."

"Oh, no!" said Vera. "That's just plain wrong—anywhere—any country—any culture."

"I totally agree," said Alan.

Vera tucked the compact mirror away and started back up the sidewalk with Alan next to her.

"Of course the sister relationship also applies to Mei too," Alan said.

"So, Nelson's pimping both his sisters?" Vera asked, anger in her voice.

"So it would seem," said Alan. "And guess who was Lynn's first customer, the man who took her virginity and turned her into a prostitute?"

"I don't know…maybe Hack Sawyer? Is that what the killing was all about?"

"I wondered that too," said Alan. "That was my first guess, but it turns out that it was none other than our own Hungry Harry. Of course Sawyer could have always gone in right after him; we don't know that part for sure. I'm guessing he was no angel."

"Aha!" said Vera. "So that's why you want to dig through their old film files. You want to find the goods on *Harry*."

"Bingo!"

"Alright, I'm good with that, but tell me more about Lynn," said Vera. "How did this nasty business happen to her? She must hate what she does here, right?"

"Well, not all of it," Alan said, careful not to disclose what Lynn had said about enjoying her time alone with him. "Can we finish this over dinner? I'm starved."

"No doubt you're hungry after all the mattress exercise while on top of Lynn, but I've already eaten—beef noodles, if you're interested?"

Alan shook his head, knowing he was going to have to put up with the teasing for awhile. "Were you wishing it was you?" he asked hopefully.

Vera rocked her head back and forth as she thought a moment. "Maybe I am, and maybe I'm not."

"Well, while you're thinking about it," said Alan, "let's go topside to the restaurant Big Ben took us to and—"

"And give you something else to eat that doesn't have two legs?" asked Vera, with a hint of sass.

Alan sucked in his cheeks, shook his head, but didn't say anything.

"Funny you should mention Ben," said Vera. "He and I are going out later tonight."

Alan stutter-stepped, almost coming to a complete stop. He stared blankly at the underground sidewalk a moment, then quickly recovered, and tried to pick up the pace again. Vera slowed a second to keep pace with Alan, while he forced a smile, hoping it wouldn't betray the wrenching feeling he felt in his stomach.

"You going to listen to jazz?" Alan asked.

"Yes," said Vera. "Up at the Black and Tan."

"Of course," said Alan thoughtfully. "Things don't start popping up there till after midnight. Give my best to Noodles and Ben."

Alan stood alone, across the sidewalk from a small Belltown shop, staring off into space. Constructed of brick and terra cotta, the shop was at the end of a one-story building next to a gravel parking lot. He shoved his hands deep into his pockets, while his back was pressed against the passenger door of the Union's Buick. At 7:59 AM a familiar hand grabbed the window shade of the front door of Mario's Tailor Shop, rolled it up, and turned the sign over to *Open*. A specter stirred behind the glass and then a short man—who, with his thick white hair, reminded Alan of Geppetto from *Pinocchio*—pressed his face against the glass, gazed for a moment at Alan, and then opened the door wide and waved him inside.

"Buongiorno, Bambino!" Mario said.

Alan forced a grin on his tired face. "Morning, Mario."

"You gotta that hang dog look, like you spent all night in the pound with no place to poop in private."

"Amen to that," said Alan. "I feel like a big dog went and peed in my food bowl."

Mario nodded sympathetically. "You're carrying nothing in your hands that needs mending, I see," said Mario, "so I'm guessing it's your inside that's aching."

"Uhm hmm," Alan groaned, as he slid past Mario and plopped down in an oaken chair.

"Women trouble?" asked Mario.

Alan slouched down in the chair and tugged his fedora down over his eyes, like he'd finally found a place where it was safe to rest. "Yes, again," he said wearily.

Mario took a pair of gray, wool slacks from a pile, turned them inside out, and picked at the seat's seam with a stitch ripper. "Last time you was here, it was because you were having too much of a good thing, wasn't it?" Without waiting for a reply, Mario continued. "It was about your friend Alice, some tomboy named Robbie, and as they say, last but not least—Miss Vera Deward. Am I right?"

Alan sighed and nodded.

"So is this more of the same, or have you become the next Rudy Valentino with so many women you don't know what to do with your pecker?"

Alan shook his head once slowly and pushed out his lower lip as if he intended to pout, but the energy just wasn't there for him. "No Valentino here," he said. "I haven't seen Robbie in two months, so she's not in the picture at the moment. There is, however, someone I met who I want to help out—that is if I can—but right at this very minute it's Alice and Vera who're on my mind."

Mario continued digging at the seam on the pants he was tailoring. "First, who's this person you wanna help out? Is she someone you like?"

"Well…yeah, you could say I've enjoyed my time with Lynn, but there are definite limitations to our relationship."

Mario glanced up and stared at Alan over his cheaters. "There's something about the big words you're using, the way you said what you just did, which makes me think you don't want to talk about her."

Alan groaned apologetically. "Lynn's a working girl, Mario."

Mario took off his spectacles and scratched at his eye. "I know what I mean when I say working girl," he said. "Does it mean the same to you?"

Alan pushed his hat back on his head, revealing his forehead. "I met her in a brothel while working a case I'm on. She's trapped inside there, and I'd like to help her escape."

"I see," said Mario. "Then it's not like you want to marry her and take her home to your family."

"No," said Alan. "It's not that at all."

"So…what are you going to do, put on your Zorro mask, climb up on a black steed, swoop down into whatever castle she's held prisoner, and carry her off in your arms?"

Alan chuckled. "Maybe."

"Well, while you're thinking how you're going to pull that off, tell me about the other two. What's going on there?"

"I'm torn in two completely different directions," said Alan. "I got a great thing going with Alice, who's more woman than I ever dreamed I'd find or thought I'd be worthy of, but then there's Vera—and you know Vera."

"You just can't walk away from a woman like that," said Mario, dreamily. "So, what's keeping you two apart?"

"There was something I wasn't sure about with her, something I thought was dangerous, but I'm fine with it now. I got it worked out. But it slowed our friendship down on whatever path it was we were traveling. I got a little off track for awhile. So she also backed off on her flirting. About the time I thought things were getting back up to speed between us, the case we're working on goes and gets complicated." Alan paused for a moment and shifted his weight in the chair. "I went further than I wanted with

Lynn, and either Vera's punishing me for it or she's found someone else she's interested in."

"What makes you say that?" asked Mario.

"She went out with a friend of ours last night."

"'Ours?'He's a friend of yours too?"

"Yeah. Name's Ben Kearney. He's not like the other police officers I've had trouble with. I've started getting used to Ben—I trust him now, and then he's got to go and ruin it by asking Vera out."

"Officer Ben Kearney—a big fellow?" asked Mario.

"Yeah," said Alan. "You know him?"

Mario nodded thoughtfully. "I tailor his uniforms and gear, and he's huge, lots of muscles."

"That's the one," said Alan.

"Well, lucky for you he's a nice guy. In fact he's a proper gentleman with real manners, not just showy stuff for when he knows people are watching him."

"Thanks for that information, Mario. I'm feeling really lucky about all that now. Maybe I should go out and buy a Chinese Lottery ticket while my luck holds."

Mario tilted his head to the side and shrugged apologetically. "Where'd they go to?" he asked. "Any place special?"

"They're both into jazz. So they went up to the Jazz Alley last night."

"And you stayed up all night worried about this?"

Alan rubbed his face with his hands, as if wiping the sleep away, pushing his fedora back on his head and out of the way. "Yeah, I did. Isn't that pathetic of me?"

"No, bambino, not at all. It's actually good, at least the way I see it. You now know how much you care for her. The last time you talked about her, you wasn't so sure about that. And besides, you could be going through all this turmoil for nothing."

"Why's that?" asked Alan, glancing up hopefully.

"Could be they just went up there for the music is all. She might've wanted company to go to a bar. Even up at Jazz Alley, it's not right for a woman to go without an escort. People see something like that and they assume the worst about a woman. It's not right, but that's the way it is."

"She could have asked me to take her."

"Well, how about you asking her, Bambino? Did you ever think of that? That's usually how it's done."

Alan shook his head lazily, like it took more gas than he had left in his tank.

"Could be your police friend called her up first and asked," said Mario. "He might not understand how close you and Vera are, because of the difference in your age and all that. He might've assumed she was available and not thought to ask you to tag along with them. Remember, Bambino, she is single and attractive."

Alan folded his hands, lacing his fingers together across his chest, seemingly more at peace with himself now than he had been in several hours.

"Besides," said Mario, "what's that old expression? Two's company, three's a herd?"

Alan snickered. "Three's a crowd, Mario. We're not cattle."

Mario nodded as he carefully threaded a needle with a long length of thread and cinched the end into a knot. "I know, Bambino. I was just checking to see if you were paying attention."

"So what am I going to do with them, Mario? Vera and Alice, I mean."

"It looks to me like you've got it pretty well figured out, Bambino—even if it's just you realizing you spent all night worrying over your friend Vera. You might want to take her out on a real date, like your police friend is doing with her. Go ahead and show her you're proud to be with her."

"I'm always proud to be with her."

"But that's during the daytime while you're on business, Bambino. It's different when you take her to a movie or a restaurant where you sit next to her, hold her hand, and people see you're a couple. What's keeping you from doing that?"

"Alice."

"Oh? Has Alice demanded that you not do this, or is it that Alice means too much to you for you to do this to her?"

"She means too much to me."

"Okay, that tells us both something. Now add in that other question I asked a minute ago. How would you feel about being with Vera and then you have someone say something about your ages? It's none of their damn business, but they might say, 'Good for you, young stallion,' because they figure you got something special to be going with a woman like Vera. But then in their next breath they'll say something bad about her, because she's a mature woman running around with a younger man. They'll think it's all about sex with you and her, and they'll attack her morals. That's too bad how people do that, but it's the way the world works. Could you handle that, or are you going to go around and break a lot of noses of people who stick them into your business?"

"The hospital will be full of trauma cases," Alan said with a scowl.

"And how long would that go on before you'd grow tired of hurting people who are just saying what comes natural to them, 'cause you're not going to be able to change the way everybody thinks? Six months? A year? Five years?"

"I don't know."

"Me neither," said Mario. "Could be you'd never grow tired of her or defending her reputation. You might even figure out some ways to deal with it while you're in public so it's not so obvious."

"That could happen," Alan said with more hope than confidence.

"And it also could happen that if your relationship with her only lasted a year or two those might be the best damn memories of your entire life."

"But it's not likely Alice is going to be keeping vigil by a window just in case Vera and I crash and burn."

"Ahhh, now you're thinking about what's really important over the long run in life, not just what you want right here and now. That's a good sign, Bambino. But are you thinking this way because you realize you see Vera only as a hot temptation, where you think Alice is the real thing, or are you hedging your bets? Is Alice just your safety net? That's what you need to figure out."

Alan slumped back in his chair and shook his head. "I'm back to square one, and what's nuts about all this is that I was doing perfectly fine until Vera waltzed into my life—without an invitation. She crashed the party I was having in my head, and now I don't want her to ever leave me."

"Vera's not such a bad thing to have running around in your head. From everything I've seen of her, I'd say she's a good woman, definitely not a conniving game player."

Alan inhaled deeply, crossed his leg, and let his foot dangle casually, finding a sense of peace.

"So, what time did she get home last night?" asked Mario.

Alan leaned forward at the waist and gazed at Mario suspiciously. "How would I know?"

"In this case, a question from you is a good answer, Bambino, and the only right one. If you'd been up at her apartment waiting in the bushes like a prowler, we'd have a whole different set of problems to discuss."

Alan grinned. "I'm not stupid, Mario. If I had waited for her, I would have sat inside the car where it's warm."

Mario shook his head, stuck the sewing needle into the

gray wool, and drew it through the fabric. "You know what
I meant, Bambino."

"Pour yourself a cup of coffee, Champ," Vera said as she rubbed black grease paint under her eyes. "We could be in for a long night."

Alan unscrewed the cap from the thermos they had brought and grunted a reply.

"Didn't you get enough sleep last night?" Vera asked him.

"Why do you ask?" Alan said, but as soon as he spoke another yawn forced its way out, despite his effort to stifle it. He shrugged, a guilty smile on his painted face, which was only faintly visible in the lantern light inside the catacombs.

Vera frowned and shook her head. "I don't know, Champ, it could be your heavy eyelids and the yawning. That's usually a clue when someone's tired."

"I was up late," Alan said, not yet willing to explain the reason why or apologize to her.

"Then you should have taken a nap in the afternoon, like I did. You knew what time we'd be starting."

Alan nodded thoughtfully, thinking this disclosure meant that Vera likely spent the night alone, which was a good thing from his perspective. "I thought naps were just for kids and old men."

"They're also for people who work night shifts or have

busy schedules," Vera said. "Winston Churchill swears by them. He says it doubles the work he can do in a day, and look how he's holding England together during all that chaos."

"I had things on my mind last night, couldn't sleep."

"I thought massages like the one Lynn gave you were meant to help you relax, but then of course you might have gone back for seconds after I left."

"It wasn't Lynn I was thinking about," Alan said.

Vera sat down on the wooden steps, the portal to the catacombs beneath the Japanese theater. She bumped her hip up next to Alan's as she tugged off her left shoe and rubbed at her toes through her wool stocking. Without thinking why he did it, Alan reached out and pulled Vera's leg up onto his lap and started kneading at the bottom of her foot with his thumb.

"Be careful with the little toe," she said. "It's sore."

"I couldn't sleep because I was thinking about you all night."

In the faint lantern glow, Vera squinted at Alan, puzzled. "Why?" she asked.

Alan pressed both thumbs into the high arch of Vera's foot, and she moaned. "Am I hurting you?" he asked.

"Not at all," she said. "What you heard was pleasure, not pain. You could do that all night long, except we have work that needs to get done."

"I was worried," said Alan, pulling Vera's foot up close to his shoulder, for better leverage, so he could work his magic.

"Why?" she asked with a pleasant sigh. "Were you afraid that Ben would break all my toes?"

Alan leaned back and stared at Vera's foot in the dim light. Then he lightly clasped her little toe.

"Ow!" she protested.

"Ben did this to you?" Alan asked.

"Yes," Vera said, drawing out the S into a long hiss,

182

"while we were dancing. He means well, but he doesn't get the concept of leading with his left foot."

"Well, that's exactly what I was afraid of," said Alan, now more alert than he had been all day. "I didn't want him hurting a hair on your head, let alone mashing your toes."

"That's sweet of you," said Vera.

"How's your other foot?"

Vera pulled off her right shoe and offered her foot to Alan, letting it drop familiarly on his lap next to the other. "Not so bad, but it could use a tune up—and then we should get to work."

Alan released Vera's left foot and pulled her right one close to his chest, and he began working the arch like he had the other. "How's that feel?"

"Absolutely wonderful," Vera cooed. "Where'd you learn to do feet? I'm certain that Lynn wouldn't waste her time counting your little piggies."

"From my mother, I suppose," said Alan. "Some days her feet bothered her to no end. I'm oldest and closest—"

"And you're the one who could do the best job," said Vera. She pulled her feet back without explanation, and dropped them to the paver floor where her shoes waited.

Alan finished his coffee, put the lid back on the thermos, and stowed it in a daypack that held their tools.

"Time's wasting," she said. "There're pictures of you in the nude worth exploring."

Alan suddenly gasped, like he'd swallowed a moth, and his eyes flared wide. "You're not going to look at them, are you?" he protested.

"If I find them first, I certainly will."

"Well, that's not fair."

Vera finished putting on her shoes, calmly stood up, and grinned devilishly. Alan hovered close to her, while searching her face for meaning.

"What's fair got to do with it?" she asked. "You shouldn't have *exposed* yourself to the risk and to the camera. Besides, you've already seen a picture of me in the buff, on Brinkman's yacht as I remember—my burlesque picture with 'tassels twirling,' as you said. You told me that a couple of months back."

Alan groaned, knowing she had him cornered.

"Turnabout is fair play," Vera said. "Isn't that how the expression goes?"

Alan growled gutturally. "Just because an expression seems to fit, doesn't mean it's always right...and for damn sure that I'll be happy going along with it."

Alan slung the pack over his shoulder, and Vera led the way down the graded tunnel to Chinatown with him close at her side. She was ahead so he couldn't see her face, but he sensed she was smiling, proud of herself for having another way to torment him. She loved having the upper hand.

"But you posed for your pictures," Alan said. "I didn't. Mine were taken absolutely without my knowledge—or permission."

"Uhm...okay, if you say so, but I have no way of knowing that for sure. For all I know you could have been waving your tool around like it was a billy club that was going to inflict a beating, showing it off for all the girls in the building."

Alan grabbed Vera's arm and stopped her abruptly on the brick pavers. He held the lantern up to her blackened face to see the playful glint in her eye, which was just as he suspected. He let go of her arm, reached around, and pulled her tightly against his frame. As he lowered his lips towards her, she reached up for his mouth with hers, pressing their lips together. Her mouth slid open a crack. He felt it happen and forced his tongue inside her mouth, chasing after her tongue, savoring the flavor and wetness of her being. His free hand slid down her back between her butt cheeks, and he clasped hold of firm muscle, squeezing it gently, holding it for a long moment, daring her to protest his brashness at some point, but she didn't. His hand continued back to the crevice between her cheeks, following it down to where her rump met her leg muscles. He cupped her bottom firmly in his hand and held onto it.

"You drive me crazy!" he said, after pulling his lips away to nuzzle her ear. "I think about you all the time, even when I shouldn't."

Vera put her hand on Alan's chest and gently pushed him back, putting an arm's length of distance between them. "I'm not sorry about that in the least, but I'm sure you've figured that out already."

"I've been hoping that I've been more than just a playful diversion for you," Alan said. "I'd go stark raving nuts if it turns out I'd become your source of amusement and nothing more."

"No, Champ. You don't have to worry about that at all. You've become much more. As it is, I spend too much time wondering about you, trying to convince myself that the difference in our ages doesn't really matter—that is to anybody but me."

"You worry like that too?" Alan asked.

"Of course I do, darling. I've taken a stroll around the block a time or two. I know how people talk and how hard things we hear will be on the both of us. If somebody accused you of just being after one thing, I don't know that I wouldn't hurt them. I might snap a few of their vertebrae. I know you think I'm a lady, but I don't always take the high road."

Alan tried to pull Vera close for another hug, but this time she protested, holding her ground, shaking her head. "Not now, we have work to do, and I don't want you distracted, because that's when mistakes happen and you could get hurt. We can talk about this later."

Alan sighed heavily, but he knew she was right. He adjusted the daypack on his shoulder, giving it another hitch to even the weight. "Remind me again: what do we do if someone catches us?" he asked.

"We're not going to get caught."

"What if they have a night watchman, somebody like Shifu?"

"There's probably somebody living in the back of the shop or close by it, and if there is, we try not to hurt them. If we can take care of whoever it is without making too much noise, we do so. We bind their hands and feet with the chord and tape their mouth shut with that gray tape I borrowed from the Navy."

"Nobody dies?" Alan asked.

"This doesn't involve national security," said Vera, "unless your pecker's a secret weapon we don't want falling into the hands of the enemy."

Alan bent forward with laughter, but then tried to suppress it. He reached up and grabbed Vera by the nape of her neck and gave her a playful shake. "You can be just plain evil at times."

Vera pulled away and pushed onward, exiting the tunnel that put them under King Street and Seventh Avenue. "Alright," she said. "We need to quiet down. I don't plan on hurting anybody—unless I have to, and that should be your position too. If this goes to hell, it's not likely anyone from Chinatown would call the police to handle it, but there're two reasons for that. First, the Chinese don't trust the police—and why should they? And secondly, they have their own ways of dealing with crimes committed against them. The problem is that their way could involve physical dissection and body dumping in Elliott Bay. So I suggest we speak only when it's absolutely necessary, because I don't want to find out what it is that the Chinese think is just and fair when dealing with burglars and thieves—because that's what we are tonight. We're not on a black bag job for the government, which means we're on our own, and we're messing with the way they do their business down here."

"Understood," Alan's whisper was accompanied by a thoughtful nod.

They quietly crept through the tunnel underneath King Street, set their lantern down, and veered to the left down the grade towards the west. Given her experience working anti-spying operations, Alan followed her lead. Instead of posing as the romantic couple, this time their goal was to be as close to invisible as possible, which meant unseen as well as unheard.

Vera crossed over the numbers embedded in the tile entrance to *Donnie Chang's Herbs, Potions, and Acupuncture Shop*. She pressed up close to the door and studied the interior of the shop carefully. Alan stayed to her left and watched her eyes to see what things she focused on, what she thought was important. To the left in the interior was a crowded display case in front of a counter with mahogany colored wooden shelves that were full of green jars with re-sealable lids. Their contents, labeled with Chinese characters, appeared to be dried roots, herbs, leaves and other vegetable matter. On top of the counter was a cash register with a crank handle, and the drawer appeared to be open a few inches. They've been burglarized before, Alan thought. Leaving the till open sends a message to would-be burglars that they'd find no cash in the drawer. In front of the counter was a small table with two chairs set opposite each other, and along the wall were more chairs.

Vera leaned close to Alan. "There's a bell over the door," she whispered. "When I open the lock, I'll need you to lift the bell out of the way to keep it from ringing. Can you do that?"

"I'd be glad to."

"On the way out, we need to also remember it's there. Other than them missing a few photos, they should never suspect anyone was ever here."

Alan nodded.

Alan kept watch as Vera knelt on one knee and brought out a small canvas pouch from her pocket, untied it, and rolled it open on top of her thigh muscle. Inside the pouch was a set of lock picks done in gun-metal blue, which reminded Alan of a set of hex keys his father kept on his workbench, only these tools were flattened out for better gripping, and the working parts were much smaller. He'd read that a pick set was illegal to possess by anybody other than a locksmith, something about it being prima facie evidence of intent to commit a crime. So if the police found them in their possession, they both could be arrested for possession of burglary tools, with little or no chance that Naval Intelligence would step forward to bail them out— that is unless Vera could convince her superior to intervene and pretend they were again hot on the trail of a Japanese spy, somebody like the White Dragon.

Vera pulled a military flashlight equipped with a red lens from her coat pocket, cupped her hand around the lens, and pressed it against the lock for just a second. She switched on the red light long enough to study the keyhole a moment, and then she quickly turned it off. As she set the flashlight down on the ground, Alan stepped back and peeked around the edge of the store's front to make sure no one had seen anything. At 3:30AM there were no signs of life in the catacombs, but Alan knew from his bread delivery days that there were plenty of early risers in the world. They didn't have much time to work before the morning people would pose a threat.

Vera withdrew two picks from opposite ends of the

canvas pouch on her knee. One pick appeared to be a flattened hex wrench, and the other strongly resembled a screwdriver, only without the fat handle. She inserted the wrenching tool into the opening away from the tumbler and flexed it slightly to the side. Then she inserted the slender pick on top of it and applied upward pressure. Within seconds the bolt withdrew and the door sprung open. Vera grabbed the handle and stopped it from swinging open.

Alan clasped Vera's shoulder and gave it a squeeze. He wanted to tell her how amazed he was at yet another skill he didn't know she possessed, but he realized the celebration would have to wait until they were done. There was still much more work to be done before their night was over.

Vera indicated the door handle with a nod of her head, and Alan took over holding it in place while Vera put her tools away. As soon as she was done, she stood up next to Alan and took possession of the door handle again. Vera caught Alan's eye and gazed at the top of the door again, indicating the bell. "Grab it and step inside," she whispered. "Just make sure you don't step on their snake."

Alan Froze. "Snake? There's a snake in here?"

Vera shook her head. "Some places keep a pet boa constrictor as a watch dog. The snake also earns his keep by eating rats, but this place doesn't have a snake."

"How do you know?" asked Alan.

"Because they have a fat old cat in the window on my right. A snake would have devoured the pussy by now, despite its promise to Adam and Eve that it could be trusted."

Alan started to chuckle but fought it. "I hate snakes."

"Can't say I ever met one I liked either," said Vera. "One of the other girls in our show wanted one for her act, but I nixed it. Wasn't going to happen while I was the headliner."

"What about the cat?" asked Alan.

"She sees people coming and going all the time," said Vera, "and if it's like the one I have at home, she'd let us cart away everything but the pillow she's camped on without uttering a mew."

Alan snuck another peek behind them and reached up through the opening to clasp hold of the shop's bell, attached to the jamb. He gently squeezed the small clapper to keep it from ringing and lifted the bell up and out of the way as he pushed the door open. Vera stepped inside the shop behind him, and then Alan closed the door carefully, again making sure the bell didn't betray their presence.

Vera put her index finger up in front of her mouth and pursed her lips, as if she was blowing the quiet symbol. Alan stepped to the side of the door and stood perfectly still, while Vera moved quietly to the area behind the counter. She glanced quickly inside each of the cabinet doors and came back around the counter to the open area that led to the back of the shop. Feeling the need to be the protector, Alan followed her to the rear of the shop, gliding quietly across the wooden floor.

The first door on their left was ajar, and Vera pushed it open to reveal a tiny bathroom with the same small white tiles on the floor as those located outside the shop's entry. The commode was the old fashioned kind with a tank and pull chain elevated above the bowl. Across from the bathroom was a closed door with an after-market deadbolt lock. Vera nodded at Alan and indicated the lock. Then she pointed down the hall at the last two doors. The one on the left was also left ajar, while the end door had a mat on the floor in front of it. Vera indicated for Alan to go ahead of her, while she knelt down in front of the door with the lock. As Alan passed, she tapped his leg and pointed directly at the floor mat, ensuring that he also saw it. She's thinking the door leads to the living quarters, he thought.

Alan approached the last door on his left and stopped short of the door jamb. He listened cautiously and then peeked around the corner into the dark room. He quietly pushed the door open to let in the little ambient light that was available and leaned inside. In the center of the room was a table that resembled what might be found in a doctor's office, only thinner and oddly shaped, like the massage table Lynn had used in Goon Dip's place. To the left of the table was a small stand with jars, cotton balls, and cruets filled with fluids that gave the room a medicinal smell. Behind the table was a coat rack with a couple of robes hanging on it, and to its right was a bare wall with a fancy mosaic sculpture of a large coiled snake with two eyes facing straight ahead. Alan recoiled and backpedalled away from the room and the duplicitous sculpture. He closed the door quietly behind him, glad he hadn't turned on any lights.

Alan caught his breath and stood silently for a minute, unmoving, and listening for hurried footfalls in the room behind the shop—but there were none. So, this quack acupuncturist is also set up to take nude photographs, Alan thought. Just like in Goon Dip's. He wondered who was first to discover this way of making extra money, Goon Dip, Nelson Wong, or Donnie Chang. And Alan figured that if he had turned on the light or used his flashlight, it no doubt would have shown through the snake's eyes into the room in the far back, letting whoever was back there know that there was an intruder in the shop.

Vera glanced over toward Alan, checking on him and what he had found. He raised his hand in front of his face, shook it cautiously, signaling to her that there was something dangerous where he was at. He motioned with his hand that he would be standing guard at this door. He slid the blackjack Ketchum had given him into his hand, which he dangled freely by his side. If someone opened the end door, he was going to whack them on the side of the head.

Vera continued to work at the door on the opposite side of the hall, again using her lock picks. After a few seconds, she twisted the heavier piece and the door gave way. Before pushing it all the way open, she put her picks back in their slots, folded the pouch, and put it in her pocket. She stood up, carefully eased the door open, and stepped out of Alan's view. After fifteen seconds, she stuck her head out the door and nodded for Alan to join her.

Alan cautiously stepped away from the end door and quietly moved down the hall to the room, which was emitting a red glow. He stopped at the door jamb and peeked around the corner, just to be sure there wouldn't be a surprise waiting. Underneath a red globe, Vera stood in front of a file cabinet drawer pulled all the way open, leafing through folders in the top drawer. It was one of three matching wooden cabinets stacked side-by-side, each four drawers high, situated next to a workbench with a photographic enlarger perched on top. Located in the back at the far wall were a deep sink, processing tanks, and several large jars of chemicals on the floor. Strung across the wall immediately to Alan's left were three rows of wire, each ten feet long, hung like laundry lines with clothes pins holding enlarged photographs in place. At the far end of the front row was a stretch without pictures, where a dozen clothes pins sat like chattering crows perched idly on a telephone wire.

Vera gazed up at Alan and indicated for him to close the door behind him. As soon as he had done so, he crossed the room and stood next to her.

"He has one of those mosaics on the wall in his examination room," Alan whispered, "just like those in the brothel."

"Chang takes pictures of his patients?" Vera asked in a hushed tone.

"Looks that way," said Alan, "and it's on the back wall, which could mean if we turned on a light in his office, somebody in the living quarters might know we're here."

"What a pervert! You know it's one thing if the person was in the business of taking their clothes off, like I was…well, just like you said earlier." Vera growled as she turned sharply and stared at the far wall, past the sink and processing tanks, studying it. She nodded quietly to herself. "I don't see anything like that here, but that's good to know."

"Where should I start?" asked Alan.

"Can you read Chinese?"

Alan scrunched his brow low into a playful scowl. "Of course not."

Vera reached to her left, picked up a handful of 8 x 10 inch glossies from a basket tray and handed them to him. "Two batches here," she said. "The ones on top were drying. They appear to match the ones in the basket which have markings on the edges…"

Alan stared wide eyed at the top photograph of him and Lynn, his bare torso and face fully visible over the top of her, bent over at the waist onto the massage table, his pelvis pushed tight against her bare flanks. Lynn's eyes were closed dreamily and she was biting pleasurably at her lower lip. Alan's mouth fell open as he quickly flipped through the stack of photographs.

Vera stopped her file search while Alan processed what he was looking through. His anger took him past the point of embarrassment at his exposure, and he slowed down on his third time through the pictures. The second picture in the sequence showed Lynn with her leg raised, knee up on the table, improving the camera's visibility of her genitals and Alan's erect penis. Alan swallowed an uncomfortable lump in his throat. "She's posing for the camera," he groaned.

"Looks that way," said Vera, "but then she's probably got her routine choreographed for her. She probably follows it without thinking."

Alan chewed on his lower lip and moved to the next picture. In this one Lynn was positioned in front of Alan, facing the camera, her back to him, straddling him as he sat against the table. His hands were wrapped around her breasts as she twisted acrobatically to the side to kiss him passionately. Alan stared at the picture a long moment.

"She's not faking that," said Vera, "if that's what's bothering you?"

Alan dropped the pictures on top of the open cabinet, grimaced, and shrugged apologetically to Vera. "Well that's reassuring," he said flatly, "but in the next one she's literally got me by the balls."

"Keep out one picture with symbols on it," Vera said. "Put the rest in your bag. We need a reference to find the file we want."

"Great!" said Alan sarcastically. "So which picture do you want to look at for the next thirty minutes? Me on top of Lynn? Me behind Lynn? Lynn tugging on—"

"How about the one where your back's to the camera, and we just see your cute butt?"

"But you can see Lynn squatting down in front of me, and you can tell that her face is in my crotch," Alan said.

"I can live with that," said Vera. "It's your cheeks I like, and she apparently does too. We might have to call you sweet cheeks after this."

Alan managed a snicker, and he reached up and gently stroked Vera's back, running his hand up to the nape of her neck. "You're a good friend, you know that? You've managed to take a lot of the sting out of how stupid I feel."

"Well thank you for that, darling, but save it for later. We've got work to do now. So study the writing on the edge

194

of the photo, pick a file drawer, and see if you can match the characters up to a folder. Since Lynn's been doing this for several years, she should have a drawer thick with files. Remember, we want prints and negatives."

"Do you think these are filed alphabetically or numerically?" Alan asked.

"The writing has stylized numbers, along with the Chinese characters, if that helps you? But what I'm seeing is not doing anything for me."

Alan stared at the characters and numbers as he dropped to his knees and tucked the extra pictures in his daypack. He opened two of the bottom drawers next to each other, set the photograph on top of one set of files, took out his Navy flashlight, and studied the tabs on the green files in the other drawer using the red lens. He ignored the numbers at first and focused instead on the second word of the text, which contained a pen stroke that reminded him of the roof of an Asian temple, making it more distinct than the other characters. He flipped through each tab, tipping the folders forward as he sought that one distinctive roof character, and as he did so he noticed that there was indeed a pattern to the files. He pulled one of the folders up far enough to catch a glimpse of who the woman was in the pictures inside. It contained pictures of Mei when she was younger, wearing pigtails, a white blouse, and an undersized pleated skirt. Apparently she went for the schoolgirl look before switching to the dominatrix leather and whip she now sported. In the back of the folder was a manila colored envelope, which Alan guessed contained the negatives for that particular file. The next folder also contained pictures of Mei in a similar outfit, but with a different customer, one who's overweight body was covered in wiry gray hairs, even over his shoulders, reminding Alan of a silverback gorilla at the Woodland Park Zoo. Behind the man on a chair was a dark colored coat that Alan recognized.

"I've got a police officer here," said Alan as he flipped back to the first photograph at the front of the file. The man in the picture wore a blue tunic with seven buttons and a cap with a bill.

"Who is it?" asked Vera. "Could it be our Hacksaw Sawyer or—"

"He's got sergeant stripes," said Alan. "I'm wondering if this is Sergeant Knuckles McMurphy?"

"Take a couple samples from the file, and we'll show them to Big Ben."

Alan selected a few photographs at random, but he found he didn't like staring at the ones involving actual sex acts, because it was somehow different now that he knew the woman involved. He felt like he was invading her privacy, especially because she was so much younger in the photographs.

"I think the characters in front of the numbers are the girl's name," Alan said. "They're alphabetized. These are all Mei's files down here."

Vera resumed checking the file drawer she had been working on. "I'm getting that too," she said, "except this drawer has a blonde with big boobs." Vera shut the top drawer and opened the one underneath. "Would she be another one of your friends?"

"That would be Ruth, and she's not yet one of my friends yet," said Alan. "I thought I would subject her to rigorous questioning next week, see what she's hiding and where."

Vera shoved Alan's watch cap sideways and rubbed his head. "You rascal!"

Alan grinned to himself, glad for the banter. He plucked at other files, held the flashlight close to them, skimmed over the tabs quickly, and pulled a folder from near the back of the drawer. Once again it was a picture of Mei, but in this one she was very young, not yet filled out. Alan doubted whether she was within reach of fifteen when the picture was taken. Again, the customer was another gray haired white male, and although he was nearly naked, Alan had the feeling from the man's longish hair cut, sock garters, and hosiery that he was old money, from Seattle's patrician class, certainly a pillar of the community. Alan skewed his face to the side, disgusted, but at the same time he wondered for a second if he wasn't above this sort of thing himself. Would he ever take advantage of his position, connections, or income to exploit a young girl who was not yet a woman? Before he drew another breath he vowed that age, maturity, and consent were sacred trusts when it came to sex, boundaries he would not cross.

Alan slid the bottom drawer shut and tugged open the one above it. Immediately, he recognized the writing symbol with the roof character appearing on the tabs. A couple files deep into the cabinet he found a manila envelope stuck out of a file, as if serving as a place marker. Instinctively, Alan reached for that folder and tugged it open. It contained a half-inch thick packet of pictures of Alan and Lynn, and it had the exact set of Chinese writing and numbers on it that were on the photograph he was holding.

Alan lifted out the envelope and flipped up the flap. He dug his fingers inside and tugged out three strips of negatives. He flipped on the flashlight again to study them. It took him a moment to imagine that the image's lights and darks would be opposites of those on the photograph, and then he recognized the sexual positions, which included several more than were hanging from the drying rack. The film developer must have printed extra sets of the dozen he liked best, the cream of the crop, so to speak. But as soon as Alan thought that, he knew not to repeat it to Vera that way. Some humor was helpful, too much was full of salt.

"Bingo!" he said quietly. "Here're the dreaded pictures and their negatives."

"Oh goodie," said Vera. "Can I see them?"

Alan dragged his daypack around next to him and inserted the whole file into it. He gazed up at Vera, smiled devilishly, and shook his head. "Then you'd know all my secrets."

"You mean there're still some I haven't seen? Did she dress up in a Little Bo Peep outfit, and you were one of her little lamb chops?"

Alan rolled his eyes. "There's not too many more secrets, but I want to hold on to the ones I've still got."

"You don't want to look at these together? Maybe later? I'll make popcorn for us," Vera teased, faux pleading.

Alan reached underneath her buttocks and squeezed her upper leg familiarly. "I just might take you up on that," he said, trying to keep a straight face.

Vera reached down and pulled Alan's hand away from her thigh. "Grab the empty folder too, Champ, so Mr. Chang doesn't discover that it's empty. We want him to forget about it or think he's just misplaced it somewhere, and then see if you can find Hungry Harry's file."

"I'm on it," he said.

Given the chronological order of the bottom file drawer, and that Hungry Harry was reportedly Lynn's first trick, Alan reached to the back of the drawer and pulled out the last green divider and all its contents. As he spread it out over the top of the other files in the drawer, Vera knelt next to him. He flicked on his flashlight and directed the filtered red beam toward the black and white glossies, which began in order with a timid, pubescent Lynn standing in her underwear in front of a seated Hungry Harry, his hair slicked back with pomade like a Latin lover. Alan dug at his eye a moment before dragging his hand downward, dry washing his face. He inhaled noisily and flipped the picture to the side so he could see the next in the stack. In this photograph, Lynn's clothes were removed and her side and bare back were exposed to the camera.

"Son of a bitch!" Alan growled through his teeth.

Vera closed her eyes a moment, shook her head, and rubbed Alan's shoulder. "Do you want me to take it from here?" she asked.

Alan sighed. "No, I've got it," he said as he flipped deeper into the three-quarter inch pile and stared at a picture that showed a naked Frantz, fully aroused, touching Lynn romantically. Alan slapped the photographs back together in disgust.

"I can't look anymore," he said, "or I'm going to toss my cookies all over the rest of these files."

Vera reached down and took the pile of 8 x 10 glossies from his hand. He didn't protest this time. She sorted through the stack rapidly, picked out several duplicate copies, and set them to the side. She scowled, inhaled deeply, and pinched her eyes shut. "These should provide all the evidence we need. Put the others back where you found them."

"Why not destroy the rest of these?" Alan asked.

"Because if we do, they'll know they're gone, that someone has been in their files, and then Chang and Nelson Wong will take steps to secure these better or move them some place we don't know about. We need to handle this in the least obtrusive way possible, in case we have to come back some day. In the meantime, they might be using these to blackmail Frantz, and I hope they squeeze every dime they can out of that bastard."

Alan nodded thoughtfully. "If they are blackmailing Harry, he knows they've got to have more pictures stashed in a safe place—which we just happened to find—and given that child molestation is a felony, he'll probably never call their bluff and demand to see more pictures as proof they still have them, because they could end up in the Prosecutor's Office."

"He's not likely to report the blackmailing to Mike Ketchum or anyone else either," said Vera.

"That's right," said Alan. "He's got too much pride and wouldn't want anyone to know what he's done. But whether these guys are blackmailing him or not, they're likely selling Lynn's photographs throughout the world, which means to me that they're continuing to exploit her, even if the pictures were taken years ago. I say we burn them."

Vera rested her hand on Alan's shoulder, as if she were restraining a boxer who was too eager to get back in the fight after having had his bell rung. "I've got another plan," she said. "It involves Mike Ketchum, but it might take a while for it to come together. Will you trust me on this?"

Alan rolled his tongue around his teeth as he thought. "You know I trust you."

"Alright then, we've got what we need. Put the rest back, and we'll sneak out as quiet as the cat that's napping in the front window."

Alan and Vera ordered cocktails before sitting next to each other in plush velvet chairs, waiting for Big Ben Kearney in the Ferry Kalakala's lounge. "Is there anything particular in Bremerton you wanted to see?" Alan asked.

"Nothing at all," said Vera. "I just have a fondness for this ferry in particular and thought the ride over and back would give us time to talk."

"This boat's really a beauty," said Alan, "but I've read where the ride is not as smooth as the old ferries, and it's tough to steer in tight quarters."

"I was only figuring on a few drinks and a little privacy, Champ. I didn't think you were going to have to climb up top, take the helm, and steer."

Alan grinned and scratched at his ear, catching the glint in Vera's eye. "I like to be prepared, just in case the helmsman keels over and they need someone to step in for him."

"You're always prepared, a regular Boy Scout."

"I was going to shoot for Eagle, but instead I went out and got a job, because I needed money of my own.

"I was never a Girl Scout, but I still keep one of their uniforms in my closet—but that was from another time. And women over forty shouldn't play those games anymore."

Alan sat back and rested his chin on his doubled-over knuckles. "You could still pull it off, you know?"

"That's sweet, darling, but my days of taking my clothes off for entertainment are over."

"Ahem," a voice cleared behind Vera. "I hate to interrupt the conversation flow, but I thought you might want to know I'm here."

"Ben!" said Vera, tilting her head as she turned to glance behind her. "I didn't think you were here yet."

"I was in the Men's room," Kearney said apologetically. "I suppose I should have made a little more noise walking up behind you. Despite my size I can still get around without making a ruckus—an occupational necessity I suppose."

Alan stood up and greeted Kearney with a handshake as the large man stepped between other chairs into the inner circle of furniture. Alan almost didn't recognize Kearney in his surprisingly well tailored civilian clothes, which included a herringbone top coat, wool slacks, well-shined shoes, and a fedora. The fit and quality suggested they were tailor made, not something picked off the rack in a department store.

Although gracious in his own right, Alan didn't offer Kearney the seat next to Vera, which he kept for himself. As he sat down, Kearney opened his coat for ease of movement, revealing a chalk-striped suit coat. When the drinks arrived Kearney was quick to pull out his wallet, "Let me get these," he said, dropping a ten spot on the waiter's tray, "and I'd like a scotch for myself. Single malt if you have it."

Alan dropped his wallet back in his pocket, sat back, and crossed his leg. Something about Kearney's manner suggested that his generosity and manners were genuine, not just a display to impress Vera and upstage him.

"In your phone call you mentioned you came across pictures you wanted me to look at," Kearney said.

"That's right," said Vera. "We won't trouble you with the details of how we got them, Ben, because that might create a bit of a conflict for you."

Kearney nodded. "Chief Ketchum asked me to come up to see him yesterday, and he told me I should leave well enough alone when working with you two. He's filled me in, and he quietly approves of your techniques. He said not to ask too many questions, and that's good enough for me."

"Well, I'm glad you're open-minded about this," said Vera.

"I'm open minded on a whole lot of things," said Kearney, "like politics, equal rights, and who can be friends with whom, but then there are other things I can't abide, which hasn't endeared me to my fellow workers. I've been told that I'd probably be better fit for in front of a college classroom than walking a beat, but I've found a lot of the real lessons in life happen right where it gets down and dirty. I'm also not worried what people might have done for their own entertainment—or for the entertainment of others, years ago."

"I'm not ashamed of my past, Ben, but I don't like to make a big deal about it either," said Vera. "So, when did you figure it out?"

"At the Black and Tan when the three of us were together," said Kearney. "You introduced Champ and me to Gypsy Rose. It was obvious you and her were very comfortable around each other, like colleagues would be, even though neither of you mentioned your past. It was like how I would be around another wrestler from back in the day. So I asked an old friend."

"Sully?" asked Vera.

Kearney grinned apologetically. "Yeah, you mentioned you knew him, so I figured he'd be a great person to start with."

Alan took two manila envelopes he had out of a leather brief case and leaned forward. He waited for a break in the conversation and thought this might be the place where he could bail Vera out. Alan glanced around quickly to make sure there wasn't anyone sitting close enough to see or hear what they were about to discuss. "We brought these for you to take a look at," said Alan, extending his arm so Kearney could take an envelope.

Kearney held his gaze on Vera a moment before acknowledging Alan's outstretched hand. Then as if apologizing for the delay, he smiled at Alan and took the envelope. He squeezed the metal tabs together and flipped up the unsealed lip.

"I probably don't need to caution you on this," said Vera, "but they're very graphic."

Kearney paused a moment, smiled appreciatively at Vera, and exhaled a sigh. "No sense putting off the unpleasant," he said.

Kearney shook the black and white glossies out of the folder into his hand, tucked the manila envelope behind it, and then glanced around the lounge just as Alan had already done. He flipped the pile over and started with the top photograph, staring stone faced at the image. "This is Knuckles McMurphy," Kearney said quietly. "From a few years back, I would say. He's a little heavier and grayer now."

Kearney took the picture off the top and slid it around to the back. "Wow, she's young," Kearney said. "Is she legal?"

"That's Mei," said Alan. "She's Lynn's older sister, and we're not sure about either of their ages."

Kearney sucked in air through his teeth and slid the photo underneath the pile, revealing the next one. "You have to be careful with these," he said. "If she was under age when these were taken, they're technically child porn, and you can't show them to anyone or keep any souvenirs for when the case is closed."

"We guessed that already," Vera said diplomatically.

"Right now, you're the only one we've shown them to," said Alan. "Chief Ketchum will be next and hopefully last."

Kearney flipped through the rest of the photographs quickly and handed the packet and envelope back to Alan, apparently glad to be rid of them.

"Here's another set," said Alan, not letting Kearney off easy. "These are worse."

Kearney took hold of the packet and glanced up at Alan, as if hoping he would change his mind and spare him from the discomfort. "Worse?" he asked.

"I'm afraid so," Alan said, glad that he didn't have to look at the pictures anymore.

Kearney slid the glossies into his hand while checking around the room again, apparently delaying the inevitable. He took a deep breath, exhaled, smiled at Vera and glanced down at the photographs. His brow instantly drew low into a scowl as he stared hard at the first picture. He growled gutturally and slid the photograph around to the back of the pile, and then quickly flipped through several others before settling on one that showed a very clear image of the face of the man in the photograph. Kearney roughly handed the pictures back to Alan, stood up for a moment, rubbed his hands through his hair, and sat back down.

"That's obviously Lieutenant Harry Frantz," said Kearney, "and he was committing a vile felony on that little girl, which should net the bastard twenty years in the state pen."

Vera reached out and touched Kearney's hand. "I'm sorry you had to see those, Ben, but we felt it was important."

The waiter brought Kearney's drink and the six dollars in change, all in singles. Kearney took his drink from the steward, and as the man reached for the change to leave it on the table between them, Kearney waved him off. "Keep that for yourself, and bring us another round please."

As the grateful waiter walked away, Kearney raised his glass and toasted his company. After savoring his drink a moment, he was ready to speak. "That wasn't the older one in the picture, was it?"

Alan shook his head. "That was Lynn. I figure she was shy of fourteen when the shot was taken."

"I'd say you're right. I'm not sure of the statute of limitations on Carnal Knowledge," said Kearney, "but I'm sure it runs several years. I'll have to look up the Revised Code of Washington. There is some kind of exception for rape if the man marries the woman, which was one way to escape prosecution in the Dark Ages, but that window of opportunity looks closed to Harry."

"You mean there's a possibility that Harry could escape prosecution?" asked Vera.

Kearney licked his lips as he thought, and then he shook his head. "I'm not positive on that. Since he's a government official the statute runs longer for him than the average Joe—as it does for me, for that matter—it's a ten year minimum, more if he took steps to cover it up."

"That leaves us with a little less than a year to work with," said Alan.

"Since we know where we can find the victim, I think the prosecutor would be inclined to work this up in short order," said Kearney. "The only problem is that we would have to protect the victim during the trial."

"From Harry?" Vera asked.

Kearney nodded slowly. "Yes, him and his friends, which could include Goon Dip or Nelson Wong."

"By the way, Nelson's her brother," said Alan.

Kearney tilted his head to the side as he stared open mouth at Alan. "Seriously?"

"That means Mei is also his sister," said Alan. "I heard

Nelson mention it to one of his cronies inside Goon Dip's."

Kearney's eyes hooded over as he exhaled in disgust. "Well, that's keeping it all in the family isn't it," he said.

"Lynn told me that she wasn't supposed to go into the business, but Hungry Harry chose her while she was part of the wait-staff. He apparently paid Goon Dip's asking price for the privilege of being her first."

Kearney set down his drink and rubbed his face with both hands. "So, you have pictures of Knuckles and Harry with these two young girls; do you think that's what's behind this case?" he asked. "Is the motive for Hack Sawyer's murder blackmail, and it's somewhere in these pictures?"

"It might be," said Vera, "because we found several drawers full of photos like these, filed chronologically, under each girl's name. We're also sure that they use these to extort special considerations from the police and elected officials."

"How far back do they go?" Kearney asked.

"As far as we can tell, they seemed to have started keeping files about the time this first picture of Lynn was taken," said Vera.

Kearney weighed this for a moment. "I wonder if that had something to do with the advancement of camera technology around 1930. That's when they started using thirty-five millimeter film in Leica cameras."

"The camera Nelson Wong had with him was a Leica," said Alan.

Kearney gave Alan a reassuring nod of approval. "It might be as simple as that, but there could be more to this."

"How so?" asked Vera.

"Back in the '20s, a police lieutenant was the mastermind behind much of the booze smuggled into Seattle through Elliott Bay. His name was Roy Olmstead. He'd figured out a way to ship Canadian booze from Victoria thirty percent cheaper than his rivals, at the rate of two hundred cases per day. He became one of the region's biggest employers of shippers, drivers, warehousemen, runners, and such. Those who couldn't compete with him turned to hijacking his and others' liquor shipments.

"Olmstead and his wife ran a radio show that sent coded messages to his fleet, mixed between her reading children's stories on the air. He didn't want anyone to get killed over liquor, so none of his men carried guns. The cops knew it, so did his rivals. He said he'd rather give up a shipment of booze than lose one life over liquor.

"Roy was finally turned in by one of his partners in a power move. The guy was playing both sides. He was a paid informant and heir apparent, until he got himself arrested. After the Olmsteads were caught and charged, along with eighty-eight co-conspirators, there was a scramble to fill the void they all left. Working the Dry Squad, Hack Sawyer had the inside track and the connections, and he made plenty of hey during the day. He also made bitter enemies of those who didn't have the same hook ups he did. From what I heard, Hack had the Goon Dip Wong concession, which all by itself would have set him up to live the high life."

"Excuse the interruption," said Vera, "but what did Hacksaw do with all of his money? Mike Ketchum estimated it was maybe a quarter million dollars, but I'm thinking it was many times that. Why hasn't it turned up?"

"I suppose it depends on if it's been found and who found it. Let's say somebody like Goon Dip came up with it. Then it's probably been absorbed into his stash, wherever that is."

Vera nodded thoughtfully. "I see," she said, "but you were telling us about Hacksaw and how the booze moved through Seattle."

"Yes," said Kearney. "Hack had rivals. He and Harry

Frantz fought it out for years, and then Frantz made sergeant. A clever man with the right connections, who's willing to pay the price, can get access to the sergeant's exam and the keyed answer sheet. Frantz is smart enough, and he's also clever. So he got promoted and Hacksaw didn't. He tried to pull rank and bump Sawyer from the Dry Squad, but as a new sergeant he didn't have enough clout at the time. But Frantz is a very determined fella, and he went through the steps and made lieutenant within two years. As a rising star, he now had clout. So he called in favors and got Sawyer kicked out of the Dry Squad. The department promptly sent Hack to the South Precinct, the department's equivalent of Siberia. There was a lot less graft in the south end of town. But…Sawyer had enough clout of his own, which means hard cash, to get himself transferred up to Twelfth and Jackson, where there was still plenty of money to be made. At any rate, Frantz took over Goon Dip's liquor concessions and had it up to the Repeal, which really wasn't that long afterward, but I don't know if he took over before or after Hacksaw's demise."

"When did Frantz make lieutenant?" Vera asked.

"About nine years ago," said Kearney.

"That's about when these photographs were taken," Alan said.

"Could Harry have been celebrating a special occasion?" asked Vera. "Could he have pulled out all the stops and celebrated it by catering to a secret fantasy, which in this case meant Lynn?"

"How lucky for her," Alan said dryly.

"There's always that possibility," said Kearney, "but I'd like to know more about the photographs you showed me. They all were taken from the same angle."

Vera leaned forward and patted Kearney's forearm. "As fast as you went through them, you still had time to notice that?" Vera asked.

"Well…yes, I can also read very fast," Kearney said, inclining his head toward Vera. "But I'm wondering where the camera would have been hidden in the room, because after all, these are smart people. They wouldn't have allowed photographs to be taken of them that might come back and haunt them some day."

"In the wall," said Alan. "Goon Dip has mosaic sculptures in the shape of animals attached to the walls. I think the camera lens fits into the creatures' eyes."

"Oh…so someone would be behind the walls in the smuggler's passage, working the camera," said Kearney.

"That's what we're thinking," said Vera.

"Would there be anything else behind the walls that would help us out?" Kearney asked

Alan grinned devilishly, glancing at Vera, who responded with a nod.

"I think we'll have to take a look and see," she said.

"You two seem to enjoy your work," Kearney said. "But I don't imagine there's much room for error in what you do, which makes me worry. When these people play marbles, they play for keeps. Is there anything I can do to help out?"

"I might have just the thing for you," said Vera, "but first I'd like to know more about Knuckles. Where could we locate him, and would anybody on the department get upset if we rattled his cage pretty hard?"

Kearney grinned broadly. "I know he's still in town, so I'll see what I can do to drum up his address," he said. "But if you don't mind my saying, he's what we in the wrestling business called a cheap shot artist, meaning he doesn't understand the concept of playing fair. He'd likely kick, bite, gouge, and hit you below the belt to get the upper hand, even when it's not necessary."

"We have skills that would surprise you," said Alan.

"I have no doubt," said Kearney. "I'm sure that's why Chief Ketchum picked you for this job, but perhaps I might be able to assist you during my off time. I made my living for years twisting guys like Knuckles into pretzels."

"Ooh, that's a tempting offer, Ben," said Vera, "but wouldn't Knuckles recognize you? And when he recovered, he'd file charges or come after you himself some night."

"Did I mention that I wrestled under several stage names?" asked Kearney. "For a couple of years I wore a mask."

"Hurricane Alley was a bad guy?" asked Alan.

Kearney nodded with a grin. "Yes indeed, and I was also the Teutonic Thunder: The Pride of Germany," said Kearney, "even though I'm not German, but somebody had to wear the black trunks to make the pretty boy in white look good."

"But Ben, you're good looking too," said Vera, patting his forearm. "In fact you're very handsome."

"That's why they made me wear a mask," Kearney said, slapping his knee with a laugh. The marquee wrestlers didn't want me stealing their show."

$\diamond$

At 11:00 PM, Officer Ben Kearney rang in at the call box at Seventh Avenue South and King Street. A moment later, he stepped aside and let John Sullivan do the same. As soon as they'd finished, Kearney removed the call box key and clipped it to his belt underneath his tunic.

Big Ben grinned devilishly. "You ready for some fun, Sully?"

"Sure thing. Let's do this."

The two men drew their billy clubs from rings attached to their belts and crossed King Street, an arm's length between their broad shoulders. Kearney was content to hold his gleaming stick by its well turned handle, ignoring the long leather lanyard attached two-thirds of the way up. Sullivan, on the other hand, twirled his baton expertly, making it dance in front of him like a puppet, before he spun it around backwards and then deftly back and forth across his body, like it was a buzz saw ready to chop lumber or anything else in its way. Sully knew how to project an image, send a message: these beat cops were not to be messed with.

Kearney and Sullivan marched directly up to the two bouncers in front of Goon Dip's main entrance. Sullivan cocked his head back and glared down his nose, across his silver handlebar mustache. "We've met before, haven't we?" he asked.

"Yes sir," said the doorman. "I'm Eddie."

"That's right, I remember now," Sullivan said. "So tell me, who'd be in charge tonight, Eddie."

"Nelson Wong," said the bouncer, concern reflected on his brow.

"Nelson is?" Sullivan repeated, as if in doubt. "What about old Goon Dip? I haven't seen him in ages."

"Goon Dip is unavailable," said Eddie, bowing his head ever so slightly.

"Do me a favor, lad," said Sullivan. "Have Nelson Wong meet Officer Kearney and myself in the lobby. We have business of an important nature to discuss with him, and don't keep us waiting."

"Yes sir," said Eddie, his brow pinched tighter and his bow more pronounced than before.

As soon as Eddie dashed up the steps to Goon Dip's, Kearney turned to the remaining doorman. "You're Jimmy, aren't you?"

"Yes sir," the man nodded.

"Do us a favor Jimmy," Kearney said. "The police patty wagon will be showing up any minute with a couple of police officers driving it. Ask them to wait right here for our prisoners, would you please? We'll be back out in a couple of minutes."

Jimmy stood frozen, his mouth sagged slack jawed, and his eyes flared wide.

Kearney nodded at Sullivan, whose blue eyes sparkled with mischief. Without saying a word the two big men shouldered their way past the lone doorman and entered Goon Dip's, stopping in the lobby area near the stairs, drawing occasional stares from the White patrons. The

214

beat cops took familiar positions facing each other, like they would on street corners, each one looking over his partner's shoulder, watching his back. Kearney rocked on his heels while holding his baton casually by both ends in front of his lower torso. Sullivan, on the other hand, dangled his billy club from its leather thong, performing a well-practiced dance routine with it, a less threatening display than the wicked airplane spins he had put it through moments before.

"You ever break a window by mistake with your stick?" asked Kearney.

Sullivan shook his head.

"About the time I thought I was pretty good at that," Kearney said with a tilt of his head acknowledging Sullivan's routine, "the thong broke and my stick crashed through the front window at Ace's Pawn Shop. Worst part was that when Knuckles stopped by, he wanted to help himself to a fancy camera in the front window before the owner arrived to secure the place. Knuckles didn't like it when I threatened to arrest him."

"Knowing what you know now, you probably wished you'd waited until he got it to his car so you could've pinched him," said Sullivan.

"A couple of coppers might still be alive if I had, but then he'd've claimed he wasn't stealing it, he was going to put it in the Property Room to protect it from the criminal element."

Kearney inclined his head the other way, tilting it toward the interior stairway, and Sullivan followed his line of sight to see Nelson Wong and two bouncers hurrying down the steps. Nelson was in the lead of the small posse as they approached the last of the steps, where they slowed to a normal pace and assumed an air of casualness and control. Nelson walked directly to the officers, stopping near them, his men waiting a few paces back. Kearney and Sullivan held their ground, keeping Nelson at a slight angle to them, rather than facing him directly, allowing for continued surveillance over each other's shoulders.

"Nelson Wong, it is my duty to inform you that we are here with arrest warrants for two of your employees," said Kearney. "Issued by Judge Wilma Goodloe. We are to find the young women named herein and present them to her forthwith."

"But it is 11:00 o'clock at night," said Nelson. "Can't this wait till tomorrow morning when we can have our attorneys surrender them?"

"No," said Sullivan harshly. "This is a Habeas Grabus, and we don't have a choice."

Kearney nodded ever so slightly to Sullivan and then gazed down at Nelson. "Judge Goodloe is waiting in her chambers as we speak, and her orders to us are specific, 'Fail not at your peril,' it says. In legal speak that means: 'don't bother coming back if you don't have the two young women with you.'"

"Which two?" asked Nelson through gritted teeth. "May I see the warrants?"

"That depends on the young women," said Kearney. "The warrants are not for you, so technically we shouldn't be telling you what is officially other people's personal business, but given your friendly relationship with the department, we thought to inform you as a matter of courtesy. It's for the two women described and named herein to disclose the nature of the warrants. As soon as we've located them, we'll officially present them with the warrants, and if *they* choose, they can advise you, their business manager, of what it says—but that's strictly up to them."

"And the judge who signed these is a woman?" asked Nelson, making more of a statement than posing a question.

"Yes," said Kearney. "I imagine she's one of the few

who's not on Goon Dip's payroll."

"You'd be surprised," said Nelson. "Money from Chinatown flows into almost every elected official's coffers."

"Well then, that explains a lot," said Sullivan. "She was appointed, not elected. She's not due to run for office for at least two years. So I imagine you'll take her off your Christmas list for the next year or two."

Kearney and Sullivan started for the stairs, brushing by Nelson and the two bouncers. Nelson moved quickly, climbed a few steps ahead and stopped in front of them, midway up the stairs. "But I protest," he said. "You can't just come waltzing in here to arrest some of my employees. You are not welcome here, and I want you to leave now."

"Mr. Nelson," said Officer Kearney. "Let me remind you that according to your license on the wall, this is a business that is licensed and permitted by the City of Seattle—a sporting house, I believe they call it. If my partner and I leave now, as agents of the City we will be forced to peel your license off the wall, take it with us when we go, padlock your doors shut, and close you down for non-compliance until the judge tells us to give your license back. That could take all of your attorneys and all of your hip-pocket judges weeks to unravel, entirely disrupting your revenue stream, especially since the Honorable Wilma Goodloe has personally signed the warrants herself. Your people will want to be careful taking her on. She could slap an injunction on you and close these doors permanently. Have I made myself clear?"

Kearney glanced up at a specter in gold silk that suddenly loomed behind Nelson Wong at the top of the stairs, accompanied by several followers. Waiting near the top step was a corpulent Chinese man with flushed cheeks that made his droopy silver mustache and thin goatee more striking. At five-foot-eight inches in height, he was as nearly wide as he was tall. His gold cassock had a high collar with red trim, worn over a white shirt. A black, puffy, pill box hat sat perched on top of his head, matching his black silk shoes that stuck out from under his robe, which had a red sash at the middle. Above and below the sash were fanciful dragon figures done in silver.

Nelson Wong followed Kearney's glance up the stairs. Then his shoulders sagged, and he quickly shut his eyes, turned around, and gazed downcast at the floor below him, as if he'd suffered a measure of defeat or embarrassment. Kearney quickly brushed past Nelson and was followed by Sullivan up the steps. The man in the gold robes moved graciously to the side, giving the beat men room to stand comfortably.

"I am Goon Dip Wong," said the man with a nod that might have passed for a slight bow.

Kearney formally introduced himself and Officer Sullivan, with each offering a slight head nod toward Goon Dip at the mention of their names, but at the same time not offering their hands to shake, a western tradition that wasn't always understood or appreciated by others.

"What is so important that brings on-duty policemen through the front door and not the service entrance?" asked Goon Dip. "You are alarming my guests."

"I apologize for that, Mr. Wong," said Kearney in a loud voice, "but this is official business. We are not here for a free meal, a drink, a handout, or money. We're here to collect two young women whom we have warrants for—so that we can produce them in front of Judge Goodloe."

"Call me Goon Dip, please."

A young Chinese man stood behind Goon Dip. He was also clad in the traditional eastern attire of upper class royalty, an ornate gold silk tunic with more red and black than the older man's. He stepped from behind Goon Dip

218

and approached the officers.

"Provide me their names," said the younger man, "and tell me what the warrants are for. I will fetch the women for you."

"It doesn't work that way," interjected Officer Sullivan. "The warrants are for the young ladies, not for you. Technically we shouldn't be telling you what is the ladies' business—that is unless we can't find them. Once we locate them, however, which I expect we will, then they are free to tell you the nature of their warrants—because they might need help making bail, that kind of thing."

"But that is ridiculous," said Goon Dip. "As soon as you arrest the young ladies, we will all see and know who they are. So what is the point of your approach?"

"What you say makes logical sense to us," said Kearney, "but we're just simple policemen who follow the laws, rules of the court, and department regulations, not necessarily in that order. As policemen we have to set aside common sense and follow orders, because we have to assume those giving them have their reasons, which they don't have to explain to us. As in this case, the judge and our superiors might want to protect these young ladies from the government needlessly soiling their reputations. We have to work under the premise that the ladies may not wish you to know what they are being arrested for."

"But this really implies that you don't trust us," said Goon Dip, laying his spread-out hand flat against his chest. "This shames me in front of my family, employees, and guests."

"Please don't take it personally," said Kearney. "I have heard nothing but the best about Goon Dip's establishment. Your gambling tables are reputed to be the most fair in all of Seattle, not just Chinatown, your drinks are generous, your ladies safe to be with, and those who have been unlucky at your tables say you have provided them transportation to their residences. There is no finer sporting house. The business we are on is simply a matter of police and judicial protocol, nothing more than that."

Goon Dip sighed, nodded, and leaned to the side. The young man standing next to him bent lower to hear the whispers. Then Goon Dip stepped away as the young man moved forward to take his place.

"I am Jai Wong, the son of Goon Dip," the man said in a hushed voice. "We pay our tributes on a regular basis and have never had trouble with the Seattle Police Department. The sheriff deputies, on the other hand, have paid us visits on their own accord, as the mood strikes them, or so the police tell us. The deputies make a loud ruckus until we can take no more, and then we pay them to go away. It happens a couple times a year. Is that what this is really about? Are you here for money?"

Kearney painfully forced a smile and glanced over at Sullivan, who stood stone faced, his blue eyes burning a hole through Jai Wong. "I know you didn't mean that as an insult, Mr. Wong," said Kearney, "and surely this is not an attempt to bribe us—but that's not why we're here. Our sole mission tonight is to find the two women described here-in on the arrest warrants that I'm carrying in my coat pocket, and to present said ladies to Judge Goodloe this evening. The honorable judge is waiting our return in her chambers as we speak. It will be up to the judge to determine if the ladies will be held in jail, allowed to post bail, or outright released. The longer we spend here talking about it, the longer it's going to take to resolve this matter, which means the ladies might end up being held overnight, when that wasn't necessary at all."

At 11:05 PM, Alan climbed the steps from the

underground sidewalk and led Vera through the green door. They quickly climbed the interior staircase, pausing at each of the landings for a moment or two to determine if there was other foot traffic coming their way. When they reached the fourth floor, Alan stopped next to the door under the last flight of stairs, and stood guard for Vera while she examined the locking mechanism to the door. She pulled the small satchel of lock picks from her coat pocket and then hesitated a moment. She gave the doorknob a twist, and it turned freely, opening inward. Vera smiled at Alan and dropped the lock picks back into her pocket.

"Somebody left in a hurry," she whispered.

Vera pushed the door open slowly, glanced quickly around, and stepped inside. Alan followed, shutting the door behind them.

"Lock it," Vera whispered. "If anyone returns, I want to hear them coming."

In the dim glow cast by red light bulbs, Alan and Vera surveyed the narrow passageway before them. It was long, full of dark spots, and cluttered with furniture and broken chairs that were being cannibalized for parts. The lath and plaster on the left side was covered with old movie posters salvaged from a Chinese theater. Few of the American titles were familiar, and they had been covered with Chinese characters supplanting the English. The White actors on these posters had eyes with a slight almond shape to them, as if the artist drawing them was unfamiliar with people of European descent. There were fewer movie posters on the right side of the passage, covering the raw bricks' coarse, uneven mortar joints. Twenty feet down the passageway, past a heavy beamed archway, was a wooden box in the middle of the bare floor.

"Do you smell cigarette smoke?" asked Vera, her voice just above a whisper.

Alan sniffed the air and nodded.

Vera continued on and stopped just past the box on the floor, indicating a rough-edged cut out in the plaster, with a tilt of her head.

Alan didn't need the added height the sturdy box would give him as a stepping stool. From his six-foot-two perspective, he could see through a blurry lens into what he believed was the room with the Tiger mosaic on the wall.

"This is useless," said Alan. "I can't make out much of anything in there. It's like looking through the bottom of a *Coca Cola* bottle."

Vera picked up a small black container with a flip top lid and opened it up. From the satin lined container she slid out what appeared to be a miniature spyglass, constructed of brass, ivory, and ground glass—except the piece where the front lens should have been was empty. Vera held it up to examine it, and Alan grinned with recognition.

"I think I see how it works," he said.

Vera handed Alan the spyglass, and he set it tight against the Tiger's eye.

"I bet that's it," she said.

Alan leaned forward and rested a hand on the wall as he put his eye up against the adjustable piece on the small end of the miniature telescope.

"Jackpot!" said Alan. "I can see clear as a bell into the room...and beyond, when I adjust the focus. The room is empty, but I can see the girls moving around out in the area by the stairs. Something's going on inside there."

"That would be Big Ben and Sully," said Vera. "Right on cue."

"The only thing," said Alan, "is that I don't understand how a camera lens would hook up to this. I'm not a camera expert, but it seems the camera would see the same blurry picture we do, unless—"

"There's some kind of adaptor."

"You know about this stuff?" asked Alan.

"I'm no Ansel Adams, but I've done camera work for Naval Intelligence. In fact my last black bag job with Gunny involved photography."

As Alan stepped back, he bumped a roll of toilet paper loose from the small cutout, and instead of landing on the floor, it fell into an open waste basket. Alan was about to bend over to retrieve it, when Vera touched his shoulder.

"Just leave it where it fell, Champ. Whoever's using that roll will have to find himself another. Those spent tissues are tossed for a reason, and they weren't used for a head cold. You don't want to get some guy's spunk on you."

Alan stared at the basket a moment. "Voyeur tissues," he said.

"Well, they're certainly getting a show back here, so I guess that's to be expected."

Alan scowled, shook his head, and followed Vera to the next opening. "I sure hope they didn't get excited watching my performance in there."

Vera spun around, a big grin on her face. "Would you feel better if you knew it was Lynn they liked watching?"

"Yeah, somehow it would...well, actually, no it wouldn't. I can't imagine Lynn's thrilled with the idea she's being watched all the time. The point is that neither of us had any say in this. It's sneaky, and it's wrong."

"But would you have cared as much," asked Vera, "if it only involved her or a customer you didn't know?"

"I don't know if I can answer that honestly. I'd like to say yes, but I seriously doubt it."

At the next opening a Leica .35 mm camera sat on the small platform below the thick lens that served as the eye for the Dragon on the wall. Vera picked up the camera, examined the brass sleeve that fit over the front lens and handed it to Alan.

"This is very primitive," said Vera. "I've never seen anything like this before, but I'm guessing it's a multiplier of sorts that fits snuggly against the lens in the wall, which might be a 135 mm."

"The Chinese are so amazingly clever," said Alan.

"But it's a German camera…"

"I know, but look what the Chinese did with it."

Next to where the camera had been was a case for a miniature spyglass, several extra containers of film, and another roll of toilet paper.

"Another spyglass?" asked Alan.

"Of course," said Vera. "Because the camera's rangefinder can't focus through the lens that's built into the wall. They need the spyglass to see what's going on before they hook up the camera. It's probably been all trial and error by the photographer, and whoever takes the pictures just needs to know when the actions hot, so he can start shooting. He's probably already established what distance to set the camera for and what shutter speed to use. They've had years to work out the details for this."

Alan put the camera back where they'd found it, took the spyglass from its container, and pressed it against the lens in the mosaic.

"There's a guy behind the door inside the Dragon room," Alan said. "He's getting dressed in a hurry."

"Is he anybody you recognize?"

"No one I know, but he obviously doesn't want Sully or Big Ben to know he's hiding back there. Do you want to take a look?"

Alan leaned back as Vera leaned in, crowding up against him.

"Remember that City Councilman you helped Mr. B get elected?" asked Vera.

Alan let out a gush of air as he rolled his eyes. "That's Jack Hardin?"

"Yes indeed. So, after you and Alice cast all those votes for him, you never knew what he looked like?"

"Not in his underwear like this. There was a lot going on that day, and much of it included champagne—but how did you hear about it? It was supposed to be our little secret with Mr. B."

"It still is, in a manner of speaking," Vera said as she adjusted the lens focus. "But I'm George's personal secretary and the one who keeps him supplied with envelopes stuffed with cash for business expenses. I need to know what he uses them for."

Alan shook his head, ashamed of the memory of the drunken voter fraud, a co-optive scheme that drew him into working for the union and Mr. Brinkman, because now more than ever, he was sure that Mr. Brinkman had played him, orchestrated the whole affair. And then to top it off, Brinkman hadn't kept it private like he'd promised.

"Well, let's just hope Jack is Lynn's last customer," Vera said, "and that she never has to do this again."

Deep in the shadows, behind them and to their right, a throat cleared as if its voice hadn't been used in decades. "Are you enjoying the sights?" asked the phantom.

Alan quickly slid sideways between Vera and the specter, instinctively taking the protective position, while at the same time defusing a pre-emptive attack by her against the shape Alan hoped he recognized.

"Shifu?" Alan asked. "Is that you?"

"Ah, so it's the young chauffeur," said Shifu, "and you've brought a friend with you this time."

Although he and Vera were deep inside enemy territory, Alan went with his instincts and tried to make the most of the situation. He slid his hand into his pocket and came up with a small handful of dollar bills. He counted out four in the dim light.

"Here're two for me and two more for my friend," he said. "I wouldn't want to cheat you, Shifu."

The phantom stepped further into the light, nodded, and extended his hand slowly from a loose silk sleeve, as if he was lost in thought. "Ah, let us please never forget the price of admission," he said, smiling as he took the money casually from Alan's outstretched hand.

Alan placed the flat of his hand reassuringly against Vera's side and followed with a formal introduction to Shifu, speaking in a hushed tone, as if they were in church waiting for the reverend to start services at any moment.

"The residence floor above us is in an uproar," said Shifu. "The casino has required Goon Dip's immediate presence. And apparently the disturbance is working its way up to this floor. Is that what brings you two here?"

"Yes," said Alan. "We're responsible for the disturbance inside the casino, because we wanted to find out more about what happens in your smuggler's passage."

"I see," said Shifu. "I suspected when we met that you were more than a rich man's chauffeur, but I still don't pick you as a policeman—because so many in their ranks are on the House payroll. It's been that way since the last century. Why would they turn against us all of a sudden and risk losing their weekly tithing? And what needs would they have that Goon Dip could not satisfy?"

"We are private detectives," said Alan. "A policeman was killed not far from here nine years ago, and we think his death has something to do with photographs that were taken back here."

"A policeman was killed?" asked Shifu. "Why aren't the police investigating it?"

"His name was Charles Sawyer, and the department

wants to leave him buried in the past. They used to call him Hacksaw Sawyer. He was part of the Dry Squad during Prohibition, and we understand he made booze deliveries here."

"Yes, he was known to us," said Shifu, "very well, in fact. He ran the business for those who were sent to prison. That was back before the man we have now."

"Is the man you have now Lieutenant Harry Frantz?" asked Vera.

"Yes," said Shifu. "Sawyer was here before all the nastiness. Even though many police went to prison, everything seemed to be going well with Mr. Hacksaw, but then it was he who brought the camera to us, which was the beginning of the nastiness."

"Hack Sawyer brought the camera here?" asked Alan.

"Yes," said Shifu bitterly. "The camera you have there. He demonstrated for Goon Dip how simple it would be to make it work, give Sawyer what he needed to control the trade. He didn't care what we did with the camera after he got photographs of his rival."

"Then he wasn't trying to set up blackmail as a side business?" asked Alan.

"No, just set up the one man: Frantz. It was Nelson who kept the blackmail going, extorting men who are in positions where we need political leverage, and now he continues to do it to build a nest egg—so he can strike out on his own."

"Nelson is planning to leave?" Alan asked, hoping to learn more that might be of help later.

"Nelson is not cautious with his secrets," said Shifu. "Watching carefully from the walls has taught me plenty about him and others."

"When did Sawyer start the photographs?" asked Vera.

"Because of the liquor, Hacksaw Sawyer used the smuggler's passage for deliveries," Shifu said. "And one day he came here with a plan for Goon Dip. He said he needed help catching a man who liked young girls coming of age. He promised that if he was successful he would help the House of Wong, which would help China—but his help has been a lasting curse and has done nothing but divide us. It is nasty business not fit to discuss."

"Not fit to discuss because I'm a woman?" Vera asked. "If that's your concern, please don't worry about it. I've seen the pictures with the young girl and can handle it."

"My poor girls," said Shifu mournfully. "Maybe you 'can handle it,' as you say, but I can't. I have much difficulty with it, because it is not right."

"Of course," said Vera. "How thoughtless to think in terms of myself. So it is Mei and Lynn we're talking about? Are they your daughters?"

"They are my cousin's off-spring, his daughters, but my responsibility. I feel shame that I had no way to protect them from the nastiness. The dollars speak louder than my protests."

Shifu paused a moment, as if weighing whether or not to continue. "You mentioned photographs," he said. "What is it you want to know about them?"

"I think you've pretty well covered it," said Vera, "but can you tell us if the ones involving Harry Frantz were used against him?'

"Yes, of course they were," said Shifu. "When Frantz became a sergeant he came to see Goon Dip. He was angry about the photographs that Sawyer used to keep him out of Chinatown. He wanted to know who took them and from where. He was incensed we would permit such a thing to happen, and he vowed that he wouldn't take this 'lying down,' as you say. Two years later he was promoted to lieutenant, and Detective Sawyer was transferred from the Dry Squad to a beat somewhere. Maybe six months later, no more than that, and Sawyer was found shot to death. That's all I know about it."

"What about Knuckles McMurphy?" asked Alan. "Is he a regular visitor to this floor?"

"Sergeant McMurphy has been known to frequent this floor, but mostly he used to go to the third floor. He was one of the crew for Harry Frantz, and each time he made a delivery Nelson gave him a five-dollar token. The House discourages police from coming to the fourth floor, but McMurphy traded or collected tokens from the other runners, and when he'd gotten enough he came up to the fourth floor to cash them in."

"Does he *know* Lynn and Mei?" asked Vera.

"You are nice to put it that way," said Shifu. "Yes, he *knows* Mei. He occasionally comes to see her, after she came to work this floor."

"What about Lynn?" asked Alan.

"I don't think so, but I'm not here all of the time—and I do not have the stomach to watch what goes on inside these rooms."

"We hate to ask these questions of you, but we don't have anyone else we can approach," said Vera.

"I understand."

Alan leaned back and gazed past Shifu into the shadows. "What's around the corner back there?" he asked.

"A passage that leads through the mop closet," Shifu said. "Why do you ask? You know the way through the front door."

"I'm the curious type," said Alan. "These passages fascinate me, with their secret entrances and all."

"On this side it's not so fancy," said Shifu. "Around the corner at the end of the hall, you will see a fist sized grip on the wall. You turn it and pull towards you, and then a door with mops and brooms screwed onto it will swing your way. Of course you'll find yourself inside the mop closet at that point. Be careful to step over the deep sink, which is built into the floor."

"Were you already here, when we came in?" Alan asked. "Back in the shadows?"

"I came down from upstairs, after making sure the floor was safe. There is a stairway around the corner, but you are not to go up the stairs."

"I can't imagine a need for doing that," said Vera.

Alan nodded in agreement and took another peek through the lens into the bordello. Without turning around, he asked, "Do both girls go on outcalls?"

"Yes, of course, if the price is agreed upon and an escort is available."

"How about nine years ago?" asked Alan, setting the miniature telescope down. "Would Lynn have gone out back then?"

Shifu nodded. "Not so much then, but yes she did."

"Was Nelson Wong her escort?" asked Vera.

"So many questions you two have," said Shifu. "Do you think Nelson is involved in the policeman's murder?"

"According to our contacts, Hack Sawyer had enemies all over the city, all across Chinatown, and on all levels of the police department," said Vera. "We're just trying to eliminate those we can."

"And Nelson Wong hasn't been eliminated yet, has he?" asked Shifu.

"No he hasn't," said Vera.

"Nor has Mei or Lynn?"

"I'm afraid not," said Vera.

"**L**adies, we need your cooperation for a few moments," said Officer Sullivan. "Please gather around and take a seat on the settee. Sit on each other's laps if you must. We apologize for the inconvenience, but we shouldn't be long. And let me assure you we are not here to enforce the City's ordinances prohibiting prostitution, so there's no need to get your lovely knickers in a twist."

"Is all this necessary?" asked Jai Wong. "If you have warrants, take the women you need and hurry on. There's no need to waste time."

"How thoughtful of you to be concerned about our valuable time, Mr. Wong," said Officer Sullivan, "but we have to make sure we have the right ladies. You wouldn't want us to make a mistake and cart the wrong girls away, would you? We'd not only ruin their night, but then we'd have to come back and ruin someone else's."

Officer Kearney pulled out a small notebook from inside his coat pocket. "Now ladies, I need for you to give me your names and dates of birth, please. We'll start with the lovely blonde lady on the left and work our way across. State your name and birth date please."

"And no shenanigans, girls," added Sullivan. "There will

be heck to pay if we get back to headquarters and find you've been less than truthful."

The blonde gazed toward Jai Wong, as if seeking his permission to speak. He in turn scowled and looked toward his father, who nodded his approval.

Kearney indicated with a roll of his large head for the blonde to get off the settee, walk over, and talk to him privately.

"I'm Barbara Ruth Dixon," said the busty young woman in a hushed tone, "but I go by Ruth…"

And on it went, Kearney interviewing Lena and then Laurie while Sullivan stood by, watching his back while occasionally putting his billy club through a dancing exhibition, twirling, spinning, fanning back and forth. Off to Sullivan's side, a gentleman in a suit with an overcoat draped over his arm, slid quietly out of a room, hoping to go unnoticed.

"How's your evening, Councilman?" Sullivan asked without so much as a side glance to the man.

"Very well, officers," said Jack Hardin. "Keep up the good work. There are things going on here that need your attention."

"Thank you, sir. We appreciate your vigilance. We'll make a note of it, and advise the Chief, should he ask," said Sullivan with a wink towards Kearney.

Officer Kearney arched his back and rolled his large head on his neck. "My back's got an ache in it, and I need to sit a few moments. You three," he said with a nod to Ruth, Lena, and Laurie, "are free to move about while we sort this out, but don't wander off too far."

The young women uncrossed their silk covered legs with a flurry of scissors kicks as they quickly stood up. Eager to put distance between themselves and the law, the young women moved to the far corner of the room, with

Jai Wong following them part way, before turning back to be closer to Mei and Lynn. As soon as the women moved away, Kearney sat down, and patted the spot next to him, indicating that it was Mei's turn to sit next to him.

Kearney repeated the same pattern of questions to Mei, and then he rocked forward, pulled out a tri-fold sheath of papers, and lowered his voice as he showed them to her. "The material witness warrant is real, but I can have it quashed in a heartbeat. You won't have to stay in jail. Now, if you want out of this place forever and want to leave the business in your past, you don't have to say anything—just nod your head. We have a safe haven where we can put you that you'll like. I promise."

Mei pushed down on her dark nylon covered knees, rolled her shoulders forward, and then sat tall on the settee. She exhaled, closed her eyes, and nodded slowly. "But what about Lynn?"

"I'll make the same offer to your sister. If she agrees, we'll escort you both to your rooms so you can find the appropriate attire for court, but I suggest you take whatever you don't want to leave behind or never see again."

Mei nodded silently, as if she was contemplating a chess board and trying to determine if her opponent had either made a costly error or was sacrificing a valuable piece to gain an advantage. "It's not *rooms*, it is *room*. We share a room."

Kearney sat up straight, grimacing as if his back was still bothering him, and he glanced at Sullivan, giving him a thin smile. He raised his voice so others could hear. "Please wait next to Officer Sullivan, Mei Wong. We'll be with you in a moment."

Kearney turned his attention to Lynn, who stared at him wide-eyed. He indicated the spot next to him with a tilt of his head and a benign smile. She approached him

233

carefully, as if she was a puppy leery of being punished for chewing a slipper. Kearney showed her a separate packet of tri-folded papers, pointing out her name, and verifying the information she provided. He had her spell her name out loud, which wasn't really necessary, but he wanted a clue to her level of formal education.

"What nicknames do you go by?" Kearney asked. "What do people call you besides Lynn?"

"I prefer Lynn, but I've been called Lien Hua and just plain Hua—Lord knows why—because that's my middle name, same as Mei's."

"Hua? Of course," said Kearney, "but Mei just told me she didn't have a middle name."

"Well, since neither of us has a birth certificate, we can add and subtract names whenever we want, and who's to say we changed what's not even there?"

Kearney exhaled and shook his head. Then he smiled. "I don't think that's ever come up before, but I suppose you're right. If you were born inside this building and lived here all your life, what documentation would there be? Have you used any other names?"

"Chastity," said Lynn, "but not for long."

Kearney resisted the temptation to challenge her on the irony of such a name. "And would you spell that for me please?"

As she did, Kearney sat up straight again and rolled his shoulders, as if working out a set of kinks. He leaned forward and opened the warrant up again for Lynn to go over the details with him. "Do you have any trouble reading this?" he asked.

"Not at all," Lynn said. "It says that this is a material witness warrant issued by—"

"That's correct," Kearney said, leaning forward and lowering his voice. "Friends of yours say you want out of here, and that you never want to come back. They've made arrangements to have you taken somewhere safe that you'll find quite comfortable. If you're agreeable to that, you don't have to say anything, just nod your head."

Lynn rolled her weight forward and exhaled. Then she snuck a glance toward Mei, who responded with a discreet nod. Lynn sighed, rolled her shoulders forward, bowed her head, and nodded.

"Wise choice," said Kearney. "Officer Sullivan and I will be escorting you to your room to fetch clothes that you will need for court. I suggest that while you can, grab the personal belongings you don't want to leave behind, and we'll take them with us. Understood?"

"Yes," said Lynn, "and thank you for doing this."

"Now keep this as quiet as you can. Don't blab it to the other girls or Goon Dip. And resist telling anyone goodbye. I don't want to have to fight our way out of here, while protecting you at the same time."

Officer Kearney stood up and escorted Lynn over to where Mei and Officer Sullivan were standing by themselves. Jai Wong soon joined the small group, followed by Goon Dip.

"Do you ladies mind if I explain these warrants to your business managers?" Kearney asked the two sisters. "I need your permission before I can start, not theirs."

Lynn glanced at Mei, who shrugged and then shook her head, indicating she didn't mind. Lynn followed her sister's lead, mimicking her gesture.

"Messieurs Wong," said Kearney, "the young ladies we have identified here have material witness warrants issued by Judge Wilma Goodloe for their arrest. It concerns a murder that occurred several years ago. Our orders are to take them into custody and present them to the good judge, who will question them about their safety before she likely places them in protective custody."

"Protective custody?" asked Goon Dip. "Protecting them from whom?"

"The Judge didn't feel it was her obligation to tell us who that might be," said Kearney, "but I would suspect it would include whoever might be responsible for the murder."

"What murder?" asked Jai Wong impatiently.

"Police Officer Charles Sawyer," said Kearney.

"Hacksaw Sawyer?" asked Goon Dip. "But that was nine or ten years ago, when these girls were just children."

"Exactly," said Kearney. "But nonetheless, they were working on this floor, and you would know that as well as anyone else, because they're your daughters, aren't they?"

Both of the Wongs glared at Kearney but didn't answer his question.

"The court is apparently aware of their ages, both then and now, and that's likely what led to the judge's determination that they need protection."

"Protection from their own family?" asked Goon Dip. "That is an insult!"

"Like the officer said, the judge didn't feel the need to state her reasons to us," interjected Officer Sullivan. "We're only guessing at her honor's motives at this point."

"You are not to take them from here," said Jai Wong. "They are family, and we have friends on the department who outrank the two of you. We wish to speak with them before you take any action."

"I'm well aware of your police connections, Mr. Wong," said Kearney, "but those friends you speak of are included on the list the judge thinks the ladies need protecting from—that is if you're thinking of Lieutenant Harry Frantz. And besides, these orders don't come from the Seattle Police Department, they come from a Superior Court Judge, who's not concerned with any chain of command.

236

That nonsense means little to her. This is what we call the separation of government, where the different branches act independently. It's designed to thwart corruption and governmental abuse."

Officer Sullivan slapped his billy club against his gloved hand for effect. "Now gentlemen, we have work to do," he said. "We will give the young ladies a moment to collect a change of clothing from their room, because I can assure you that Judge Goodloe will not appreciate their coming to her chambers wearing skimpy outfits meant for the bedroom. So my caution to you is: Allow us to do our jobs, and this will go smoothly for everyone concerned, with nobody getting their feathers plucked, their beaks clipped, or their noggins bopped."

Jai Wong and Goon Dip glared darts at the officers.

In an exaggerated movement, Officer Kearney reached an arm around Mei's shoulder as a guiding gesture, steering her away from her father and half-brother, with Lynn soon following behind her. "Is your room nearby?" Kearney asked.

"Against the back wall there's a set of rooms for those who work the floor," said Mei. "But we need Jai or Nelson to come with us."

"Why's that?" asked Kearney.

"They have the key to the rooms."

"You don't have you own key?" asked Kearney.

Mei shook her head.

"They don't want you straying far," said Kearney under his breath. He caught Jai Wong's eye and indicated with a commanding thrust of his head that he was to come along with them.

They passed the Dragon and Tiger rooms on the way to the back, and then the carpeted hallway branched to the left. "Ours is the last one on the right," said Mei.

When they reached the room, Jai Wong stepped forward and produced a key from somewhere inside his robes, pressed it into a deadbolt lock, and pushed the door open. He was about to step inside, leading the way, when Kearney stopped him.

"For our safety," said Officer Kearney to Jai Wong, "one of us will accompany the girls while they're inside their room. We can't have them fetching a gun or knife, jumping out a window—that kind of thing—because we're responsible for their safety from this point onward, and if there's more than one of you inside the room, that's too many for us to watch. You'll just have to wait outside."

"But you're not going to stay in there and watch them get dressed!" protested Jai Wong.

Kearney smirked and then scowled. "That should be the least of your worries, Mr. Wong, given how you've made your sisters earn money for you, but no, they're not going to change clothes here. They'll grab what they need and take that with them. They can get dressed on their way to meet the judge. That's the best we can do."

Mei closed her eyes a moment and chewed on her lower lip as she thought. "Okay. Lynn you go first. I'll wait here."

Lynn slid past Mei and ducked under Kearney's arm which propped the door open, before he followed and closed it behind them, leaving Sullivan to watch Mei and Jai Wong in the hallway.

Lynn knifed between the two small beds and went straight for the open closet door, which had its contents divided neatly in half. Kearney stepped up close behind her, and she grabbed a handful of dresses and proffered them to him to hold for her.

"Hold on a second," Kearney said. "You can carry one outfit over your arm, and whatever else you want you can throw into a pillowcase—but you'll have to carry it."

"Can't you help?" Lynn asked, wide-eyed.

"I'd love to, miss, but I have to keep my hands free in case we need them. I'm not so sure your extended family is going to let you out of here without putting up a fight. Losing you and your sister is going to put a dent in their revenues. So pick something that's warm and comfortable. You might have to wear it for a few days."

"Does all this have something to do with someone named Alan?" asked Lynn.

Kearney stared into Lynn's eyes, sizing her up. "Apparently you told him you wanted out of here more than anything else," he said.

A faint smile creased Lynn's lips, and she flipped through the outfits Kearney was holding, pulled three away by the coat hangers and tossed them on the bed, leaving him holding one. Then from a bottom bureau drawer she took out a clean pillowcase and stuck in two pair of women's shoes, panties, hose, garter straps, and a blouse. From the top of her bed, Lynn picked up a bisque porcelain china doll, dressed in a blue and white silk kimono with lips painted into a small red V. Lynn drew the doll close to her, kissed it gently on the shiny forehead, and stuffed it inside the pillow case. She spun the pillow case around a couple of times, giving her a handle to grab onto while she gazed around the room.

"Excuse me," she said to Kearney, indicating a need to slide past him, but instead of waiting for him to move his big frame out of the way, she stepped into the narrow space between the beds, where he was standing, and brushed by him, her eyes gazing innocently into his as she squeezed past him. She stopped at the closed door and lifted an overcoat from a hook and climbed into it, pulling it tight around her.

"Alright," she said. "I'm ready."

"You're going outside without a hat?" Kearney asked, gazing over her head to a shelf above the door.

"I'm sorry," she said, "I have a lot to think about. Would you get down the puce one for me?"

"Puce?" asked Kearney.

"Yes, it's sort of like purple, but not quite."

Kearney reached up, grabbed the hat, which reminded him a bit of a man's fedora, only with the brim turned up on the side. He handed it to Lynn, who again was staring up at him with her big innocent eyes, her openness and vulnerability competing against suspicion, which made Kearney feel self-consciously responsible for her and her welfare. He glanced away, gazing past her, and he stared blankly at the dead bolt lock, which was visible now that she had removed her coat from the door.

"Where's the knob for you to unlock the door?" he asked, irritation straining his voice.

Lynn looked at the eye-level lock where the thumb toggle had been sawed off.

"It's been this way the whole time I've been here," she said.

"So, they lock you inside at night, is that it?"

Lynn nodded as if that was the only reality she had ever known.

"But what if there's a fire in the building—or on this floor?" Kearney asked sternly.

"Someone would let us out…"

Kearney scowled. "I'm not so sure about that. From what I've seen here, it's every man for himself and to hell with the rest of you. This is a flagrant fire code violation that's going to require direct intervention and strong action, even if the Chief Fire Inspector has been getting his nozzle polished and his pockets lined while making his tours through here. This isn't right!"

Lynn shrugged, as if apologizing for the House's practices.

Kearney shook his head and slowly lowered it in contrition for his angry outburst. "Right you are then," he said. "Wait outside with Officer Sullivan, and send your sister in, please."

As Lynn stepped into the hallway, Kearney wandered out from between the beds and backed into the small area next to the white porcelain sink, the only plumbing fixture in the room. This meant the young women were required to take care of their bathroom chores in a shared toilet somewhere down the hallway, before their hosts locked them in their rooms for the night.

Mei entered the room and shut the door cautiously behind her, gazing at Kearney suspiciously.

Kearney forced a smile, trying to keep the situation friendly. "I understand you're both locked in your room at night. So what do you do if you need to use the bathroom? Are you forced to hold it until the morning? How long would that be?"

"There is a pitcher and basin under the sink for night soil," said Mei.

Kearney leaned his big frame away from the sink far enough so that he could see what was underneath it. When he looked back for Mei, she was already over at the closet, pulling out clothes on hangers and tossing them on the bed.

"Take just what you can carry, Mei, nothing more. You'll want something that will be comfortable, in case you have to wear it a number of days."

Mei stared at Officer Kearney, either expecting more information or processing what he had said. "Are two outfits okay?"

"As long as you're carrying them. I told Lynn that Sully and

I have to keep our hands free in case we encounter trouble."

"I understand," said Mei.

"Take whatever else you need and stuff it into a pillowcase, like Lynn did. Now's the time for you to grab keepsakes, family photos, jewelry, that kind of thing."

Mei paused, sat on her bed, and crossed her legs. "Has this got something to do with that old murder you mentioned, or is this about my sister's new client who she thinks likes her?"

"All I can tell you is that your sister told someone—I imagine it was her new friend—that you both wanted out of here more than anything else in the world. I don't know if promises were made, money changed hands, or how it was arranged, but we were instructed to come and get you by Judge Goodloe—fail not at our peril, the judge said."

Mei scratched her head, got off the bed, opened the same drawer Lynn had earlier, and took out a pillowcase for herself. She also stuffed in a couple pairs of shoes, stockings, hose, and women's undergarments. From next to her pillow she picked up a pink-faced, bisque porcelain doll, with a matching red silk tunic and Chinese hat that had multi-colored tassels hanging from the sides. Mei checked under its collar, examining something, and then stuffed her doll in the pillowcase. She picked up two outfits and moved them to the edge of the bed and smiled up at Kearney.

"Would you do me a favor, please, and lift the foot of the bed up in the air for me?" she asked. "It's not that heavy, but it works better if you help."

Kearney puckered his mouth into a knowing smile, stepped to the edge of the brass frame bed and easily lifted it a foot off the floor.

"That's plenty," said Mei as she dropped to her knees and grabbed the flared footing of one of the legs and gave it a twist. With little effort the footing slid off, and she set it aside. She reached underneath with her fingers and poked them into the hollow of the frame's tube. Almost instantly a large wad of green bills appeared. Mei tugged on the thick roll and pulled it out on the floor in sections.

"Your tips?" Kearney asked.

Mei nodded, again sticking her fingers into the brass tube opening.

"How much do you think you have there?" Kearney asked.

"Four thousand, three hundred eighty-two dollars."

"Your life's savings?"

"Mine and Lynn's both. She doesn't care about the money, and wouldn't know what to do with it. She never thought we'd ever be free to spend any of this. So I've kept it for us, just in case."

"Looks like your 'just in case' is finally paying off."

"Thank you for making it so, and please pass our thanks to Lynn's new friend," Mei said, re-arranging and packing the cash tightly. "So, Officer Kearney, if you ever want a free session, it's on me—literally—with the whip or without, your choice. My only requirement would be that you wear a prophylactic."

Kearney smiled wryly and glanced away for a moment, staring at the dusty lace curtains that hung over her bed and drawn shades. "I couldn't do that," he said. "I know you mean well, but I'm not doing this because I'm expecting something in return. I was told you and your sister are good people who needed a break in life. That's why I'm doing this."

"Alright, suit yourself," said Mei, and then she stared again at the money in her hand. "This probably works out to a dollar a trick over the years," she said, shaking her head. "But not everybody tips us, and the House would take it all if they knew how much I had here. It's because of guys like Lynn's new friend, who tips well, that we have this much.

Most of the rich banker types are tighter than a cockroach's behind, just like the cops. They never tip either—except for one. The police we see figure they're entitled to whatever they can get. I hope my saying that doesn't offend you, because I can see you're not like the others."

Kearney forced a smile but didn't respond. He knew the sort she was talking about. There weren't many carnivores like that on the department, but those who were all seemed to be in positions of power, able to inflict their way of doing business on the hunter-gatherers and herbivores that filled the ranks. Mei got to her feet, went to the door, and grabbed her winter coat. "Would you get the black Coco Chanel down for me, please?"

"Coco Chanel is a hat, right?"

Mei nodded. "It's also the little black dress I picked out," she said. "Chanel is the best designer in the world!"

Kearney reached for a black hat that was shaped like a soft helmet with matching large petals on one side and handed it to Mei. "This looks expensive," he said.

"They want us to dress nicely on our outcalls," she said. "It's not that they care about us so much, it's more so that we can cater to a higher class clientele and charge more."

Mei stuffed the roll of money in her coat pocket.

"You mentioned cops as clients," said Kearney. "Have you had many of those?"

Mei reached for the door handle and stopped. She thought a moment and then gazed into Kearney's eyes. "I've had a few over the years, but awhile back they discouraged their coming regularly. Whoever was running things told them to stay off this floor."

"The one who gave that order, was he running things at the police department, or was he running things here?" Kearney asked.

"Both," said Mei. "Because we couldn't open our doors if

the bosses at the police department didn't say we could."

"Was that said after Hack Sawyer was killed?" Kearney asked.

Mei sucked in her cheeks as she thought, and then she finally nodded, as if answering might be painful for her. She opened the door, sad faced, and stepped into the hallway, with two dresses draped over one arm, a pillowcase gripped in the other like a refugee.

Kearney stared after her, wondering if Mei was feeling sentimental about leaving her home of twenty-five years, or did something about his last question get to her? She mentioned another cop having tipped her in the past, but she didn't say who that was or when, but it would have had to have been years ago if the girls were no longer servicing cops.

It was after 11:30 and the doorman at the Sorrento Hotel had already gone home, when Alan held the front door open for Vera. Alan gestured as if he was tipping his hat to the receptionist as they passed the front desk and headed straight for the elevators.

"You come here so often that they recognize you, even when you're with a strange woman?" Vera smirked.

Alan chuckled as the elevator doors opened and they stepped inside. "Sure," he said. "Alice and I come for the prime rib and roof top dining. Then there's dancing afterward. Makes for a nice evening. But since you brought it up, I find that there's nothing strange about you."

Vera pushed the button to the sixth floor and then leaned back against the interior railing. "This isn't one of those moments where you've got me alone, so you're going to try and kiss me again, is it?"

Alan placed one hand against the panel in front of Vera and the other to the side, trapping her in the front corner of the elevator. He leaned forward to kiss her, but she turned her face to the side and presented her cheek instead. He kissed it softly, nuzzled her ear, and kissed her jaw line that he liked so much.

"Kiss you 'again?'" he asked. "I hadn't yet kissed you for the first time—first time today, that is."

Vera smiled and glanced up at the lights marking the floors they were passing.

"You should be careful, Champ. What if I kissed you back and then the elevator doors opened wide? What would you say if your dear Alice saw us? Would you put the blame on me?"

"You're right. I'm sorry. I lose all perspective and don't know how to behave when I'm around you, so I end up acting like a sixteen-year old kid."

"You don't have to apologize, Champ. You know I like it. I'm just telling you to be careful."

Alan nodded but didn't say anything. And her mentioning being careful reminded him that Mario had said the same thing. Whatever happened, he wondered, to unabashed mindless lust?

Alan pushed away from her, weighing what she had said and staring up at the floor numbers as they passed, checking the elevator car's progress. Within a few seconds the ride stopped, and the doors opened onto a carpeted hallway. He walked alongside Vera to just around the first turn to the corner suite, which he already knew had a commanding view of Elliot Bay. He knocked softly. A moment later, Alice Mahoney answered the door, stepped back, and showed them in.

Sitting directly across the room on the sofa in front of the window were Mei and Lynn Wong. Standing next to an over-sized chair near the girls was Chief of Detectives Mike Ketchum. Opposite him, on the other side of the sofa, was Gunny Manheim, wearing his trade-marked leather flying jacket. Marring his rugged good looks was an arm sling that hung around his neck and left side. Seated at the desk to their immediate right was a woman dressed in dark worsted wool. She glanced up from paperwork that she was reviewing on her desk.

Greetings were exchanged with Gunny, and then Ketchum introduced Judge Wilma Goodloe and her bailiff Charles Boyer, neither of whom Alan or Vera had met before. Judge Goodloe remained seated, but spun half–way around in her chair, dangling a pair of reading glasses in her hand. Boyer stood near Goodloe's desk, waiting with more documents at the ready.

"I'll be with you shortly," the judge said. "I just want to make sure that the Police Department's Affidavit of Probable Cause is legally sufficient. I thoroughly expect Mr. Wong's attorneys to protest this unusual action, particularly at this hour of night, and if they can't get the young ladies back immediately, they'll complain to the Judicial Review Committee. We all have people looking over our shoulders."

Chief Ketchum crossed the room to meet with Alan and Vera, as Judge Goodloe returned her attention to the paperwork. They were joined by Gunny and Alice, while Mei and Lynn remained seated on the couch. Ketchum raised his arm and draped it in a fatherly way over Alan's shoulder, while somehow squeezing in next to Vera and giving her a hug around the waist.

"What took you so long?" Ketchum asked. "Sully and Kearney left here twenty minutes ago. I was getting worried."

Vera reached out and clasped Gunny's freehand. "Thank you for coming," she said. "I wasn't sure you were up to helping." She turned to Ketchum. "The Wong family wasn't very happy about our maneuver in their den of iniquity. So we waited until Sully and Ben cleared the front door before we left, just in case they needed us. And then we just couldn't waltz out onto Seventh Avenue with the street in a buzz, so we had to drop down a level and navigate through

249

the catacombs to get back to our car."

Behind Ketchum and Gunny, Lynn called out. "Alan? Is that you?"

Alan froze for half a second, and then he felt a gentle squeeze above his elbow from Vera. He hoped she was sending him encouragement and good luck. He excused himself from the circle, which had gone quiet, and moved over to the sofa, where Lynn slid over, making room next to her.

Alan could sense that Alice was watching his every movement, but he dared not look in her direction, lest she would give him a look indicating that he had better not talk to these women, a gesture they either might not understand or conversely would understand only too well, take offense to, and come out fighting.

Alan stopped next to the sofa, took off his fedora, and forced a gushing smile of encouragement to the young women, who had already found time to change out of their bordello wear into well-tailored evening wear that was tasteful but still sexy. Lynn patted the cushion next to her, indicating she had made a place for him. He sat slowly, and as soon as his bottom touched the cushion, she reached out and grabbed his leg familiarly, well above the knee, and tried to pull him closer to her.

Alan quickly grabbed her hand, lifted it up and slid back slightly. "It's good to see you two," he said softly. "But I'm with someone who's here in the room."

He gazed into Lynn's expectant eyes, and then glanced toward Mei, hoping he wouldn't have to repeat himself.

A flash sparked in Mei's eyes, and she suddenly started speaking rapidly in Chinese to Lynn, whose eyes registered disappointment, sorrow, and then anger. A shadow suddenly appeared next to Alan, apparently blocking Lynn's view of the room, and it of her. She leaned to her side, pressing against her sister as if trying to peek around the shape that had stepped forward.

Alan felt a hand clasp his shoulder firmly, while at the same time Mei raised her voice, as if scolding her sister in Chinese.

"Can I get you a drink, Champ?" asked Gunny, speaking loud and clear from next to him.

"Would you, please? Scotch on the rocks."

Gunny tweaked Alan's shoulder playfully and leaned down close to him. "Same place your love life is about to end up?"

"Let's hope not," Alan said through a clenched jaw.

"Ladies, is there something I can get for you while I'm up?" asked Gunny.

"We like Coca Cola," said Mei. "Can we have that?"

"Sure," said Gunny, "but the caffeine might keep you up all night."

"That's okay," said Mei. "We're always up at night."

"If that's the case then," said Gunny, "you can have Coke, and you can stay up with me while I watch the door tonight. We'll play cards and listen to the radio until morning."

Alan stood up, and sidestepped in front of the young women. "We'll talk more later," he said, "after the judge has finished and the others have left."

As Alan turned around, Gunny slid a tumbler of scotch into his hand, grinned knowingly, and then moved on with the colas for the girls. Alan re-joined the group with Ketchum, Vera, and Alice, who was staring hard at him.

"The ladies are very grateful for your getting them out of Goon Dip's," Alan said. "I didn't have a chance yet to tell them this is all your doing, Vera. Would you like me to introduce you now?"

"I'd like that too," Alice said. "I didn't have a chance to formally meet them yet."

"Sure," said Vera. "I'd love to say hello, but do us a

251

favor, Champ, and don't bring up mine or Alice's days in burlesque. This is their chance to start over. We want to encourage them to stay out of the spotlight, not dance in front of it and draw attention to where they're hiding."

Crossing the floor, Alan did his best to put on a smile, but it wasn't working as well as he'd hoped. He had told Alice the general details of the case, but had omitted the sexually explicit, except for the photographs of Hungry Harry and Knuckles McMurphy. The parts that included himself he thought would be better left unsaid.

"Mei and Lynn, this is Vera and Alice. It's Vera who's seen to the arrangements, including here at the Sorrento, your plane ride tomorrow, and then to where you'll be staying until things quiet down. Alice has been—"

Mei and Lynn's faces burst into smiles, and they popped off the couch to give Vera heartfelt hugs. She responded in kind, blushing noticeably.

Alan smiled over the top of the pig pile to Alice, whose response was more measured, as if she was not convinced of Alan's noble deeds or intentions.

"Excuse me," said the bailiff. "Judge Goodloe is ready, and this session will come to order."

Judge Goodloe took off her reading glasses and turned around in her chair to face those gathered in the room.

"Let me address the two young ladies first," said Judge Goodloe, "after all they are the reason we are here under these unusual circumstances. I can start by telling you that I am a Superior Court judge, but for the purpose of this investigation, I'm serving as an Inquiry Judge. That probably doesn't mean a hill of beans—or rice for that matter—to you, but what does matter is my concern for your safety.

"The affidavit prepared by Chief Michael Ketchum— himself no less, with the aid of Sergeant Watkins and Officer Benjamin Kearney—lays out a tangled web of corruption that we will likely never be able to root out completely—and that poses a risk to you young ladies. This case potentially involves current and former police officers, as well as members of your own family, who I understand have forced you two young ladies into a life of prostitution. A hand written addendum from Officer Kearney on this hotel's stationery informs me that you were locked into your room at night and not allowed to leave the premises without an escort. This is appalling!

"President Lincoln signed into law the Abolition Agreement in 1864, the purpose of which was to forever remove from this country the abomination of slavery, and yet here in 1941 we find that it still in fact exists right under the nose of our own police force, federal agents, and elected officials, whose duty it is to prevent such outrages, not exploit them by taxing them via a systemic payoff scheme."

Judge Goodloe glanced toward Chief Ketchum. "I'm sorry for the strong words, Michael, but your agency needs to do more to protect the citizens of this town and worry less about how much under the table graft it can take in at their expense. It's time for your police officers who are working vice to get off their wallets and get to work. I do, however, applaud your personal efforts and integrity for bringing this matter to me, despite the continued opposition you face from the highest levels. Lord knows I'd never have seen this if it was left to your boss or the Mayor."

Returning her gaze to the young women on the sofa, Judge Goodloe sighed heavily and then continued. "Back to the matter at hand," she said. "I'm not at all satisfied that you ladies would be safe in the City Jail, which is run by the Police Department. Just two years ago, three detectives arrested and murdered a Black man, while walking him the two blocks from Occidental and Yesler

253

to Police Headquarters. They claimed he fell down stairs while trying to escape. What stairs? It's an uphill walk. Fortunately for justice, a hairdresser witnessed the beating, but he was bought-off by the detectives and chased out of town, while other witnesses were threatened with arrest if they cooperated with the NAACP. When the hairdresser came back to Seattle a year later, Federal officials and the NAACP had to hide him in the County Jail, which is run by deputies who are friends of the police detectives. I'm not going to take that kind of chance with you on this case. So therefore I am releasing you to the care and control of Chief Ketchum, who I understand has Federal connections ready and willing to assist him, upon his request. Chief Ketchum is satisfied with the arrangements and has asked me to keep the details confidential. So they will only be released by him or me on a need to know basis. Therefore, I am not recording them in my case notes, because it has been my experience that anything that is written is retrievable, despite the best of intentions and promises. And if people learned where you will be staying, your lives could very well be at risk until the case has gone all the way through the courts and exhausted the appeals process."

With that, Judge Goodloe stood up, said her goodbyes, and Alice and Chief Ketchum showed the judge and her bailiff to the door. As the door closed behind them, Ketchum nodded assuredly. "I think that went very well, don't you, Alice?"

"Given what little I know of the case, I'm inclined to agree with you," she said. "It's a good thing that you and Vera are doing for the young ladies."

Ketchum stopped, as if an idea had just occurred to him.

"Her bailiff is a fine looking young man," he said quietly. "In my day we'd call him 'strapping,' but then I suppose a girl as pretty as you would already have a fella, wouldn't you?"

Alice smiled and lowered her eyes. "I'm seeing someone," she said.

"Oh yes, well of course you are, darling, and I'd say he's a very lucky fellow. I hope he knows it."

"I hope so, too," said Alice.

Once drinks were refreshed, Chief Ketchum sat on the chair next to the young ladies, perched on the sofa, crossed his legs, and dangled his drink, giving the ice a chance to chill the scotch.

"Here's what I'm thinking," he said, addressing Mei and Lynn, but saying it loud enough so that the others in the room could hear. "You will spend tonight in the bedroom suite, under the watchful eyes of Gunny Manheim and Alan Stewart, who will stand guard out here. Tomorrow morning, Mr. Manheim will fly you to a secret location, which might involve a stop or two along the way. Our goal is to get you out of Seattle and out of the reach of those who might harm you."

"How long will this take?" asked Mei.

"We're not sure at this point," said Ketchum. "We've got more digging to do, a lot more questions to ask before we've identified the shooter and are ready to make an arrest. But since we have you here, I've asked Detectives Stewart and Deward, along with Detective Kearney to interview you tonight, take your statements while we can."

Ketchum turned towards Alan and Vera. "Ben will be back within the hour. I've appointed him to police detective, effective an hour ago."

"That's wonderful!" said Vera. "Does he know?"

"I told him as much, just before I asked him to notify his sergeant and report back to me forthwith. He will be working special investigations, directly reporting to me. I'll let the Chief know in the morning, tell him I've got concerns that need looking into. So obviously this will be Ben's first investigation, as such. I want Ben here because he already has a feel for how the courts and prosecutors want our statements to look, what kind of information they need to make their cases stick, et cetera. But I want you two here, because you know how to play rough when it's necessary to do so. As private investigators, you have demonstrated that you have a nice feel for when pain compliance is necessary, despite what the courts tell the police."

"Are you going to hurt us?" asked Mei, urgency in her voice.

Ketchum smiled apologetically and shook his head. "I'm sorry, ladies, I should have saved this conversation for later," he said. "I was referring to life in general, police work in particular, and the interview of whoever it was that shot Hacksaw Sawyer, specifically."

Mei nodded politely and gazed down at her drink. "May we have another *Coca Cola*, please?"

"I'll get those," offered Alice.

Chief Ketchum stood up and arched his back, as if working out a kink. He returned his gaze to Vera and Alan. "You two have already shown me that I don't need to tell you how to do your job, so I'll leave you in peace. I'll give Alice a ride back to her apartment, which is on my way home."

While Ketchum fetched his hat and overcoat, Alan helped Alice into hers. She wiggled her shoulders getting into it, glanced over her shoulder, and smiled at Alan.

"I left you a couple decks of cards, per your request," she said. "I hope I don't have to remind you: No strip poker."

Alan smiled wryly. "You got pinochle cards, right? That's what I asked for."

Alice spun around and cinched her coat tight at the waist while facing him. "I got you pinochle cards all right, but my experience with boys tells me that the type of cards wouldn't make a difference. You'd play three cards short of a full deck if it meant seeing pretty girls in their panties."

"All right, young lady," said Ketchum standing by the door, "your driver awaits."

It was 1:30 AM before Kearney arrived back at the Sorrento Hotel.

"Congratulations on your promotion, Ben," said Vera, as she leaned forward and gave him a hug.

"It's actually an appointment," said Ben, almost apologetically, for clarification. "It's not really the same as a promotion. It's a lateral move. Same basic Civil Service pay grade, and they can move me out if they don't like the job I'm doing."

"I get it," said Alan. "Like with Hacksaw Sawyer, when he got bounced from the Dry Squad."

"That's not the example I was thinking of," said Kearney, "but yeah, that works. The point is, I'm not going to get bounced."

"The point is," said Vera, "this is what you've always wanted to be. That's what's important."

Kearney grinned broadly. "That's the point alright."

With a tilt of her head, Vera indicated for Alan to move in closer, so they could speak in whispers.

"So Ben, how do you want to do this?" asked Vera. "We waited for you before saying anything to the girls."

"Rule number one is we separate them. So let's do that. It never works to interview two people at the same time.

One can always hide behind what the other is saying. And that plays right into rule number two, which is: start on the person you think has the least chance of involvement, learn what you can from her, and work towards the middle. Have you got a thought about who would know the least? And before you answer, I should let you know that both girls' middle names are Hua. Lynn uses hers more than Mei, if that makes a difference?"

Vera glanced at Alan, and he nodded, knowing already what she was thinking. "That makes us feel better about all this," he said. "We know we're getting close. So my vote is that we start with Lynn. Mei is older and the leader. Lynn checks with her first before saying or doing anything."

Vera nodded along with what Alan was saying. "I've seen the same thing."

"We're in agreement on that," said Kearney. "It's Mei who takes care of them both. She has the stash of money they had hidden in their room. If it had been left to Lynn, she might have walked off and left it."

"How much cash?" asked Alan.

"Close to $4,000. She credits some nice tippers, who shall remain nameless."

Alan suddenly felt Vera's elbow digging playfully into his ribs. He forced a smile and a nod. "That should help them get started," he said.

"Mei complained that cops never tipped her, except one," said Kearney. "I tried indirectly to get her to tell me who that was, but she didn't say. I'm wondering if it wasn't Hack Sawyer, because what I know about Hungry Harry, he always feels entitled to whatever he gets."

"We've seen that before," said Alan.

"Oh yeah?" said Kearney. "What'd you see? It might be helpful."

"We'll save that for later," said Vera, "because it also

might pose a problem for a number of people, but there is a problem we haven't discussed yet."

"What's that?"

"One of these girls was there when the shooting happened," said Vera. "We're pretty sure of that. We don't, however, know what her role was at this point. What if she was actually the shooter and not just a witness? Are we prepared for that?"

"Actually, I've thought about that for awhile," said Kearney. "There's plenty of motivation for either of them, especially if they blame Sawyer for turning them out, making them prostitutes—even if he only had a little something to do with it."

"But wasn't it Hungry Harry who turned them out?" asked Alan.

"Lynn? Yes," said Kearney, "but do we know if that's true of Mei? Or could it really have been Sawyer who did the same thing with her, and she's held a grudge? To this point, we're just assuming it was Harry."

"I see what you're saying," said Alan.

"Alright," said Ben. "Let's not overwhelm the girls with too many of us. So why don't you two draw straws or flip a coin to see who sits-in on the first interview with me and Lynn." The other one should wait in the next room with Mei and the other fella you have here."

"That's Gunny," said Vera. "Did you have a chance to meet him yet?"

"Just the handshake," said Kearney. "That's about all I remember, because that's when Chief Ketchum broke the news that he was making me a detective."

"We've worked with Gunny on other projects," said Vera. "He can be trusted."

"He's a war ace," said Alan. "He was shot down over France."

"Is he still recovering?" asked Kearney, glancing past them at Gunny's arm in a sling. "That would have been over twenty years ago."

"No," said Vera. "This is new. He got shot helping us with a nasty little problem a few months back. He's just now getting up to speed."

Alan and Vera stepped back, and she whispered in Alan's ear. "Given that you've had sex with her—twice no less—it's probably best that I take this, not you. I can be more objective."

Alan nodded but didn't say anything.

Vera gazed into his eyes verifying their agreement. "If you can keep from pouting, I'll give you a kiss later that'll make it all worth your while."

Alan smirked and then raised his hand to hide his smile.

"I'll take the first shift," she said to Kearney. "Alan gets Mei."

Alan helped Big Ben move furniture around the suite, arranging it for the interview. Although they didn't need to, the girls got up off the sofa and stood nearby as Alan and Ben slid the coffee table back a few feet and then pulled the side chairs up close to the empty sofa. Lynn stared after Mei when she left the front room, as if she wanted to run after her.

Vera clasped Alan's arm and pulled him close. She pressed her lips against his ear lobe. "You keep your pants up, darling. If I go in there and find them down, I'm going to tie your pecker into a knot."

She kissed his earlobe and let him go, but before she could pull away, he grabbed her arm and tugged her close to him.

"You're a deliciously evil woman, Vera. I'm going to spend the next hour wondering how you possibly could do that. Then the hour after that I'll be wanting you to try it out on me."

Vera pulled away, put on a friendly face and quickly filled the void left by Mei's departure, offering to refresh Lynn's cola. She hugged the smaller woman reassuringly, like a mother would do.

"It'll be alright," she said, flashing a winning smile. "We just need a little information to make sure the police are on the right track and not wasting their time."

Gunny led the way into the suite's bedroom and hitched his leg up on a corner of the bed. As Mei followed him into the room, she glanced back for Lynn, who was already engaged in conversation with Vera. Mei shrugged, crossed the room to the bed, kicked off her heels, and plopped her rump down near the pillows. She drew her legs up under her to sit on, before pressing her dress down in a gesture of modesty. As Alan shut the door behind them he couldn't help but think back to his watching her strut around the bordello in her leather outfit that exposed all of her thighs and much of her body. Her willingness to show skin then but not now had to be all about the time and place, he thought, which was fine with him. He just found it curious.

He tossed a new pack of cards on the bed in front of Mei.

"You ever play pinochle, Mei?"

"I don't know how."

"It's really pretty easy," he said. "I just learned a few months back. Gunny and I'll show you."

Mei took to pinochle quickly, just as Alan suspected she might. Although she claimed that she had never played it before, she had a lot of experience with cards and knew tactics and strategy. She displayed a knack for remembering the bidding and who had laid down what card combinations for meld, which made it easy for her to later anticipate which cards would be played and when. She was also aggressive in bidding, which allowed her to control the trump suit and tempo of most of the games. Alan decided never to play her, or anyone with latent skills like her, for money.

An hour and fifteen minutes later the bedroom door opened, and Lynn stuck her nose into the room. She smiled evenly at Mei. "You're next," she said, like she'd just survived three fillings while at a dentist appointment.

Alan slid off the bed and offered his hand to Mei, giving her an easy tug off the bed. She landed softly on the carpet, and he followed her into the front room. She stopped along the way and took something out of the pillowcase stuffed with her belongings, before plopping down on the sofa. Vera stopped Alan at the door, drew close to him and spoke in hushed tones.

"We learned a lot more about the bordello, the inner workings, and hopefully enough for Chief Ketchum to shut it down, but Lynn didn't give up anything about Hungry Harry or Hack Sawyer. But that photograph we have of her and Hungry Harry could cost him fifteen to twenty in the state pen, if we can get Ketchum's approval to move on it—and that's a big *if* by the way. That's what took up the bulk of our time."

"But nothing on Sawyer's murder, then?" asked Alan.

"She either doesn't know or isn't saying. My hunch is that she simply wasn't involved."

Alan glanced over toward the sofa, where Mei had already taken a defensive sitting position, again drawing her legs up under her. This time she held a doll in a red outfit close to her chest, squeezing it tightly under crossed arms.

"So it's either Mei or we got no case?" asked Alan.

"That's the way I see it," said Vera.

"The way I'm seeing it from here is that she's got something to hide."

Vera went into the bedroom, and Alan chipped off more ice for his drink and added scotch to his glass before sitting across from Mei. He slid back in his chair and casually crossed his legs the European way, letting one knee drape over the other so that his ankle hung low.

After re-introducing himself and explaining the reason for the interview, Kearney leaned forward and handed Mei a black and white glossy. "I'm sorry for having to show you this, but it's important. Do you recognize this picture?" he asked.

Mei's eyes flashed wide, as did her nostrils, before she sighed and let her hand with the photograph flop to her lap. "I've never seen this picture before," she said, closing her eyes for a moment, "but that's me when I was much younger, if that's what you're asking."

"And the man with you?" Kearney asked.

"He's some police sergeant that used to come around all the time back then."

"Do you remember his name?"

"Not his real name. He had a boxer's nickname... *Knuckles*," she said. "The others around the House called him Knuckles."

"How old were you when this picture was taken?" Kearney asked.

Mei pulled her red clad doll up to her face, spun it around, and nuzzled it. She groaned as she thought. "I would have been fourteen."

"How certain are you of that?" asked Kearney.

"I wore that outfit when I first started working the fourth floor. And I remember it was during Chinese New Year of my first year. So yes, I'm sure."

"Did you have sex with other policemen back then, Mei?"

Mei pushed the doll down into her lap and dug at a chain of red glass beads that hung around the doll's neck, nervously rubbing the little nodes between her fingers, while her eyes stared unfocused at the floor between the detectives.

"What's your doll's name?" asked Alan, while Kearney jotted notes patiently.

Mei gazed up, as if interrupted from a distraction. "This is Mei Ling."

"Pretty name," said Alan.

"It means Beautiful Bell, which is actually funny, because unlike a bell, Mei Ling can't make a sound, of course."

Kearney wrote quietly for a moment before speaking again, giving everyone time to collect their thoughts. "Did you need me to repeat the last question?" he asked.

Mei shook her head and rubbed the ruby colored beads intently, like they were prayer beads and she was doing penance.

"There was another policeman before that, which I'm sure you've figured out."

"Why do you say that?" asked Kearney.

"Because that's why we're sitting here waiting, isn't it? You want to find out what I know about Charley."

"That would be Charles Sawyer?" Kearney asked, for clarity.

"Yes. You want to know about his murder and what I had to do with it."

Kearney nodded.

"I didn't have anything to do with it," Mei said passionately, while shaking her head. "What I mean is: it wasn't my fault. He'd been shot, but he was still alive when I left."

"No one's fixing to blame you—at least not yet, anyway,"

266

said Kearney. "We'd like to hear your side of it, what you saw happen in the garage, from your perspective."

Alan felt a rush of adrenalin course through his veins. It was like setting the hook on a trophy sized steelhead. The trick now was not to let his excitement show and scare her off, losing his and Kearney's chance to draw her into the net.

"It was supposed to be an easy outcall," said Mei. "Charley knew about the camera, because he's the one who first put it there to catch another policeman he didn't like."

"Was that policeman Lieutenant Frantz?" asked Kearney.

Mei nodded. "Is he the one they call Hungry Harry?"

"That's what a lot of police call him," said Kearney. "I wasn't sure you'd know him by that."

"Then, that was him."

"Go on…" said Kearney.

"Normally we would take a taxi up and back to Twelfth and Jackson, but this time we got a ride."

"You'd met Charley before on outcalls?"

Mei nodded, and then glanced toward Alan. "Is it alright if I have another *Coca Cola*, please?" she asked.

"Certainly," said Alan as he got up from his chair. "You're not worried about staying up?"

"I don't know life any other way," she said.

"Most people call it a *Coke*," said Alan. "I take it you don't get to drink *Coke* in the House."

"No," said Mei. "We drink cha, which is black tea. We drink it hot, we drink it cold, and we drink it warm, but we never drink *Coca Cola*. We see the red and white signs from our bedroom windows. They're everywhere in Chinatown, but we're not allowed *Coke* in the House, even though it's in the restaurant and bars, unless we sneak it."

Alan quickly fetched another bottle, uncapped it, and as he handed it to Mei, he saw the beads in her hand clearly. They were set in sections on a thin chain: ten beads followed by a long space before a single node, another long space, which was followed again by another set of ten beads. There was also a medallion of sorts where the beads yoked together. Attached to the medallion was another shiny object that dangled lower and had edges like a key. It was a Catholic rosary wrapped around the neck of a Chinese doll. His detective magazines would have called it "matter out of place."

"You pray the rosary?" Alan asked.

Mei glanced at the beads in her hand. "I try to, but I don't know all the words."

"The rosary you have is very pretty," said Alan. "When we're done, maybe you can show it to me, and I'll teach you some words that a friend taught me. Between the two of us, we might get it right."

Alan sat down again, while Kearney gazed patiently at Mei.

"I saw him once a week, every week," Mei said. "Same time, same place, same garage."

"How long had that been going on?" Kearney asked.

"For about two months, maybe a little more. It started right after he got transferred from the South Precinct to Twelfth and Jackson."

"Do you remember seeing me up there?" Kearney asked. "I used to have the beat just south of his."

Mei shrugged her shoulders. "Not really, but I think Charley took precautions. It seemed like we always got dropped off on a side street where it was dark."

"So Charley was what you'd call a regular customer?" asked Kearney.

"I suppose that's one way to look at it. Nelson certainly looked at it that way, but I saw him as my special friend. He would slip me extra money that Nelson wouldn't know about."

"Was Nelson nearby, or did he watch you two when you and Charley were being romantic?" asked Kearney.

"He waited outside the garage. He was only interested in the business end of things. He made sure we were paid first—or sometimes it was a trade off for some deal he'd worked out with the House—and then he'd stay outside and smoke, while I would be inside with Charley. But Charley didn't trust Nelson at all, so he would lock the door to keep him out. I think he was worried about Nelson picking through his wallet when his pants were down, like what happens with street whores and pimps, or something like that. And of course Nelson didn't like the garage door being locked, keeping him out. He said he wanted to make sure Charley didn't get seconds without paying for it, and he wanted to make sure I didn't get hurt, that kind of thing. When Nelson thought we ran over the time limit, he'd knock on the door, which meant I was supposed to hurry up and do what was needed to satisfy Charley."

"What was the time limit you had?" asked Kearney.

"Enough time for Nelson to smoke three cigarettes. What's that take…maybe a half hour?"

"What happened on this night?" asked Kearney. "You mentioned you got a ride."

"Nelson came for me, and when we got to the door, a police car was waiting for us. But Nelson wasn't surprised at all, so I figured he'd made an arrangement. Either the sergeant owed Nelson a favor, or it was the other way around. I didn't ask."

"And that sergeant would be…" Kearney let the question hang in the air.

"Knuckles, as always. I wasn't sure what his payment would be that time, if I would have to fuck him or— I'm sorry, I know there's another word for that, but that's what they call it in the House."

"I'm not a prude," Kearney said, "but it will read better in your statement if I put 'sexual intercourse' instead of that."

"Okay," said Mei. "Put down what you must, but the other thing he likes me to do is suck his cock, so how do you want me to refer to that?"

Kearney gave Mei a polite smile. "I'll figure something out."

"So I figured I would have to do one or the other," said Mei, "but that's not the way it turned out at all."

"Go on," said Kearney.

"The sergeant drove us up to South Main, but he dropped us off down by the corner. So we had to walk the last half block. Charley was waiting inside with the door closed, but he was mad at Nelson. He asked what the deal was with him involving the sergeant, letting him in on what we were doing. Nelson told him we just happened to meet Knuckles in Chinatown, and he volunteered to drop us off in the area so that we could see a headliner backstage, at one of the jazz clubs. He lied and told Charley that Knuckles never asked who it was or where we were going."

"I see," said Kearney.

"And then Nelson told Charley he'd brought the package that he'd asked for. He gave him a manila envelope. Charley opened it inside the garage and studied some photographs under the light over the door. Then he said he should be the one with the negatives, the price was too high, and something else. I wasn't really paying attention to what they were saying. To me it was just more business, but I do remember Charley wasn't especially pleased."

As Mei took a sip from her cola, Kearney stuck up his hand, indicating he had a question and for her to wait while he formed it.

"Remind me how old you were when this happened," he said.

"Fifteen."

Alan computed the math in his head. According to state law on Carnal Knowledge, Hack Sawyer was also committing a series of felonies with Mei, which could have garnered him fifteen years in the state penitentiary, and charges probably could be laid against Sergeant McMurphy for Aiding and Abetting that felony, if the police could prove he knew that Mei was going to sexually service Hack Sawyer.

"So I went inside," said Mei, and Charley closed the door and locked it—or so I thought. We went over to an older car with a large back seat that had all the windows open. Charley tossed the envelope on the front seat and held the back door for me. He climbed in behind me and undid his pants and tugged them down so I could get at his… what do you want me to call it? At the House we call it a cock, but I'm sure you don't want me saying that for your report."

"I'll write down penis," said Kearney.

"Alright," said Mei, "Some of the customers call it that, but most of them like talking dirty to me. They like calling it their cock."

Kearney nodded patiently.

"Charley undid his belt and dropped his pants so I could perform a sexual act that helps excite him."

"Do you remember how he wore his gun?" asked Kearney. "Was it on his belt, or did he wear a shoulder holster?"

"It wasn't on his belt. It was tucked up under his arm. That's a shoulder holster, isn't it?"

Kearney nodded. "That's right, and what was it he liked you to do?"

"Do you want me to name it or describe it?"

"Whatever you're comfortable with."

"He wanted me to start with a blow job. That's one of Charley's favorites, which was no surprise. Most men like that. If I do a good job with that, the rest goes much faster,

271

which means I've done my job well, and everyone goes home happy."

"The pictures show Sawyer's tie undone. Did he do that, do you remember?"

"He loosened that as soon as he closed the door to the garage, which was pretty standard for him. I got the feeling he hated wearing the tie, and so he loosened it whenever the sergeant wasn't around. He said Knuckles was looking for any excuse at all to give him a couple more days suspension."

"What about his hat?" asked Kearney. "Was that on, or did he take it off?

"Uhm, it was on. I don't remember him ever taking his hat off because he's balding, except maybe the first time we had sex, and that was inside the House."

"You said something about Nelson worrying about your getting hurt, did that kind of thing happen with Charley?" asked Kearney.

Mei pushed her doll down into her lap, shrugged her shoulders, and pulled tight on the rosary she'd been playing with. Alan sensed that Kearney had hit an emotional mark with her, something painful. After a moment she picked the doll up and held it to her face, as if shielding herself from the world. The rosary crucifix was pulled tight against the doll's neck, as if Mei was choking it tightly. Her knuckles showed white. After a moment she relaxed her grip and lowered the doll.

"Well not exactly...but sort of," said Mei apologetically. "I can see why Nelson thought he was hurting me. To someone who doesn't know that kind of thing—or like that kind of thing, it looks rough."

"How's that?" Kearney asked.

"Nelson wasn't supposed to come into the garage. He wasn't supposed to see us and what games we liked to play."

"Go on," said Kearney.

"When I pulled up my dress and straddled Charley, he was sitting in the back seat."

"Did you have to take your undergarments off?"

"I don't wear panties on out calls. It would be just one more thing to get in the way, and then you'd have to search for them when you're done. So, I never saw the point."

Kearney nodded. He got it.

"Charley started rubbing my neck as the frenzy built for him, and then he began squeezing it. Before long he was choking me...sort of...but we had done it before—and I didn't mind. What we do is called erotic asphyxiation. It was one of the things I liked doing with him, because I could trust him to take me to a place where I could forget about my life for awhile. Some girls use drugs to do the same thing, but they always end up with them controlling their lives—not the other way around. Nelson watches Lynn and me closely so we won't do drugs. He won't let us near the opium."

"Did Nelson know you liked your sex rough?" asked Kearney.

"He'd seen the marks around my neck before and complained about them, so I thought he knew all along what we were doing. I think that's why he came into the garage, because he was worried and wanted to make sure I was okay."

"How did he get into the garage?" asked Kearney.

"He never told me. But over the years I've thought about it, and I think it had to have been with a key."

As she spoke, Alan flashed back to how quickly Vera had picked the lock on the front door to the photography studio. Maybe this was a talent that Nelson also shared.

"But the more I thought about it," said Mei, "the more I think it was Sergeant Knuckles who opened it."

"Why's that?" asked Kearney.

"Because of how things ended up."

"Alright then," said Kearney. "Let's back up to where you were having sex with Sawyer and keep things in order."

"Since I was almost unconscious when it happened, I didn't see or hear Nelson creeping up on us in the garage. I was in that little wonderland deep inside in my head. I vaguely recall Charley's hips thrusting up against mine from below, but that's about it. And then I was interrupted by this awful roar right over the top of my head. It was deafening, and my ears started ringing. Right after that Charley plopped backward on the seat, and I felt Nelson drag the pistol across my head, like he was parting my hair with the blunt end of a brush. Everything was moving in super slow motion. When I opened my eyes, I remember seeing Charley with this horrible hole in the front of his face, and blood was spurting out his neck on the side, right around his ear."

"Where was the hole in the front of his face, Mei?" asked Kearney. "High up, in the middle, or down low?"

"Right here," Mei said, pointing to her cheekbone, just to the side of her left nostril. "Charley just sat there dazed. I thought he was dead at first, but it turned out he wasn't. Nelson grabbed my hair from behind and tugged me hard, like he was trying to drag me into the front seat to get me away from Charley, but then Charlie suddenly grabbed my arm and pulled me back, keeping me from leaving. It's funny in a way. The choking didn't hurt, but the hair pulling did. But it was almost like Charley was trying to protect me from Nelson, before he died. In some weird way they were both trying to protect me."

Mei released the rosary and used the coarse hem of her doll's tunic to dab at her eyes.

"So Nelson let go of my hair, stepped back, and opened

the door. While he was doing that, Charley must have pressed the rosary in my hand. I don't remember where it came from, I just remember it being there and him saying something."

"Do you remember what it was he said?" asked Alan, as he stood and opened the bathroom door.

"It was garbled, I couldn't be sure. One of the words sounded like 'tran,' but I couldn't tell you the others."

"Do you remember how any of the other words started?" asked Alan, handing Mei tissue from the bathroom. "A first letter? Anything like that?"

Mei sniffed and dabbed at her eyes again, this time using the tissue Alan had handed her.

"'Nar'…," she said making a sound like she was thinking. "That's about the best I can do."

"Northern Pacific?" asked Alan.

Mei shrugged. "Maybe. Like I said, it was garbled."

"Alright," said Kearney. "What happened next?"

"Nelson yanked me by the arm, this time from the side. He was pulling me off Charley's lap. As I stepped down, I missed the running board, and he caught me. He took my hand and led me over to the front door."

"Did Nelson still have the gun out?" asked Kearney.

Mei thought for a moment. "Yes, he tucked it in his coat pocket when we got to the door."

"So, to be sure I'm clear on this," said Kearney, "Nelson shot Sawyer once in the face, but no more than that?"

"Just the once."

"Alright. So then what happened?"

"Sergeant Knuckles opened the door and came inside the garage. His eyes were wide, and he was staring at Nelson. He asked, 'Was that what I thought it was?'"

"So Knuckles had heard the shot, then?"

Mei nodded. "Yes, and he must have had a key to open the door, because it's one of those that locks by itself when it closes. That's what I couldn't think of before. That must be why I was thinking he let Nelson inside, because he must have had a key."

Kearney glanced sideways at Alan and nodded.

"What happened then?" asked Kearney.

"Nelson said that Charley was choking me, that my eyes were bugging out, and Charley wouldn't stop—so he shot him to save my life. Sergeant Knuckles said, 'That's convenient,' or something like that, and then he said, 'the courts would call that excusable homicide.' I think those were his words."

"Were those his exact words?" asked Kearney.

"Yes, except for 'excusable.' He might have said 'forgivable' or something like that. I'm not positive of that."

"Okay, then what?" asked Kearney.

"Knuckles told me to stand right there, near the garage doors, while they went over and took a look at Charley. I was to tell them if I saw anybody coming. They stood next to the car for a few moments, and then Knuckles told me to go wait inside his police car, which is what I did."

"Did you see or hear anything more?" asked Kearney.

"I'd just gotten to the car and was sitting down, when I looked back and saw a flash inside the garage and heard another gunshot. I remember seeing the flash before I heard the gunshot, which must have been instantaneous. It's funny how the brain works."

"How long was it before they came out to the car?" Kearney asked.

"Maybe two minutes or so."

"Did anyone turn on the shop lights inside the garage?" asked Kearney.

"Oh yeah, they did. It was after the second shot, a little while before they both came out. The lights came on for only thirty seconds or so, probably not even that long."

276

"What did they say when they got back inside the police car?" asked Kearney.

"I remember that Nelson was sort of mad but not quite, because he was kind of happy too, which I didn't think was right. He said he was mad that Charley was hurting me, and he said he was mad because he got blood all over his clothes, but then he seemed excited too, like he'd done something he was proud of and wanted to brag about to his friends."

"What about Sergeant McMurphy?" asked Kearney.

"The first thing he did was sit back and let out a great big groan. Then he said, 'I thought he was dead,' and Nelson said, 'Well he is now. That's what counts.' Then Knuckles said something about Charley coming to and trying to pull his gun on him, so he swatted his hand down, took the gun away and shot him with it himself."

"Do you remember his exact words?" asked Kearney.

"Yes, give me a second to think." Mei said. She inhaled deeply and nodded that she was ready to go on. "He said, 'The fucker pulled his piece, and I thought he was going to shoot me. So I took his gun and put him out of his misery.'"

"Those words, my dear, sound a lot like the Sergeant McMurphy I know," said Kearney. "Did either of them say anything about making the shooting look like a suicide?"

"Not that I recall," said Mei, "but then we sat in silence most of the way back to the House."

Kearney glanced toward Alan. "Have you got any questions for her?" he asked.

Alan drew his brow low as he thought for a moment. "What about the manila envelope with the pictures?" he asked. "Did either Knuckles or Nelson bring it out to the car?"

Mei shook her head. "I didn't see them do it, but I was pretty shook up. I remember crying a lot, and that's about it."

"Is it possible Nelson had it with him later, when you got out of the car?" asked Kearney.

"I'd say that he didn't, because it seems like I would remember that part," said Mei.

"That rosary you're praying on, Mei, is that the one Charley gave you?" asked Alan.

Mei nodded and dabbed her eyes again with the tissue.

"Can I take a look at it?" asked Alan. "And as I was saying, if I don't know the words, I have a friend who'd be glad to teach them to you. I'm sure you'll take to it like you took to pinochle."

After Ben Kearney called it a night, Mei and Lynn scurried off to the bedroom, while Gunny made himself comfortable on the sofa with a pillow and extra blanket. The hotel staff had delivered a fold-away day bed for Alan, which he said he would use right after he walked Vera to her car, but first they stopped for a visit in the Fireside Lobby. Although no one was around, they kept their voices low and intimate.

"How'd you talk Mei into giving you the key?" Vera asked.

"I told her that it didn't belong on the rosary. That it was bad juju to mix something secular with something holy, especially when you see what happened to its previous owner. The key should really have its own chain, because from what Alice tells me, the Catholics put a lot of stock in their beads, their crucifixes, and statues of the saints. Personally, I don't know if it's sacrilegious or not, but I don't think it's a good mix. At any rate, I told her I would find her a chain for it."

"I admit I'm superstitious about religious symbols," said Vera. "I also agree there's something inappropriate about not treating them with respect. I'm glad you picked up on that 'matter out of place.' Every time I hear that expression

I think of a brothel madam crowding into the front pew of church on Sunday. Sure, she's welcome, but the congregation hopes it was her knickers she remembered to wear and not the cheap perfume."

"Alright," Alan said with a smile, twirling the key and catching the glow from the fireplace. "That's certainly 'matter out of place,' and it works too."

"The point is, Mei gave you her key," said Vera. "And I suspect it's probably important. It might even lead us to Hacksaw's fortune, but at this point we don't know what it opens."

"It's not the same as the safety deposit key I have stashed away," said Alan. "I'm guessing this is more like a locker or trunk key. And since Mei said that Sawyer's last words were 'tran,' that's a big clue. Huge, in fact. Do train stations have storage lockers, like the Greyhound Bus Depot?"

"I'm sure they do," said Vera, "but if the key is to a locker, I don't know how long you can leave things there. The rate was a dime a day the last time I checked, but I believe the railroads want turnover, at least once a day—but I'm not sure. They wouldn't want a sailor shipping out to sea for a year or two, tying up one of their lockers, and what about people losing their keys or forgetting to come back and fetch their belongings? They'd never make any money if they ran their business that way."

"There're two train depots in town, two blocks apart. After we're done interviewing Knuckles, we can start with the Great Northern and see what's there. Maybe we'll get lucky."

"And what if we do?" asked Vera. "Even though Mei would probably never know the difference, we'd have to cut her in on it, don't you think?"

"I agree completely," said Alan, "but I don't think it should come out of our finder's fees. It should come out of the widow's side."

"So, you're saying we should tell Mrs. Sawyer that her

husband was banging a Chinatown hooker when he was shot," said Vera, "but the girl should get a cut of the dough, because he entrusted her with the key to his fortune? And we know this because the hooker told us so?"

"Mei's actually a pretty nice gal, Vera. 'Hooker' just doesn't seem to do her justice."

"I know. I'm being sarcastic and mean."

"But you raise a good point," said Alan. "What would we tell the missus?"

"If we don't find Hacksaw's treasure, we don't have to tell her anything," said Vera.

Alan shook his head. "We'll deal with it when it comes up."

"Alright then," said Vera, "I should be getting home."

"I'll walk you to the car, if you'd like."

"Of course I'd like," said Vera, "but you've been awfully amorous lately. Are you going to try and kiss me again?"

"Sure. Isn't that the point?"

"Alright then," Vera said thoughtfully, "but this time keep your hands off my breasts, Champ. I don't want you getting your hopes up, praying for something that's not going to happen."

"Are you just saying that because Alice was here tonight?"

"Yes, because of her, but not just because she was here helping out. She's such a sweetheart, and I don't want to see her getting hurt. You really should take care of your relationship with her first, and leave me out of the equation, because I might not be a part of it. So decide what you want to have with her and let her know. Then, if and when you're free, we'll see what happens between us, but in keeping with my belief in total honesty, I can't promise you the moon and the stars, and whatever else is out there. In relationships there's never a guarantee of utopian bliss."

"Which means what for now?"

"For now you can have a kiss, not a fondle."

"Alright, I promise," said Alan, knowing full well that as soon as he got the chance he was going to grab both her rump cheeks and squeeze them firmly.

Alan and Vera exchanged morning greetings with Ben Kearney, who was wearing a wool suit, overcoat, and fedora, waiting patiently at his old call box on King Street. "I don't know about you two, but I could've used a little more sleep," he said.

Alan grumbled, not bothering to hide his weariness, while Vera flashed a chipper smile. "It only seems early because you were up so late last night," she said. "But that's also true of Nelson and his thugs."

"That's true of most of the low-lifes of the world," said Kearney. "It's a police maxim that it's easiest to catch crooks before noon, because they're still in bed. We catch Nelson now, and we don't have to deal with his cronies. We wait till later, and we could be staring down the entire Chinese Army…well, at least those who aren't fighting the Japanese in Manchuria."

"Speaking of an army, Ben; who do we have to watch our backs?" asked Vera.

"Sully should be here any moment," said Kearney. "Otherwise, we're on our own. If we were to put out a call for back up, we could end up with police officers who're cheering for the other team."

"Really?" asked Vera. "I thought all the boys in blue stuck together, through thick and thin, and all that."

Kearney shook his head slowly. "That's mostly true. Cops won't rat each out other over everyday sins, sexual indiscretions, and even when thievery and mayhem are happening in front of them, but they do draw the line when you break the blue code. So if they figure they can't trust you—which really means me—to look the other way when I really shouldn't—because I'm trying to solve Sawyer's murder—then they might not be there when we need them."

"But at this point, nobody really knows what we're doing here, do they?" asked Vera.

"No," said Kearney. "At least I hope not, but if they'd show up here because I summoned them, the first thing they'd ask is: what's this about? They're smart thinking men, and they'll want to know it's a fight that jibes with their values, whether good or bad, before they put their lives and limbs on the line. We can't count on blind allegiance because we're doing 'God's work.'"

Kearney gazed over the top of Alan and Vera's heads and nodded a greeting. Alan turned around and did the same, although he knew that Officer Sullivan would have eyes only for Vera. But then as if to prove him wrong, Sullivan reached up and gave Alan an affectionate squeeze on the shoulder.

"How you doing, lad?" Sullivan asked in his Irish brogue with a twinkle in his eye.

Alan returned the greeting, knowing it was well meant. As he thought about it, he realized that this time Sullivan hadn't arched his back and stared down his nose, as beatmen were wont to do.

"The bouncers aren't up and out front yet," said Kearney, "but the kitchen's fired up and the hired help should be eating soon. The restaurant doesn't open until 11:00 o'clock, so that gives us about an hour to work with. Any questions?"

"Do we have a warrant yet?" asked Sullivan.

"I talked to Judge Goodloe," said Kearney. "She doesn't want to give us an arrest warrant based on the say so of a witness with a dubious reputation. At least that's how she put it."

Sullivan exhaled and blew at the edges of his mustache, causing them to flutter. "So we've got no warrant. We can't go after Nelson in his living quarters then, so do we lure him outside?"

"If we can take him down on the gambling floors or in the restaurant area, Goodloe is fine with a probable cause arrest. She calls the floor 'an area open to the public.'"

"Works for me," Sullivan said.

The foursome crossed King Street and marched down Seventh Avenue until they came to the lonely glass doors which had been left unattended.

"No money on the tables this time of the morning," Kearney said, as if explaining the absence of security.

Officer Sullivan tugged one of the doors open, shoving it wide for Kearney to hold. "Uniformed police first, Vera," he said matter-of-factly. "Those inside need to know it's the police who've come a calling. We don't want them opening fire on us, claiming later they thought they were being robbed."

There were eight to ten people gathered around two large circular tables near the restaurant entrance. As Kearney's posse worked its way across the red carpet, heads turned in their direction, and when the door finally closed behind them, eliminating the backlighting, one of the older women from the kitchen staff stood up, a puzzled look on her face.

On the tables were several serving dishes full of steaming hot food. Alan inhaled the delicious aromas, recognizing several of the dishes by their smell and what they looked like. He decided that Chinese food would make the perfect lunch as soon as this matter was settled. At the tables some of the wait staff selected and added items to their rice bowls, while others sat hunched over similar bowls held close to faces, chopsticks working furiously.

"We're here to speak to the manager," said Sullivan. "Is Nelson Wong available?"

"He not up yet," said the woman begrudgingly.

"It's a matter of importance," said Kearney, forcing a smile that wasn't overly friendly. "It's police business. Would you have someone get him for us, please?"

The elderly Chinese woman stood silently for a moment, as if she was interpreting the information in her head, decoding it in her native language, and preparing an appropriate response. Finally she nodded and turned to the table to her side, saying something in an Asian dialect. A girl of about ten wearing kitchen staff apparel glanced up attentively. After listening to the elderly woman, she got up from the table and hurried up the carpeted stairs and out of sight.

The elderly Chinese glanced sideways at Kearney and then Sullivan, staring up and down at his tall frame or uniform. "Mai Ling will wake Nelson. Could be few minutes. You wait here. Would you like tea while wait?"

Kearney glanced at his companions for their response. Sullivan, who was holding his nightstick by both ends in front of his hips, blinked long and shook his head. Vera shrugged a "why not," and Alan said, "Sure." Kearney turned back to the elderly woman and nodded politely. "That would be nice, please."

The elderly woman spoke to another waitress at the round table, who got up and disappeared into the kitchen. A moment later she returned with a well used metal teapot in one hand, and a tray with small porcelain cups in the other. She set the tray on a nearby round table and poured steaming tea into four cups, just as the messenger girl returned from upstairs.

"Nelson will be down shortly," the waitress said with a bow.

Kearney thanked her and sat down at the table. He was joined by Alan and Vera, but Sullivan continued to stand sentry. Kearney held up a cup of tea, offering it to the veteran beat cop, but again Sullivan shook him off.

A few moments later, the thudding of footsteps on carpet drew their attention to the staircase. Sullivan stepped away from the table so that he was conspicuously visible, and Kearney rose from his too small chair. Vera and Alan followed behind as Ben stepped close to Sullivan.

A silhouette came into view at the top of the staircase, legs moving rapidly. He was quickly followed by another shadow, and then another. The dark shapes turned the corner quickly at the rail to race down the steps to the lower level. But halfway down the man in the lead suddenly slowed as he emerged into the light. Those behind him were forced to do likewise, but they had to make an obvious effort to catch their balances and slow their momentum. Dressed in cream-colored suit pants, and calf-colored dress shoes, Nelson Wong paused theatrically to size up the room below as he fastened the gold cufflinks on his white dress shirt. Behind him, dressed in a black shirt with a gray vest and matching slacks, the one called Charlie tucked in his shirt into his waistband. Next to him was Louie, the one Alan and Vera had trailed to Chang's shop. He was also pulling together his outfit, which consisted of a light gray woolen suit with two-toned leather shoes.

Nelson glanced first at Ben Kearney, and then shifted his gaze to Officer Sullivan. He nodded a greeting to him and then glanced at Vera and Alan. He met Alan's eyes and stared intently. "Mr. Stewart, isn't it?" he asked.

"Good morning, Nelson," Alan said.

"I see you brought your very charming lady friend with you this time," he said, "the one who is so tolerant of your appetite for the special services we offer here. So was there a problem with the woman you visited while you were here?" Nelson asked. "I believe she was one of those the police officers arrested last night."

"Your sister Lynn is fine," said Alan, "but that's not why we're here."

Nelson smiled indulgently. "Then why are you here?"

"We've come with another Habeas Grabus," said Kearney, "and this one's for you."

Nelson shifted his glare to Kearney. "And why would you have a Habeas—whatever that is—for me?"

Kearney glanced around the room conspicuously, as if making a point. "This is a conversation we really should be having in private, Nelson. I'm sure you don't want the whole world to know your business. We should discuss this downtown."

"The House of Wong is not the whole world," said Nelson. "You have my permission to discuss this publicly with me, in front of family and friends, in the here and now."

Kearney glanced back to the others with him, as if giving them an opportunity to interject an idea that would keep him from heading down the inevitable path they were taking. "Alright Nelson, have it your way. We're here to talk to you about the murder of Police Officer Charles Sawyer, otherwise known to you as Charlie or Hacksaw Sawyer. Do you still want to talk about it here?"

Noisy chatter erupted behind them at the tables where the kitchen help was eating. The conversations were in Chinese, but they had understood what Kearney had said to Nelson Wong in English.

Nelson raised his brow and glared disapprovingly at the

kitchen staff, his glare sufficing to quiet them.

"What makes you think I would know anything about Hack Sawyer's murder? I believe that happened when I was a child, perhaps a teenager, no more than sixteen."

He redirected the question, Alan thought. *He didn't answer it.* Alan remembered discussing interrogations with his father, Mackie, who had told him that good detectives were alert for that ploy when interviewing a suspect. "A man with something to hide won't answer you directly," Mackie had said. "He'll ask you something far less important, to keep you at a distance, like what's the basis of your knowledge or something abstract in a detached way. A guilty man avoids saying the obvious, such as: 'I didn't do it,' because he needs to work himself up for the lie. Instead, he saves his clear denial until long after it should have been made."

"Your age at that time might be of interest to the courts who'll decide your fate at trial," said Kearney, "but common knowledge tells us that even a young man is capable of pulling a trigger and shooting a man in the face."

Again the tables behind them with the kitchen help erupted with raised voices. In front and to their left, up the stairs, Alan sensed the presence of more people arriving. The audience was growing.

"After all," Kearney continued, "just look at Billy the Kid. By most accounts he was a nice enough fellow who shot a score of men, his first while still in his teens."

"I am not a cowboy," said Nelson, "and this is not your Wild West. I am a civilized Chinese man. You should know better than to believe anything Mei told you about me. After all, she is a common prostitute."

"But she's your sister," said Vera. "How could you call her that? You pimp her and would throw her to the dogs, but she stuck up for you. She made excuses for you. She said you shot Charlie because you thought he was hurting her."

"He was hurting her!" Nelson snapped angrily. "He was a vile man who had his hands around her…"

"Throat?" asked Kearney.

"Yes, her throat," said Nelson, sighing with resignation. "Her eyes were bulging out and rolling upward into her head, and her face was turning blue."

"Not a pretty sight indeed," said Kearney, "but you shouldn't have shot Charlie.

"What would you have had me do?" asked Nelson scornfully. "I had warned her that he could be dangerous."

"We understand you're quite skilled in Kung Fu," said Kearney. "I imagine that if you had used some of that while yelling at Sawyer to stop him, we wouldn't be here now."

"How did you get in the garage?" asked Alan.

Nelson glared at Alan again. "So, you are with the police?" he asked.

"Private detective," Alan said. "Miss Deward and I have been retained by an individual, whose name we can't divulge. We're working this case independently of the police. Today, however, we happen to be working together."

Again, he re-directs the question, Alan thought, *but then I gave him a roundabout answer too.*

"Sergeant McMurphy opened the garage for me," said Nelson.

"Why?" asked Alan.

Nelson brought up his hands like a music conductor getting his orchestra's attention. "No more questions," he said, as he beckoned for Charlie and Louie to join him on the floor.

"I'm sorry to disappoint you officers and detectives," Nelson said, "but I have other business that demands my attention this morning. Charlie and Louie will see you to the door."

Nelson turned sharply and his eyes betrayed the

direction he intended to go. Officer Sullivan sidestepped quickly and blocked the route to the stairs that led below, as well as keeping Nelson away from the hallway that led to passages unknown. Kearney also shot forward, like a huge defensive lineman at the snap of a football. Nelson countered his move and brought him to a halt by dropping low and putting up his hands up in a bladed fashion, assuming a martial arts stance, alerting everyone that there would be a battle before he allowed himself to be taken.

Nelson's friend Charlie took a similar position to his leader, jumping in-between Kearney and his quarry, indicating that the big man was going to have to go through him first to get at the young boss. Vera had also reacted quickly and was now circling the group—tiger like, herding her prey—while also approaching Kearney's side.

"Don't let him get inside the walls!" Alan shouted past the others to Officer Sullivan, "or we'll never find him."

Louie struck a similar martial arts pose to his compatriots and glared menacingly at Alan, who brought up his fists like the Golden Glove boxer he was. "So, you know Kung Fu," said Louie, evaluating Alan's hand position as he balled them into fists, while rolling his shoulders and squaring them to him.

"Kung Fu, my ass!" said Alan, seeing that Louie was focused on his hands, not his eyes. *Big mistake!* Alan thought, seizing the moment and driving his right fist through the opening provided by Louie's bladed hands and vacuous stare, crashing a powerful haymaker on the thug's nose, snapping his head back, dropping him like a sack of rocks on the stairs behind him.

Next to him, Charlie's eyes bulged wide and his head jerked quickly to the side to watch his playmate's collapse, and his jaw moved just in time to catch the full force of Vera's left foot as she kicked upward ferociously, planting the side of her foot on the bottom of Charlie's face, cracking teeth and sending him reeling. Charlie staggered backward a few steps, before his legs buckled and he dropped to the floor, landing in a kneeling position, wavering a moment, then keeling over on his side and flopping to the carpet like a sea lion on the beach.

Sullivan spun his baton back and forth rapidly, fanning it menacingly in front of Nelson, before catching it and spinning it again, while he jockeyed to keep the young man away from the stairs and back from the side hallway. As Kearney raised his huge leg to step over Charlie, who lay like a giant sequoia on the brothel's floor, the big thug lurched and wrapped his fat arm around Kearney's leg, tripping the over-sized detective. Kearney's momentum caused him to fall forward, crashing to the floor in front of Nelson Wong.

Vera deftly leaped over Kearney's sprawled out figure, and she unleashed a wicked kick that struck hard at the side of Charlie's head, catching him solidly on the ear, rattling his noggin with a whump. Charlie's eyes rolled shut and his arm fell away from Kearney's leg, flopping limply to the floor.

Behind the pile of bodies littering the carpet, Jai Wong, clad in regal silks, jumped over Louie's unconscious form and landed on the floor close to Alan, forcing him to pivot around, stand his ground, and raise his fists again to protect Detective Kearney.

"What's the meaning of this?" Jai roared.

"Stay out of this, lad!" Sullivan yelled. "This is police business, We mean to take Nelson into custody for the murder of Hack Sawyer."

No sooner had those words left Sullivan's lips than Nelson dropped close to the floor in a squat, put his hands down for balance, and with one leg extended he spun around lightning quick and caught Sullivan from behind, sweeping his feet out from under him, which caused him to fall backward and crash ingloriously to the floor.

Almost before Sullivan landed on his back and elbows, Nelson was already springing to his feet. He dashed down the short hallway, slowing briefly to grab a fire ax from the emergency display, which also held a pressurized fire-extinguisher can. Nelson raced ahead with the ax, put a hand down on the railing that protected the stairs, and leapt over it, landing several steps down the flight that led to the lower level, which would take him out into the catacombs.

Alan tore off after Nelson, running toward the hallway. He stomped hard on top of Charlie's back, like it was a boulder in a stream, using him to skip across the other bodies that were covering the floor. Not knowing the staircase as well as Nelson did, Alan ran to the end of the wooden railing, where he grabbed the post and pulled himself around it, launching his body down the stairs. As he was letting go of the stair post, he felt Vera's hand grabbing the well-polished chunk of wood where his had just been. She was hot on his heels. Half way down the stairs Alan saw what was ahead and he came to an abrupt stop, with Vera doing the same.

Just beyond the foot of the stairs and to the left, Nelson Wong was again squatting into a Kung Fu stance. He scooted to the side crablike, trying to get past someone who was blocking his way. Instead of his hands being in the open bladed position, this time they were wrapped around the end of the red handle to the ax, which he was swinging in large arcs, crisscrossing on either side of his body, keeping a figure in silk robes away from him.

Alan inched lower on the steps, and his hand grasped the hilt of his .45 semi-automatic, making sure he was ready, just in case Nelson decided to retrace his steps and come his and Vera's way with the ax.

As Alan stepped far enough below the main floor, he

recognized the specter in the silk robes beyond him. It was his old friend, Shifu. Alan knew better than to call his name, because that might serve only to distract him, giving Nelson the little opportunity he needed to gain an advantage.

Vera slid up close to Alan and spoke in a low tone. "Keep your pistol in the low ready position. If he attacks with the ax, take him down immediately. Don't take any chances."

Alan nodded and drew his Colt, as Vera had suggested, never taking his eyes off of Nelson Wong, who abruptly stopped swinging the ax. He now took to making thrusting motions at Shifu's face and arms, trying to push him away from the front door. To Alan's side, Vera slid over the railing and dropped to the floor, landing softly as a cat.

"You have again dishonored the House of Wong," said Shifu to Nelson. "You are to lay down your weapon and surrender."

"Don't give me that crap, old man," said Nelson. "I see nothing honorable about spending my life in a prison cell, especially since what I did was a favor for someone else, and it benefitted the House. I have beat you before, and I will beat you again."

"You are young and you might be able to beat me, since you refuse to fight with honor and dignity, but it will come at a price for you. If you get by me, you'll know you have been in a fight."

Alan heard a clanking to his right, but his mind tried to ignore it, knowing full well that Vera was there and quite capable of taking care of herself. But then, this was Vera, and he had to know how she was doing, what she was up against. He brought the pistol up a little higher, aiming it now at the floor just in front of Nelson's feet, and then he stole a sideways glance in her direction. She was standing next to a mannequin in full Chinese armor, on the side of the staircase, where she had just finished prying a spear with a bladed edge from the menacing figure's gauntlets. Vera took the weapon, a pudao, by its long shaft and heaved it blunt-edged first towards Shifu, like it was a piece of driftwood for a beach fire. The pudao bounced on the carpet and skipped toward the Kung Fu master. Nelson Wong spun on his heel and stared in Vera's direction, apparently to assess the new threat, and then he instantly realized his mistake. By the time he turned back to face Shifu, the smaller man had the pudao firmly in his grip and was assuming an en garde position.

Shifu stood erect, set the butt end of the pudao on the carpet, and spun the weapon in his hands so that the bladed edge moved in a blur.

"Of course you know the armor was my grandfather's, and he taught me how to use this when I was a young man," Shifu said thoughtfully. "I see it still has the keen edge I put on its blade. The advantage is now mine, and I would suggest you surrender while all of your limbs remain attached to your body."

Shifu thumped the butt of the pudao on the carpet, brought it up, twirled it in a circle, tucked the shaft under his arm and thrust the blade out towards Nelson. "Lay down the ax now!" he demanded.

Nelson's shoulders sagged slightly, and the grip on his ax softened, but otherwise he didn't budge.

Shifu took three steps forward, his weight on the balls of his feet, which never crossed one in front of the other. He kept the bladed weapon pointed at Nelson's face. Nelson exhaled heavily and lowered the fire ax from port arms to where it crossed just in front of his hips. Then he let the bladed end sag toward the floor and dropped it noisily, the heavy end making a thud, and the handle a thwap as it struck the carpet.

Shifu spun the pudao in his hand, the edged end still

pointed at Nelson's face. "Step away from the ax and lie down on the floor," he said. "Do it now."

Nelson stepped backward, one pace and then another. Shifu matched him step for step. Nelson knelt down, first one knee, and then the other, like a priest saying mass at St. James Cathedral, or so Alan thought. Then he rolled forward and caught himself with his arms, lowering himself to the floor.

Knowing that Vera would watch his back, Alan holstered his Colt and descended the stairs rapidly. He took out the handcuffs Chief Ketchum had given him, when he had presented Alan with the "tools of persuasion." He grabbed hold of Nelson's left arm and drew it down behind his back, and ratcheted a handcuff around it. He then reached up for the other hand, pulled it down to match up with the other, and cuffed it securely in place.

Alan slid his hand between Nelson's right arm and his side, cupped him around his bicep, and helped lift him to his feet. "Let's head on upstairs," Alan said, "and see what carnage you left on the floor."

When Vera and Alan reached the top step and turned the corner at the rail post, Big Ben Kearney squinted in their direction and called out to them. "Are you two all right?"

Alan pushed Nelson slightly ahead of him and Vera on the narrow hallway, showing off their prize. Kearney smiled broadly and nodded his approval. "Good job, you two."

"We had a little help," Vera said, as they caught up to Kearney and Sullivan.

Sitting handcuffed on the staircase in front of them, Charlie sat with glazed eyes, the crotch of his pants torn out, exposing his meaty thigh and his boxer shorts. Next to him Louie sat slumped over, a trail of blood coming out of his nose. Over by the kitchen Jai Wong stood next to Goon Dip, who was also attired in regal silks. Goon Dip was animated, gesticulating heavily with his arms to make a point. He was either giving Jai a piece of his mind, or he was instructing him emphatically on his new responsibilities as manager.

"Nice right cross," said Kearney to Alan. "You clocked him a good one. His nose will either have a new bump or a crooked bend to it, which just might keep him from being the new starlet on his cell block."

Louie glared up at Kearney and shook his head foggily.

"How're you doing, Sully?" Vera asked.

"I've got a pain in my tailbone, darling. I'm sure it's broken."

"I'm sorry to hear that," Vera said. "Is there anything I can do for you?"

Officer Sullivan grinned painfully. "You don't want me to answer that right now, do you" he asked. "I could think of a few dozen possibilities, especially given the nature of my injury, but you're a lady, one I've always admired, so I won't press the matter."

Vera smiled with a bit of a blush. *She's embarrassed*, Alan thought. *Another rare moment where she's been caught off guard. How about that?*

"And Vera," said Kearney. "That was a wicked roundhouse kick you gave Charlie! It caught him and me by surprise. I'm very impressed. I don't think I ever saw anything that spectacular in all my years wrestling. Of course all our moves were choreographed and rehearsed, but still, that was a thing of beauty."

"Thank you, Ben."

Ben reached out and clasped his paw firmly on Nelson's shoulder, his finger and thumb securely clamped into Nelson's trapezius muscle. "We'll finish our discussion later in the holding cells, but right now I want to know where our old friend Knuckles McMurphy is staying."

"You mean you don't know?" asked Nelson.

Kearney shook his head. "No, Nelson, why would I?"

"He tells me he sees you all the time when you're walking the beat."

Kearney knitted his brow low as he thought. "I've run into him a few times down here," said Kearney, "but we're not what you would call tight friends."

"I suppose he sees you from his room window then," said Nelson. "He's staying around the corner at the Milwaukie, room twenty-five."

"Of course he is," said Kearney, letting go of Nelson's shoulder. "That makes sense. Before the paddy wagon hauls you away, is there anything you'd like to add about Sawyer's shooting—like which one of you fired the second shot?"

Nelson closed his eyes and shook his head. "I've said too much already."

"That second shot was the fatal one, by the way. The coroner told us that Sawyer would have survived the first one. He would've been horribly scarred, like a war veteran, and might have had to wear a tin mask, but he would've made it."

Nelson's mouth sagged open and he stared at Kearney vacuously for a long moment. "I've got nothing more to say."

"Suit yourself."

Big Ben led Vera and Alan through the front door of the Milwaukie Hotel on King Street and headed straight up the stairs. "There's that old expression 'strike while the iron's hot,'" said Kearney, "and although we could use a break, you can't afford to take one in Chinatown. Word's probably already getting around the district about the confab at Goon Dip's. It won't take Knuckles a New York minute to figure we're coming fast for him, and then he'll scoot town."

"I totally agree," said Vera.

Kearney paused on the steps a moment. "The Chinese have their own way of numbering the rooms in these old hotels," he said. "Since the first floor is divided into small shops and retail spaces, the numbers for the rooms on the second floor start with one, and then on the third floor they start with two. It's screwy that way, but of course this building also has a few fake rooms, which are part of the smuggler's passage."

"I've been in those before," said Alan. "Different building but same idea."

Kearney raised an eyebrow. "Is there a story you want to tell us about?" he asked with a knowing smile. "Or is that something

299

you want to keep between yourself and your confessor?"

"Uhm…I think I'll hold onto that story, at least for the present," said Alan and added, hoping to change the subject, "I'm curious why Knuckles would be living in Chinatown."

"You mean living in the heart of the district with all of the Chinese, as opposed to living on Queen Anne Hill where it's all White?"

"Yeah, exactly," said Alan. "I have a friend who used to spend a lot of time down here, but generally speaking, he and I always stood out in the crowd, at least that's the way it was whenever I came down to see him."

"I'm sure he lives here because the rooms are cheap, and so is the food. As I told Nelson, I used to bump into Knuckles every once in a while on the beat, but it was only ever a head nod, nothing more. We were never chummy enough to ask him how he was getting by without a pension. He lost that after he got nailed at the border for smuggling. But back in the day, Knuckles did a lot of bootlegging down here, so he still has his nefarious contacts, like Nelson Wong and the other dirt bags who'd like to be the Taipan of Chinatown."

"Any chance he's living off the stash that should've gone to Sawyer's widow?" asked Vera.

"I'd say no to that," said Kearney. "After all, look at this place. If he'd come into serious money, like what I'd imagine Sawyer would have left, he'd be living uptown in one of those hotels with a view of the bay, like the Sorrento."

The trio stopped before they reached room twenty-five. Kearney indicated for Vera and Alan to stand behind him and not in front of the door. "Safety precaution," he said. "You never know when some bird is going to open up with his .38, shooting through the door. Lath and plaster do a better job of stopping slugs than a thin sheet of pine, but not much."

Kearney rapped on the door with authority. "Open up,

Knuckles. It's Ben Kearney to see ya."

Inside the room a voice rattled and a throat cleared. "Ben?" the voice asked huskily, before clearing again. "What do you want?"

"To talk, of course," said Kearney, "but make sure you're decent. I brought a lady with me who wants to see you."

"A lady?" the voice called out, and the bed springs squeaked.

"Yes indeed. Pretty as a bonnet on Easter morn."

"Thank you, Ben," Vera whispered, and then she smiled sideways at Alan, as if to show off.

"Alright, give me a moment," the voice inside the room said. "I'll put my pants on."

Kearney leaned back and spoke softly. "So far, so good, but keep your hand near your piece," he said with a nod toward Alan's hip, "just in case he opens the door and points one of his own at us. My hands are quick enough, if that happens. I should be able to slap him around a little, should it come to that, but I'd feel bad if this went south, like over at Goon Dip's, and I hadn't given you a heads up first."

Inside the room, the floor squeaked and then the door knob shook slightly, accompanied by the metallic sounds of a bolt being drawn back. The door opened a crack and a face peeked around the door's edge.

"So, where's your uniform?" Knuckles asked.

"In my locker," said Kearney. "This is more of a social call."

The door opened a few more inches.

"Who's the broad?" Knuckles asked.

"She's a lady," said Kearney, "not a broad."

"I'm right here," said Vera, standing behind Alan, both of them in Kearney's shadow.

The door opened wider to reveal the backlit silhouette of a pot-bellied, middle-aged man in need of a shave and a haircut, wearing a suit vest over a sleeveless undershirt

301

tucked into well worn slacks. Knuckles stuck his head out into the hallway as Kearney stepped back and moved closer to the wall.

"A bit late in the day to be getting up," said Vera from the shadows, using her sultry voice.

"Do I know you?" Knuckles asked.

"I'm sure you probably caught my show down on Second Avenue," said Vera, turning on the charm. "Seems like all the coppers dropped by back then. Most of the Dry Squad for sure."

"Burlesque show?" asked Knuckles, brow drawn low. He gazed up at Kearney, whose arms were crossed casually in front of him, stepped past the detective's large frame, and squinted into the darkness at the alluring specter. As Knuckles moved away from his door, Kearney stepped sideways in front of it, spread his feet wide, blocking Knuckle's retreat.

Vera moved forward into the light. "I'm Detective Vera Deward," she said, flashing her private investigator's badge, and this is Detective Alan Stewart. We have a few questions we'd like to ask you."

Knuckles glared at Kearney. "I thought you said this was a social call," he said.

"If you mean 'social,' as in exchanging pleasantries and such, I can do that. How you doing, Knuckles? How's the family? How're the kids? How was the divorce? How're they hanging between your legs? Is that social enough for you?"

Knuckles lowered his head, like a boxer getting ready to bring up his dukes.

"Now that the pleasantries are over," said Kearney, "we've got more pressing questions that need addressing."

"Questions about what?" asked Knuckles, the words almost spitting out of his mouth.

"The night Hack Sawyer was killed," said Kearney.

Knuckles shook his head defiantly and moved toward his door. "The Homicide Captain ruled it a suicide," he said wearily, as if even he doubted it. He made it clear that he wanted to get back in his room, trying to slide around the big detective, but Kearney stood his ground, like a football lineman refusing to give the linebacker a shot at the quarterback.

"Let me by, you big oaf!" demanded Knuckles.

"Hands against the wall and spread 'em," said Kearney. "We've come with a Habeas Grabus for you."

"Don't give me that shit, Kearney. You can't come grabbing me out of a private room. That cockamamie detective shit doesn't work with me. You need a real warrant, not some make believe gibberish—"

"But you're not inside your room anymore," said Kearney. "You're outside in a hallway, which means it's a public area, even if this is a hotel. Therefore, we don't need a warrant."

Knuckles was ten to fifteen years past his fighting prime, but that didn't stop him from sizing up Kearney's jaw for a haymaker. Alan had boxed enough to know the searching gaze, know where the opponent's punch was going to land, and he was eager to jump into this fray as soon as the fists started flying. He already had one knockout this morning. Two would make his day.

"Hands on the wall NOW," Kearney barked, "and if you're thinking about trying one of those cheap shots you're famous for, you better think again. I've already rolled around on the mat this morning, and I've had enough foreplay. You piss me off, and I'll tie your arms and legs into a knot that Houdini couldn't unravel."

Knuckles' shoulders sagged and he slowly spun in place and reached out for the wall, leaning into it slightly.

"Step back further," said Kearney, moving up to reach around the front of Knuckles' left side and begin patting him down. Suddenly, Knuckles dropped his right hand toward his waist and pushed away from the wall with his other hand while trying to spin. Kearney reacted quickly, and with a powerful shove he knocked Knuckles off balance, face first into the wall.

BLAM! A pistol shot roared in the hallway and a bright light flashed under Kearney's arm.

Kearney clamped onto Knuckles' left arm, wrenched it behind his back and punched at the back of his head with his open hand, pounding it into the lath and plaster wall.

Without conscious thought, Alan drew his pistol and stepped in front of Vera, bumping her with his hip, forcing her into Knuckles' room. He brought the Colt .45 up with both hands and moved to the far side of the hallway. He aimed the barrel of the pistol around Kearney squarely at Knuckles' back, high up between the shoulder blades. He slid his index finger into the trigger guard. The pad of the first digit found a familiar spot on the trigger, making itself comfortable and lethal.

BLAM! Another pistol shot rang out, again echoing through the hallway, and bright light flashed against the wall in front of Knuckles' stomach.

In the periphery to Alan's left, sunshine now poured out of twin bullet holes in the room Alan had just shoved Vera into. *So much for lath and plaster offering protection*, Alan thought. There was no margin for error here. Alan determined he would not allow Knuckles another opportunity to hit Vera, wild shot or on purpose.

As Kearney struggled to control the ex-sergeant, he glanced over his shoulder at Alan and shook his head quickly. Without waiting for a response, Kearney wound up for another powerful strike and uncorked an open-handed slam that smashed Knuckles' head into the wall again, this time breaking loose paint and chunks of plaster from the trembling lath work.

Alan watched pensively, ready to squeeze the trigger at any moment, but Knuckles dropped his right arm impotently to his side. Alan followed the hand that posed the greatest threat, adjusted his sights, and focused on Knuckles' shoulder now, still prepared to squeeze a .45 round into the large mass, should the former sergeant try to bring his hand up and shoot from behind his back.

After forcing Knuckles head into the white plaster hole that was now rimmed with blood, Kearney cocked a leg and drove his knee hard into Knuckles' kidney. Knuckles let out a sickening gasp, his knees buckled, and he dropped the pistol to the floor, where it made a double thud, one from the barrel strike of the .38 Colt and the other when the grip tumbled to the carpet strip.

Kearney let go of Knuckles' oily hair, reached down, and grabbed his empty right hand. He jerked it up high behind Knuckles' back, causing him to wince in pain and stand on his toes.

"My nose is broken," Knuckles whined.

"From this angle," said Kearney, "I'd say you're right. That's the second one for us this morning, and the day's still young. But doing it my way probably saved you your miserable life, you pissant. I was half-tempted to step out of the way and let Detective Stewart here dump a full clip into your ass, but I didn't—although I'm not sure why."

Kearney glanced back to check on Alan and then spun the other way to see that Vera also had her .45 out in a high-ready position.

"Champ, why don't you holster your piece and gather up Knuckles' revolver? Vera can cover you while you're at it. Once we know his gun's safe, we'll handcuff him, and then finish the frisk. You never know with a bird like this, he might have another piece tucked away somewhere, like in his underwear."

As Alan picked up Knuckles' revolver, his mind flashed back to when he'd first met Mister Brinkman, the union head, several months ago at Mario's Tailor Shop. While Mr. B's former bodyguards were helping him get fitted for a suit, Alan had spotted a derringer clipped to the union boss's boxer shorts. In retrospect, Alan could see that it was an early warning of the man's dangerousness, but at the time he first saw it he'd chosen to overlook that possibility and simply considered it a part of Mr. B's quirky nature.

Alan slid Knuckles' .38 Colt Police Special into his coat pocket and grabbed hold of his right hand, taking it from Kearney, while the big man pulled handcuffs from somewhere behind, under his suit coat. Kearney brought the cuffs around and drove the case-hardened steel against Knuckles wrist bone, causing the half-moon shaped ratchet to spin through the other side, over the top, and finally latching on Knuckles' wrist. Kearney brought Knuckles' left arm down and repeated the process. Then he stood Knuckles up straight and looked at Alan.

"Do you want to pat him down from here, detective, or do you want me to finish this up?"

"I'll give it a go," said Alan.

Kearney spun Knuckles into the light that was shining through his door. He smiled at Vera. "While you're in there, madam detective," he said, "would you take a quick look around and tell us what you see?"

"For the record, Ben, I was a headline performer, not a madam," Vera said. "Are we looking for anything in particular?"

Kearney grinned at her and wrapped his fingers around the links and swivels to the handcuffs on Knuckles' wrists, while at the same time he tucked his thumb inside the rear waistband of Knuckles' suit pants. He leaned close to Knuckles' ear. "Here's something you're going to hear a lot of in prison: Spread 'em wide, Chuckles."

Knuckles sneered and was slow to respond, like a grade school brat refusing to move without a prod from his teacher. Kearney lost his patience and kicked with the side of his right foot at the soles of Knuckles unlaced shoes, knocking his feet farther apart. First one ankle and then the other, until Knuckles resembled an upside down Y planted in the middle of the hallway.

Kearney nodded to Alan. "Check around his nut sack carefully, and don't be afraid to squeeze anything that seems to be dangling where it shouldn't be. A guy like him couldn't have much of a pecker, but Knuckles will probably call you a queer, to get you to stop your frisk—because he's that kind of guy—but you're better off taking a little name calling now than getting bullied out of doing your job."

Knuckles sneered through lips covered with a bloody discharge from his nose. He blew out contemptuously at what was dripping into his mouth, spraying a bloody mist out in front of him and down on his undershirt.

Kearney spun back toward Vera and tilted his head to the side, as if he was ashamed. "Sorry for the strong language, Vera, but…"

"Don't worry about it, Ben. By now you know what I used to do and where I used to work, so you can imagine that I've heard a lot worse, all before the first intermission."

Kearney nodded his understanding, while Alan went about the pat down, working his way up and down each side of Knuckles. "So, about the room search," he said. "Look for anything that might be a link to Hack Sawyer, because that's why we're here, but if you see any guns or contraband, like narcotics or Chinese lottery tickets, we'll take those too."

"He has another pistol on a stand by the door," Vera said.

"Why am I not surprised?" asked Kearney.

"Hey! Careful with the family jewels!" Knuckles said as he flinched spasmodically.

"Detective Stewart's just late giving you your Christmas goose," said Kearney.

Alan chuckled, letting the tension from the shooting and the earlier fight dissipate with laughter. "I thought while I was down here," he said, "I'd measure your inseam."

"Get your jollies while you can, you little queer," said Knuckles.

Alan glanced up at Kearney, who smiled and shook his head. It was just as he had called it. For an instant the idea of giving Knuckles "jewels" a serious slap with a blackjack occurred to him, but then he thought better of it. There was no sense taking a cheap shot now while Knuckles was so vulnerable. The purpose now would be to make Alan feel better, not help the investigation, so he knew it wouldn't be right. There would be plenty of opportunity for pain compliance later, if he still felt the rage.

Alan finished the pat down, finding no other weapons. As in the other shootings in which he'd been involved, his mind started to replay what had just happened in the hallway. It was like newsreel footage spliced together by a schizophrenic art student. In the first flash, he remembered stepping in front of Vera and bumping her with his hip into Knuckles' room. He realized immediately why he had done that—he wanted to protect her and get her out of harm's way as far and fast as he could. She meant so much to him that he wouldn't be able to stand himself or his life if she wasn't in it. He would gladly take another bullet to save her, but as had happened before, he knew she would scold him later for his actions, reminding him that she didn't need protection during a fistfight, a gun battle, or a profanity duel. She was a savateuse, master of la canne, an excellent marksman, black bag operative, and former headline stripper. She wasn't a delicate flower, or so she had told him, but to him she was his favorite blossom, the finest bloom in any garden he had ever seen.

Kearney pinched hold of Knuckles' waistband and lifted up, allowing Knuckles to draw his legs together again and stand up. "While we have your attention," he said, "is there anything you'd like to say about what happened with Sawyer?"

"You were there when we found the body," said Knuckles. "You know as much as I do."

"So you want to play it that way, do you?"

Knuckles shrugged. "Who's playing? I've got nothing to add?"

"Of course you know you're in for an interrogation, and it could get rough, just like the old days when you used to dish it out."

"But I know all the detectives," Knuckles said, "and cops don't beat on guys who once wore the uniform. I've got nothing to worry about."

"You're probably right about the cops," said Kearney, "but you haven't considered that we have more options. *Two* of us here are not the police."

Kearney spoke to Alan loud enough to make a point with Knuckles. "When we get downstairs, I'll leave *you two* to watch Knuckles while I call Sully and ask him to bring the wagon back for another haul." Then, as if the thought had just occurred to him, "On second thought, Headquarters is just up the hill. A little walk might do us all good. The only problem is that it's raining."

"Come on, Ben, this is Seattle," said Vera with a sly wink. "It's always raining here. You act like you're surprised."

Ben grinned knowingly and then directed his conversation at the back of Knuckles' head. "I was just thinking," said Kearney, "we wouldn't want our prisoner's hair getting all wet, would we? That's all."

"Well, there is a shortcut of sorts," said Vera. "The Champ and I know one that's covered, and it runs all the way up the hill."

"That should work," said Kearney. "But my goal right now is to make sure this dirt bag's attempt to shoot the three of us gets properly reported and thoroughly investigated. He should draw fifteen years in Walla Walla for three counts of felony assault with a firearm, for our assaults alone. So we want it done right. Later, Chief Ketchum, and most likely Sergeant Watkins, will need our statements."

"I wasn't trying to shoot the three of you," said Knuckles. "Just you, you turncoat asshole."

"Aw, Knuckles, why do you have to be that way?" asked Kearney. Now, I'm okay with you calling me an asshole, but why turncoat?"

"Yeah, turncoat," said Knuckles. "Men in blue stand behind men in blue, no matter what—even for the ones who no longer wear the uniform anymore. You don't try to stick a brother officer with some old murder that no one cares about—not then, not now."

"Right you are about loyalty, Knuckles—but that only applies when high crimes, murder, and thievery are not involved. But your logic escapes me here. Personally, I make exceptions when it comes to *fired* coppers who shoot at a *brother officer* in the hallways of the Milwaukie Hotel. Where's your loyalty to the man in blue that you talk about? What you just did goes beyond turncoat to treacherous, you vermin slime.

"So be sure to correct me in front of the judge if I get the loyalty thing wrong, would you please? I'm sure it'll put you in a favorable light when you tell the judge at sentencing that you're above the law, because you once wore a blue uniform once upon a time. Maybe they'll take that into consideration and give you Lieutenant Olmstead's plush cell at McNeil Island Penitentiary."

As they marched down the front stairs of the Milwaukie, Kearney held tight to Knuckles' handcuffs, which were covered over by a suit coat, which Vera draped over the ex-sergeant's shoulders. She and Alan had each tied one of their prisoner's shoes, ignoring the snide remarks about sexual favors he tossed Vera's way. When they reached the bottom step, Knuckles turned to the side and shouldered through the door into the late morning daylight. They traveled another thirty feet, when Kearney steered Knuckles through the door of the last business on the block.

"I thought you might like to sit in on a gambling game," said Kearney with a wicked smile, "while I report your shooting. The gambling's downstairs where they play for chips that don't mean anything, but of course you know that."

Vera winked at Alan, who nodded with a broad grin, not ashamed that he was enjoying this.

"What the hell are you talking about?" asked Knuckles.

Kearney steered the handcuffed Knuckles through the shop's wares and shoved him against the counter in the back, where a Chinese man and woman stared wide-eyed at Kearney.

"I'm not sure you folks remember me," Kearney said

with a forced grin. "But I've been in here with the lovable Irishman, John Sullivan. He's your beat cop. Now my friend and I have a little wager going. I told him that the card game going on downstairs is played just for fun, not high stakes gambling, and that he'd be welcome to sit in and watch a few hands while I take care of some necessary police business upstairs with Officer Sullivan. I brought along two babysitters to make sure Mister McMurphy doesn't wander off into the down-unders and get himself lost or hurt. So drop whatever it is you can afford to break down your brass tube, let the people downstairs know we're coming. We'll give everybody a minute to tidy up: pick up the trash, get the garbage off the floor, sweep up, that kind of thing."

Knuckles twisted angrily in Kearney's grip, but then realized his energy was wasted.

"What the hell do you think you're doing, Kearney? Are you angling for a psych pension?"

"If you were listening, Knuckles, I just told the shopkeepers what we're up to," said Kearney. "Try to keep up with the rest of us, you're lagging behind."

Kearney pulled Knuckles away from the counter and pointed him toward the door at the rear of the shop. Reaching it, Kearney stood Knuckles to the side, pulled the door open, and nudged the ex-cop toward the dark opening, but Knuckles dug in his heels. Kearney quickly raised his thick leg, let go of the handcuffs, and caught Knuckles from behind with a knee spike, lifting him off the floor and sending him reeling into the inky blackness, his feet scrambling to keep his face from doing a plant on the wooden steps below. Knuckles bounced hard off the sidewalls as the stairs turned a ninety degree angle, which led to a dimly lit card room. The only lights that were turned on hung low from the ceiling and had green hoods that directed the light onto green felt covered tables.

314

Vera and Alan followed as Kearney pushed Knuckles again, shoving him out into the middle of the room between the four card tables which were surrounded by surprised Chinese men. The gamblers were mostly older men, and many had their hands placed protectively around their stacks of poker chips, arranged in neat piles in front of them. Unlike any card room any of the detectives had ever been in before, in the middle of the tables upside down fedoras held large quantities of poker chips. *They've taken precautions,* Alan thought, now noticing that each of the players discreetly held cards in their hands. *The hats contain the pot, the wagers from the current hands,* he figured. *The house is ready to pick up the pot and run, if necessary.* Alan snickered quietly, remembering Kearney's story of Sullivan raking all of the chips into the middle of the table in a fit of righteous anger.

Kearney paused and stared at the poker tables. He nodded approvingly.

"This is just as I figured," said Kearney. "There's no gambling going on down here. These men have mended their ways. So I could leave you here, in good conscience, Knuckles, and not worry about your morals being corrupted. But the problem is there is no room at these tables for you to sit in on a few hands. So we'll have to move somewhere else and see if we can find you another game."

"What kind of game are you playing, Kearney?" asked Knuckles.

It's called rattling your cage, Alan thought, but kept it to himself.

Kearney steered Knuckles through the table and pushed him up against the far wall. About four feet up the wall was a varnished trim board that ran across the wainscoting. Kearney studied the trim board for a brief moment, slid his hand across it, and pulled it down like a lever. A door sized section of the paneling swung open toward Kearney, and he

315

pulled Knuckles out of the way of it. As soon as it was all the way open Kearney pushed Knuckles in part way and stopped.

"I really should be getting back upstairs to wait for Officer Sullivan," he said. "Do you mind watching our prisoner for me?" he said with a nod to Vera and Alan.

"I think we can handle it from here," said Vera.

"We know a shortcut that will take us most of the way there," said Alan, "near the Panama anyway. He grabbed hold of the handcuffs in the same place Kearney had held them, while he also palmed a blackjack in his other hand. "Give us a head start, and we'll meet you outside the police garage entrance on Fourth Avenue, below the Yesler overpass."

Vera took a lantern off a wooden peg, shook it, and listened to the fuel sloshing around inside. Satisfied she had one that had enough for their purposes, she adjusted the wick and struck a match. As the level of light came up in the spur tunnel leading to the catacombs, the door behind them slowly closed. Alan pulled Knuckles' handcuffed arms out straight behind him and lifted them up, which bent the ex-policeman over at the waist. Alan nudged him forward, and they followed Vera out of the spur.

"There's no need for the rough stuff!" Knuckles said in protest.

Just setting the tone, Alan thought. *I don't need to show him how clever I am. We just need some answers.* Having Knuckles bent over from the waist would make it difficult for their prisoner to retrace their route, Alan figured, should that become an issue.

Vera turned to the right, which Alan figured was north. He and Knuckles followed close on her heels. Judging by the wear on the brick pavers and old fashioned dead reckoning, they were under the alley at the west end of the Milwaukie Hotel building, on their way to Jackson Street. Ahead of them were underground sidewalks, a reminder of Seattle's early re-grading. When they reached the Jackson Street underground sidewalk, Vera turned right, and again Alan and Knuckles followed her closely. Out of curiosity, Alan glanced behind them to the west. That section of sidewalk ran to the end of the block and disappeared. It looked like that was where it became a tunnel, exactly as Kearney had described it. Alan's concern in heading east and then north up the grade was that they were likely to encounter people who habituated the area as regular customers, the fringes of Chinese society.

"What's really going on here?" Knuckles protested. "What kind of game is this?"

"Save your energy," said Alan. "You'll have a chance to talk soon enough, but while I'm thinking of it, do these tunnels look familiar to you at all? From your bootlegging days?"

"I didn't do deliveries or grunt work," Knuckles said. "I was in distribution and management, but I can tell we're heading east, which isn't right. Headquarters is up the hill between Fourth and Fifth."

"We might make a stop on the way," said Alan. "Did you have a fancy title to go with your distribution responsibilities?"

"Yeah—people called me *Sergeant*. So why all the questions, wise guy?"

"I'm the curious type," said Alan, "I was born asking questions."

"Spare me," snapped Knuckles.

"You'll want to save that plea for the judge," said Alan.

"Remind me again: Why aren't we using the paddy wagon?" Knuckles asked, as they trekked up the tunnel underneath Seventh Avenue to South Washington Street. "This isn't proper police procedure."

"We're not the proper police," said Alan, "and the

wagon's tied up with the three arrests we made at Goon Dip's," said Alan.

Knuckles stopped abruptly, and Alan prodded him with a light slap of the sap on his shoulder.

"Was that a blackjack?" asked Knuckles.

"Yes, a gift from a special friend on the department," said Alan as they crested the hill and turned west under Main Street.

"Who was arrested at Goon Dip's?" Knuckles asked. "A customer?"

The walk was easier now that the grade sloped again towards the saltwater, which they could smell on the light breeze from the harbor that coursed through the tunnel. In a moment they would be passing the Buddhist temple they had used on other occasions, although not for the purposes it was intended. Much blood had been shed inside there, mostly that of foreign agents. Alan walked softly, his senses alert for sounds or signs that the temple might be occupied by their enemies. They passed it silently and continued west, down the stretch that Alan knew would lead eventually to the Panama Hotel and its secret portal to the baths underneath the building, but they stopped about a half block short of the hotel's tunnel and turned into a darkened spur that had a thick post with a shelf attached to it. Japanese characters were painted in black on the beam above the post. The shelf held a small white bowl containing sand that had several burned out incense sticks sticking out of it.

Vera ran her hand over the top of the incense stubs. Alan knew she was checking to see if any of the sticks had burned recently, indicating guests might be paying their respects to bodies interred inside.

"We arrested Nelson Wong and his two sidekicks, Charlie and Louie something-or-other," said Alan.

318

Knuckles stuck his jaw out defiantly toward Alan and tilted his head angrily. "No one from the House of Wong has ever been arrested before," he said. "They've paid good money and have earned their protection."

"All that money they've paid over the years didn't seem to help them this time," said Alan.

"Your friend Ben Kearney is full of himself, and he's gotten in way over his head," said Knuckles. "Do you two amateurs know what the hell you're doing down here in Chinatown where people disappear, die tragically, and sometimes both? Do you know who you're going to piss off?"

"Right now, I figure you, Goon Dip, Nelson, Charlie, Louie, and why don't we throw in Hungry Harry," said Vera. "Who're we missing here?"

Knuckles worked his mouth like he was chewing on something hard to swallow. "Most of the police department brass, the Mayor, two thirds of the City Council. Do you want their names?"

"You'll get a chance to name names with the Inquiry Judge," said Vera. "We weren't retained for that part of the business."

Vera unlatched the heavy black door and pushed it open into the haunting darkness that seemed to suck them inward. The hinges groaned wearily, indicating their lack of use. Knuckles scrunched his nose, frowned, and moaned loudly. "This place stinks of death," he said.

Vera swung the lantern ahead of them, and its dim light cast a fleeting glow over a crowded chamber of skeletal bodies wrapped in shrouds, stacked one on top of the other, piled high on shelves carved out of the hillside rock under what was left of Seattle's First Hill.

"It's a Japanese burial crypt," said Alan. "If you think this is bad, you ought to smell the new one where the decay

319

is in full bloom." Alan prodded Knuckles forward into the claustrophobic little room, spun him around, and pushed him backward against a stack of bodies.

"I thought the Japanese cremated their dead," said Knuckles, his voice wavering for the first time.

"I believe their families do that when the bodies are shipped home to them," said Vera as she pushed the door closed behind them. "I have no idea what they do for their sons when they die on foreign soil and everyone wants to keep that fact hidden."

Knuckles scowled momentarily, and then his eyes darted around, as if he were looking for an avenue of escape. "All right," he said, taking short shallow breaths. "There's not much air in here, and it doesn't seem like there's been any for a long time."

"These fellas don't seem to need it," said Alan.

"I'm not interested in your jokes or your tomfoolery. I just want to know what the hell's going on, and what you want from me."

"Cops handle shooting and dead body calls all the time," said Alan, "We're here about one you mishandled."

"Is that right?" Knuckles asked weakly, his obvious attempt at sarcasm falling short.

"Yes, it is," said Alan. "We want to know what you did after you found Hack Sawyer the first time—before you found him again with Ben Kearney? We know Nelson Wong shot Hacksaw in the face. He admitted that, but we have two people telling us that Sawyer wasn't dead until you got to him."

"Sure he was," said Knuckles.

Alan shook his head and slapped his hand lightly with the back end of the sap, having learned the hard way that a similar slap with the business end could be quite painful. "You gave Nelson Wong and his sister Mei a ride up there

320

so they could meet with Sawyer and deliver a package of photographs, isn't that right?"

Knuckles eyebrows flared high on his brow, and then as if he realized that his body language was giving his inner thoughts away, he forced a frown and shook his head. "She's his sister? I didn't know that."

"Oh? We thought you did," said Alan, "but maybe you just never asked." Alan leaned closer, the lantern giving his face an eerie glow with exaggerated shadows. "Now what about the ride up there—and the package that you took from the car after Sawyer was shot?"

I don't know...what you're...talking about," Knuckles said, short of breath.

Alan sighed heavily, and his exasperation echoed throughout the tiny room of nearly skeletal corpses. "Sure you do," Alan said. "We have a signed statement from Mei. She said that right after she went out to your car she heard the shot and saw a muzzle flash inside the garage."

"That could have been Nelson..." said Knuckles.

"We don't buy that," said Vera. "If Nelson would have shot Sawyer a second time—in front of you—then you would have been derelict in your duties if you hadn't arrested him, you being the good copper you keep telling us you were. And since you covered up the shootings, we figure there was more going on here than what Nelson told us. The two of you went up to the garage intent on whacking Hacksaw while he was having sex with Mei. However, we don't think she knew what her role was to be in Hack's murder."

Knuckles head lowered, he grimaced, and a high-pitched wheezing accompanied his breathing. "Do we have to... have this conversation...in here?" he asked in a voice just above a whisper.

"We know you unlocked the door and let Nelson inside the garage. Why'd you do that?"

"This must be what…hell is like," Knuckles said in a painful whisper. "I need air,"

Vera held the lantern close to Knuckles' face. "Do you have asthma?"

Knuckles nodded with a grimace. "Not often. Just when I'm around dust and mold."

"Well, there's a lot of that here," Vera said. She glanced at Alan and rolled her head, indicating the door behind them. "This is worse than a beating for him."

Alan reached up, touched her face, and pulled it close to his so he could whisper in the tight quarters. "It's painful to watch. He's likely to topple over and give up the ghost right in front of us."

Alan raised his voice slightly for Knuckles benefit. "I vote we head toward the waterfront. If he still won't talk, he can take a harbor swim with the handcuffs on."

"I'll talk," said Knuckles. "I just need air…but you can't tell anyone…about my condition."

"Your asthma?" asked Vera.

"Exactly," said Knuckles. "No one is to know…about my weakness."

"Deal," said Alan, "as long as you don't hold nothing back."

The trio walked painfully slow down the low grade toward the saltwater in the brick-lined tunnel, with Alan helping to hold Knuckles up. The ex-sergeant's high-pitched breathing gradually began to improve the farther they got away from the crypt and the closer they got to the Panama Hotel's side spur. Alan and Vera knew this area well, and again they walked softly as they passed the familiar entrance, with Vera holding the lantern close to the brick pavers, checking for recent foot traffic. Gunny had shown them how to do this on another occasion at this same location.

They continued down the tunnel, past Sixth Avenue, and here the slope increased. Knuckles breaths grew deeper and the wheezing lessened as the tunnel leveled off at Fifth Avenue. "Police Headquarters should be two blocks up the hill," Alan said, "but we're not going there until we're done talking—in case you need a reminder."

"My chest is still tight, but I can talk."

Vera slowed to a stop, and Knuckles leaned back into the slope of the arched tunnel walls. He slid down the wall to the brick pavers into a squat, his legs spread wide to allow his diaphragm and belly to expand freely.

"You remember the question?" Alan asked.

"Yeah," Knuckles said. "Why I let Nelson in… Someone, and I ain't going to say who—but you know him—told Nelson and me to take care of a problem for him. It was about the pictures, but you know that. I was just supposed to supervise is all, make sure the kid did what he was supposed to do, and then make sure the pictures didn't get left behind.'

"What did you two get out of it?" asked Alan.

"For me, it was securing a spot in the new organization, the one that replaced Sawyer's, which was essentially Olmstead's. For Nelson, it was his coming out party—his chance to stick it to his old man, whom he hates, by the way. I think he got two grand and favorable terms from his new partners, but you'll have to ask him about that."

"So who pulled the trigger the second time?" asked Alan. "You never said."

Knuckles head dropped forward and he shook it sadly. "I'm a dead man, so what does it matter? Anyway you look at it, I'm going to prison, and the boys will be waiting for me with their cocks in their hands, smiles on their faces. Do you know what they do to ex-cops in prison?"

He's being deliberately evasive, Alan thought. *He doesn't want to touch that question.*

"We've heard," said Vera.

"I might as well pack a dress in my suitcase, because I'll be the new princess bride for anyone big enough to reach my behind."

"Like the lady said, we get the picture," said Alan.

"The gallows just might be my ticket out of there," said Knuckles. "I'd rather drop through the trap door with a noose around my neck then have to spend a week in the general population at Walla Walla."

"I heard that coppers go to McNeil Island," said Alan,

324

"but it's probably the same difference."

"Walla Walla is where the executions are," said Knuckles. "That's what the Prosecutor would want."

"So, what about it?" Alan asked. "Who fired the second shot?"

"What's it matter?" asked Knuckles. "I'm going to die anyway."

"It matters to us that this case is solved correctly so the widow gets Sawyer's pension," said Alan. "The police can't take their case to court and say, 'It was sort of like this and kinda like that.' That just won't work."

"He's right, you know," said Vera. "To convince a jury, the police will have to show what really happened. Half-told tales and theories about what should fill in the blanks doesn't work, otherwise a rookie attorney could run circles around them."

Knuckles sighed heavily, his lungs working better now. "Me," he said. "I'm the one who betrayed a brother in blue."

"Why?" asked Alan.

"We were going to move Sawyer to his car and then drive it into the ship canal, at least that was our plan. I grabbed Hack's legs, and Nelson was going to lift him from behind, reaching under his arms, and pull him out his side of the car, because he had the heavy end. But as soon as we spun him around, Hack kicked at me with his legs, pushing me back, and his hand went inside his coat. He pulled his piece, and at first I thought he might shoot me. So I grabbed his revolver, took it away from him, but then I got to thinking it was time to end this. Nelson knows this. I'm surprised he didn't tell you. His face was just over Hack's shoulder, so he saw it coming. If I had missed Hack, I would've drilled him a good one."

"So, there was no pretense that you were there to help Sawyer and it was some kind of self-defense?" asked Vera.

"I wasn't there to help him," snapped Knuckles. "We went there to ice him, and the kid screwed up. It was my job to fix it, and to do it quickly. I know this sounds hollow, but I actually thought I was speeding up the process and saving Hacksaw from more misery, like when you put a dog down that's been hit by a car and hurt so bad you know it's going to die no matter what you do."

"Sawyer may not have had a lot of friends, but he was no dog," said Vera.

"Of course I realize that, and I know a jury would have no sympathy for me using that as my reason. I'm not trying to excuse what I did, I'm just explaining to you what I was thinking. If I had waited for Nelson to pull out his piece again and shoot Sawyer a second time, there would have been undue suffering."

"You're quite the humanitarian," said Alan.

"So what you're saying," said Vera, "is you just wanted to end this nasty business quickly?"

"There's no other way to sweeten the bitter taste," said Knuckles. "After all, I'm a logical man. I've always been. I know what I did was wrong, and I deserve to die. With that said, I'm not in a particular hurry to get it done. But knowing what's in store for me in jail, the newspapers, the trial, and what my time in prison would be like before they hang me, quicker might be more humane for me too. One of you could do me a favor and end it for me now."

"I'm afraid that's a service we don't provide," said Vera. And then she leaned close to Alan's ear. "Be careful with him," she whispered. "Listen carefully to what he's saying. He's desperate, and he might deliberately instigate something to make us do what we don't want. Like he said, if we shoot him, we spare him the agony."

Alan chewed on his lower lip as he listened to Vera, and then he nodded his agreement.

"I've got a couple more questions that need answering," said Alan. "First, where did Nelson get the gun he used?"

"I gave it to him."

"And where did *you* get it?" asked Alan.

"From the man who asked me to take care of his problem," Knuckles said. "And to cut right to the point, knowing where you're headed, it's a department gun. Somebody in the property unit loaned us a gun a retired officer had just turned in. Later, I returned it to where I got it, and it's been re-issued since. Some cop who doesn't know the difference is walking around with it on his hip."

"Were you going to frame somebody?" Alan asked.

"That was a possibility, yes, but it didn't happen. Now you've got me, so it really doesn't matter."

"How about the pieces of the slug that went into Evidence," said Alan, "what happened to them?"

"We got word in '32 that J. Edgar Hoover and the Feds could do wonders with bullets in the lab they were making. They could tell what gun they came from, if they had left or right twist to the rifling, that kind of thing, so a friend made sure the pieces disappeared."

Alan nodded thoughtfully at Vera. This meant that Chief Ketchum was wrong about their disappearance, and the problems on his department ran deeper than he might have imagined.

"Doesn't sound like the department put much effort into this investigation," said Vera.

"Not at all," said Knuckles.

"How about the spent shells?" asked Alan. "How'd the first one that Nelson fired end up in Sawyer's revolver?"

"When he gave me the gun back, I switched it out."

"And since you shot Sawyer with his own gun," Alan said, thinking out loud, "you didn't need to make it look like the gun had been fired, because it actually had been."

"To be honest, I really didn't worry about that," said Knuckles. "I'd already figured that Sawyer had probably fired his gun recently enough and not bothered to clean it, and at the same time our crime lab was nothing to brag about. I bet right now if you were to pop a surprise inspection on any squad of officers around the department, probably thirty percent would have dirty guns—and half of them would have empty cartridges in their cylinders that they hadn't bothered to replace."

"Why's that?" asked Vera.

"Anything from boredom, to drinking, to chasing hobos on the rails, to target practice on wharf rats, to shooting at fleeing suspects who got away—when you don't want anyone to know you missed. A lot of that never gets reported."

"Alright," said Alan, "are you able to walk now?"

"Yeah, thanks for getting me out of there," said Knuckles.

Alan nodded, not knowing what to say to Knuckles, after all it was he and Vera who had put him in the claustrophobic crypt.

"And just so you know," said Knuckles, "that tough guy treatment doesn't work on me. I've dished out my share of abuse during my days. I've busted knees and noggins. I know how to drag confessions out of the unwilling. Doctors would say I'm a mean cuss because I took a shit pot full of beatings as a kid. The point is: I know how the game is played. You could've beat me until I was unconscious, and you still wouldn't have gotten diddly squat. I would take a beating just to prove my toughness. I wouldn't have given you the satisfaction of breaking me. My satisfaction would've been in proving you couldn't do it. I'm contrary that way.

"I only told you what I did because I could see you didn't

have it in you to hammer on me—which means you have a heart—which I always thought was a weakness. You have your soft sides—both of you. You had me on the ropes with my asthma and could have let me suffer and die inside that hell hole, but you didn't. But because you didn't, that as much as anything else is why I talked."

Vera leaned closed to Alan's ear and whispered. "There's no sense cracking his knee just to show him he's wrong, but still, I've got a lot to learn. Who would've thought kindness would have worked on him?"

"Double that for me," said Alan.

"So where's this tunnel come out?" asked Vera.

"Under the Mount Fuji Hotel," said Knuckles, speaking up. "Occidental and Yesler."

Vera and Alan both stared, puzzled, at their prisoner. "You've been through here before?" asked Alan.

"Yeah, this part of it, anyway, but telling you why is not part of our deal."

Knuckles' information about there being a portal to the catacombs under the Mount Fuji Hotel was accurate. Vera and Alan brought him up through its basement out onto Yesler Way, half way between First Avenue and Occidental, while catching only a curious glance from a tenant in the lobby. They walked him up to Third and cut across to Terrace Street, a direct route to the police garage entrance underneath the overpass. Detective Kearney was already waiting for their arrival. He smiled patiently as they crossed Fourth, and Alan was relieved that Kearney didn't badger them with the expected taunt: "What took you so long?"

Kearney scrutinized Knuckles from head to toe, checking for new injuries, ignoring the obvious broken nose. He gazed at Alan and Vera and shrugged his shoulders, "You get what you needed?" he asked.

"Most of it," said Vera. "We'll catch you up, after he's booked."

"Speaking of which," said Kearney. "Jail's no place for a lady. I'm not trying to be chivalrous here, it's just a fact of life. The Champ can go with me, the jailers won't care, but someone as pretty as you would cause a cell block riot."

Vera smiled self-consciously. "Well thank you, Ben, but

I'm not sure whether I'm flattered or not."

"Why don't we meet you in the lobby, instead, or up in Chief Ketchum's office." said Kearney.

"Let's make it the lobby," said Vera. "That way we can all walk up together and give Mike the news."

A turnkey opened the heavily greased lock of the wrought iron door and greeted the trio with a pleasant grin, nodding a hello to Kearney and Knuckles, calling the prisoner by his name. Then he gazed at Alan, questioningly.

"He's with me," said Kearney preemptively, with a nod towards Alan.

Kearney pushed Knuckles ahead of them into the reception area, and the turnkey's eyes dropped down Knuckles arms to where his hands should be, following the empty sleeves around to his back where his hands were manacled, hidden under a suit coat. Kearney prodded Knuckles ahead to an open booking window. The turnkey followed them to the counter, like a curious puppy.

The booking officer, whose sewn-on name tag said Meyer, nodded at Kearney and greeted Knuckles by name, who responded in kind. A sergeant rose from a table somewhere in back and moved up next to Meyer.

Meyer licked his lips and stared blankly at Kearney. "First, Sully brings in a load of your fish from Chinatown," he said. "Didn't you catch your limit with the Chinese, Ben? Couldn't you just leave it at that?"

"Felony booking," said Kearney flatly. "Suspicion of Murder."

Meyer rolled his tongue around his cheeks as he thought. "And what murder would that be?" he asked. "The Chinese guy was already booked for murdering Hack Sawyer."

"That information's not necessary for the booking

forms," said Kearney. "What's required is the date, time, location, charge, and suspect's identifying information."

Meyer shifted his weight and glanced toward his sergeant.

The sergeant leaned forward. His nametag identified him as Qualls. "Who's screened these arrests you're making?" he asked.

"Chief of Detectives Michael Ketchum," said Kearney in a loud clear voice.

Qualls closed his eyes and nodded as he thought. "So you won't mind, Ben, if I give him a call?"

"Well, Sarge, actually I do mind," said Kearney, "but go ahead if you must. You could also check with your jail commander, if you'd like. Lieutenant Harry Frantz, isn't it?"

Meyer spread his hands out and pushed away from the counter, as if he were trying to work up the courage to glare at the much larger Kearney, who smiled back contentedly, like a poker player with a pat hand, one which really held all the cards.

Alan swallowed automatically, felt his face flush, and the hairs on his scalp tingle with anticipation. This was a chance meeting he hadn't anticipated. He glanced back at the turnkey behind him, knowing whose side he would take if Frantz wanted him arrested for assaulting him in the months back. Alan had tried to kill Frantz, shooting him twice, no less—both times head wounds. The last shot, with a rifle, was nearly fatal. Alan's actions had crashed much of what was left of Hungry Harry's empire, exposing him as vulnerable to his legion of supporters.

Alan had forgotten that Chief Ketchum said he was going to assign Frantz to the jail as its new commander, when Harry recovered well enough to return to duty. Although Alan and Frantz had never met face to face, Harry would obviously recognize Alan because of the strong resemblance to his late father, McAlister Stewart. Alan had learned from his sister Margie's snooping through the family home that Harry had once been the rival for the affections of Mary, Alan's mother.

Qualls picked up the phone on the desk behind the counter and dialed four numbers and turned away to face the window. As he talked, Qualls' hand moved up and down emphatically, before he ran it through his hair, and then bunched it into a fist and planted it on his hip. A moment later he nodded and glanced to his left through an open door into an adjoining room. He acknowledged someone inside with more nods. Finally, Qualls set the phone back in its cradle, and the man in the office walked out casually, sipping a cup of coffee.

Hungry Harry tilted his head back as if he'd just asked Meyer a question and was expecting an answer. Qualls said something to him, accompanied by a head shake that showed disgust, not disagreement. Frantz stared at Meyer, frozen in place, as he listened, and then his head suddenly spun on a swivel to stare through the jail's booking window at the new prisoner. Frantz's mouth fell open, and his brows flared high and wide.

Always dapper, Hungry Harry was wearing a white dress shirt, red silk tie, gray wool slacks, bright suspenders, and shined shoes. He had lost a few pounds during his hospital stay but otherwise looked trim, fit, and dangerous. The middle of the right side of his clean shaven jaw was scarred, and the cheek was thinner than the left, which also had a scar, lower down and more jagged. Alan had imagined that Frantz would be horribly disfigured by the bullet wound, but that wasn't the case by far. Harry's mug had healed very well, giving Frantz's clean features the rugged roguish look, like a cavalryman of the last century whose face was slashed by a saber during combat or a duel of honor.

The question lingered whether he could talk clearly and well. The doctors had predicted he would never be able to sing again, like in the picture Alan had seen of him in a speakeasy, where he was singing his heart out, thrilling an audience and the much younger version of Alan's mother, who was accompanying him on the piano.

Frantz moved slowly, making his way up to the front counter. As he drew close, he glanced down at the paperwork but did not acknowledge the prisoner with a greeting. Knuckles also ignored him, his actions appearing deliberate, forced, and unnatural as he glanced off into the distance, his eyes lost in a thousand yard stare.

Frantz was now separated from Alan by no more than six feet and the four foot high counter that a reasonably athletic man could scale with ease. Harry glanced down at the booking form again and then up and quickly past Knuckles to Detective Kearney, and then to Alan.

Harry's eyes flashed wide and locked on Alan's. He glanced away quickly, and then they returned with a fiery vengeance. Alan held Frantz's stare firmly, as if the two men were boxers confined in a ring, both waiting for the bell to signal the start of their bout. Alan gazed unblinking, as if sending a message without speaking: "You think you can take me, you child rapist and murderer, jump over the counter and come and get it!"

After a long moment, Harry's eyes softened, but his nostrils continued to flare wide, as if the tension in his body was once again under control.

What's it going to be? Alan thought, almost hoping that Harry would throw down his coffee cup and come after him.

Frantz moved his jaw as if chewing on something grisly. "Go ahead," he said to Meyer. "Book him."

"Those are your orders?"

"Those are mine and the Chief's," said Frantz.

"Come on, boss!" said Meyer, like a recalcitrant child. "You want us to book a police officer for toasting that lowlife—"

"Get it done, Meyer," Frantz said impatiently. "I expect orders to be followed, as does Chief Ketchum. If we were to say no, he'd likely come up here himself, put a boot up your ass, then mine, before he booked Knuckles himself."

"But, this goes against everything I—" said Meyer.

"I understand," said Frantz, touching the coffee cup to his lips, but not taking any of it in.

"How about I relieve the new guy, Al Gustin, and send the Reverend Rookie up here for this?"

"Don't disappoint me on this," said Frantz, while turning toward Knuckles and tilting his head back, like beat cops do when they're making their point clear to street hoodlums. "I expect loyalty," he said, "even when it hurts. We've all made decisions in life and on the job that we've had to stand by, now we have to live with them. Life's never fair to coppers. No one ever told us it would be easy when we hired on and took our oaths. You need to take what the Master Chef in the big kitchen has dumped on your plate, even when it looks like slop."

Vera led the way up the steps to Chief Ketchum's office, a spring in her step. Ketchum's office was on the top floor of Police Headquarters with a western view that swept over the roof tops below them on the hill, except for the Smith Tower, which was still the tallest building on the West Coast. The view encompassed most of the water front, the shipyards to the south, cradled at the base of the Duwamish River, and the Olympic Mountains, across Puget Sound.

Ketchum's door was already open, and Sergeant Watkins was in there visiting. Ketchum waved them in, hearing their approach. "I've been expecting you!" he said. "The jail called and ruined your little surprise. That's unfortunate but couldn't be helped. So, I understand you have good news for me."

The trio took turns getting Ketchum caught up on the morning's arrests and case development.

"But what about Harry?" Ketchum asked.

"Knuckles wouldn't roll over on him," said Kearney.

"Yes," said Alan. "He admitted that he'd fired the fatal shot and why, but he wouldn't give up Harry."

"Knuckles ain't stupid," said Kearney. "He might save that little nugget for a bargaining chip in a plea deal. As this gets closer to trial, if the Prosecutor offers him life in prison instead of the gallows, he might be willing to pin the hit on Harry."

Vera shook her head. "I'm not so sure, Mike," she said. "Knuckles knows what prison life would be like for a former cop, especially one who's made as many enemies as he has. A lifetime of wearing a male chastity belt on his hind end might not be to his liking. He might choose the gallows instead of that."

Ketchum grinned self-consciously, as did Kearney. Alan was used to Vera's tart humor enough that he took it in stride.

"What about the Carnal Knowledge charge?" asked Alan. "Shouldn't Harry get fifteen to twenty for that?"

Ketchum closed his eyes and shook his head, trying to put on a happy face. "Ben's given me the pictures, and I've gone over them with Spud. The problem with photographs is that we can say it looks like Harry and we're sure this is Mei or Lynn, but that's just not good enough."

Ketchum glanced to Sergeant Watkins and raised his head, indicating for him to take it from there and help explain the law.

"The Chief is right on this," Watkins said. "First of all,

everyone here believes the girl in the pictures was one of the young ladies, Mei or Lynn, when she was much younger, but which one was it really? How old was she when the pictures were taken? Do we have a birth certificate so we can prove her age at the time of the event?

"Personally, I have trouble telling the sisters apart," said Watkins, "and who's to say there aren't more girls in Goon Dip's House who look a lot like them? And as far as the age goes, we would need their personal physician to come forward and testify about their physical development, because puberty doesn't automatically come at a standard age. The problem here is that as far as we know, the girls have never been to a doctor, so there're no medical records to subpoena. A good attorney would argue that the anonymous girl in those pictures was really of age, she was just dressed up to look young because some customers like that kind of thing—like with the one sister wearing that school girl outfit."

"So what you're saying is that Harry's getting a free pass on this?" Vera asked, anger in her voice.

Watkins shook his head. "Not necessarily," he said. "The Chinese characters and numbers are helpful. We could possibly use these if you can bring in the photographer and film developer and get them to testify against Harry. Meanwhile, the pictures'll have to stay in the Chief's safe."

Alan glanced to Vera, while thinking of the developer, Donnie Chang, knowing that she was also considering him. She met Alan's gaze and shook her head. Not this time, not yet, is what she's thinking, he thought.

"Great job by all of you!" Ketchum said. "I really mean it. Now tell me, is there any hope finding the widow's fortune for her?"

Alan drove the union's big Buick west on Jackson Street to Occidental, where he stopped at the light before making a left turn toward King Street.

"You're quiet this morning," Vera said. "Did you get enough sleep last night?"

Alan shook his head. "Everything that happened yesterday kept dancing through my brain," he said. "Nelson, Knuckles, the shooting, and Hungry Harry gave me a lot to think about." He swung the car into the turn. "And of course I want to find Sawyer's money, and I want it to be right here, not over at Union Station, not up at the Greyhound Bus Depot, and I want it to be now."

"I'm not as picky," said Vera. "I'd settle for just finding it."

Alan parked at the curb and held the door.

"You're such a gentleman, Champ," Vera said. "But you don't have to do that for me anymore. We're partners—and detectives at that."

"Detectives or not, I still think of you as a classy lady."

"As opposed to a brassy detective hussy?"

"Yeah, exactly."

"You put it that way, you sweet talking darling, and you can keep at it," she said, taking him by the arm, while entering the King Street Station, home of the Great Northern Railway and the Northern Pacific. They crossed the large compass in the foyer, the bank of telephone booths, and worked their way through the crowd of new arrivals and porters carrying luggage to a bank of lockers situated between two large pillars at the edge of the waiting area.

Alan let go of Vera's arm and held the key out and compared it to the ones sticking out of the lockers that remained unused. "Looks the same as these," he said. "According to the tag, ours is forty-three."

"Alright," said Vera. "You take the left side and I'll take the right. We'll meet in the middle."

Alan scanned the locker numbers in front of him, quickly seeing the pattern. The lockers on his end started at one and ran to five going down, like on a Bingo card. He moved quickly over the rows and realized the lockers were stacked in eight columns. Unless the numbering system changed, forty would be the maximum number. Vera was waiting for him in the middle, her usually confident smile pulled into a puzzled frown.

"Forty is all they got," she said. "Nothing higher."

Alan read the sign on the pillar out loud: "Lockers are for day use only. Management is not responsible for items left over twenty-four hours. Items left unclaimed beyond twenty-four hours will be removed to Lost and Found. Items not redeemed in thirty days will be disposed of at owner's risk and/or expense."

Alan's stomach suddenly sank. "Disposed" to him meant sent to auction so that the railroad could recover their costs. If that's what happened here, some lucky bidder claimed what was in Sawyer's locker and has probably retired to Tahiti and its warm beaches, sun, and exotic drinks with rum in them.

The sinking feeling soon settled down and inexplicably a

340

feeling of hope and unwarranted optimism began to replace it. Alan grinned to no one in particular, nodded to Vera, and inclined his head toward the large pillar bracketing the lockers, indicating they should walk around to the other side. Vera followed his lead, but as they turned the corner and reached the back, they found that there weren't any more on that side. That sinking feeling returned with a vengeance, making him think this excursion was a hopeless longshot that fell short.

Alan's sideways frown mimicked the one Vera had worn a moment earlier. "Well, what do you make of that?" he said.

An old sign posted on the pillar was similar to the one on the other side. Alan stared at it vacuously and then decided to read it again. "Lockers are for weekly use only. Management is not responsible for items left over seven days. Items left unclaimed beyond seven days will be removed to Lost and Found. Items not redeemed in thirty days will be disposed of at owner's risk and/or expense."

Alan gazed curiously at Vera, who was also reading the sign. "So which is it?" Alan asked. "A twenty-four hour limit or a seven day limit?"

"That's very odd," she said.

Alan stared at the back of the lockers and then down at the floor. He walked over to the large pillar and examined it closely. "There used to be other lockers here," he said.

Vera inhaled deeply and nodded. "I agree."

Alan squatted low and examined the white tiled floor next to the pillar. "It's got that old grime buildup," he said. "The kind that never goes away, no matter how much they scour and polish the floor. It's taken the shape of something rectangular. I'm sure of it now."

"What do you suppose happened to them?" Vera asked.

Alan cocked his head to the side, put his hands on his hips, and slowly gazed around the room, taking it all in.

There were no more lockers in view, just people wandering through the high-backed benches that reminded him of church pews. Doubting his eyes, he retraced the room and began wandering toward the eastern doors and the raised railroad platform, where the train was unloading its passengers. Along the way Alan and Vera passed a raised shoeshine stand, where a well-heeled customer was getting his money's worth from an elderly shoeshine man. They worked their way out onto the platform and scanned the length of the platform. There weren't any more lockers outside.

Alan brought his fingers up to rub the top of his nose. Then he dug at the corners of his eyes and shook his head. "Obviously not here," he said, "but somehow I don't think the railroad would just get rid of them when they have all this space for them. What sense would that make?"

"I agree," said Vera. "I'm sure they're already paid for and have earned their keep, and any space concerns the station would have are minimal."

They walked back inside as the shine customer was counting out his coins to tip the man. The old gentleman took the coins, thanked the customer, and slid the change in his pocket. Then he gazed around for waiting customers, but there weren't any, so he climbed up into the raised chair and crossed his legs comfortably, one over the other, like someone used to watching people.

Alan smiled wickedly at Vera. "Do you mind?" he asked. "I think I'll take a minute for a shine?"

Vera nodded knowingly. "Of course not, darling. Be sure to tip well when you're done."

Alan and Vera stopped in front of the stand, and the gentleman gazed down at them and tipped his snap-brim hat to Vera.

"Good day to you, folks," he said as he spryly climbed out of his chair. "My name's RJ, and I give the best shines in town. Yes, sir and ma'am, people come from all around the world for RJ's shines. I've shined the famous and the greatest, the rich and the poor, the shady and the righteous. So, which one of you's first?"

Alan grinned as he climbed into the shine chair, amused by the knowledge that Vera hated being called "ma'am," but he also knew she wouldn't correct RJ about that like she would him. She'd just take it out on Alan later...that is if she caught him snickering or otherwise enjoying this at all.

"It's just for me," said Alan. "Thought I could use a touch up."

RJ stretched back and stared at Alan's shoes. "They look mighty fine already," he said, "but I'd be glad to touch 'em up, make them something you'll be proud of. You'll tell all your young friends, and they'll come down here to see me."

"How long have you had your stand here?" Alan asked as he settled in the chair.

RJ opened a small tin, dabbed two fingers into it, and he began rubbing the polish around Alan's shoes, working the waxy gel into the leather without a brush or cloth. "Oh, you're going to make me feel old, young man, but I suppose I am, so there's no sense trying to hide it from you. I won this concession in a card game back in 1914, about eight years after the station opened. You'll have to do the math for me on that. They didn't have school for Colored people back then. Still don't, for all I know."

Alan nodded and flashed a grin to Vera over the top of RJ's bent-over frame. "I'm thinking you're the perfect man to help us out and answer our question," said Alan.

"Oh, yeah? What question's that?"

"We're curious about the storage lockers over there," Alan said with a tilt of his head to the bank of lockers between the marble pillars.

Intent on the work in front of him, RJ didn't bother to

look up at all. "Yes, sir, what about 'em?"

"I've got a key for a locker that doesn't appear to be there anymore. We got the feeling the key belonged to another set of lockers that might have been behind those, but we can't seem to find any others."

RJ stood up straight, all five-feet-six-inches of him, and shifted the weight on his feet. "Let me see your key," he said with a serious gaze.

Alan handed the key to RJ, who studied it carefully for a moment. Then he handed it back to Alan and resumed shining shoes. "That's one of our keys alright," he said. "So how did it come into your hands?"

"We're private detectives," Alan said, fishing his badge out of his pocket and showing it to RJ. "The lovely lady standing next to you is Vera Deward, and I'm Alan Stewart."

RJ turned towards Vera, and she held out her badge for inspection, and RJ flashed her a broad grin. "Pleased to make your acquaintance, Mr. Stewart and Miss Deward. I told you I've shined the shady and the righteous, and I'm thinking you fall into the latter category."

"We hope so," said Vera.

"A widow, who was left high and dry when her husband died, retained us to see if we could find this key for her," said Alan. "And we only came up with it a couple of days ago. Let's just say that it had fallen into the wrong hands."

"And how do I know you're the right hands to hold that key?" asked RJ as he furiously worked the buffing cloth around the cap toe of Alan's shoe.

"I'm not sure how we could prove that to you."

RJ stood erect again, admired his shine on the first shoe and then commenced to buffing the second. "Can you describe the original key holder for me?" he asked. "That would be a start."

"We never met him personally," said Alan. "The only pictures we ever saw of him were in the police files, and what was left of his face was covered in blood, same as his uniform."

"Uniform, you say?"

"Police uniform," Vera said.

"He walked a beat up around Jazz Alley," said Alan. "Across the street from Noodles' place on Twelfth, the—"

"Black and Tan," said RJ.

"Exactly," said Alan. "Except that the shooting was around the corner in a garage on South Main."

"I remember when that happened," said RJ. "Noodles told me all about it. He used to get along fine with the deceased—Hacksaw Sawyer is what they called him up there."

"That's right," said Alan.

"Noodles and him had business dealings," said RJ. "We should probably just leave it at that."

RJ worked the buffing cloth again on Alan's other shoe, snapping and cracking it as he drew out the shine. "The radio says arrests have been made in that case."

"That's right," said Alan. "We made those yesterday."

RJ stood back and admired his work. "That'll be a quarter, Mr. Stewart."

Alan craned his neck and gazed down at his shoes, over his knees. "Very nice work, RJ. I thought I did a pretty good job on these myself, but that's the best these shoes have ever looked."

"Keep the change," Alan said, as he slipped a five-dollar bill into RJ's hand.

"Thank you sir," said RJ. "You're a gentleman and a scholar."

"I try to be," said Alan.

RJ reached behind his stand, pulled out a small placard,

and placed it on the seat of his shine stand. It read: "Back In Five Minutes."

"Now, about that locker," RJ said. "If you folks would be kind enough, follow me please."

RJ led Vera and Alan through a short hallway to a shiny oaken door, he tugged on a key ring that was fastened to a retractable chain fob on his belt, selected a key and opened the door. He flipped on the light, and immediately Vera and Alan could see the missing bank of lockers, lined up in a row, against the left wall. They followed RJ inside the room, and he closed the door behind them.

"Welcome to my office," said RJ.

To the right of the narrow room was a workbench with shelves segmented into sections big enough for pairs of shoes, which customers must have left for RJ to shine at his convenience. In the back of the room was a coat tree with a small assortment of apparel and surprising to Alan, a saddle with an exceptionally high cantle.

RJ must have followed Alan's eye or was prepared for the inevitable question. "That's from the police department's horse patrol," he said. "It was custom built for one of their bigger horses, and I can't tell you why I have it anymore. The cantle in the back is extra tall to keep the rider from getting thrown, if the horse reared back."

"You can't tell us why you have it? Or is it that you don't remember?" teased Vera.

RJ cackled, happy with the banter. "I believe it was another card game," he said, "but it was legit. The horse had been retired, and they didn't need the saddle anymore."

Alan stepped in front of locker forty-three. "May I?" he asked, holding up the key.

"Be my guest," said RJ. "Usually this is about the time the police officers ask me to leave the room, but I'm guessing you two don't mind if I see what's inside there."

346

"Now, what was that you said about the police officers?" asked Vera.

"This whole bank of lockers belongs to police officers," said RJ. "Goes back to the early days of Prohibition, but I don't ask questions. Some high ranking types bought the lockers, destroyed the extra keys, and they tip me for taking care of them, making sure no one sees them or asks what's inside. The rest of it is none of my business."

Alan stuck the key into number forty-three's lock, wondering if the locker had been picked or cleaned out by the host, but then if it had, why would RJ be so gracious about helping them now? If he had something to hide, he could have denied there were any lockers. How could they challenge that?

"Has anyone asked about this one?" asked Alan as he twisted the key in the lock.

"Can't say they have," said RJ. "I think the boys got it worked out so that no one knows who's got what locker, and when those who have them move on, they *bequeath* them to other officers. That's a good word, *bequeath*. One of those important policemen taught me that."

The tumblers clicked, Alan opened the lock, and flipped the door open. Inside in the dark was a heavy duty canvas bag, similar to the ones hidden under the floorboards in the Stewart's garage, where Mackie Stewart's arsenal was still hidden. Alan reached inside the locker, grabbed a cloth handle, and tugged the bag out toward him. His stomach churned noisily with excitement. He could tell by the heft of the bag what it contained, and it was chock-full, just as Ketchum had speculated.

Alan grinned from ear to ear, as he pulled the bag free of the prison that it had been locked in for the past nine years. He grabbed the second handle to the bag, swung it around, and tossed it up on the counter. He reached for the heavy duty zipper's tab, but then Vera clasped his arm gently.

"I think we should do this part in private," she said, directing her comment to RJ. "It would create less problems that way, if you don't mind?"

RJ nodded. "I suppose you're right about that," he said. "I'll leave you two here with your discovery, but when you do come out, I'd appreciate knowing if you're pleased with what you found. That's all. You don't have to tell me what it really was."

"RJ, you're a darling," said Vera. "Do you mind telling me what your take would be from one of these lockers, in a typical year?"

"I'd say the average policeman would come by here twice a month. Typically they'd slip me a couple, two, three bucks each time. Again, I'm not good with math, but I suspect that'd be about fifty, sixty, seventy bucks a year, depending on the officer."

"So you're owed some back rent," said Vera, "and you were honest enough not to go prying into this locker."

"I appreciate you saying that, Miss Deward" said RJ, "but the truth is I didn't know which locker was Hacksaw's. I knew he'd not be coming back, but I didn't know if there was enough in his bag to risk my life and all that I got going down here. If I had took to messing with the locks in here, the boys in blue would've spotted that sure enough, and they wouldn't have been forgiving about it—even if it weren't their box. I'd be chopped up and feeding the Elliott Bay crabs before the next sun rise."

"Alright then RJ," said Vera. "Give us a few minutes alone, please, and we'll come settle up with you when we're through."

RJ nodded with a smile, stepped out of the room and closed the door. Alan's eyes flared wide and he grabbed for the bag's zipper, but again Vera stayed his hand, leaned closed to his face, and raised her forefinger in front of her lips, making the quiet sign. Alan's brow lowered in puzzlement, and then Vera pointed to the shadow movement underneath the door.

"He's listening," Vera whispered, her lips touching Alan's ear lobe.

Alan reached an arm behind the small of Vera's back, squeezed the top side of her rump, and tugged her against his body, while tilting his head low, knowing that she would reach up for his lips with hers. She kissed him firmly with wet lips, and he savored her flavor, wanting more, while at the same time weighing that passion against the potential discovery of what was inside the large utility bag. Vera decided for him, putting her hand up to his chest and pushing him gently away.

"Save that for later," she whispered. "Now open that damn bag, would you? But be careful about any noise you make."

Alan tugged the zipper's tab, pulling it down the entire length of brass teeth that gave way without a snag, all the way to the bottom stop. He inserted his fingers into the opening, grasped the brass vislon, and spread the bag open wide, revealing its bounty: bundles of green joy. From what he could see through awestruck eyes, the stuffed bag was full of high denominations, hundreds of stacks of notes wrapped together in bundles of tens, twenties, and fifty dollar bills. Hack Sawyer apparently hadn't bothered with low denominations, like ones and fives. Vera grabbed Alan's upper arm with both hands and squeezed it tightly, like a bettor at a horse race watching the winner cross the finish line.

"I think I'm going to pee my pants!" she whispered.

Alan chuckled and then glanced at her face to make sure she was kidding. She was, he was sure, so he snuck a kiss, planting it on her left cheek.

Alan inserted his hand further into the bag, probing,

and flipped and pulled bundles up from its deepest parts, and as he hoped there were some that consisted of one-hundred dollar bills, also wrapped in banker's tape. He sunk his hand into the bag again and hit something hard, out of place, near the front. It was wrapped in oily paper, but he knew what it was. He guessed that if he found a large stash of money, there would also be a gun nearby, an exit strategy.

Alan pulled out the wrapped package and folded the paper back, revealing a Colt .45 from the last century. "I wonder whose this was?" he said.

"And what it was used for?" asked Vera.

"If Ketchum doesn't want it for evidence of some crime," said Alan, "I'd love to have it. At any rate, it looks like Mrs. Sawyer is going to be one very happy woman," said Alan.

"Now are you sure that's what you want to do with the money?" asked Vera.

Alan nodded. "I'm sure. It's her money…except for the ten percent and something for Mei Hua."

"Good for you, Champ! Sawyer may have come about the money dishonestly, but it's not like he stole it. People willingly paid him for a service he provided. So she gets ninety percent, but I say we also tip RJ generously from her ninety percent—let's say a bundle of tens for him. That would be five-hundred dollars for his troubles."

"I agree," said Alan, "Then we show Ketchum what we found, count it with him as a witness, and then put it in the safety deposit box Vic left at the vault, not the Police Property Room. After what I saw going on in the jail yesterday, I don't have any confidence that this much cash wouldn't disappear."

Vera hurried the last few feet, trotting ahead of Alan down the hallway to Chief Ketchum's office. She stepped into the open doorway and rapped lightly on the jamb, as Alan caught up to her and plopped the bag down on the floor behind her, so he could rest his arms.

"Top of the morning to you, lass," said Ketchum, who was seated behind his desk with Sergeant Watkins planted in a chair across from him. "Come on in, Vera, and bring that bright young detective with you."

Watkins and Ketchum both stood up, and the Chief's gaze quickly fixed on Vera, as it inevitably did. Alan reached down, grabbed the large utility bag by both handles, and toted it into the room. Watkins watched Alan carefully, his brow knitted low thoughtfully, while Ketchum's brow jumped high with expectation.

"Well, what's that you have with you?" he asked, and before Vera or Alan could respond, he shook his head and said, "Never mind, I think I know. I'll wager you two have been up to your old tricks again, finding everyone and everything that's ever been reported lost."

Vera smiled broadly, as did Alan. This was one of the rare moments, however, that he had ever seen her blush.

That just didn't happen with her. She was too cagey and wise to the world to be surprised often.

Alan carried the bag across the room, and Ketchum waved graciously at the top of his desk. "Throw it there, lad. Let's have a look-see, shall we?"

Sergeant Watkins also stepped back, giving Alan the room he needed to swing the bag, which he did artfully, as if he'd had a lot of recent practice tossing the large grip. It landed on top of Ketchum's desk, and without waiting to be told, Alan grabbed the zipper's tag, and paused.

"There's an old fashioned Colt .45 in there," Alan said. "Looks like it was a cowboy's gun. It's wrapped in oil paper and still has two live rounds in the chamber."

"The others are spent?" asked Ketchum, and he looked to Sergeant Watkins for concurrence.

"Looks that way to me," said Alan.

Ketchum nodded thoughtfully. "Alright, we'll deal with that later."

Alan tugged the zipper down to the brass stop and pulled the long fly wide open, as he had done earlier in the train depot, exposing bundles of greenbacks and the package wrapped in paper.

"Saints be praised!" said Ketchum, stepping forward, grabbing a bundle of Ben Franklins and tossing it up and down, playing catch with it like a boy on the schoolyard with a ball and mitt. "You two have done it again!"

"How much is in there?" he asked.

"We haven't counted it yet," said Alan.

"We were waiting to do that when we had witnesses present."

"Ah," Ketchum sighed. "Good idea, but be sure to keep whoever it is at arm's length, or this package could end up a lot lighter than when you brought it in."

"We were hoping it would be you, sir," said Alan.

Ketchum grinned self-consciously. "Thank you for that, lad. I appreciate your faith in me, but I am not without sin. I'd feel better if you'd put a door between us when it's all laid out there. How about we use my secretary's office? Connie would be a perfect witness for you, and we'll bring up Ray Holms from Fiscal to help with the counting."

Alan glanced to Vera and nodded that he was okay with that, and she followed suit to Ketchum.

"When you're done, I'd like to get a photograph of that as a keepsake—but not for the papers. I also suggest that you call Mrs. Sawyer and let her know you've found what she's been searching for. That way you can prepare her so she doesn't have a heart attack when you show up on her porch with the loot. Of course I've already talked to her about the arrests, and she's very pleased with those, because she always knew it was a murder. Now she'll get the pension she deserves. She asked about Hacksaw's money, and I told her you were working on that, but your finding it would come with a fee. She was fine with that. So you can tell the reporters who show up at her house that you were working on a commission basis."

"I'd like to have Ben Kearney with us when we do that," said Vera, "if that—"

BANG! A gunshot roared in the hallway, coming up from somewhere lower down in the building.

Alan instinctively pulled his coat back and placed his hand on the outside of his holster, over the grip of his Colt. He glanced up and both Ketchum and Watkins were doing the same thing, while Vera's hand went inside her purse, seeking the handle of her .45.

"Gunshot," Watkins said softly, announcing the obvious.

"From inside the building," said Ketchum, standing alert, his senses focused.

Suddenly there were shouts from outside and down below on the sidewalk. **BANG! BANG!** Two more gunshots echoed off the walls of the building to the north.

Alan and Vera followed Chief Ketchum and Sergeant Watkins over to the windows and glanced down to Terrace Street, four floors below them. Sprawled spread eagle, his body overlapping the curb and rain-filled gutter, was a man in a gray suit without a tie. Two red blotches were spreading over the middle of his chest. Blood was also oozing out slowly from a hole in the middle of the man's forehead, between eyes that were wide open. The blood trickled down the left side of the man's face.

Standing nearby him was a young man in jail worker clothing, his bloody hand pressed to the side of his head, as if he was holding his ear, or the spot where his ear should have been. It was difficult to tell from this height and angle. He was being consoled by a man in shirt sleeves and suspenders, whose hair was slicked back. The dapper man was holding a pistol down by his side. On the ground in front of him was a crude shiny object, perhaps a knife.

"Holy Blessed Virgin!" said Ketchum. "We've had an escape attempt from the jail."

"This can't be happening!" said Alan.

"Don't worry, lad. There'll be a lot of explaining to do before this one's put to rest. I want you and Vera to wait right here. Spud and I will have to run down to find out what's happened. But I've got to tell you off the top of my head, I can't imagine how a prisoner, who's been in police custody less than twenty-four hours, has managed to craft himself a jail-house shiv and hatch an escape plot."

Sergeant Watkins shook his head gravely, as if he too knew what had really happened.

"And it would appear that our illustrious lieutenant has found a way to save the day," said Ketchum sarcastically.

"Not only has he foiled Knuckles' bid for freedom, it appears he's saved our young jailer's life in the process. I can see the headlines now."

➤ THE END ➤

NEIL LOW is a captain with the Seattle Police Department and is the agency's Night Commander, responsible for coordinating the police handling of large emergencies, trajedies, and serious crimes. He was the agency's first commander of its Ethics and Professional Responsibility Section and has commanded sections in almost every other area of police operations, including: Metropolitan Section, which has K-9, Mounted, Harbor, and SWAT; Homicide and Violent Crimes, which also has Robbery, Fugitive, and Gangs; Advanced Training and the Range; Internal Affairs; and Domestic Violence and Sexual Assault. He is a Vietnam War veteran and a cum laude graduate of the University of Washington's Bothell campus, where he also wrote for the school's weekly newspaper, The UW Bothell Commons. A Seattle native, he now lives in Snohomish with his wife and three daughters.

Also by Neil Low

SIGN OF THE DRAGON

UNREASONABLE PERSUASION

THICK AS THIEVES

...from Tigress Publishing

ACKNOWLEDGEMENTS:

I am eternally grateful and wish to acknowledge those who have helped to make this, my fourth novel, possible. As always I have been blessed with the continuing support I have received over the many years from my lovely wife, Lesley, as well as from our three daughters, Amanda, Michelle, and Meghan. As with my other three novels, portions of this novel were written at the University of Washington's Bothell campus, where I can still find solitude and freedom from interruptions inside my favorite nook in the school's library (second floor south end), which is managed by Sarah Ledley. Special thanks go to Jim Ritter and Judy at the Seattle Police Museum, who have been very helpful with my historical police research, some of which includes correspondence and files they provided for my review so that I could capture the feel of this corrupt "bygone era" at the Seattle Police Department. Kudos go again to Cold Case Detective Mike Ciesynski, for his assistance in researching the primary case file that this story is based on. Special thanks, again, go to the amazing Steve Montiglio for his original cover art and interior designs. I also wish to acknowledge first draft readers Nancy Gratton, Marie Trujilo, and Maggie Olsen for their keen eyes and attention to detail. I'd also like to acknowledge, again, Dr. Jeffrey Abrams, my chiropractor for his wonderful stories and anecdotes about old fashioned police work (comparing Philadelphia to Seattle), which has been very helpful to me in my characters' development. And of course there is Peter Atkins, whose subtle hand at editing helped smooth out the rough edges in my manuscript. He was kind enough to thank me for writing cleanly and not making his work especially onerous and taxing. Of course none of the above would have been possible without the expert help and guidance from my very wonderful publisher, Kristen Morris, of Tigress Publishing. She has been the perfect sounding board for character and plot development. Again, to all of you, thank you.